KV-429-180

BOND OF PERFECTION

The setting could hardly have been more lovely: an English country house with an age-old view of distant downs, and a garden breathing gratitude for years of human care. Nathalie had had little reason to guess of the condition of the man she had married until his elder sister Vera came to live with them, the barren virginal Vera whose hatred of life was shown even in the way she planned the garden. The visits of her Aunt, the Baroness Olga, and of Felix whom she might so easily have married, and then the birth of a daughter, seemed at first to promise Nathalie a rescue. But in the end they were to prove only stages on the twisted path of enlightenment that culminated in the night when Nathalie received her first intimation of the terror, the absolute terror, that is love.

BOND OF PERFECTION

A NOVEL BY

STELLA ZILLIACUS

London
SECKER & WARBURG
1959

Printed in England by
The Camelot Press Ltd., London and Southampton
and
first published 1959
by
Martin Secker & Warburg Ltd.
7 John Street, London
W.C.1

For

G. A. W.

St. Paul to the Colossians, Chapter III

Brethren: Put ye on, as the elect of God, holy and beloved, the bowels of mercy, benignity, humility, modesty, patience; bearing with one another, if any have a complaint against another; even as the Lord hath forgiven you, so you also. But above all these things, have charity, which is the bond of perfection: and let the peace of Christ rejoice in your hearts, wherein also you are called in one body; and be ye thankful.

BOND OF PERFECTION

Part One

"Why are you so worked up just because your sister's coming to stay?" Nathalie asked her husband.

Arthur said nothing, but went on dusting the drawing-room with rapid, nervous movements. He straightened ornaments, stacked papers and puffed up cushions, and his narrow mouth was set and sulky.

"Are you afraid Vera may not like the house?" she went on. Still he did not speak, and Nathalie began to grow tense with the feeling of apprehension that had already become so familiar during those first months of marriage.

"What have I done wrong this time?" she wondered, already knowing that her thoughts must be censored and shaped before being expressed, but still forgetting this from time to time. "Or is Arthur really only irritated because I haven't dusted the drawing-room this morning?"

"Mrs. Dennison can do that," she tried. "She's coming in for a couple of hours today, even though it is Sunday. I've made the beds and tidied upstairs, so there'll be plenty of time for everything else."

"Everything else except work," snapped Arthur. "I can't think why you don't get someone efficient, instead of that parturating chatterbox."

"I thought she amused you."

"She can do that in the pub, instead of at 2*s*. an hour while the house goes to rack and ruin!"

"It's not as bad as that, is it? She seems to enjoy scrubbing and is quite a good cook as well."

"I suppose it is something that I don't have to put up with your cooking all the time."

"Is there anything I do right?" Nathalie asked miserably, and Arthur checked his mood.

"Silly," he said, patting his wife on the head. "I was only joking."

"You meant every word of it."

"The trouble with you is that you've no sense of humour!" He wondered irritably why she could not be more robust and resilient. "Still, I suppose you can't help it, being a woman. It's a pity you don't show your femininity by being house-proud, though."

At one time, Nathalie would have felt near to tears by then. In these bickerings, it was not so much Arthur's words that depressed and discouraged her, as his hostility. Trying to cajole him, she said: "Tell me the worst, darling. Is this sister of yours so very fierce?"

Arthur suddenly put an arm affectionately around his wife's waist and drew her to sit beside him on the sofa.

"You're not a bad little thing, really," he said, remembering that although this girl was now listless and colourless, when he first knew her she had been bright-eyed, and glowing with a challenging serenity. "I'm a tiresome old bear," he added.

"Only sometimes."

"You mustn't pay too much attention to what I say."

"There'd be hell to pay if I ignored it, wouldn't there, now?"

"Don't ignore me. Just be nice to me, as you are being at the moment."

"Aren't I always nice to you?"

"No."

"Aren't I?"

"You can be most tiresome."

"Oh?"

"Still, we won't go into that now." He used a tone of voice that was on the border-line between cruelty and mockery, thus being free to commit himself to either.

"Tell me what you don't like and I can change it," said Nathalie.

"No, that wouldn't be kind."

"I don't mind. After all, however much people may love one another, they have to learn to live together."

"You must learn by experience, and if you care sufficiently for me you'll be able to do that."

"But its rather cosy to talk about things." Arthur's arm was still round her waist, but Nathalie now felt it to be dead. She tried to establish some kind of contact with her husband by snuggling her face into his shoulder, but he jumped up and stood by the fireplace. Even when he stopped moving, he was never still. There was a tautness about him, an impression of deliberate and difficult control that seemed to be holding back almost superhuman energy. His vitality was all-embracing, but more like an insatiable appetite than a sign of strength, or even enjoyment.

"You always think everything can be solved by talking!" he exclaimed, without looking at her.

"Well, it does help, don't you think?"

He looked angry, and so cold that once again she began to feel unsettled and said quickly:

"Do tell me about Vera. You never have much, you know, and I so want everything to go well."

"You will be nice to her, won't you?" It was more of a command than an exhortation; nevertheless, Nathalie knew that Arthur was anxious.

"But of course I will. What do you expect?" She already felt an immense, unreasonable affection for this woman she had never seen, simply for being her husband's sister; anything that was so much a part of him seemed to her especially lovable.

"You mustn't think I'm frightened of her," Arthur went on, still looking straight ahead and choosing his words with care. "It's just that she's determined to be reasonable at all costs, so she often gets hurt and baffled, and . . . well, one just had to be careful, that's all."

"Do you think she'll like me?"

"Of course she will. Just be nice to her, the way you can be when you choose, and everything will be all right." He suddenly looked much younger as he talked and became boyishly eager. He had a curiously lopsided, creased face. When he was sad, it was quite ugly, but when he laughed, or was happy, it suddenly became extremely attractive in a rather puckish way. Yet, however warm his smile might be, his little, pale-blue eyes remained as opaque and unyielding as seaside pebbles on a cold winter's day.

"She hasn't had an easy time, you know," he went on. "She was fifteen when I was born and my mother died, and so she more or less took me over and sacrificed her life to bringing me up."

"How do you mean, 'sacrificed'?"

"I mean, she gave up everything to be as good as a mother to me."

"What did she have to give up to do that?"

"Now you're being tiresome again."

Nathalie's own nature, as well as the sort of people who had brought her up, had taught her that unusual commitments and responsibilities might frequently be undertaken but as well as, and not instead of, other facets of living. She could see no contradiction in a Vera married and with children of her own but also helping to bring up a small brother; or even a Vera with such a responsibility launched on some career, since old Professor Bateman-Brown had continued to keep a comfortable establishment and a housekeeper until his death at the beginning of the war.

"Did she give up going to University so that you could go instead?" Nathalie asked, thinking that perhaps it had been a question of money.

"Something of the sort, I believe. You'd better ask her yourself, if you're so anxious to know. She doesn't like to talk about it much, but I know I owe her a great deal. She really was as good as a mother to me in many ways, and not only when I was small. I was miserable when I first went to Harrow, but Vera always saw to it that I had plenty of letters and cakes and all the other things that matter so much to a schoolboy. I didn't get on awfully well with my father in those days, either. He rather wanted me to become a scientist—which was odd, come to think of it, considering his speciality was ancient history—and I wasn't keen on the idea, even though I was quite good at stinks. Vera smoothed things out between us and made him realise that it would be more useful if I stuck to classics. She always organised things for my holidays, too, so that even if I couldn't see my friends I was never at a loose end. She was the most companionable of sisters. I never needed anybody but her, really, and we had a lot of fun. We used to come up to London for a week or two of theatres, or go motoring in Scotland, and several times we went abroad together. Its an example of devotion you could well learn something from, in fact."

"It's funny that we've both got that in common, isn't it? I mean, both of us losing our mothers when we were born."

"Yes," Arthur answered, now smiling at Nathalie. "It's only one of the things that makes me realise that we were meant for one another. Goodness, I was right to marry you."

"In spite of everything?"

"In spite of, indeed! *Because* of everything!" Although their eyes never quite met in unguarded intimacy, this was one of their rare moments of harmony. Nathalie wanted to put her arms around her husband, to complete the moment with the reassurance of physical contact, however innocent, but she knew from experience that Arthur would not respond, so she stayed where she was and asked:

"What happened to Vera after your father died?"

"She went to take care of an aunt of ours, in Scotland. I've told you that already."

"Oh, of course. The one who died a few months ago, you mean?"

"You know quite well that's what I mean. Why don't you ever listen to anything I say?"

"Darling, don't get cross, it's too silly. I just meant I wasn't sure if Vera had been there all the time, that's all."

"You should learn to express yourself more clearly, then."

"She must be terribly kind, to devote herself to other people like that."

"Yes, she is." Arthur knew that common sense, as well as kindness, had sent Vera to Peebles, but there seemed to be no point in explaining that. His sister had known that she and Arthur were their aunt's only heirs, but she also realised that old ladies were apt to get eccentric ideas and be easily influenced, and that it was up to her to see that the will was not altered at the last moment in favour of a cat's home or an orphanage.

"Vera's come into quite a bit of money as a reward for her pains," Arthur went on.

"Oh, good," said Nathalie.

"We don't quite know how much yet, but it shouldn't be far short of £5,000."

"That will be nice for her."

"Should be able to draw about £150 a year from that, with luck and good management."

"Really?"

"You're only pretending to be interested." He thought her indifference feigned and a cover for jealousy, because he did not yet understand that Nathalie could not discuss money any more than she could dissert on aerodynamics or higher mathematics. She could not think of a £150 a year in terms of a bigger car, or a house in a more respectable street, or saving for a really good fur, or even a holiday abroad every summer. There had been occasions in her life when £150 had seemed like riches beyond the wildest dreams, and other times when it had merely helped to cover a grocer's bill.

"It's just that I don't feel money," she tried to explain.

"Only because you've never needed to worry about it, like ordinary people."

"We were terribly poor sometimes, before father became a fashionable painter," Nathalie said thoughtfully, "but it's quite true that we never worried much. So it seemed, anyhow. We had so many kind friends, and somehow we could always laugh."

Arthur was suddenly overcome by a powerful jealousy. He fiercely begrudged success; indifference to what others thought; a world in which people might be poor, but never took poverty seriously; and above all, a form of basic confidence which he longed to share but could not even understand. His own wife had been brought up in all this, and he both envied and resented everything she stood for. At that moment he wanted to strike her, but instead he shouted:

"You're just a slut! You haven't any idea how to live decently and respectably! People like your father and your other fine friends may have had some kind of talents—no credit to them, since they were born with them—but the law of the jungle is the only thing they understood! Oh yes, I know its fashionable not to have a good word for the bourgeois virtues, but where would civilisation be without them, I'd like to know? You can't run a country, or an office, or even a house, for that matter, without any kind of order or organisation!"

"Artists have to be rather more highly organised than most people, even though they may have unconventional methods because their work comes first."

"Don't you try to be clever with me, my girl, because I'll always get the better of you. 'Be good, sweet maid, and let who will be clever.' It's just as well you married me, even though I am only a business man, because you'd never have made any headway in that precious intellectual set of yours!"

Nathalie began to cry softly, now too tired to resist tears.

"I might have known you'd start snivelling sooner or later!" Arthur's rage abated to exasperation, and he wondered irritably why it was so necessary to have women when they were so impossible. If this one had stood up to him, called him names or even slapped his face, he would have preferred it. She would not have been allowed to get away with it, but he could respect defiance. Nathalie's gentleness irritated him, and her almost pathetic desire to please acted on him like an open invitation to bullying. When he married her, he had taken her remoteness to be an indication of worldliness and sophistication, but soon found it to be the dreaminess of an irresponsible and over-affectionate child.

"If you must cry, go and do it somewhere else," he exclaimed. "Someone might see you here." The sight of her quite genuine grief made him feel uncomfortable and ashamed, so he added: "You needn't trouble to switch on the tears just for my benefit. I'm impervious to that sort of blackmail."

"I didn't switch them on," Nathalie sobbed. "I just couldn't help it. You're so *beastly* sometimes. Why do you go at me like that? Why? I can't bear it!"

Arthur, suddenly frightened, went down on his knees at her feet, buried his head in her lap and blurted out: "What a brute I am! I don't know what gets hold of me. Can you forgive me? What on earth would I do without you? Nobody else would put up with me. You can't imagine how I need you. Please, please forgive me."

Nathalie tenderly stroked his wiry locks and murmured reassuring endearments. Both the firm texture and the vivid sandy shade of Arthur's hair, which was exactly the same all over him, had a compelling fascination for her. At that moment, she remembered how often, before they were married, she had stroked the curly wisps on his sturdy arms, for the contrast of them against his exceptionally white skin had delighted her even then.

"What have I done to deserve someone like you?" Arthur asked almost humbly.

"What I should like to know is what you did to deserve such divinely curly hair! Just look at it!" Smiling through her tears, she pulled out a mesh and it snapped back into place again as soon as she let it go. "Why haven't I got curls like that?"

"Now then. . . . Jealousy!"

"I think it's *most* unfair. You could quite well do without them."

"Then I wouldn't be so beautiful."

"I'd love you just the same."

"Really? Would you?"

"I'm afraid so."

"You're a wonder, you are. But I'll make it up to you one day, you see if I don't." Arthur smiled happily for a moment and then stood up, saying briskly: "No time for that sort of nonsense now, though. We've got to get on, you . . . you . . . Mary! Still, we'll make a Martha of you yet. Have you remembered to put flowers in Vera's room?"

"I was going to do that after lunch so that they would be fresh for her."

"You'd better do it now, otherwise you're sure to forget."

Nathalie felt a slight tautening and waited for apprehension to assail her again. She need not have worried, however, for Arthur always felt better after a scene, and it was with comparative blandness that he said: "By the way, there's one more thing you should know. Vera was engaged to someone who was killed in the war."

"Oh, I *am* sorry!"

"I thought I'd better just mention it."

"It makes me almost ashamed that I should have been so lucky."

"If I'd been killed in the war you'd never have known the difference, since we didn't meet until 1946."

"Well, you know what I mean. . . ."

"Silly thing!" Arthur patted her awkwardly on the cheek and added: "I'm just going to collect some books for the spare room."

"All right. And I think I can hear some Dennison brats in the offing."

There were shouts, slamming of doors, and then the crash of something enamelled falling on to the tiled floor of the kitchen.

"My goodness, yes! You don't think . . . But no, it doesn't matter."

"What were you going to say?"

"Nothing. It can't be helped, anyhow."

"What can't?"

"Forget it," said Arthur, and he walked into the library, leaving his wife feeling uncertain again.

Nathalie wondered at this power Arthur had of taking her with him in every variation of his moods. She could see it happening and deplored it, and yet, for the first time in her life, seemed to have no will of her own. Sometimes she could see quite clearly the reactions that dignity, rather than defiance, demanded of her, but only with another, unreal self. Unable to appease Arthur, unable to even stand up to him, she was powerless to resist the degradation of being totally possessed by someone who yet did not really want her. Moreover, she felt resentful, and even ashamed, at being so profoundly committed to an intimate relationship which did not fit into any of her ideas about love. "Yet how much do I really know about love?" she wondered. "Although I'm twenty-five, I've only once before been at all seriously involved." That situation had been so different from this concentrated warfare that it now seemed to have happened in another life, almost to another person. "Was that because I wasn't married to Felix? Or because he was nearly twenty years older than I was? Or simply because he was a different kind of person, and basically gentle and peace-loving?" She reflected that perhaps she had still been a child then, living instinctively and happily, and now she was growing up and finding the process difficult. Arthur was contemptuous of her disappointments and maintained that unhappiness was an inevitable condition of mankind. For all she knew he might be right, but then she did not know anything for certain any more, and possibly that was an aspect of growing up too, just as living by calculation seemed to be. Shrugging her shoulders with philosophical resignation, she went to face Mrs. Dennison in the kitchen.

Arthur, meanwhile, selected a few books from the library and then sat down. He was filled with a mixture of shame, relief and apprehension: shame because his self-control had deserted him once again that morning; relief at his wife's easy acceptance of the prospect of his sister's visit; and apprehension as to what Vera's reactions would be. The more he speculated on these, the more nervous he became, until finally he opened the cupboard where the drinks were kept and poured himself a stiff gin. Now he felt guilty as well, for it was only just after ten o'clock in the morning. In order to prove to himself that it was ridiculous for a grown man to have inhibitions as to when he had a drink if he felt the need for one, he poured himself another gin and drank that just as quickly.

Nathalie did not find herself alone with her sister-in-law until the following morning, after Arthur had gone to London. At ten o'clock she knocked softly at the spare-room door, and was surprised to find her guest already dressed, the bed stripped and the used breakfast-tray discarded on a nearby table.

"You should have stayed in bed, and rested a little after your journey," Nathalie said.

"I don't need to rest, my dear," replied Vera. "I've always had twice the energy of people half my age. Besides, I'm so looking forward to seeing everything."

"I'm longing to hear what you think of the garden. Arthur says you have incredibly green fingers and I'd be so grateful for your advice. I know nothing about gardening."

"Well, you've plenty of time to learn," Vera said. "You look absurdly young this morning. . . . Arthur never really told me how lovely you were."

Nathalie blushed and looked away. "Thank you so much," she smiled. "You're being most complimentary, but I could say 'same to you'."

"I always say fair people come into their own at middle age, and sometimes even later, but you dark ones are at your best in early youth."

"I can't get over how like Arthur you are," Nathalie exclaimed. Both had the same sandy colouring, the same shaped head, the same rather long nose, the same thin-lipped mouth that went up on the left when they smiled. Vera's eyes, however, although also pale blue, were larger and softer than Arthur's.

"Well, we are brother and sister, after all."

"Yes, I know. I suppose every wife thinks her husband is

unique, and it's curious to find someone so like him. It's jolly nice, though," she added, with genuine enthusiasm.

"Shall we go down, now?" Vera asked abruptly.

"Yes, do let's."

"What about this tray? Do we take it down?"

"Yes, all right. Here, give it to me."

"And the beds? Does your woman make those?"

"No, but I can do them later. The sun is so wonderful, and I can't wait to get out."

"Very well, but do let me help you with that tray, won't you?"

"No, it's all right. You're a guest after all, so just relax and enjoy yourself."

Nathalie was walking carefully in front, peering over the breakfast tray and easing it around corners, and could not see Vera's expression harden when she answered: "It seems odd to think of myself as a guest in Arthur's house."

As they left the kitchen, Vera said: "There's nothing like an Aga, is there?" and then she stopped in the hall, in front of a mahogany table. "How pretty that blue bowl looks with those daffodils!" she exclaimed. "I love daffodils. I nearly bought a table very like that before the war, but by the time I'd made up my mind to have it, it had already gone. It was a real bargain, and would be worth three or four times as much now, I should think."

"This isn't a real one."

"Its made of old wood, isn't it?"

"Yes, but that's not quite the same thing."

"I always think it's what counts, though." Then, going into the drawing-room, she exclaimed: "What a pretty room! I was too tired and excited last night to really take anything in, but I *am* enjoying this." She fingered the brocade curtains and peered closely at the weave. "You can't get stuff like this these days, and if you could, it would come to the best part of two or three pounds a yard, I shouldn't be surprised."

"Really?"

"Still, this ought to last a while yet. That's the beauty of it. It does rather show up the carpet, though. What a shame it's so faded."

"That *is* real. It's a Savonnerie."

"I always like a fitted carpet, myself."

Vera wandered around the room peering, commenting and

asking questions, and then stood in front of the fireplace and looked up at a large portrait of a strong-featured Edwardian beauty.

"And who is that?" she asked.

"That's my Aunt Olga, the owner of this house. She'll be back from America any day now, so I hope you'll meet her soon. Of course, that was done years ago. Father painted it as a wedding present for her second marriage. It was before he became famous and he couldn't afford to give her anything else."

"Quite a valuable present after all, as it turned out."

"I suppose it is."

"She was a fine figure of a woman."

"She hasn't changed all that much since then. She's older, and has put on quite a bit of weight, but she's still the same in herself. You'll like her. She's a darling."

Vera walked on into the library and exclaimed: "What a nice room! I always think those Toile de Joule chintzes are in such good taste."

"I'm glad you like it. We mostly sit here, when we're alone."

"We?"

"Arthur and myself, I mean. In the old days it was Walt's—my uncle's—study."

"I see."

The library had french windows. These opened on to a stone-flagged terrace level with the lawn, and extending round the south-west of the house and under the Regency drawing-room windows. Nathalie opened them, and she and Vera stepped outside. The garden was saturated with sunshine—still weak, as it was early spring and the young leaves were small and pale. As they walked around the lawn, Vera peered into the flower beds and discovered one little treasure after another. Then she and Nathalie returned to the terrace and looked across the hills beyond.

"Its a nice garden," Vera said at last, "but it needs tidying. It's been rather neglected, I should think."

"Yes, I suppose it has," Nathalie said, though she could not imagine it any different. It had always been rather overgrown, thus seeming luscious and mysterious. She did not really understand what Vera meant by 'untidy' or 'neglected', so she took herself for ignorant.

"Do you have a gardener who comes regularly?" Vera asked.

"Oh, yes. He's been working here for nearly thirty years, and the only condition made about our having the house was that we should keep him on. My aunt doesn't know much about gardens either, but she adores Jacob."

Vera frowned. "Perhaps he just needs a little direction," she suggested sternly.

"I expect he does," Nathalie laughed, "but he's an obstinate old devil. He even decides what we eat and when, as far as vegetables are concerned."

"We'll have to see about that!" Vera exclaimed, and then added, "I expect he's taking advantage of your extreme youth."

"He's just the same with my aunt," Nathalie smiled, remembering the screaming matches between those two that had so often turned into sudden peals of laughter.

"Does Arthur pay the rent into a bank over here?" Vera asked.

"We don't pay Olga any rent. She just lets us live here."

"But is that altogether satisfactory?"

"How do you mean?"

"Isn't a rather difficult situation?"

"I don't think so. We like living here and she doesn't, so it seems rather a good arrangement."

"But it's putting you in the position of caretakers."

"Is it?" Nathalie was trying to understand what Vera was driving at, but she was not equipped to do so.

"You've no security of tenure, like this. I dare say that's why she's letting you live here without a contract."

"I'm not quite sure what you mean, but the thing is that Olga has quite enough money as it is, and Arthur and I find it a help not to have to pay any rent. That's all."

At that moment, Mrs. Dennison appeared at the french windows. She stood with a duster dangling from one hand a small child from the other.

"Sorry, dear, I didn't see you was out 'ere," she said, smiling cheerfully.

"That's all right." Nathalie turned to Vera and said: "This is Mrs. Dennison, who looks after things for us here."

"Good morning," Vera said, smiling only with her mouth.

"Morning, Miss. Say good morning to the ladies, Reggie-boy." She tugged at the child, but failed to pull him out of his trance. "He's shy, that's what it is," she explained. "Oh, and look at me! I've forgotten to put my teeth in this morning! Whatever will you think of me?"

Even her set of shiny, symmetrical teeth would hardly have counteracted the look of a bloated Medusa that was characteristic of Mrs. Dennison. Her hair had at some time been permanently waved, but looked as though it had been neither washed, nor cut, nor even combed since then. She wore a grubby floral overall that was tied round the middle with one of Arthur's old ties, thus emphasising her large, low-slung bolster of a bosom.

"I'll just leave 'im out 'ere while I do the drawing-room," she added. " 'E's a proper monkey and I wouldn't want 'im to do no damage, but 'e'll be as good as gold out 'ere. Lily'll look after 'im. LILY!" she screeched. Almost immediately another, slightly larger, Dennison child sidled into sight.

"Hullo, Lily," Nathalie said, but Lily out-stared her with the same glazed look as her little brother's and never uttered a sound. Her face looked as though someone had hit her on the head, rather to one side, while pulling the outward corners of her eyes downwards, and then the wind had changed. It was difficult to tell what those children would have looked like without traces of chocolate biscuit all over them, or in clothes that were not frankly filthy and several sizes too small, but in any case, their total lack of response did not increase their charm.

"Lily, take 'im orff for a bit, will you? There's a good girl. Over there, in that nice corner of the lawn. That's it." The children trotted off hand in hand without a backward glance, as Mrs. Dennison gazed fondly after them and murmured: "The loves! Did you ever see such bonny children? Don't they make you long to see what you can do? Never mind, you don't need to be in any 'urry, but the spring's a great time for falling, so you watch out!" She laughed merrily and then added: "Well, I'll get the sack if I stand 'ere chattering all morning. That Jacob'll be 'ollering for his tea in a minute, but I must get straight in 'ere first." She turned back to the drawing-room, humming loudly and unmelodiously.

Vera looked as she might have done if she had found a dead mouse in her bedroom. It was an expression of refined distaste which Arthur never had, because when he was displeased, he became either sulky or angry. Nevertheless, brother and sister were sufficiently alike for Nathalie to realise that all was not well at that moment, although Vera did not frighten her in the same way.

"Mrs. D. is rather overpowering," she said quickly, "but she works like a beaver and doesn't mind turning her hand at anything."

"That's a great asset, I must admit," Vera smiled. "In these days, it is rather a question of what one can get."

Nathalie had never made any attempt to get anyone else, for Mrs. Dennison had become a friend. She did not say this, however, but asked her sister-in-law if she would like to walk down to the village.

"I'd rather see the rest of the house first," Vera said. "I haven't really been upstairs yet. But don't bother about me—you must have hundreds of things to attend to."

"No, really! It's much more fun talking to you, anyhow."

"What about those beds. Shouldn't they be made?"

"Oh, they can wait. After all, it isn't every day that Arthur's sister comes to stay. . . . Nor that the sun shines like this, for that matter." Nathalie suddenly stretched out her arms towards the sky. The movement only lasted an instant, but it was at once graceful and passionate, and Vera turned away.

"First things first, my dear child," she said briskly. "If we do our chores in the morning, then we can enjoy the afternoon."

Nathalie privately felt that the morning, especially early, was the best part of the day and should be treated as such, not wasted on doing boring things, but she merely said: "All right, I shan't keep you waiting long."

"That's the way," said Vera. "I'll give you a hand, then we'll be through in no time."

First they made Vera's bed, and did what little tidying was needed in her room; then they went into the master bedroom. Vera took one look at it, and paused on the threshold before bracing herself to go in. Nathalie did not miss this hesitation and laughed: "It is rather a mess, I'm afraid. Arthur's awful about hanging things up, and I'm not much better."

"He never used to be particularly untidy."

"I expect it's just that he's in a hurry in the mornings, having to catch that wretched train."

"Perhaps." Vera hesitated once more by the side of the large double-bed, and then forced herself to help draw the bedclothes back one by one, turning away from the faint, but distinctive human odour that came from them.

"You really should strip your bed before you come down in the morning," she said, rather sharply.

"I mean to, and then sometimes I forget. I always seem to be in rather a rush and a muddle."

"A little simple organisation would soon put that right!" Vera smiled again.

"Yes, I know." Nathalie had many times devised systems for improving her housekeeping methods, but she would either forget all about them, or be interrupted by outside influences. She would omit to strip the bed because Arthur suddenly needed a button tightened. ("You ought to get up in time to check my clothes before I put them on!"); or breakfast would be late, and badly-cooked, because she had enjoyed listening to him talking. ("You ought to remember your responsibilities and break away."); but then those early morning talks, before and during breakfast, were the only times they never quarrelled, and such moments seemed too precious to interrupt. Sometimes, she would be unable to get up on time because a pleasant dream still held her back from waking; or she woke with one of the curious, sick headaches that had begun to afflict her lately. Later in the day, she would go for a walk and forget the time, or get lost in reading a book and leave some job undone, or simply sit, and then an hour, or sometimes two, or even three, would somehow get lost. She had begun to know more or less what she ought to do, but so often could not make herself do it, or simply forgot.

When the bed was made, Vera folded up Arthur's pyjamas and was just about to put them under a pillow when Nathalie said: "Could you just hang them on the door? He prefers it that way?" Vera did as she was bidden without a word, but her mouth was very straight and thin. Then she picked up a flimsy nightdress from a chair, asking: "And this?"

"I'll put that in here. . . . thanks." Nathalie pushed it under her pillow in a bundle.

"You'll catch cold if you don't wear any more than this," Vera said, forcing a smile.

"It's warmer than it looks," Nathalie answered. "It's nylon. They wear nothing else in America now, apparently. My aunt sends me underclothes from time to time and that helps with coupons."

"It looks most inadequate to me."

"Well anyhow, I've got Arthur to keep me warm."

Vera suddenly caught her breath as though she had been winded. "Do you find you get a proper night's rest, sleeping in a double-bed with someone else?" she asked quickly.

"Good heavens, yes. After all, there's plenty of room in this one. My aunt is twice the size of either you or me, and she was never cramped for space here. One of her husbands was enormously fat too," Nathalie added.

"It can't be as restful as it should be, for a man who has to go to work every day."

"Quite a lot of people sleep in double-beds, after all," Nathalie said, a little surprised. "Anyway, what's the difference? It's just more cosy, that's all." She knew that the warmth of such nearness was more important to her than to Arthur, however. He merely shared the double-bed with her because it was there, but it did not unite them in any special way. He made love to her, but to Nathalie that was only one part of physical intimacy. She craved the kind of unity of which physical pleasure is only an extension and confirmation, and he never understood that it was affection, rather than passion, that she lacked. If she put out a hand to touch him or tried to lie closer alongside of him, merely for the warmth of contact, he always assumed that she wanted him to respond entirely, and often upbraided her for making unreasonable demands on him. She knew nothing at all of what his private life had been before he married her, but her own experience, limited though it was, had taught her about a kind of tenderness of which he seemed to have no idea. With Felix, almost the best moments had been after they had made love; then, they had lain in each other's arms, sometimes dozing and sometimes talking softly, feeling so close that it was hard to tell where the one of them ended and the other began. Between herself and Arthur, however, there was always an unbridgeable gap, and it seemed that he did not want whatever it was she had to give, although he made so many demands on her in other ways. Even so, Nathalie considered herself fortunate to have had at least one experience of happy and satisfying love. At the time it had seemed to her quite natural; an inevitable, though miraculous extension of her contented and generous nature, which had made astonishingly vivid all the beauty of life that she had always been aware of. Lately, however, she had begun to wonder whether anything so whole-hearted were not, perhaps, rather unusual. Had Vera, for instance, ever known anything like it? Had she memories that made it possible for her to accept her fiancé's death and feel: "Well, at least I had that." Nathalie hoped so, but felt instinctively that her sister-in-law's experience had been of a different order to her own, however deep. Vera did not give her the impression of a serenity that indicates fulfilment, of whatever kind, although she was already forty-five. Feeling a glow of sympathy and affection, Nathalie exclaimed warmly: "You are a darling to help me like that! Now I can devote myself entirely to you. What would you like to do first?"

During the next few days, Arthur was in a better humour than he had been for a long time. Vera and Nathalie seemed to be getting on well, and he assumed that his irritability, during those first months of his marriage, had been due to niggling anxiety about the reconciliation of the two principal responsibilities of his life. Now that this was turning out well, he felt an immense relief. He congratulated himself on his handling of the situation and was well-disposed, both to Nathalie for her warm-hearted acceptance, and to Vera for showing so much common sense.

Arthur knew that his sister had felt piqued at his marriage, since he had presented her with a *fait accompli*, thinking that she would be less upset if it were too late to interfere. Nathalie had gone to live with her Aunt Olga in Paris soon after the war and had met Arthur there, shortly before his demobilisation. He and several other young officers had been entertained at the Baroness Bergerander's house, and the sense of freedom that the whole atmosphere seemed to convey enchanted him. Nathalie had intrigued him with her peculiar combination of unself-conscious vitality and shy awareness. He had found her restful and impressionable, and yet romantically exciting, and became convinced that she would give him the key to a world where he knew he belonged, but which he had never been able to find. Through her, he hoped to know the kind of self-assurance that would give him unlimited power. Only after their marriage, when they had known each other barely three months, did Arthur discover that Nathalie knew too little even to help him maintain his own illusions. In fact, on the contrary, she had a way of always wanting to know the truth, of trying to probe beneath appearances and asking direct questions to which she expected straight answers. He found this as maddening and childish as her capacity for being easily hurt, so that his sister's presence soon became reassuring to him.

"I do so want you to be happy," Vera said on her first Saturday morning at Walton House, when Nathalie was out shopping. "I'll do all I can to help her."

"Thank you, darling."

"She's not very practical, I'm afraid, but I suppose it's hardly surprising, when one considers her upbringing. We must try to be patient with her." Arthur said nothing, so Vera went on: "I know that her father was most distinguished and that her aunt is rather remarkable, but I don't much care for that set, myself."

"What exactly do you mean by 'that set'?"

"The cosmopolitan lot. I realise they often have looks, and money, and brains, and even influence, but they never strike me as having much solidity."

"They don't pretend to." Even though he wanted to be in harmony with Vera, Arthur could discern her limitations too clearly, and he experienced a sudden pang of nostalgia for his Paris period. "There's something very attractive about them, just the same."

Vera flinched and changed her tactics: "It's odd that with all these advantages, Nathalie should be so . . . well, so diffident, one might almost say."

Arthur's sense of propriety had now been outraged, and he exclaimed angrily: "Are you suggesting that my wife is insignificant?"

"I'm simply saying how fortunate it was for her that she met you, as she probably wouldn't have been able to fit into that set at all happily. I hope the child realises how lucky she is to have found someone with such good prospects." Her voice became husky with sentiment as she said again: "I do so want you to be happy, and you can always count on me, you know."

"You do like her, don't you?" Arthur asked, almost shyly.

"I think she's lovely—quite lovely. And so young. Young enough to develop sensibly, at any rate. I'll help all I can—if she wants me to, that is. I do so hope she values us all being together like this as much as we do."

Nathalie, in fact, did find this arrangement pleasant. She was by nature gregarious, and since Arthur invariably seemed bored and irritated by her own friends, she now saw less and less of them. Having another woman living in the house made her realise how much she missed the kind of effortless relationships that had always been so enjoyable to her before her marriage, and since she connected Arthur's present phase of exceptional good humour with Vera's presence, her sister-in-law's company seemed doubly welcome. Vera was unfailingly helpful to her about everything connected with cooking, cleaning, shopping and the other intricacies of housekeeping. It is true that they talked of little else, but Nathalie hoped that their happy exchanges on the best cuts of meat and the most advantageous lines in biscuits would lead to more personal talks about deeper things. She had never yet come across people who made their whole lives revolve around the mechanics of existence; her sort either took joints and biscuit in their stride, or else did without. Nathalie assumed that the offspring of a professor who had been brought up in a university town, even in the Midlands, must like nothing better than to curl up in front of a fire (or lie in the grass in the sun, according to the season), and discuss life, or aspects of the human soul, or just people, places and books. She was wrong, however, and as time went on she became more and more mystified. Vera numbered among her friends—or at least, acquaintances—many learned people. She read the papers assiduously, was punctilious in changing her library books, and appeared intelligent. Yet her comments on people, places and books were so trite that, to begin with, Nathalie thought they were satirical, and she firmly resisted any attempt to talk about life or the human soul. At the first hint of danger, of anything going down beneath the surface, she smiled in an enigmatic way and changed the subject.

Vera had been at Walton House nearly six weeks when Baroness Bergerander telephoned from Southampton to invite herself to lunch. Her ship had docked that morning, and she would be on her way to London.

Nathalie had not seen her aunt for nearly a year, but the thought of their reunion hardly moved her. Previously, she had always loved Olga's company, but now, rather to her surprise, she felt nothing except a slight apprehension. Although she did not realise this, it was her aunt's perception that she feared, and the energy with which the Baroness exposed any situation that came her way. All Nathalie admitted to herself was that she was extremely tired, as so often these days, and so any deviation from routine was an effort. She simply asked Mrs. Dennison to lay one more place for lunch and warned her that the chauffeur would also have to be given something to eat. The charwoman exclaimed happily: "Just you give me time to slip home and put me teeth in and then leave him to me! But I don't know what Mr. Dennison'll say, I'm sure!"

Vera, however, was thrown into a turmoil about everything. She worried about the meal not being adequate, as they only had two courses at lunchtime and there was no wine. She also complained that the house looked grubby, and exclaimed that as the best china had been put away and had not been used for so long, it would need washing. As she spontaneously poured out her doubts to Nathalie, her tone became more and more unfriendly, and she was especially irritated because the girl did not seem to take the situation seriously.

"Olga won't want more than two courses," Nathalie said laconically, "especially after stuffing herself on board ship for the past week. And she doesn't mind about things like dust and china."

"We can't let her think we don't know how to do things properly. Besides, its inhospitable. Oh, what a pity Arthur has to be in London today!"

"If you really think it's necessary, I'll open a tin of soup."

"That would be better than nothing."

"And we can give her whisky and soda to drink. She'd prefer that to the kind of wine you get in grocer's shops, anyhow."

"Personally, I've never had cause to complain of a reputable grocer with reliable stocks," Vera said primly. Then she added: "What will you wear?"

"What I've got on, I suppose." Nathalie was a little puzzled: she had put on a clean shirt that morning and her skirt was one of her newest and best cut.

"I should have thought a dress would be more suitable."

Vera had never spoken to Nathalie in such an icy tone before. Agitation had completely dispelled the almost fawning sweetness of the past few weeks, and there was something different in her expression as well. Up till then, she had conveyed smiling affability, misty sentimentality, or a coyness which, if embarrassing, was at least a facet of contentment. In more serious moods she looked attentive, or even politely puzzled, but never anything but confident. Now, caught unawares, her eyes seemed to grow larger and deeply opalescent, but these depths merely betrayed an emptiness, and a kind of desperate hunger, that was almost haunting in its desolation. Her resentment increased in observing that however tired or untidy Nathalie was, her slight figure, her youthfully compact features and her colouring of black hair, green eyes and golden skin still made it possible for her to look attractive. "Besides," Vera added, "it can't be healthy to constrict your waist like that."

Nathalie was prepared to accept criticism of the way she ran the house, or even how she looked after Arthur, but became impatient at being told how to dress for luncheon with her own aunt.

"If someone drops in in the country to take pot-luck, they don't expect to find everybody trussed up as though at a garden party," she exclaimed without a smile and turned to walk away. Halfway out of the room, she heard her sister-in-law mutter: "That girl will have to watch her tongue, or she'll become a shrew."

When Vera had spent half an hour in the kitchen supervising Mrs. Dennison she began to feel better, and by the time she had changed from her skirt and twin set into her good wool dress, her confidence was completely restored.

"I must apologise for getting into such a fluster," she said to Nathalie, while they were waiting for the Baroness to arrive. "I awoke with a bit of a head this morning, and that always makes me touchy."

"I am sorry. Would you like some aspirin?"

"I've taken some, thank you. I'm a martyr to migraine, I'm afraid, but this was only the slightest of attacks, I'm glad to say. I've been so looking forward to meeting your aunt, and I was anxious that everything should go well."

"You don't have to worry about Olga. She always sort of takes over, wherever she is."

Vera did not seem to find this altogether reassuring and her fingers began to twitch nervously, but she merely said: "Well, we ought to have quite a lot in common, anyhow. I like travelling too."

In spite of this eager anticipation, however, Vera's first sight of Olga Bergerander was a shock to her, as well as a surprise. The little she knew about the Baroness had seemed revealing enough, and the idea of a thrice-married Russian aristocrat who had, in one way or another, acquired wealth and property, led her to expect dignity, and even mystery. She was not prepared for a tubby and crumpled woman, whose face was more like that of an inquisitive bulldog than a haughty enchantress.

Vera had been upstairs putting a final dab of powder on her nose when the car arrived, and by the time she reached the front door, the situation was out of her hands. The Baroness had not so much come into the house as invaded it, and the hall was already full of her personal belongings: a portmanteau, coats, baskets, books and a fur rug. Vera wondered why these could not have been left in the car, since their guest was only staying to lunch. She had yet to learn that the Baroness did not organise her way through life but charged through it, thereby always surrounding herself with the sparks and shavings that had been let off in the process.

Nathalie introduced her sister-in-law to her aunt, but before Vera had any time to make the Baroness feel at home, Mrs. Dennison emerged from the kitchen, grinning broadly.

" 'Ullo, 'ullo, 'ullo—look who's 'ere!" she burst out. "Well, it is a treat to 'ave you back, and no mistake. 'Ow've you been keeping?"

"Margy Porter? I can hardly believe it!" the Baroness exclaimed.

"Margy Porter as was. Mrs. Ronnie Dennison, now, tra la la! Course I was forgetting it's bin ten years, and we're none of us getting any younger, are we!" Her laugh was like a cheerful neigh. "Still, I didn't think you'd 'ave forgotten the Porters in an 'urry!"

"I certainly remember how you and those ruffian brothers of yours used to climb into the orchard and pinch the apples! How are you, Margy?"

The Baroness held out a smooth, strong hand, and Mrs. Dennison wiped a red and chapped one on her apron before taking it.

"Not so bad, considering, and I've got myself a brood of bonnie bairns, as they say, since I last saw you."

"So Miss Nathalie told me. I'd love to see them, sometime."

"Well, I'd 'ave brought Reggie today, but I thought we'd be too busy, what with all this posh company, so 'e's gone orf shopping with 'is auntie. And Marlene and Lily are at school. Still, they'll keep."

Vera was making stern faces, first at Mrs. Dennison and then at Nathalie, but no one noticed her. The girl was looking at her aunt, and the Baroness was encouraging the charwoman to be what Vera termed 'too familiar'.

"Are your children as naughty as you were?" she was asking.

Mrs. Dennison laughed again, loudly and merrily. "They got spirit, the loves, but we were proper cards, weren't we, even though we did get belted now and then."

"Won't you take your coat off and come into the drawing-room?" Vera said suddenly. The atmosphere, which had been billowing warmly, suddenly became precise and cold. Nathalie stopped smiling and Mrs. Dennison said: "Well, mustn't stand 'ere gossiping all day, or we shan't get any dinner." The Baroness patted her shoulder and said: "It's lovely to see you again," and then followed Vera into the drawing-room.

All through luncheon, Vera talked about the places she had visited abroad, yet this did not seem to lead to the sense of solidarity she had visualised between herself and the Baroness. Olga listened, but was not especially responsive, for she thought of places in terms of people, and often the same people in different places. She had never been interested in the monuments, the fauna and flora, the annual rainfall or even the historical associations of any town or country. When Vera was describing a walk among alpine flowers in the spring, or the carving of a rood screen in some Florentine church, or the legendary origins of an ancient wall near Arles, the Baroness would say: "Indeed," or "How interesting!" and then turn to Nathalie with some remark like: "By the way, I saw Nicky Holdenstein in New York. He asked after you," or "Do you remember that absurd house Nina de Billancour used to have near there?" After luncheon, while they were having coffee in the drawing-room, the Baroness looked at her niece on two occasions and said: "It is so lovely to see you again, my darling", but Vera still talked; first about the Black Forest, and then about some interesting buildings at Nancy. Finally, the Baroness said: "There are one or two things I must discuss with Nathalie, so I hope you won't mind if we move to the library." Smiling as though she had just bitten into an unripe quince, Vera jumped up and said: "Please don't move, I was just going in any case. I've lots of little things to attend to in the garden."

The door had scarcely closed behind her, when Olga exclaimed: "How do English women get that shape?"

"Shhhh, she'll hear you."

"It will do her good. Really, that behind! And those legs . . . straight up and down. And even if her bosoms *are* round her waist, why doesn't she do something about it? It's disgusting!"

"You being an example of what a woman's figure should be like in middle age, I suppose," Nathalie smiled.

"Oh, I know I'm fat—fat and gross. But at least I'm all in one piece. That woman is thin, and yet sticks out in all the wrong places. Besides, I'm not such a bore. How can you stand it?"

"She's not so bad, really. So full of information, too, and I'm sure it's correct."

"It's always a mystery to me how some people can know so much, and yet understand so little. I'm just the opposite, myself. I know nothing and understand everything. How long is she staying, anyhow?"

Nathalie remembered how often her aunt said what others merely thought. She herself had begun to wonder how long Vera's visit was going to last, but nothing whatever had yet been said about her leaving. All she replied, however, was: "After all, she is Arthur's sister. He likes having her here."

"How is Arthur, by the way?"

"Fine. He'll be sorry to have missed you."

"Are you happy?"

"Yes, of course I am." Nathalie looked away, feeling an unusual need to hide her private life from her aunt.

"Well, you don't look it," the Baroness said emphatically. "I've never seen anyone change so much. You've no life left in you any more. What does he do to you?"

Nathalie laughed: "Oh Olga, I'd forgotten how you exaggerate." She thought: "It's the strain of always watching myself, trying not to say what I think, and saying things I don't mean", but out loud she explained: "I'm just finding it rather hard work learning about housekeeping and things, that's all."

"Does *she* teach you?" The Baroness pointed a thumb at the door.

"She's practical and helpful, and that keeps Arthur sweet, which is the main thing."

"She looks a vampire to me. You watch out."

"What *do* you mean by that?"

"I shouldn't be surprised if she's the kind who lives on human sacrifice, and can only exist by sucking the life blood out of other people."

Nathalie felt piqued at her aunt's downrightness and protested: "She's a most self-sacrificing person herself."

"They're usually much the worst," the Baroness replied at once. "They implore you to trample all over them, and all the time they've got their teeth firmly clenched in your throat." Then she completely disarmed her niece by adding: "My darling child, I do so hate you to be unhappy. You seem to have a flair for attracting trouble." She spoke with so much warmth and affection that Nathalie wanted to throw herself into her aunt's arms and sob her heart out. This impulse was momentary, however, and left her with no emotion and no thought.

There was a long silence before the Baroness spoke again. Then she said: "I saw Felix in Washington."

"Did you?" Nathalie still felt nothing, rather to her surprise. "How is he?" she added.

"I think he misses you." The Baroness watched her niece closely, for Nathalie betrayed a momentary flutter of feeling. It was an awareness of something pleasant that might even lead to a hope of some kind, but it passed and left her feeling as flat as before, and as though they were discussing something that was not quite real. She had put Felix away in a separate compartment with many other things that Arthur disliked about her, whether thoughts, memories or friendships. In a few months many of these, which had taken years and years to create, had almost been forgotten.

"Surely he's found another girl friend by now?" Nathalie said, with surprise rather than bitterness.

"He's tried several, but they don't seem to last long, these days."

"Well, that's nothing new, is it?"

"Stop this nonsense, my darling. What went wrong? Why did you go and marry Arthur, like that?"

Nathalie suddenly felt an overwhelming desire to talk about Felix. Her aunt's presence made her feel that she belonged to herself again, and therefore had a right to do this. Slipping down to sit on the floor at the Baroness's feet and putting her head on the comfortable lap she had known for so many years, she exclaimed: "I couldn't help it. I've thought about it often enough since then, but I still can't really explain it. It was so strong, so compelling. People imagine one has a choice in these things, but I never have had. I never had any choice about loving Felix, and I had no choice about marrying Arthur. If someone had gagged and bound me and taken me to the other end of the world for ten years, I would still have felt that I'd left something unfinished."

"And if Felix had been here instead of in America? Would you still have chosen Arthur instead of him?"

"But Felix wasn't here. . . . You never tried to stop me marrying Arthur at the time. Why all this now?"

"At that time I thought you knew what you were doing."

"I was hypnotised. I don't know whether it was right, but it was inevitable."

"And I didn't know then that you and Felix had been lovers."

"Oh, he told you, did he?"

"Yes. Now many things are more clear, except the one thing that really matters. Why did you marry Arthur, and not Felix?"

"Felix never asked me to."

"But you knew how he felt."

"Yes, *I* knew, but did he?"

"He certainly does now, anyhow. Why didn't you at least wait until he came back?"

"He never asked me to do that, either."

The Baroness looked at her niece incredulously, and exclaimed: "Are you the fool, or am I?"

"I expect I am," Nathalie smiled, "but I'll try to explain. It won't make much sense, but I expect you'll understand just the same. I've loved Felix ever since I can remember, and when I was fifteen I fell *in* love with him. It was rather a joke, do you remember? Nathalie Corrand's teen-age infatuation, and so on. Touching and amusing. It didn't worry Felix, though. He'd always had rather a special spot in his heart for me, and that just went on. It developed and changed, but it never flagged. We always had fun together, whether I was ten or twenty. Goodness, how we giggled—about everything, even his girl friends. He helped me with my homework, and in return, I'd help him get out of one affair after another. I was always on the inside with him and that was where he needed me most. When I became his mistress, it seemed as natural and as beautiful and inevitable as all the rest, only a little while after that, he was suddenly sent to Washington. If he'd needed me then, either as a wife, or to wait for him he could have had me, and he must have known it. He didn't seem to want either, though, and that was all right by me, but I'm still on the inside with him, and I always shall be. The fact that we can't now be lovers doesn't matter. It was only a small part of the whole." She looked out of the window, knowing that what she said sounded false. It was therefore no surprise to her that the Baroness exclaimed:

"My dear child, your self-delusions would be funny if they weren't so pathetic! Do you suppose that Arthur will accept Felix for one moment, even as a friend? Arthur's sort are not ours, you know. They never really know about love. It gets so muddled in their minds with sex, and paternity, and income levels, and respectability, and Heaven knows what else. Their hearts become distorted, and love to them acquires a quality of exclusion that makes nonsense of all our ideas. You must understand that and be patient with it, or you'll never make a success of your marriage."

This time, Nathalie welcomed such brutal honesty and said wistfully: "Well anyhow, I'm not likely to see Felix again for ages, so that's all right."

The Baroness caressed her niece's hand and said, "My poor darling."

"Why poor?"

"Oh, because you're so innocent and so brave that it's heart-breaking, and because you still have to learn how to fight for your happiness in this world."

"I can't fight for *people*. I can only try to give them what they want."

"It's only the brutes who know what they want and go all out to get it, but there aren't so many of those. With the rest, it usually takes a woman to make them realise what they're really after."

"Well, you should know if anybody does. How many lovers have you had, Olga? Somebody once said—I can't remember who, now—that you made Catherine the Great look like an inhibited novice."

"An Englishman, I've no doubt. They have a vulgar respect for quantity, but quantity implies superficiality. It is quality that teaches you; the quality of your enchantment, of your intellectual excitement, of your ecstasy, of your suffering, even."

She followed her memories in silence, while Nathalie relaxed a little in the warmth and security of her presence. It was the first time she had had a conversation of this kind, aimless but unfettered, for many months. Then the Baroness went on: "I expect you'll suffer a lot before you get yourself sorted out. Slavs have a capacity for suffering, but also for making an ally of it."

"I'm only a quarter-Slav after all; quarter-Russian, quarter-French and half-English. What a horrible mixture! I suppose my mother took after the French side?"

"Yes, she was quite different from me in every way. Perhaps that was why we got on so well. She was so beautiful—so beautiful that her admirers hardly dared to come near her. With me, it was just the other way. Mine used to sniff round like naughty little dogs, and I sometimes longed to inspire awe the way she did. I think she would have been quite as gay as I was if she'd been stronger, but even so she managed to have a lot of fun."

Nathalie had never really been able to imagine her mother as a person, rather than as a sitter for some of her father's early portraits. Now, for the first time in her life, she was beginning to think a great deal about her. Her own dissatisfaction was making her aware of herself in a way that called for a continual reassessment and examination, a perpetual attempt to understand what was happening to her, and why.

"Am I at all like her?" she asked her aunt.

"In a way. In looks, you miss something she had that put her quite out of the ordinary, but in character, I should say that you are more complicated. Your mother already seemed a complete person when she died, although she was younger than you are now, but I have a feeling that you've only just begun to show what you will eventually become."

"How complicated it all sounds!" Nathalie laughed. She was reassured by her conversation with her aunt, and so much off her guard that when Vera suddenly appeared at the door with a laden tea-tray, she felt a pang of irritation.

"I thought you'd like some tea before you go back," Vera smiled stickily, "and I've made one of my special sponge-cakes. I do hope you'll try it."

When Arthur heard about the Baroness's visit, he was sincerely sorry to have missed her. His admiration for Olga was not tainted with the same sort of jealousy as he felt of his wife, so it was with imaginative enthusiasm, at dinner, that he began to talk about the Baroness's parties in Paris.

Nathalie laughed readily at his remarks, encouraging him to do imitations (which he did excellently), and seemed more lively than she had been for a long time. This pleased Arthur. He liked her to chaff him and provoke him into making the kind of remarks which he felt were worthy of him. When she seemed to be taking things in her stride, and lost the dull look in her eyes, and the pallor and dejection that had so often settled on her lately, he was, for a time, released from the cloud of guilt that so quickly turned to irritation. But however much he was enjoying himself, Arthur always remained acutely aware of the atmosphere in his audience, and he realised that Vera had not smiled once.

"Well?" he said, turning to his sister halfway through dinner. "You haven't got much to say for yourself."

"I've never even heard of the people you're discussing, so it's not awfully easy for me to say anything."

"You might at least take an interest."

"I do, but I don't want to intrude on you two. Besides, compared to all your interesting friends, I must seem very dull." Vera looked sulky, with her thin mouth turned down at the corners and the expression in her eyes that of a dog which has been beaten but does not understand why. Arthur smelt danger and said:

"You could never be dull, darling. Only restful." Vera smiled soulfully at her brother but said nothing, so he continued: "If you want to know what being dull really means, you should meet Poldi Puppenheim, one of the Baroness's favourite courtiers.

Now there's a bore for you, if ever there was one!" He turned to Nathalie and asked: "Don't you agree, darling?"

"Poor Poldi," said Nathalie.

"*Poor* Poldi, indeed!" Arthur exclaimed. "The man positively stinks of money, yet he can do nothing except get more and more pompous every time he opens his mouth. I don't believe he has any sense of humour at all. You should see the way people ask for their hats the moment he walks into a room." As Arthur went on with his mockery, Vera began to look happy for the first time that day.

Later, when Nathalie lay in bed reading while Arthur went to say good night to his sister, as he always did, she felt calmer and more hopeful than for months past. Taken as a whole, the evening had been an agreeable one, and Nathalie was beginning to understand that a kind of domestic intimacy could exist regardless of what a personal relationship might be. She saw that the knowledge of what another person liked to eat, the repetition of routines, the shared responses to an obstinate boiler or a pattern on a curtain, and a hundred other trivialities, could add up over years to create a bond that might be quite as compelling as a deep spiritual affinity. She had yet to realise that, although many people think they crave deeply exciting relationships, most of them, when it comes to the point, prefer to feel comfortable and secure; yet, she began to blame herself for her unhappiness.

"A relationship is rich because of the worlds that friends or lovers share, but these must obviously differ in every case," she told herself. "Felix and I knew heavens and havens of the mind and heart, which we could find together wherever we were, but I haven't succeeded in providing a world in which Arthur and I can find each other. The trouble is that I don't really know what he wants. Perhaps he and I really do have different ideas of intimacy, and my failure to sew on buttons, or do the dusting properly, or get meals on time really does undermine him in exactly the same way as his coldness and lack of purpose does me." These past weeks, since Vera had been in the house, had taught her that Arthur did not want her at his beck and call, in case he should want her to come for a walk, or read to her, or just talk. He preferred to be told to drop something he was doing because it was tea-time, or forbidden to have baths at certain times because the hot water had to be eked out, or even sent off to do some shopping. No men that Nathalie had ever known would have responded to such things except by ignoring or forgetting them. To most of them, these were the mechanics of living; they might prefer them well organised, since this made them less noticeable, but they only took up a small and minor part of their consciousness. "But Arthur isn't like that," she thought, "and since it's him I have to live with, I must try to make him happy in his way. I mustn't be depressed because he seems to need a combined nurse and housekeeper, rather than a lover or a companion. I mustn't worry because he doesn't seem able to give himself in any way, and except when we're quarrelling, we behave as though we were at a tea-party. I must try not to be resentful that, ever since Vera's arrival, we've hardly had any time by ourselves. I must just try a bit harder."

Arthur seemed to be taking rather longer than usual saying good night to Vera that evening. Their bedrooms were adjoining, and Nathalie could just hear their voices coming through in a series of jerks, rather than a murmur. Presently, she was distracted from her reading because the voices got louder, and it became obvious that Arthur and Vera were quarrelling. The sound of his voice came through in angry bursts, but his sister's were higher and higher pitched wails of hysteria. Nathalie could not hear what they were saying, but she had to put down her book. Discord of any kind always upset her, and she felt herself stiffening with apprehension, longing for the row to stop, yet dreading Arthur's return. The scene next door seemed to go on and on, and at one point, Nathalie thought she heard the window being banged. Gradually, the voices became quieter, and at last she heard Vera's door softly opening and closing. Then, Arthur came in. At first, she did not even dare to look at him. It had occurred to her to pretend to be asleep, but she knew from experience that this would be futile. If Arthur wanted to talk, or make a scene, he would rouse her even if she were genuinely asleep. He began to empty the contents of his trouser pockets on to the dressing-table with abrupt and noisy movements, and it struck Nathalie as yet another remarkable facet of domestic intimacy to be able to detect a person's mood in so commonplace an action. She could even tell, by looking at his back, that he had his tight-lipped, sulky expression, the one that also denoted self-pity. Then her heart went out to him, for she felt his unhappiness, and without premeditation she said: "Are you all right?"

This broke the tension. Arthur wheeled round with suppressed fury and rasped: "What the hell have you been doing to my sister!"

Nathalie at once felt the old fear again, so that instead of giving a jocular, or even aggressive answer, she almost cringed as she said: "What's the trouble?"

"Trouble!" Arthur said, still quietly, but with his voice full of hate. "No trouble at all, except that she's in such a state about something that happened today that she tried to throw herself out of a window!"

He knew very well that this was nothing new. This sort of scene had occurred with almost predictable regularity ever since he could remember. During his childhood they had not been so violent, though they had affected him quite as much. Only since he had grown up, and begun to acquire interests that Vera could not share, or friends to which she took inexplicable dislikes, had the suicidal note been added to them. He had learned how to deal with these crises, how to calm and reassure Vera until gradually her hysterics were replaced by quiet sobbing, and finally she smiled bravely through her tears and forgave him. The scene that had just taken place, however, was the first he had had to deal with for a long time, and he was more upset by it than he could ever remember being on similar occasions. Serving overseas during the war had widened his horizon and made such tantrums now seem the more intolerable. Besides this, Arthur had hoped that somehow, in some miraculous way, the fact of his being married would make a difference; what difference, he had never clearly thought out, but he felt that this must put him in a new category, that it confirmed his maturity and independence, and therefore Vera would show him some respect. The disappointment that he now experienced was really bitter, and his dissatisfaction with himself, profound. Since he could not castigate Vera, and Nathalie provided such a sitting target, it was on his wife that he directed the blame for everything that had gone wrong. When Nathalie asked: "What did she say?" she betrayed such a failure to grasp the situation that his anger and resentment increased. What did she say, indeed! How could anybody tell what Vera was saying on these occasions? What did coherently get through the mass of disjointed accusations and almost flagellating self-pity was so wounding that it was better forgotten as soon as possible.

"What is more to the point is what you've been saying," he said angrily. "You, and that aunt of yours!"

"Olga may be downright, but she's never unkind." Nathalie was puzzled, rather than frightened. She could not imagine what had gone wrong, for the day had seemed to her so pleasant.

"I gather that this time she seems to have been condescending and inconsiderate."

"I'm terribly sorry Vera should have felt that. They seemed to be getting on so well."

"You can't ever see anything beyond the end of your nose, and the Baroness is obviously far too cunning to let you do so, but at least she might have appreciated the trouble my sister went to on her behalf. It was extremely discourteous of her to refuse to eat tea, when she knew that Vera had prepared it all herself."

"But she never has tea. It's a very English meal, you know, and she hasn't lived in England for years."

"Evidently good manners is also a prerogative of the English."

"Arthur, we never asked Vera to get any tea, you know. It's such a silly thing to be upset about, anyhow."

" 'We', is it! I might have known there was a conspiracy between the two of you."

"I only meant that Olga and I were talking together when Vera came in."

"Having been dismissed earlier, I gather."

"Not dismissed, but Olga wanted to talk to me alone."

"What about?"

"Nothing in particular. It's just that I haven't seen her for so long."

"About what hell your marriage is, I suppose!"

"I wouldn't dream of discussing my marriage with anybody."

"What about, then?"

"Well, you know what it is, if you haven't seen someone you're especially attached to for a long time—for instance, like you and Vera meeting after so long. There must have been things you wanted to talk about that were of no possible interest to me. . . . You *must* know what I mean."

Arthur did not see that, however. His conversations with Vera could be overheard with impunity by anyone, because they only concerned trivialities. Even their criticisms, whether astringent or mocking, were never concerned with anything beyond appearances: whether so-and-so's taste in cretonnes was acceptable, or how much a dinner-party must have cost to give, or how loudly, or ignorantly, somebody spoke. Arthur had occasionally tried to speculate about what went on under the surface, but Vera invariably disagreed with him. She made him feel that his judgment was puerile, so he developed the habit of keeping such thoughts to himself. His contact with people apart from his sister was so different from Nathalie's experience of friendship that he could not conceive of the kind of relaxed cosiness that she meant. Once Nathalie made friends, she never lost touch with them; or at least, that had been the case until her marriage. Arthur, on the other hand, lost interest in anyone the moment any kind of intimacy became an established fact, rather than something his imagination could play with. The jealousy he experienced at that moment came out of his assumption that any kind of relationship must always be as highly charged as his own were.

They went on wrangling, as they had done so often before, and Arthur's abuse became almost ludicrously exaggerated. After twenty minutes of this, Nathalie burst into tears. She had not yet learnt to hide her emotions, as well as control them, and the contrast of this scene, coming so soon after her moment of hope and determination, made her feel all the more desperate.

"Oh, for Heaven's sake stop behaving like some female Ferdinand!" Arthur exclaimed. "I know far too much about blackmail to be impressed by it, anyhow." He was disappointed that she never proved an opponent worth his metal. He craved the elation of conflict with someone who matched him in vigour and outrageousness, some kicking creature who continually escaped him, only to give as good as she got whenever he mastered her for a moment. He had rightly judged Nathalie to be passionate, but could not have foreseen that, when assailed, she would dissolve into sadness, instead of being raised to savagery. He demanded her absolute devotion, and yet was bored by the unconditional way in which she totally surrendered herself. Once she had collapsed into crying, there was no point in going on, and then he left her alone.

It was from then that Nathalie noticed a distinct change in Vera's attitude to her. Previously there had existed an easy affability between them, whatever their private speculations about each other may have been. When the Baroness's visit had shown Vera that she was not of exclusive importance to Nathalie's life, however, all the suspicion and jealousy that she had not faced up to now came to the surface.

Her first action, the morning after Olga's visit, was to ask for the return of some things she had given Nathalie during the previous weeks: a brooch she had had since childhood ("It would look exactly right on that blouse of yours"); a bright mohair scarf ("It goes so well with your dark hair"); and a knife-sized nail file, nearly thirty years old. (Nathalie had merely asked to borrow the latter, but Vera had said, "Why don't you keep it? I'd like you to have it.") Now, it occurred to her that she might want to wear the brooch again; that with a bit of a throat she had no warm scarf to go out in, apart from the mohair one; and that the nail-file might as well come back to live in her own drawer, though Nathalie would be welcome to borrow it.

Nathalie took this change of heart without being too perturbed, and what seemed to her far more serious was the difference in the general atmosphere. Atmosphere is created by and through the combined emanations of people, yet it affects all those who partake in it differently. Nathalie, for instance, began to feel that the air was full of hatred; not a mere absence of conviviality and harmony, but as though some destructive force had pervaded their midst. She became increasingly puzzled and absent-minded. Vera indulged in more and more extravagant displays of self-pity. Arthur, in a sense, had the worst of it. Being away from the house most of the day, he came back to it more impressionable than the women who had fed, and fed off the air all day. Besides, he was so sensitive to atmosphere that if it did not immediately reassure him, he became uncertain and aggressive.

Believing that any situation could be handled by correct attention to the details of its framework, Arthur decided to start taking Vera out a good deal. She would meet him in London and they would go to theatres, as they had done in the old days before the war. He took trouble not to neglect Nathalie altogether and was scrupulous in taking her out just as regularly, if only to the cinema in Oxford, or for walks on the hills. Yet, the moment they had left the house, he was already apprehensive about Vera's reactions on their return, so it was almost like having her along with them, and neither enjoyed themselves. Nathalie preferred it when Arthur and Vera were away, and found quiet satisfaction in the few hours of having the house to herself. Those moments of solitude did not solve anything, but they enabled her to come off her guard for a while. If the sun was shining, she could have her lunch off a tray at the bottom of the garden, or go for a walk without worrying about the time. Yet somehow, there was no longer any pleasure for her in doing such things. She could not now rejoice in the beauty of sights or sounds; from sheer habit, she noted all these things, but as though from the other side of a glass wall, and they meant nothing to her any more.

One morning, early in April, Nathalie decided to tidy the house. The coming of spring had always made her restless, but this time it did not fill her with exhilaration. She did not want to go out and be reminded, in countless ways, of the upsurge of new life all around her; it was something she could no longer feel part of, so she rejected it altogether. Also, at the back of her mind was a vague hope that she would endear herself to Vera and Arthur by such a pronounced symptom of domesticity, so she set herself to her task with thoroughness. Starting in her bedroom, she carried out basket after basket of waste: empty match boxes, used cigarette cartons, old medicine bottles, finished toothpaste tubes, punched bus tickets, out-of-date newspapers, and torn clothes that were waiting to be mended or cut up, but which would obviously never be touched.

When she started on the bottom drawer of Arthur's tallboy, she found his service revolver. It was jumbled up with some shirts that were now too small for him, a sweater that he disliked, and half a dozen pairs of khaki socks that were kept in case they came in useful. She tidied the drawer and was about to put the revolver back, when it occurred to her to shoot herself. Although not so acutely unhappy that to live seemed an intolerable burden, or even a pain, she was experiencing the kind of numbing despair that makes people think, not that there is no point to life, but that there is no point in their living. She did not feel that this would solve her problems, or absolve her from facing the future, or even that nobody really cared, in any case, whether she were alive or dead. Her real trouble was that she did not feel anything at all. Convinced that she had now lived out all that life held for her, there appeared to be no reason for going on with it. She sat down on the bed and began to examine the revolver, ascertaining that it was loaded and could be handled without difficulty. It did not occur to her to wonder whether suicide were wrong because she considered herself already dead. The presence of her body, with its absurd appetites and exigencies, seemed to her no justification for existence when her heart and her soul had already gone. Since there was nothing more she could contribute to life, it seemed, in fact, right to complete her death. "How long have I felt like this," she wondered. "Is it, perhaps, that I really can't live without Felix, as they would say in books?" But she knew that this was not so, and that whatever way their parting had affected her, she had gone on feeling that the life they had both loved with such intensity was well worth living, though more complicated than she had once supposed. Even the previous spring there had been no such feeling of despair. "I didn't know Arthur existed then," she suddenly realised. "Is it just being with him that has driven all the joy and purpose out of living? In less than a year? What is a single year, after all, out of the seventy or eighty of one lifetime, out of all the lifetimes of all the people in all the centuries since man began? How is it possible that one man can make me feel like this within one year?" She could find no answer to this. Confusion and doubt, as well as straightforward misery, had weighed her down so that she could not think, but suddenly a great curiosity was born in her. "What a fool I am!" she thought and putting the revolver gently back in the drawer, buried among the khaki socks, she went on with her work.

As Vera's visit to Walton House was indefinitely prolonged, various local families began to call on her as though she had become an inhabitant. The village of Compton Fawcett was small, but it had two big houses: the oldest, Fawcett Place, where the Hammonds lived, and the Manor House, which belonged to Lady Bates. When General Sir Alfred Bates bought this place in 1900, the social ramifications of Compton Fawcett had been clearly established, and Lady Bates had known where she stood. She was not a snob, but both her character and her upbringing made it impossible for her to take people as they were until she knew who they were. She did not automatically like people just because they had money and came from respectable families, but it was difficult for her to accept them unless they qualified in both these categories. A more sensitive person might have become rather lonely and even melancholy; a relic of her time. As it was, Lady Bates was robust enough to feel that it was somehow others who had gone wrong. There were still a few old ladies in the neighbourhood—as well as Sir James Featherstone, a retired colonial governor—with whom she was on visiting terms, but except for gentleman farmers, the younger generation no longer really settled in the country as they used to, for most of them now had to earn their livings. Anthony Hammond she had known ever since his babyhood, but to her mind, the Hammonds had always been a mixed blessing: they loved the country, while the Bateses put up with it as a necessary requisite for position; they had many friends, and the visitors at their frequent house parties were often distinguished, but they detested the kind of social round that the Bateses found necessary; they liked the village people, knew them as individuals and gave them help or advice when they got into difficulties, but the Bateses sat on innumerable committees of charitable and welfare societies. The Hammonds had always been Liberals, while the Bateses were Conservatives, and fifty years beforehand, when political tempers flared up so violently, there had been several occasions on which Henry Hammond and the General had quarrelled so violently that they had not been on speaking terms for many weeks.

All this belonged to the good old days, however, so that even the rows of the past had now become cherished memories. Lady Bates even forgot how much she had disliked and distrusted Olga, and now looked forward to her calls at Walton House with pleasure. She was a large woman with a heavy, florid face, and a deep, loud voice. Her clothes had been bought, rather than chosen, so that her whole appearance gave an impression of tasteless opulence, yet there was something rather pathetic about the sight of her stumping through the village, eagerly hoping to find in Vera someone who would share her point of view.

A great deal can be said about the meaning and characteristics of true friendship, but a relationship can be considered satisfactory with far less. Lady Bates and Vera contrived to use each other as mirrors to their own aspirations and prejudices, and so achieved the illusion of mutuality. Vera gushed with unconcealed respect and admiration, making the old woman feel not only important, but also that she had found a person with the correct outlook on things, and Nathalie watched all this with interest. The low ebb in morale that she had reached over the revolver incident and her temptation to commit suicide had marked a turning point in the development of her state of mind. From that day, she began to use her head, as well as her heart, following up a resolve to try to piece together the fragments of her understanding. A more thorough knowledge of Vera, for instance, seemed to her obviously desirable, and the latter's conversation with Lady Bates was proving something of a revelation.

"I always think your house far the loveliest one in the village," Vera twittered. "There are other fine ones round here, of course, but yours looks so cared for, somehow."

"Yes, it's a nice place," boomed Lady Bates. "You must come and see it, one day. I've found a very pretty new chintz for the hall. It looks well."

"There are *such* pretty chintzes about now. That's something that can still be had, I'm glad to say. And I've often admired that yellow rose that does so well on your east wall; It's a Mrs. Perkins, isn't it?"

"Yes, it is. Would you care to see the garden, some time?"

"I'd simply love to. I hear it's a real show place, and I would so appreciate your advice. Arthur and Nathalie have asked me to help them with this garden, but I'm afraid I don't know much about Oxfordshire soil." She smiled at Nathalie with a shining, conspiratorial look, as though to convey: "We all have such jolly times together," but Nathalie could not bring herself to respond, and looked away.

"Mrs. Walton never seemed to be much interested in the gardens, I'm afraid," sighed Lady Bates.

"They were my uncle's great delight, and after he died, she hadn't really the heart to do more than just keep them up," said Nathalie.

"Really? I always thought it so odd of her that she wouldn't even open them, like the rest of us did."

"I think she felt they weren't good enough any longer after Walt—my uncle—died." Nathalie turned away then, unable to stop smiling as she remembered her aunt once saying: "Why can't my friends enjoy it in peace, and without that interfering old bitch and all her boring committees trampling about all over the place!"

"Our English customs must sometimes be rather difficult for foreigners to grasp," Vera said, her conspiratorial look directed at Lady Bates, this time, and her implication shutting out not only the Baroness, but Nathalie as well.

"How is Mrs. Walton, by the way?" asked Lady Bates.

"She's very well, thank you," answered Nathalie.

"I suppose I should really call her Baroness Bergerander now, but I always forget."

Nathalie could almost hear her thinking: "But of course, to be a Baroness abroad doesn't really count, in any case."

"When did her third husband die?" Vera asked.

"He's still alive as far as I know," said Nathalie.

"Oh, of course," Vera exclaimed, as though she knew all about it, but it had just slipped her mind for the moment.

Nathalie suddenly felt thoroughly exasperated, but she said calmly: "I believe that after they'd been married about a week, Olga decided it was all rather a mistake, and when the Baron came down to breakfast one morning, he found a one-way ticket to Buenos Aires on his plate. Luckily, he took the hint."

When the Baroness next invited herself to stay for a week-end, Arthur took great trouble to ensure that she was given a suitable welcome. He laid in various wines (from a wine merchant), made sure that Nathalie had ordered the kind of food he felt they should provide, and arranged flowers in original places all over the house. Vera was more changeable: at times she seemed to look forward to the visit and spoke of the dishes she would prepare (since the Baroness apparently did not appreciate cakes); then she would suddenly become discouraged and depressed, and sulk at the thought of having this guest for several days.

The day after the Baroness's arrival, she and the three Bateman-Browns were on the terrace waiting for Sir James Featherstone to come to tea. It was a beautiful day. The flowers and shrubs were richly colourful, and the trees by the stream at the bottom of the garden seemed dark and cool, but beyond the end wall, the downs looked parched and hazy in the distance.

"Dear Jimmy," said the Baroness. "How is he?"

"He potters around quite happily, being frightfully busy about nothing," Arthur said, and Nathalie added: "It's rather pathetic to think of him all by himself in that hideous great house. I suppose he's got used to being a widower by now, but it seems a bit hard that his only son should have been killed in the war."

"I always think he looks so distinguished," Vera gushed. Then she blushed, for at that moment, the man himself suddenly appeared round the corner of the house. The Baroness jumped up and embraced him, exclaiming: "How lovely to see you again after all this time. You are a naughty man to hide yourself like this."

"Well, I'm not as young as I was, you know," smiled Sir James. "We don't all have the secret of eternal life, like you."

When the formalities were over, and the tea had been brought, poured and distributed, he emphasised this point to Nathalie, saying: "You know, Olga really *is* amazing. I don't believe she's changed at all since she and your uncle stayed with us in the South Seas, all those years ago."

"And you're still the perfect gallant, I see," the Baroness said happily. Then she added wistfully: "Oh, what fun we all had that time. Do you remember how jealous Walt got, because I kept insisting that you had such beautiful legs?" She turned to Vera and explained: "Jimmy is the only man I've ever known who looks perfect in knee-breeches."

Vera said nothing, but her expression became disagreeable.

Sir James did not stay long, and as he took his leave, Nathalie said: "Must you really go?"

"I have several things to attend to before dinner."

"I wish you'd come to dinner here, so that we could really see something of you."

"It's very kind of you, my dear, but I don't go out much, these days. Some other time, perhaps. When one gets to my age, routine becomes a necessity, as well as a luxury."

"Well then, I shall have to come and see you," Olga said, "to stop you getting too pompous."

"That would be very nice," answered Sir James, but without much enthusiasm. Then he walked away, a stiff and lonely-looking figure.

Suddenly, Vera asked: "What sort of person was Lady Featherstone?"

"Alicia? She was ambitious, good-looking, efficient . . . and cold like a fish," the Baroness answered promptly.

"He must have been heart-broken when he lost her." Vera could never bring herself to mention death.

"He had his compensations."

"A man's work can, of course, be a great consolation to him," Vera said unctuously.

"He never had to work very hard for them. He was always a very good-looking man. I was a little in love with him myself once—oh, nothing serious, but it was nice while it lasted."

"Why did he never marry again?" asked Nathalie.

Vera said, with surprising venom: "It may seem odd to some people, but there is such a thing as loyalty to a memory. I find it rather beautiful, myself. I'm sure he wanted to keep his memories of happiness unspoilt."

"Good gracious!" exclaimed Olga. "If he had been as happy as all that, he would certainly have married again, and at once. It is only the disillusioned who say 'Never again'. Poor Jimmy!"

Vera could not think of Sir James as "Poor Jimmy", but then whatever affection and admiration she had had for him abruptly vanished. Moreover, her suspicious resentment of the Baroness now turned into an attitude of hard hostility.

Shortly after six that evening, Arthur said: "Well, I think I'll go for a stroll."

"Good idea!" exclaimed the Baroness. "You two young things go off and enjoy yourselves."

Vera smiled stiffly, and said: "I can see to supper."

Nathalie looked uncertainly at Arthur, but since he did not want to appear unfavourably in the Baroness's eyes, he said: "Right, come along then, darling."

"Are you sure that's all right?" Nathalie looked quickly at Arthur and at Vera, and then added: "There are some things ready in the larder that we can have if you like."

"What had you arranged for dinner tonight?" Arthur asked, although he knew perfectly well, as he had insisted on working out all the menus for the entire week-end himself.

"Leave it to me," Vera said.

"Yes, get along with you, you two," the Baroness exclaimed cheerfully. "Heavens, if I were in love and your age, I couldn't wait to be gone! And don't hurry back. It's much too good an evening to waste."

Arthur's manner to Nathalie changed as soon as they were outside the front gate. With the air of an exasperated grown-up trying to be patient with an exploiting child, he asked her where she would like to go.

"Wherever you like," Nathalie answered, not caring where they went or what they did, so long as it pleased him.

"Can't you ever make up your mind about anything?"

"Where would you have gone if I hadn't come along?"

"I had intended to call in at 'The Traveller's Rest', but that can wait."

"Well, let's go there, then." She was even prepared to sit in a pub on a warm June evening, if only Arthur would be in a good mood.

"All right, since you insist," he said. Even when he was getting his own way, his expression was that of the thwarted and long-suffering. Nathalie saw it, and was upset by it, and somehow knew that this was what Arthur had intended. Even though she had got used to most of her husband's reactions, the evening was so beautiful that this one depressed her more than usual. The warmth of the sun, the young green of the trees, the bright flowers in the cottage gardens, and the mellow solidity of old stones in walls and houses found a perfect setting for softness and intimacy, relaxation and peace. Missing a sense of harmony with everything around her, Nathalie recalled her recent discovery that Arther lied to her often and blatantly, and the acute distress she had experienced at this affirmation of the gulf and lack of trust between them. This memory was so painful and frightening that she impulsively took her husband's arm and exclaimed: "It *is* fun going out together."

Arthur smiled at her quite affectionately, and said: "Good." He was, in fact, also being affected by the beauty of the evening, but found its provocativeness depressing, and even dangerous. He yearned wholeheartedly for something, but did not know what, and despaired of ever being able to find out. It was with relief that he merged into the reassuring normality of the crowd at the local pub, for there he felt at home; it had become his habit to fortify himself there every evening for his return to Walton House.

"The Traveller's Rest" had at one time been a genuine Elizabethan building and still bore the marks of it, in spite of the restoration made by the brewers' company that owned it. The innkeeper, Bill Corker, was a fine looking man of about forty, who obviously enjoyed his work. He was the kind of person whom Lady Bates found it difficult to place, and belonged to that no-man's-land between gentlemen and bounders. People assessed him according as to where they saw themselves in the subtle and complicated hierachy of social distinctions. He could not be written off as a mere publican, because his speech was meticulously (even too meticulously, some might say) that of a gentleman, though his vocabulary was all his own. He knew how to chaff the boys and girls of the village, swap racing tips with the stable lads, listen to grunts from the farmers and cap the stories of commercial travellers. He was on Christian name terms with the week-end casuals who relaxed from their managerial duties in Oxford factories. Most of the county never came to "The Traveller's Rest", but some of those who passed as gentry did look in from time to time. Then, it was still a case of serve everyone and all alike, but Bill stood up a little straighter, gave his moustaches an extra twirl, and watched his language.

There was a garden at the back of "The Traveller's Rest", and Arthur and Nathalie took their drinks out and sat down at a table under a lime tree. All around them were others doing the same thing, and occasionally, the soft drone of voices was broken by the louder sound of a laugh, or a mother shrieking for a straying child. The scene was a peaceful one, yet vibrating with life. Since there was no cinema in the neighbourhood, this was the principal community-centre of the village. In summer children could accompany their parents and run around the garden, sipping fizzy drinks in deplorable colours, although they were not allowed inside the actual building. Mrs. Dennison, wearing her teeth this time, sat with her family at a table not far away. As soon as she saw Arthur and Nathalie she called out: "Look 'ose 'ere! Innit a luvly evening?" Both she and her children were so tidy and clean as to be almost unrecognisable. Her husband, looking scrubbed and sunburnt and slightly uncomfortable, sat beside her, as though a mere chair was somehow inadequate to hold his healthy bulk. He smiled shyly, obviously rather proud of his family, but not attempting to get a word in edgeways. He might be the master in his own house, but once away from it, his wife put herself, wholly and uncompromisingly, in charge of public relations.

Suddenly, Nathalie felt her eyes being covered by two hot and sticky hands, while giggles came from somewhere just behind her.

"I wonder who that can be?" she laughed. There were more giggles from behind. "Let me see. . . . It can't be Marlene Dennison, because she's smaller, and it can't be Serena Hammond, because she's bigger, and would never be so sticky. . . . It must be Annabelle." The hands dropped, the giggles burst out, and Annabelle Hammond came round to face Arthur and Nathalie.

"How could you guess so quickly?" she laughed with delight.

"I can't think."

"Would you like a crisp?"

Annabelle pulled a battered packet of potato crisps out of her pocket.

"No thank you."

"I'm afraid I've thrown the salt away. It's such a nuisance, always."

"You here by yourself?" Arthur asked.

"No, Mummy and Daddy are just getting drinks," and she darted off to the garden door of the saloon bar, and looked back and waved while waiting for her parents. Annabelle was then an attractive child of eight with a long-legged grace that was just awkward enough to be touching, and a compelling facial mobility. Her blue eyes were huge, and always alert; her hair, thick and reddish-gold, hung down to her shoulders, and her skin was perfect. The moment her parents came out of the house, she stuffed her potato crisps back into her pocket and offered to carry the glasses and bottles they had brought with them. Then, she led them over to where the Bateman-Browns were sitting. Arthur helped Anthony Hammond to draw up chairs, and then they all sat down together. Anthony's wife, Susan, was the person Nathalie liked most in the village. She was rather gaunt, wore thick glasses and took little trouble over her appearance, yet she was extremely attractive. Nathalie found her both restful and stimulating, for she had such a fixed idea of right and wrong that life seemed to her quite straightforward. She loved the country, yet thoroughly enjoyed her periodic visits to London; she was not an intellectual, yet would go miles to hear a concert or see a play that had been well reviewed; and although she was guileless and charitable, her summing-up of the essence of a person was usually unerring and outspoken.

"What have you done with the rest of your litter?" Nathalie asked her friend.

"The boys are in bed, and Serena's reading, as usual."

"She's no good for playing things any more. It's rotten."

"Well, you've still got the boys."

"Julian will be going to school next term and Henry's only five. It's not the same. Will I be like that when I'm twelve?"

All the grown-ups smiled, and Anthony said: "There's no telling about that, you rascal. But whatever you're like, we shall know all about it—of that I *am* sure."

"Oh, *Daddy*!"

Then suddenly she darted off, saying, "There's Mrs. Potter and her new baby. I must go and see it."

"Such a restful child," Susan sighed.

"I think she's absolutely enchanting," Arthur said, and then he smiled at Nathalie with an affection that was both unguarded and shy. This was so unusual that she blushed.

When Arthur and Nathalie woke up the next morning, they felt happy and light-hearted. It was again a beautiful day, and they went down together to get the breakfast ready. Leaving his wife with precise instructions as to how the bacon and eggs should be cooked, Arthur went out to pick some flowers for Olga's tray. The garden looked tidy, for Vera had taken Jacob in hand, as well as putting in many hours of hard work herself. The two large herbaceous borders looked a little bare, but she had explained that this was part of a long-term policy which would repay in time. There were still several areas that she had not yet got around to, however, and some of the flowering shrubs looked luscious and abundant.

Arthur picked a bunch of flowers, and then walked through the dewy grass, amused that he could look back and see his footprints. From the end of the lawn, he looked back at the house. The mellowness of the stone, the proportions of the Regency architecture and the care with which the garden had been created, not only to set off the house, but to be part of it as well, all made a rich and satisfying harmony.

"This house is exactly what we wanted," he thought, and then he remembered that it was not theirs, for the Baroness could turn them out at any moment. He had no rights at all on any part of the property. Vera had several times pointed out what a responsibility this was for him, since accidents could happen to anybody, and many of the Baroness's possessions were valuable treasures, and now he began to wonder what to do about this. He wanted to stay there, for he not only liked the house and the village, but it also seemed to him absurd not to take advantage of the situation. He decided that the sensible plan would be to rent the house from the Baroness for a nominal sum, and for Vera to occupy the east wing, which he and Nathalie would never use; in that way, he could make use of the furniture which belonged by rights as much to himself as to his sister, and she could contribute a share to the rent. He considered it pointless not to keep what money there was in the family.

The more he thought about this idea, the more sound it seemed, but he decided not to broach it to Vera until he had made sure that the Baroness would agree to let him the house, and to move whatever belongings she wanted from it. It never occurred to him to discuss the matter with Nathalie. He did not find her practical, and in any case, he considered it his job to make decisions of this kind. The matter preoccupied him all the morning, and he finally decided that he must talk to the Baroness about it before she returned to London. He found himself strangely nervous at the prospect of this, however; to make a decision came to him easily enough, but to take the responsibility of acting upon it was something that needed all his courage.

In spite of his preoccupation, Arthur carved the joint at Sunday lunch with his usual flair for staging and dramatic tension. He felt this ritual to be the pivot of his domestic existence, and the whole ceremony epitomised for him the kind of authority and respectability that he considered to be the foundation of English family life. In order to do it justice, however, the rest of the cast had to play their supporting roles conscientiously, otherwise the whole performance suffered. Vera knew her part well. She had learnt when to leave him the stage to himself, and at what point to follow up his first soliloquies with the carving knife by the addition of vegetables and gravy to the plates he had distributed. Nathalie, on the other hand, seemed unable to regard the solemnity of the occasion with sufficient awe. She frequently forgot to provide what props he needed, and once he had even been forced to walk out and make a re-entry, because the stage had not been properly set the first time. The Baroness was even more difficult. She upset the rhythm by chattering and laughing, and generally distracting the others, so that he might have been playing to an empty house. When her plate was presented to her, she hardly looked at it; it might just as well have contained a few spoonfuls of stew, instead of the choice pieces he had carved especially for her. Worse still, she went out to fetch her handkerchief, just as Arthur was about to take his own place. There should have been a reverential pause of sorts then, a polite ignoring of his: "You go ahead, don't wait for me", and a general turning towards him, to see if he had all he needed before he started on his own meal.

It was this inability to feel a master in his own home that made Arthur determined to speak to the Baroness about the house that very day. They all had coffee on the terrace, and when Vera and Nathalie had gone off to wash up the luncheon things, Arthur put his case. The Baroness heard him attentively, and seemed to be so understanding that he felt encouraged to express himself fully and lucidly. He was purposefully vague about Vera's position in his proposed arrangement, but gave his listener to understand that he was concerned about a lot of furniture that was his, although at the moment in his sister's care. When he had at last finished, the Baroness said: "You have made me see a lot of things that had never occurred to me before, but I need to think all this over."

"Yes, of course," Arthur replied at once, thinking how sensible she was at heart. He credited her with a business acumen that would have surprised her, and assumed that she wanted time to work out in exact detail the suitable rent to charge. Going into the library for his afternoon rest, he felt how pleasant it was to be a man of the world, and able to discuss things in a straightforward way with such an intelligent and capable woman.

Arthur did not keep these illusions about the Baroness for long, however. It was not only her decision that shocked and enraged him, but the fact that she should throw it out so casually, during dinner that night, with Vera and Nathalie present. He had thought she would respect their little discreet and adult conspiracy; that she would take him aside on his own at some suitable moment, or even ask him to lunch with her in London, perhaps after having consulted her solicitors. However, without warning, without it even being relevant to the conversation they had just been having, the Baroness suddenly said: "I have been thinking over what you told me this afternoon, Arthur."

"Oh, yes?" Arthur's politeness was exaggerated.

"Nathalie, my darling," the Baroness said, turning towards her niece, "Arthur was saying that you both like living here, but feel uncomfortable that none of it is yours in any real sense."

"Oh, no," Nathalie protested. "That doesn't matter a bit. Of all the houses I've ever lived in, this place has always seemed like home to me, and I can't imagine it any other way."

"The Baroness has been most understanding about everything," Arthur said firmly, and Vera turned towards Nathalie to say: "You see, my dear, I don't think you quite realise what a responsibility it is for Arthur, living here like this, like a—well, without any sort of arrangement."

"Responsibility?"

"Yes. If there should be any damage or—or any unforeseen circumstances, Arthur wouldn't know where he stood."

"You had better leave me to settle this matter with your aunt," Arthur said to Nathalie, quite kindly. Then he turned to the Baroness and added: "Perhaps we could go into my—into the library after dinner, and decide on what arrangements to make?"

"That is not necessary," Olga said. "I will simply tell my lawyers that I am giving the house and its contents to Nathalie, and they can see to the details. I am so bad about business, myself," she added with a confidential grimace at Vera, but Vera did not respond. Her electric smile vanished, and she looked at Arthur in a startled way, as though seeking direction. He, however, was looking first at the Baroness and then at Nathalie. He had foreseen a number of difficulties, but a development of this kind had never occurred to him. He tried to make out Nathalie's expression, but even he could not really say that it was either proud or triumphant. She was saying to her aunt: "You *are* a darling! You know, if it had been any other place, I wouldn't have wanted it," and blushing with pleasure, but more like a child who has been given an unexpected bonus with its pocket money than a newly-endowed heiress. Arthur wondered irritably if she would ever grow up and develop a proper respect for the value of things. Vera was reacting in much the same way, but she wanted to get the position clear. "Are you quite certain you may not regret this? After all it is a considerable property."

"Ach, what do I want with this little house!" the Baroness said, with a vague wave of her right hand. "When I had husbands or lovers to enjoy things with, it used to be fun to go from place to place, but I am not so energetic now. And you know, I have never found the English countryside very amusing. It is no place for an old woman living alone, anyhow. No . . . I have my house in Paris, and friends all over the world that I can visit, so it makes me very happy to give this place to Nathalie. She always loved it so much."

"With everything in it as well?" Vera asked.

"Why not? If you don't like anything, Nathalie, my darling, you can give it away, or sell it, or something."

Arthur was still speechless, for two major emotions were wrestling for first place in his consciousness. The first was his relief at realising that he would not, after all, be required to pay anything in rent. As against that, however, were the not altogether desirable implications of having a wife with property. In principle, the more assets there were in the family, the better; but he considered that it gave a woman an unfortunate advantage, a sort of impregnable sense of independence, to be in control of her own money. And Arthur felt certain that, however vague the Baroness pretended to be, she would see to it that Nathalie was in control of the house and all that went with it.

Vera seemed to sense his dismay, and almost as though she considered the Baroness to be fair game, with only herself to blame if people took advantage of her, she said: "Are we to take it, then, that Arthur will be responsible for rates and Schedule A?"

"Ah, yes, rates and Schedule A," the Baroness said vaguely. "Let me see . . ."

Then after only a moment's hesitation, she added: "My lawyers can arrange that too. I don't want to make any difficulties for the young people."

"And what about the gardener's wages?" Vera went on.

"Oh, I'll see to that too. . . . What a perfect tomato salad! Such delicious dressing."

"I was going to suggest that I might possibly be of some help," Vera insisted.

"You?" said the Baroness, in a tone that clearly meant, "And what has it got to do with you?" Then she added, with the warmth that inevitably radiated from her on all those around her: "No, no, Vera, my dear. After all, you have yourself to look after. Why not keep anything you don't need for when these two start a family? They may be glad of it then, you know."

Later that evening, when Arthur and Nathalie were in their bedroom, he said to her: "Well, what does it feel like, being an heiress?" She could not quite fathom his mood, for his tone was a non-committal mixture of cajolery and awe, so she risked telling the truth.

"It doesn't feel like anything. I love this place and I love living here, but then we were living here anyway."

"Don't bother to say 'we'." Nathalie was looking out of the window, beyond the garden and towards the hills, at the view that had been a part of her so long.

"There wouldn't be any point in living here without you, now," she said. "It's become our home."

"Yours, you mean; lock, stock and—but no, not barrel. That barrel of cider is mine, come to think of it."

Nathalie turned to him and said: "Darling, nothing is 'mine' or 'yours'. It's all 'ours', surely." Then she added anxiously: "Don't you feel that too?"

Arthur did not feel that he and his wife shared all their worldly goods; that seemed to him a sentimental notion. Everybody knew, he considered, that marriages were not made in heaven, but based on property settlements and an acute awareness, on the part of each partner, about what the other had to offer. He had not yet had time to reassess the situation in terms of this new development, but, whatever the outcome of it, Nathalie must be kept loving and malleable. Going over to where she stood, he put an arm awkwardly round her shoulders, and said: "Goodness, I do love you. You can't imagine how much."

At the end of September, Nathalie discovered that she was going to have a baby. It was what she and Arthur had been hoping for for some time, yet it surprised her that anything as wonderful could be so unpleasant. Apart from feeling sick, she was almost frightened at the thought that, through her, a new person would come into being, grow up and take its place in the world. She had alternate moods of basking in the marvel of all this, and feeling restless and irritated at being an instrument in a process that was so powerful, and full of mystery.

Her confidence increased when she had told Arthur her news. He suddenly looked so young, so boyishly excited, that she felt deeply happy at being able to give him this experience. For a while he lost his pinched look and nervous restlessness, and she noticed that his hands were trembling as he smiled and said: "I'm not quite sure what I'm meant to do on such an occasion."

"I'm not either. It's never happened to me before."

"I think I'd better just kiss you and say, 'Darling, I'm so glad.'" He did, and then added: "Let's keep it to ourselves for the moment. I feel I don't want anybody else to share in this, just yet."

"Of course, if that's what you'd like." She would have agreed to almost anything at that moment.

The tension that had always existed between them suddenly disappeared, and they experienced a peaceful relaxation which they hoped was a foretaste of better things to come. The promise of parenthood presented them with a new situation so full of nuances, that their attentions and energies were necessarily diverted from themselves and their relationship. Several times during the next few days, Arthur said something like: "I wonder what I ought to do? There must be all kinds of things a prospective father should attend to." He teased her without cruelty now. "I wonder what sort of craving you'll develop," he said one day. "Pregnant women are always supposed to have them, aren't they?" And also: "How on earth will you ever manage to get a layette ready, when you can't remember so much as to sew on a button?"

The atmosphere was so pleasant for almost a month that it was all the more of a shock when Arthur failed to return from London one day, and throughout the long evening, no message of any kind came through from him.

"What can have happened to him? He must have had an accident," Vera said for the tenth time, wandering restlessly about the house.

Nathalie was feeling sick, and said nothing. The two hours or so before dinner always seemed to her worse than the more conventional sickness in the mornings, and now that she suffered from nervous worry as well, she felt so ill that she could hardly speak. At half-past ten, Vera said. "Shouldn't we phone the police?"

"Surely we'd have heard if he'd had an accident," Nathalie managed to reply.

"They do say no news is good news, don't they? But I don't know how much longer I can stand the anxiety."

"Should we have dinner?" Nathalie suggested, hoping that food might help her to feel better.

"I couldn't eat a thing myself, but let's dine by all means, if you're hungry."

"It's not that I'm hungry, but a little food might help to give us some bright ideas. We could keep Arthur's hot for him."

They prepared to eat, which was at least a way of occupying half an hour. For somebody who felt unable to touch a thing, Vera put up a creditable performance. It was, in fact, Nathalie who was unable to eat much, after the first few mouthfuls of food had made her think that things were bearable.

By midnight, there was still no sign of Arthur. Vera rung up the exchange to make sure that the telephone was not out of order, and then tried to get through to Arthur's office, but there was no reply from there. Then she wondered which of Arthur's friends to get in touch with.

"Who do you suggest?" Nathalie asked.

"I don't know his London friends as well as you do, these days."

"I can't think of anyone," Nathalie said, realising with a shock how little she knew about Arthur. He never talked of his friends, and only casually mentioned the people he met in the course of his work. She had never been able to get any sort of picture of his life as it had been before she met him, or even as it was now when they were not together.

"My aunt left for Italy over a fortnight ago, so there's no point in getting on to her," she added.

"No, that would be no use," Vera said hurriedly. "I'm going to ring up the police."

"I wonder whether Arthur would like that. If he'd had an accident we'd have heard by now. If he hasn't, it's going to be difficult to know where to start looking. He might be almost anywhere, and even if they did find him, he might resent being tracked down."

"Might! Might! How can you be so calm and calculating? I don't believe you care at all."

"I don't feel calm, I promise you, but what can we do except wait?"

Vera's almost hysterical agitation made everything seem like a nightmare, but Nathalie affected calmness as a sort of protection for her husband. It was almost as though she were saying to her sister-in-law: "Supposing he has gone on a binge and is too drunk to ring up, what has it got to do with you, anyhow?"

The next morning, Vera woke up with a bad headache, and Nathalie felt so sick she could scarcely stand up. It was a Saturday so there seemed to be no point in ringing up Arthur's office. As a rule, he was never in London at week-ends, and for his wife or his sister to admit ignorance of his whereabouts would be to risk humiliating him. Both women were too agitated to think of trying to telephone without betraying their identity.

The time dragged on. Every hour seemed a whole day of conflicting reactions succeeding each other. By lunch time, it was impossible to believe that this uncertainty had only been going on since the previous evening. Vera was no longer bent on taking action of some kind, and relapsed into a coma of misery and discomfort. She was frightened as well, now, and instead of resenting or criticising her sister-in-law, turned to her for support and reassurance. Nathalie was feeling far too ill to respond, however. For a while, she felt it necessary to keep up some semblance of control, and got through her routine jobs with surprising efficiency. She also decided to go round to "The Traveller's Rest" and ask Bill Corker what he thought about the problem.

Shortly before six o'clock, she went up to her bedroom to tidy up before going out, but getting up from her dressing-table stool, she fainted. When she came to again, her hands and feet were tingling, and the dust from the carpet was nauseating and choking her. At first, she could not even make the effort to get up. It was so pleasant not to bother about anything. Turning her head, she now looked directly under the bed. The dust there had not been cleaned for weeks, or possibly months, and coated, rather than rested on, carpet and bedsprings, and more or less thickly on such objects as a book, a reel of cotton, a couple of odd shoes, a plate, and a sweater that had disappeared some time ago. "Really, Mrs. Dennison is hopeless," she thought wearily. "Or is it my fault? It's my responsibility, at any rate. How wonderful it would be not to have to face all the problems that seem to fill my life these days. There seems to be so much to struggle with, battle against, and fight out, that even a little dust (well, quite a lot, actually) is just more than I can cope with. Where on earth is Arthur, and what is he doing? Is he drunk? And if so, is he very unhappy?" Nathalie suddenly felt so tired that she could bear it no longer, and making just enough effort to get up, she flopped on to her bed and relapsed into a state of thoughtlessness.

Vera found her there half an hour later, and seeing the girl lying full-length with an arm across her eyes, she exclaimed: "It doesn't do to give in, you know." Then she noticed that what she could see of Nathalie's face was practically green with pallor, and added: "Are you all right?"

Nathalie slowly lowered her arm and looked around her with dull, dazed eyes.

"Nathalie! Are you all right?"

Finally Nathalie brought a remote and unconcentrated look round to Vera. Then she smiled, and sitting up, tried to swing her legs round over the edge of the bed. The movement was too sudden, however, and after a moment, she collapsed backwards again.

"Come child, you mustn't take it like that!" Now that the emergency was nearer home, Vera became calmer.

"I'm terribly sorry," Nathalie said, in a voice that seemed to go up and down in all the wrong places. "I'll be better in a moment." She sounded quite sensible, and yet looked very ill indeed.

"What's happened?" Vera asked.

"I'm not quite sure. I fainted when I got up from my dressing-table, and now I feel terribly sick."

"Do you want me to send for the doctor?"

"Don't bother," was all Nathalie said, but she thought: "Why do I have to make decisions like that? Why can't there be someone who knows whether or not the doctor should be sent for?"

"You don't look at all well, and it might be sensible to get him out now, instead of in the middle of the night."

"There's nothing he can do. You see, I'm going to have a baby. Arthur didn't want me to tell anyone just yet, so I shouldn't really have told you, but I wanted you to know so that you'd realise about my being so sick all the time. It's quite normal, I believe."

To Nathalie's surprise, Vera exclaimed: "My poor child! How *dare* Arthur behave like that at a time like this! Stay where you are, and I'll bring you up some milk and biscuits."

"Please don't bother. I'll come down in a moment." Milk made her feel sick at the best of times, and she felt that biscuits would choke her just then.

"Nonsense! An empty stomach is the worst thing for morning sickness." Vera briskly left the room, and went down to the kitchen, returning five minutes later.

Nathalie forced herself to drink the milk so as not to hurt Vera's feelings, but she could not manage the biscuits. Then, to her surprise, she suddenly began to feel miraculously better.

"How clever of you to know about such things!" She felt so grateful for not feeling sick any longer that she added: "You're always so competent."

"Think you can sit up, now?" Vera asked. Nathalie slowly began to get up, and found with relief that this time her head and stomach stayed still, and in their proper places.

"How wonderful! Thank you so much. That milk made all the difference." Arthur suddenly seemed to her rather remote; he still had the power to hurt her, but was no longer depriving her of all reason in doing so.

The rest of that evening was easier to get through. Both women now accepted that it would be best just to wait and try to carry on as normally as possible. Vera no longer considered the possibility of disaster, and kept saying that there must surely be some explanation. Nathalie still felt wretched, but no longer worried. She also lost her sense of time, and waiting was now a state, rather than a process. Moreover, she was relieved that Vera did not seem to mind about the baby, and showed interest in all the details, even making plans about what knitting was to be done.

Before going to sleep that night, Nathalie decided that Arthur's awe for his sister was exaggerated. "Poor Arthur," she thought. "How unnecessarily he tortures himself, and how incredible it is that people living together day in and day out can misunderstand each other to such an extent. I'll make it up to him somehow, when he comes back. If he comes back."

There was no message of any kind throughout Sunday but on Monday, Vera telephoned Arthur's office twice, and was told both times that he was in conference, and not available.

At about seven o'clock that evening, the telephone rang, and Nathalie, who happened to be nearest, answered it.

"Mrs. Bateman-Brown?" asked a vaguely familiar voice.

"Yes."

"Are you alone?"

"No, I'm not."

"Well then just listen and don't talk. This is Bill Corker, speaking from 'The Traveller's Rest'."

"Oh, yes."

"Can you come round here, please, and without saying anything to anybody about it?"

"Yes, of course."

"Right away?"

"Yes."

"I'm to tell you there's nothing to worry about, only keep this to yourself. Get it?"

"Yes, all right." She hung up, and tried to avoid Vera's piercing look.

"Was that Arthur?"

"No, it was Bill Corker."

"What did he want? Did he say anything?"

"Not about Arthur. There was something I wanted to discuss with him and he wondered if I could spare the time now."

Nathalie deplored her inability to be straightforward with Vera. "Why can't I just refuse to explain," she wondered. "Or simply say: 'I'm going out for a few minutes,' and leave it at that? Why do I feel forced to tell little white lies to this woman? If it's like this for me, what must it be like for Arthur?"

Once out of the house, however, she felt light-headed with relief and happiness, knowing somehow that her husband was waiting at "The Traveller's Rest". She found him in the Saloon Bar, looking tired, lined and untidy. He stood up the moment she came in, and his expression was so worried and uncertain that she smiled and went straight towards him. She was feeling sick again, but that was unimportant compared to the relief of seeing him again, and knowing that he was back. Arthur, who had been waiting for recriminations, assumed that her confident smile indicated a decision on her part.

"You can do it on desertion," he said. "Or I'll arrange for a trumped-up Brighton case, if you'd prefer that."

"What are you talking about?"

"You'll want your freedom now, presumably."

"My freedom?" Nathalie said stupidly.

"I can tell by your expression that you've decided to leave me."

She was touched by this childish resort to melodrama, but exclaimed in surprise: "The idea hadn't even crossed my mind."

Arthur did not know whether to feel relief or disappointment. He was relaxed and tired after his "lost week-end", and yearned for the comfort and oblivion of familiar surroundings; on the other hand, he needed to wallow in the rock-bottom of humiliation and loss. Nathalie had not even reproached him for his lapse, and he therefore supposed that she had either no moral sense, or else no idea what he had been doing during the past three days. In order to avoid having to say anything yet, he sat down again, clutching his head between his hands, and Nathalie swooped down and put her arms around him. Arthur thought of saying: "Do be careful! Somebody will see us," but he was too tired and bewildered, and the words did not come out. "What have I done?" he moaned instead.

"It doesn't matter what you've done. You're home now." Nathalie rocked him gently in her arms.

"Yes, I believe I am home—really home, for the first time in my life." This did not sound quite sincere even to him, but she did not seem to have noticed, and went on holding his head to her. After a moment, he suddenly felt stifled: she was too near to him, in more than one sense. Disengaging himself gently, but firmly, he asked: "How did Vera take it? Is she very angry?"

"Well . . . miserable, rather than angry."

"Does she know you're here?"

"Yes, but she doesn't realise I'm with you. And, darling, I'm terribly sorry, but I had to tell her about the baby."

Arthur looked sulky. "I particularly told you not to, just yet," he said crossly.

"I know, but I've been so sick that she wanted to send for the doctor, so I had to tell her, to stop her. She'd have found out either way."

"I see. Well, she'll have had plenty on her mind this week-end, then. No doubt she's having one of her sick headaches at the moment."

"No, I don't think so. In fact, she seemed rather pleased at the thought of being an aunt, and I think it helped to take her mind off you." Nathalie had still to learn that this sort of remark was bound to annoy Arthur, for he had to be the centre of attraction, but when they were on their way home, he said: "You won't leave me alone with her, will you?" and then did not speak again until they reached Walton House.

Vera heard them the moment they closed the door in the garden wall behind them, but she went on sitting in the drawing-room with *The Times* twitching between her fingers. Even when they were inside the house, she did not look up until they came into the room, though her ears were straining for every sound.

"Good evening," she smiled uncertainly as Arthur came towards her.

"Good evening, darling," he said. He took both her hands and kissed her forehead. Then, standing back to look at her, he said: "It's like a miracle to be home again. I don't want to break the spell, so let's leave it at that, shall we?"

Vera who was conscious of Nathalie's presence, merely smiled again, and said: "Dinner's ready when you are."

"Good! I'm starving." And, indeed, he was suddenly ravenously hungry, anticipating his meal with pleasure, and feeling master of the situation. Entering the dining-room, and gently pushing Vera and Nathalie in front of him, he exclaimed: "What wonderful women I have! I must be the most fortunate man in the world."

The evening passed quite easily. Arthur was now almost hysterical with relief, and exerted himself with skill to keep everybody entertained. Nathalie felt tired, but happy, and Vera was unusually charming. After dinner they all played cards, and then agreed amicably that an early night for all three of them would be a good idea.

When Arthur had taken as much time as he dared downstairs, he finally went up to say good night to his sister. The Vera he now found had become a different being, however. Her eyes were hard and bright, and her mouth a straight slit. Arthur knew the signs well, but he could not yet be sure whether he was in for a performance of hysterics or of abuse.

"Why couldn't you have sent a message of some kind?" Vera said, in a voice full of hatred. He knew that she was really asking: "Where did you go? What did you do? Who were you with?", but instead she enlarged on how wicked and inconsiderate he was to make both her and his wife so wretchedly unhappy. Arthur still felt sufficiently detached to say: "Stop that now, will you? The matter is over and done with, and I refuse to discuss it any further." He could not quite bring himself to add: "If my wife chooses not to make a scene, I don't see what right you have to carry on like this."

Vera's abuse turned to hysterics, and then to self-pity. She looked so ugly that Arthur could not bear the sight of her, and turned away.

"You think you can get away with it, don't you?" she shouted. "You filthy swine! You're no better than the rest of them! You think I don't know what you've been up to, but I knew all about men before you were even born."

"You can't have known much about them at fifteen, especially leading the sheltered life you did," said Arthur.

"What do you know about my life! How can you know what I'm really like inside! You're too dirty to appreciate me properly! You're just as filthy as the worst of them. How I *hate* men—low beasts, all and every one of them. Oh, why did Mother have the luck to die, and yet I had to be stranded with a devil like you? You're a devil, that's what you are—a devil! To think I gave up everything for a devil."

"Don't let's start that again, please. I never asked you to 'give up everything'."

"And I didn't ask to have my fiancé killed."

Arthur flinched. Their conflicts now always went back to that. She did not often say so outright, but it was always in both their minds and between them. She never reproached him, or even betrayed that she thought of doing so; in fact, at times, when a sense of guilt overpowered him and he wallowed in remorse, it was she who sweetly reassured him. He tried once to tell her what he had done, and to what an extent he considered himself responsible for that death, and became determined to drag her below the surface and into reality; but she had refused to listen, merely saying: "Well, at least the war spared you for me. I'm sure it was all meant for the best." That had been before his marriage, however, and now her anguish even made him feel guilty that he had dared to take a wife. "Yet," he reminded himself, "most men marry and have families. Why should it be different for me? Why should the thought of being a father fill me with such terror and apprehension that it drove me to three days of debauchery? It's all most unfair, and too hopelessly involved." He felt too tired to think, to bluff or to fight, and so allowed himself the luxury of giving in to a childish gesture of despair. Clutching his head, he moaned: "What do I do to you? Of course you can't forgive me! How could you? You're quite right, I'm absolutely worthless. I have no right to adore you as I do." He was, in a sense, playing the part that was required just then, yet he quite genuinely hated Vera to be angry with him. At that moment he needed her reassurance, but although Vera was passionate and could be sweetly attentive, there was not a trace of tenderness in her. Tenderness is a form of giving that is both wholehearted and undemanding, and she could never give anything wholeheartedly or with no thought of return. Even when she threw herself completely into her tantrums, she was in a sense selling herself, and the price demanded was an Arthur in an abject mood, an Arthur bound to her by the realisation of his many-sided guilt. When he had become almost childishly helpless he was altogether hers again, and she could afford to calm down and smile once more. It worked every time, however long the process might take. She even admitted that it was almost worth quarrelling with Arthur, since reconciliation with him afterwards was invariably so sweet.

Arthur was so exhausted by the time Vera finally let him go that he fell asleep as soon as he got into bed. He woke up at about two the following morning. Nathalie was sleeping deeply, and lay like a child, her arms above her head, slightly bent at the elbows, with the hands almost touching her hair. He watched her for a moment, thinking how incredible it was that any adult could appear so young; she was married and pregnant, yet looked withdrawn into some world of innocence and peace that he had never known. It annoyed him that she should be so remote, especially as he felt lonely and worried; the small hours of the morning were always full of terrors for him. He leant over and kissed her cheek, but she merely turned her face and went on sleeping. He kissed her again, this time on the mouth, and she slipped away from him, but still did not wake up. Piqued, he began to fondle her, but she rejected him and seemed almost to shudder at his touch. Then the increasing frenzy of his love-making woke her, and putting her arms out to her husband, she smiled sleepily. As soon as Nathalie became responsive, however, Arthur no longer wanted her; the essential was that she was now back within his orbit.

"You looked so sweet asleep, I couldn't resist kissing you," he said, settling back on his side of the bed. "It was selfish of me to wake you, but I didn't really mean to."

"That's all right, darling."

Arthur could not believe that she felt as contented as she looked.

"How're you feeling?" he asked.

"Blissfully happy, now you're back." She really looked as though she meant it, and Arthur thought that perhaps a woman who knew she was going to have a baby experienced such a promise of fulfilment that nothing else could seriously affect her.

"And how are you?" she asked him, still smiling.

"I feel awful."

"Can I get you anything? Some tea, or something?"

"Later." He wanted her to stay with him just then. "Don't you want to know anything about what happened?" he added. "Or do you just not care?"

"Of course I do, if you want to tell me."

"You don't seem very interested."

"I don't want to nag, that's all." She knew that no amount of questioning would get the truth out of him, and that he would tell her just what he wanted her to know, when it suited him.

"You find it better to chalk it all up as a black mark against me, I suppose." He took her to be smug because he was so much in the wrong, and she so much the wronged wife.

"Don't be silly!" Nathalie exclaimed.

"I'm not nearly as silly as you suppose," Arthur said. "Since you appear neither to want to leave me nor to make a fuss, I can only assume that you're storing up ammunition."

"Ammunition for what?"

"Oh, any emergency that might arise."

"If you really want to know, I was desperately worried and utterly miserable as well, but now you're back, I prefer not to think about it any more."

"Ah, so that's what it is! You haven't the courage to face up to things. Now I begin to understand."

"Darling, listen to me. I have no right to judge you. All I'm concerned with is our life together. You're my husband and the father of my child and the important thing for me is that that part should work. It's unsettling to have you disappear for three days without a word, and I admit I hated it, but now you're back. Surely, if I'm prepared to concentrate on the present and not harp on last week-end, that's a good thing, isn't it?"

Her calm maddened him, and he was unaware that what helped her to be dispassionate was a determination not to react as she had heard Vera doing. He considered it more human to make a fuss, and disliked the idea that she did not feel responsible for him at all times. Besides that, her attitude hinted at a type of experience that he did not share, and he wondered what human situations she had witnessed and drawn conclusions from that enabled her to be so philosophical. Determined to shake her composure, he said: "I think you'd better know what happened."

"I don't particularly want to—not unless you really want to tell me, that is."

"I think you should know. It wouldn't be fair to let you eventually reproach yourself for having been a coward."

Nathalie, who was finding it difficult to keep a hold on herself, felt that it would now take little to pitch her into fear and despair, yet she realised that if Arthur saw her unhappiness he would be brutally insistent. The more she betrayed her vulnerability, the more he lashed out, hurting himself in the process. "Poor Arthur," she thought, and smiled tenderly at him, but he sensed a certain tension in her now, and it excited him.

"I got too drunk to come home on Friday," he went on. "On

Saturday, I had a few drinks to pull myself round and then ceased to care, so I got drunk again. By Sunday, I couldn't stop. You can guess what else there was—wine and women, though not much song, I must say. The usual story, in fact." In the strange world, combined of filth and fantasy, that he was immersed in on these occasions, he always hoped that some clue, some solution would suddenly emerge, strong and clear, out of the darkness. He wanted violence to be met by violence, so that if he hit the depths of degradation he might finally find himself, or break completely, to re-emerge quite new. Yet, all he ever got out of these orgies was an increasing blackness of humiliation, disgust and despair, which drove him on to escape an ever-increasing fear. He could not imagine why debauchery was supposed to come into the category of fun.

Arthur was about to punish himself by inflicting all the most unsavoury details of his escapade on Nathalie, but he broke down. Burying his head in his pillow, he almost sobbed: "I don't know what gets hold of me. I have to do something—to break out, to lash, and smash, until I can go on no longer from sheer exhaustion. What is it? Why do I do it? What will become of me if I go on like this?"

Nathalie suddenly felt so sick that for a moment she almost vomited. She was afraid of moving, partly so as not to betray her extreme revulsion, but if he had touched her at that moment, it would have been unbearable to her. Feeling ashamed of her disloyalty, she kept saying to herself: "It's he who is suffering most, not me. It's he who needs sympathy and help," and forced herself to ask: "Does it happen often?"

"Every now and then," Arthur replied evasively.

"Since when?"

"Since the war. . . . Since I killed Vera's boy friend."

This was something so unexpected that Nathalie now quite forgot about herself, and put aside the implication of Arthur's confession until later.

"*You* killed him?" she exclaimed. "But I thought he was killed in action."

"He was, but he needn't have been. It was I who sent him on an unnecessary reconnaisance from which I knew he'd never return. Now you know the sort of cad I am."

Nathalie had never seen Arthur betray himself to this extent; he seemed so childlike all of a sudden, bared of his brusqueness and using schoolboy terminology, that she felt an immense tenderness for him.

"But why, darling? Why?" she asked.

"I must tell someone. . . . John was one of my best friends, and we were brother officers in the same racket together. I took him home with me once for a forty-eight-hour leave—it was not long before my father died—and the result of that was that he and Vera got engaged. He was eight years younger than she was, but that was their look-out. As far as I was concerned, he was all right; not very bright, but worthy and reasonably well off. After they'd been engaged a few months, we were both posted to the Middle East and he wanted to marry her before leaving. Vera wouldn't agree to this, though. She wanted to wait until after the war, when they could do things properly, and John gave in with good grace, I may say. But what with spring, and the war, and one thing and another, he was a bit restless, and perhaps that accounts for what happened. We were both at home on embarkation leave, and one evening he and Vera went out for a walk together. When they came in again, she went straight upstairs without a word, and I went up after her and found her sobbing. She became quite hysterical and started calling John names, and saying that she didn't want to marry him, and so on. Even after I'd calmed her down, I couldn't find out what had really happened. She kept saying he'd been 'horrible', and suddenly I wanted to kill him—just like that."

Arthur paused for a while, and then went on: "John was a good chap, though, and he soon made me see sense. Apparently, he'd kissed Vera rather more thoroughly than ever before, and she'd been frightened. He assured me that he hadn't forgotten himself in any way, and I'm certain he was telling the truth. He pointed out all sorts of pertinent things, however; that we were all nervous and under a great strain at that stage of the war, that Vera was a very emotional person who had been woken rather late in life, and so on and so forth. He was a sensible, decent, patient man, and I killed him."

Nathalie gently stroked Arthur's shoulder and asked:

"Was it in the Middle East that it happened?"

"Yes. When we got abroad I was promoted, and John stayed a captain, even though he was older than I was. I was put in charge of an operation and he was one of the people allotted to me. It was I who was responsible for sending him off on his last job."

"But why do you blame yourself for something that was an accident of war? After all, it was sheer chance that you were the one who had to give the order, and he the one who had to take it. It might have happened to anybody."

"No, that's not true. I pretended that that particular exercise was vital, but I had to admit to myself afterwards that it had not really been necessary. It was a mistake I got away with, as war is full of mistakes people get away with, but I know I'm guilty."

"Everybody is guilty, in a way, specially in war, but why you so much more than the others?"

"Because I wanted him dead. He was upsetting Vera and I couldn't have that. I must have had all that in mind when I sent him off, don't you see?"

"And she can never forgive you for it, I suppose?"

"No, that's not true," Arthur said indignantly. "She behaved splendidly about the whole thing. No, it's no use trying to pin anything on Vera. She's never in any way reproached me for what happened."

"No," thought Nathalie, "of course not. She doesn't need to, for the whole of her life is one long reproach. Every time she balks at something, it's a slap in the face for Arthur, with scenes about anything but John thrown in to sharpen his sensibility. Whether deliberately or not, she sees to it that he never stops paying for his mistake. Even her unselfishness has a destructive quality about it; its very negativity is a withdrawal from challenge, and he is forced to stand between her and life, both as a buffer and as a link."

Arthur was lying quite still, facing away from her.

"You must forgive yourself," she said at last. "Nobody else can do it for you."

"Can you forgive me, now that you know?"

"It's not for me to condemn you, but to stand by you."

"So long as you get what you want, anyhow."

Nathalie knew that this was bravado, and ignored it. "I'm not saying that you've nothing to reproach yourself with," she said, "but what's the point of wallowing in one's failures? It's surely better to try to make amends, isn't it?"

Arthur said quietly: "Go on."

"You have so much to give." For the first time, Nathalie felt in communication with her husband. "You're intelligent, well-educated, good-looking, full of energy, and often terribly amusing.

Besides, you're still quite young. All that surely helps to give you a tremendous advantage in making a success of life."

"Success! For one moment I thought you were on the verge of something quite helpful, but like all women, you only care about success. You want me to do well so that you can be rich and eminent."

"I mean success in terms of achievement, not necessarily riches or power."

"What's the difference?"

"Quite a lot, I should have thought. Doing something you consider worthwhile doesn't necessarily mean making a lot of money."

"You'd be the first to complain if I didn't set you up in the style to which you're accustomed, as they say."

Nathalie could not believe that she and Arthur were really at such cross-purposes, and thought he was being sarcastic. Yet, being aware of his uncertainty, she wanted to reassure him, and said: "What I need most is that you should do what you want to do, what you feel is right for you."

"Provided I make enough money?"

"Is that all your job means to you? Simply a way of earning a living?"

Arthur flung himself round to face her, and exclaimed in exasperation: "Do you suppose that most people's jobs mean any more to them than that? What other incentive do you imagine the majority of men have in spending their time the way they do, than to provide food and shelter for whoever may be sponging on them? You must emerge from your sheltered life sufficiently to understand that most people detest what they're doing, and only do it because they have to."

This did not make sense to Nathalie. She had always assumed that whether or not people enjoyed life had little to do with their incomes. They lived and suffered, and loved and learned, and their jobs naturally affected the way in which they did these things; yet, dissatisfaction or unhappiness had never seemed to her the prerogative of any particular walk in life.

"Do you dislike your job?" she finally asked.

"Dislike it? I hate it."

"Why?"

"It bores me. The work bores me, the people bore me, and the general scramble of rush-hour tubes, trains and all the rest of it, bores me very much indeed. And so it goes on, day after day."

"There must be compensations, surely."

"For instance?"

Nathalie could not put into words what she felt. Once, she had believed that whatever a person did was part of a whole; any given experience had seemed just one moment between the past and the future, a fragment of several dimensions, levels or facets. There had always been something to see, to wonder at, to puzzle out, to reflect back on or look forward to; even among bores, there had been degrees of boredom.

"What would you rather do?" she asked.

"Almost anything else."

"Darling, listen to me. I don't care how little money you earn, or where we go, so long as you do what you want to do. The most important thing in the world for me is that things should go well between us, and that can never be if you're neither happy, nor even satisfied."

She became convinced that it was because Arthur had given up his heart's desire, just to make money for her sake, that things had gone so badly between them. "Don't you know that?" she added eagerly, looking so radiant that Arthur had to believe in her sincerity. Her childish faith seemed to him absurdly irresponsible, however, and he said: "What I do know is that we're about to start a family, and that costs money."

"But people have children whatever incomes they earn. We can manage, darling . . . of course we can! What is it you want to do? Tell me, and then we can work it all out."

Arthur turned away from his wife again. Her generosity touched him, but it also bored him. He wanted her admiration, but within a shell of self-sufficiency, and craved a devoted submissiveness which could be relied on, but was always veiled in mystery; a response able to be complete, but also to remain coolly aloof. The wholehearted way in which Nathalie tried to give herself made demands on him which he neither could, nor would, fulfil. At that moment, he had no idea what to say to her, for he scarcely knew himself what he wanted. There had never been any alternative for him but to do what various others expected of him: his schoolmasters, his father, Vera, the Army authorities, his wife. Now all these had disappeared, except Vera and Nathalie. He knew that his sister wanted him at the top, wherever it might be and in whatever way he managed to get there, and had always assumed that his wife felt more or less the same. At times, he had had visions of becoming Prime Minister, or Archbishop of Canterbury, or even a really famous artist, but these had been private dreams, not specific plans, and based more on the eminence and pageantry than the actual work involved. The only thing he had ever felt able to do really well was act. He remembered, for the first time in years, the serious encouragement given him by a famous actor who had seen him play Hamlet in a school performance. He had been sure, then, that he must become an actor himself, but when he told Vera this, she had quenched his excitement with a single stroke, simply by treating the idea as a quaint and childish whim. After that he had somehow lost heart. He could have joined the O.U.D.S. or something, but never got around to it; there had been so many other distractions at Oxford.

"What are you thinking about?" Nathalie asked. It was the sort of question that usually infuriated him, but this time he did not seem to mind.

"I was just remembering that at one time I was going to be a great actor. Actually, I was quite serious about going on the stage."

"Well, why didn't you, then?"

"There was a world war, remember? It made fun of many plans besides my own. It made no difference to the lives of people like you, of course, but then we can't all afford to live so remote from reality."

Nathalie instinctively knew that she would hear more on these lines if she were to say, "Why don't you take up acting again," so instead she said: "Well, we must think of something you'd like to do now."

"I want to make a lot of money so that I can sit around quite happily drinking in pubs and reading poetry, without a sense of guilt about my family."

It was one of the few occasions on which he spoke the truth, but Nathalie thought he was joking, and said: "I don't mind what it is you want, darling. Really. You don't have to be afraid of saying."

"Supposing I said I wanted to be a garage mechanic?" Arthur teased her.

"I wouldn't believe it because you know nothing about engines. Still, you could learn, I suppose."

"And have a nice mock Tudor filling-station on the Great West Road?"

"Why not? And I could make a little on the side, by providing teas with the 's' back to front."

"That'd soon break down, because you'd always be running out of supplies."

"No, I wouldn't. Being in the trade, we'd have lots of contacts, and large lorries would always be drawing up, absolutely bulging with brick-dust and chocolate biscuits. There'd always be lots of people to chat with, and we could have little flower beds round the pumps and put the children in charge of the chocolates and cigarettes."

"And they'd become juvenile delinquents in no time, smoking round the countryside in our second-hand Bentleys. Still, as you say, I'm no mechanic."

"What else, then. Farming?"

"I can just see you getting up at dawn! Farmers' wives have to work, you know."

"You'd be surprised how hard I can work if I put my mind to it."

"I have noticed that you're capable of effort when it suits you, but you'd have to do better than that."

"Yes, I know—feeding animals at night, helping to deliver lambs in storms, cooking huge meals for all the farmhands, making butter and cheese, and so on. I could learn, darling. Really I could."

Smiling, her head and shoulders leaning forward towards him, and her eyes shining, Arthur realised that she would, indeed, follow him anywhere.

"You really do mean it," he said, both pleased and surprised.

"Of course I do! Anything you say, only please, please be happy."

"What a dear old thing you are," he said, feeling strangely moved, but when she persisted:

"Well, what shall it be?" his affection turned to irritation. He wanted Nathalie to spot exactly where his trends lay, and propel him unobtrusively in the right direction. That seemed to him the essential function of a wife.

"I don't much care," he answered, "so long as I don't have to grind up to London, day in and day out, year in and year out. You can't imagine how tedious it becomes."

"Yes I can, but I never dreamt that you only stuck it for my sake. Well, we're going to change all that. I'm sure you could get a job near here, somewhere—Oxford, perhaps—then you could even have a shot at acting as well. It would be just a hobby to start with, but one never knows. Look at Eileen Herlie, after all."

Arthur felt a sudden surge of optimistic well-being. He put his arms around his wife and said: "I've never seen you like this; so clear-headed and confident. Everything's going to be all right, now." Then he put his hand on her breast, and whispered, "Oh, darling! What have I done to deserve someone like you? It's your tough luck, but it's my only hope."

Nathalie rested her cheek on Arthur's head and stroked his hair, feeling calm for the first time for months, and knowing now why she had been compelled to marry him. She was convinced that he needed enough understanding and tolerance to counteract his sense of guilt and the rigidity of Vera's attitude; a sort of mother love that was firm, but warm and undemanding, but reliable.

"There'll be no more nerves, and no more nonsense," Arthur went on. Then he broke away from her, and added in a voice which was now normal: "But that doesn't mean that I'll never be thirsty again. In fact, I could do with a bucket of the stuff right now. Don't look so dismayed, though. I'm going to make some tea. Then we'll drink—or sip, I should say—to the real beginning of our marriage."

He climbed briskly out of bed and put on his dressing-gown.

"No, don't move," he said, as Nathalie made to get up. "I'm going to start looking after you a bit better now. Anyhow, you still haven't learnt to make tea that's drinkable, and this is by way of being a celebration."

When he got to the door, he seemed to change his mind, and came round to sit on Nathalie's side of the bed. Taking her left hand in both his, he said solemnly: "You've helped me to liberate myself in one important respect, you know."

"Oh, what's that?"

She knew he had waited for her to say this, even though he now snapped: "If you'll wait just one moment, I'll tell you. I've always had rather a complex about being a small-town boy who had to make good, and that got worse after I married you. I felt I simply had to get on, whether I wanted to or not, just to live up to you."

"What an unfortunate delusion! I hope I've shaken you out of that one, at any rate."

"I think you have, that's just what I'm saying, but it still doesn't make things any easier for me."

"In what way, darling?" Arthur felt the familiar pang of irritation at her mania for asking questions, instead of deducing what he meant, but he merely said: "Being the grandson of a village blacksmith has its drawbacks, you know."

"I think it's rather romantic. Besides, it does your father great credit that he should have been bright enough for the local squire to pick him out and give him an education. A humble origin never stood in the way of greatness, after all."

"Even so, the self-made man is let in for a great many humiliations."

"Are they so very serious?"

"Oh, how can you possibly understand! Your family's always been at the top."

"What exactly does that mean?"

"You know perfectly well."

"I don't think I do. We never had any money, and we didn't lead a fashionable life."

"It's the old boy net that does it, I suppose. That's what enabled your father to manage very nicely, thank you, even when he hadn't got a bean. There was always someone, somewhere, who was glad to help him out, and did it without humiliating him. You can't know how awful it is to feel that one doesn't belong anywhere. I have nothing at all in common with those of my family who still have their roots in a country village, I can't really see myself fitting into the life of a provincial town, and I'm an upstart among the people I most want to be like."

"That's absurd. You went to a good school and to Oxford, and the rest is up to you. Even among old families there are individualists. It's a question of temperament more than anything. There are lots of people who don't altogether belong anywhere, and their company is usually far more interesting than those who always remain in one kind of rut. One learns so much more about life by being a bit on the outside in that way."

"I'm not so sure," Arthur said uncertainly. Unlike Nathalie, he could never be satisfied with being an observer or partaker; he had to be a dominator, and preferred to be a cock on a small and insignificant dung-heap, rather than a worm in a large and vital one. "Where did you pick up all that stuff, anyhow?" he added truculently. "Some book, I expect!"

Nathalie smiled, but after Arthur had left the room, she realised that the notion came out of a past now so remote that it hardly existed any longer. Yet at that moment, she could see, quite clearly, herself and Felix sitting on the steps of the Sacré Cœur, one hot evening in July, and gazing into the haze over Paris. She was then fifteen, so Felix must have been nearly thirty-five. Earlier that afternoon, he had grabbed her by the hand after a long telephone conversation, exclaiming: "Will I *never* learn? Come on! Let's get out of here." She knew he was involved in an affair that had unexpectedly turned serious, and supposed he must be worrying, for he was unusually silent. "Are you wondering whether to marry Marion?" she had asked at last.

He had laughed, and answered: "I'm wondering how to get out of marrying Marion, if you want to know."

"Is there someone else already, then?"

"What do you mean, 'already'?"

"Well, you do seem to have a lot of girl friends, don't you? Why don't you ever marry any of them?"

"There has to be something very compelling to make you feel that one person is the one for evermore, in all circumstances, *and* to the exclusion of all others. I've never felt that compelled, I suppose."

They had started talking, then. She had stimulated him into telling her a lot more about himself, and for the first time he had become curious about her, and had ceased to consider her simply as "that sweet niece of Olga's".

"Some of the girls at the convent mystify me," she had confided to him. "They seem to know exactly what they want in life. They've got it all worked out what they're going to do, where they want to live, and what sort of husbands they hope to marry. They think I'm odd because I haven't an idea on any of those things. I just want to love a man, that's all, and how can I tell what sort of man I'm going to love? Perhaps I'll never marry."

"You? You'll be a terror with the boys! A little, Tartar terror."

"No, but Felix, seriously—do *you* think I'm odd?"

"Not odd. Just different."

She had thought for a while before saying: "I suppose it's because I don't really belong anywhere. I don't just mean that I have no geographical roots, but I never feel completely at home with any one sort of people. However much I may like them, I'm always a little on the outside—in everything, really."

He suddenly turned to look at her then, saying: "There are quite a lot of people like that, you know. It's hardest when you're young, but in time you acquire good friends in all sorts of funny places, and then you belong to the excellent company of those who don't belong. It's more fun in the long run, really, because you get to know so much more about life that way."

"Are you like that, too?"

"Yes, I suppose I am."

And that was the moment that Nathalie had fallen in love with Felix. They had talked until it was nearly dark, and then he had taken her out to dinner. It was her first restaurant meal as a woman, and from that day, nothing was ever to be the same again.

Remembering all this now, and beginning to understand for the first time what her husband wanted of her, Nathalie felt hopeful of failing him less in the future.

"[illegible] I suppose, I am."

Remembering all this now, and beginning to [illegible] and for the first time that she [illegible] instead of the [illegible] hope of [illegible] him [illegible] in the future.

BOND OF PERFECTION

Part Two

Everybody agreed that Elizabeth Bateman-Brown's second birthday party was a success. The children were too young to enjoy each other's company, but some of them liked being dressed up, and most of them had done justice to the food set in front of them. The mothers enjoyed meeting each other, and the three Nannies happily swapped outrageous boasts about their charges.

Annabelle Hammond, now nearly eleven, had been there too, partly to help, but mostly so as not to miss anything. She often came to Walton House to see Elizabeth, and Arthur had a strange affection for her. He found her easy, friendly, and adequately polite, without being at all in awe of him. Her independence and self-sufficiency had a quality of strength that he greatly admired, and the mobility and fragility of her unself-conscious loveliness appealed to his sense of poetic beauty, and often touched him.

After all the other guests had gone, Annabelle asked: "Can I put Elizabeth to bed, now?"

"You'd better go home," Vera said, "or your mother will start worrying."

"Oh, she never worries."

"Little girls mustn't be inconsiderate!"

"Really, she doesn't. She gave it up for Lent, one year, and has never done it since. Do let me bath Elizabeth."

"Hop it," said Arthur. "We all want to relax and do nothing for a bit."

"You can come and take Elizabeth out tomorrow afternoon," Nathalie put in. "How would that be?"

"Oh, good. Good night, Elizabeth darling." She hugged the baby passionately. "Good-bye, and thank you for having me. It was a lovely party."

When Annabelle had gone, Nathalie exclaimed: "What a delightful child!" but Vera said primly: "I can't help feeling there's something rather common about her."

"Rubbish!" said Arthur. "That's the last thing she is." He flopped into his armchair and made as though to mop his brow, exclaiming: "Why does one do it? Why?"

He had not only supervised all the arrangements for the party, but also organised various games for the children. It was a hot day in May, and he was tired and thirsty.

"You were marvellous, darling," Nathalie said. "I heard one of the nannies say to the others: 'Isn't that a wonderful Daddy? Not like some we could name.' "

"The children didn't seem to think so. I've never known a more unresponsive lot."

"They're very young, Arthur," Vera said. "You can't expect them to co-operate at that age."

"Well, you two girls were splendid, anyhow. Lovely eats, lovely birthday cake, lovely table, and both of you lovely to look at as well. I think we all deserve a most enormous drink." He sprang up, and opened the door to the cocktail cabinet. "Darling, you've even remembered to restock all this," he said, as he poured out two gins and tonics and a glass of sherry. "It just shows what a little training will do. A dog, a wife, and a walnut tree; the more you beat them the better they be."

"And what about my inborn intelligence and goodwill?" Nathalie smiled.

"Ah, but it took my firmness and determination to uncover them. There you are! One sherry coming up, and here's your gin and tonic, darling."

"I think it's time Elizabeth was put to bed," Vera said, taking the glass that was handed to her.

"Just relax for a moment. She's had it all her own way since three o'clock this afternoon, so she can jolly well wait another ten minutes."

"Do you realise what the time is?" Vera persisted.

"Yes, it's a quarter to seven, but it won't hurt her to be

up late just for once. She doesn't seem to mind, anyhow."

That was certainly true. Elizabeth sat quietly on her aunt's lap, and although Vera was holding her, neither seemed to have anything to do with the other. When Nathalie saw them together, like this, she often wondered why they looked so completely unconnected, and what was missing that usually made the sight of a woman with a child convey so much more than just two figures. Elizabeth might have been sitting astride a chair, and Vera could just as well have had a stone on her lap, for all the impression they made as a unit.

Yet, Vera was devoted to the pale little girl, with dark, curly hair, large grey eyes and a small thin mouth. She frequently expressed delight at her being so docile, easy to manage and obedient, but Nathalie was concerned at the lack of vitality in a child who never laughed, and seldom smiled. Arthur was pleased that Elizabeth looked proud and pretty, but he could still not adjust himself to being the father of a daughter; having been so certain that his first-born would be a boy, he was almost unable to regard this child as quite real.

When Vera said: "It's now seven o'clock," Nathalie jumped up and exclaimed: "Yes. High time you were in bed, young lady." She put her arms out to Elizabeth, but the child merely looked at her with a completely unfathomable expression.

"I'll take her up," Vera said. "You have a rest. You must be tired."

"It's quite all right, thank you." Nathalie welcomed the idea of getting away for the next half-hour, if not by herself, at least with her baby. "Besides, you must be tired too. You worked jolly hard all this morning."

"Nonsense, I'm never tired," Vera protested, and picking Elizabeth up, she went upstairs with her.

"So sucks to me!" Nathalie sat down again.

"Well, you ought to be jolly grateful to have someone as competent and obliging as Vera about the place," Arthur said.

"Of course I am." There was no alternative, so Nathalie thought it best to be appreciative. She no longer wondered what life would be like without Vera living at Walton House. Since it had become obvious to her the night after Arthur's escapade, two and a half years before, that he had to have Vera with him, she had accepted the situation. The moving of Vera's belongings into the east wing had been a mere formality, the sealing of a situation that could no longer be avoided. "It might have been worse," Nathalie reflected. "Vera's easy to live with. She's tidy and methodical, and becomes unobtrusive when people she doesn't want to meet come to the house. Also, she's a help in lots of ways, especially with Elizabeth."

Nathalie and Arthur still had frequent quarrels, but there was now a more established framework to their lives, and neither of them took these as seriously as before. His new job as Bursar at an Oxford college seemed to satisfy him and gave him enough time to spend in studying the theatre. Even his drinking bouts had become part of a regular routine. He had alcoholic jags, lasting about ten days, once every three months or so. Then he drank heavily outside office hours and finally disappeared for two or three days, usually over a week-end. He made no pretence to Nathalie about what went on then, and, in fact, relied on her to cover up for him, especially with regard to Vera. After these escapades, he would return thankfully to the security of his own surroundings, remorseful and exhausted, but relaxed.

This equilibrium worked so long as it existed in a vacuum, but it was inevitable that outside influences should test the balance from time to time. Such catalytic distractions had been reduced to a minimum, however. Nathalie had cut herself off from all the people she had previously known; Vera appeared to have no friends; and Arthur, although he was becoming more communicative about his life, and often talked of the people he met, seldom brought anyone home. Contacts with the village had become established, but casual. After the first flush of enthusiasm, Vera no longer gushed about anybody, and had become resentful of the Hammonds, suspicious of Sir James and bored with the Coxes. She and Lady Bates still had tea together from time to time, but even in this relationship, the honeymoon was over. Lady Bates had succumbed to the inevitable fate of turning from a symbol and a figurehead into a mere person, a metamorphosis that Vera found almost impossible to accept.

The only real threat from outside was the Baroness. She would disappear for months on end and then suddenly turn up, often with little warning, and upset the whole house for days afterwards. Vera now scarcely concealed a passionate dislike for her, and this both annoyed and worried Arthur. He felt forced to take his sister's side, partly through loyalty and partly because he was jealous of Nathalie's affection for her aunt; at the same time, he often wished to share in this family relationship. There were always tensions and quarrels after the Baroness left, because she brought with her a life force which Vera could not ignore, Arthur failed to dominate and Nathalie found pleasantly stimulating. She was, it is true, partly responsible for the episode which was to shake up the entire new order of Walton House so thoroughly, but it would be neither fair nor relevant to blame her for this. Life has a way of asserting itself, and it is better to come to terms with it, than to deny its existence.

One afternoon at the end of June, Nathalie looked out of the kitchen window and saw Felix Hamilton in the garden. A strong shock of excitement made her tremble violently, but at the same time she felt furtive and fearful, until remembering that Arthur was still in Oxford, and Vera had taken Elizabeth for a walk. She rushed to open the kitchen door just as Felix was coming towards it. They stood for a moment, gazing at one another; then, still without saying a word slipped into each other's arms. Almost immediately, he held her away from him and said: "Let me have a look at you. How are you?"

"Fine. And you?"

"I'm all right." Felix put his arm in hers and drew her into the garden. As they strolled across the lawn, he added: "It's so good to see you again."

"Where are you leading me to?" Nathalie asked, as they went towards the gate that gave on to the downs. "I can't go far, as I must get the tea ready." She realised how odd this remark must have seemed to him; such domestic details had previously always been made to fit into their lives, and had never determined their actions. He made no comment, however, and merely said: "I want to have a quick look at the view from the end of the garden again. It's such ages since I last saw it."

"I'd almost forgotten that you know this place," she exclaimed, realising suddenly that that was one of the reasons why Walton

House meant so much to her. Yet, such a lot had happened since the days of the young Balliol don and the solemn little girl, that their ghosts hardly belonged there any longer. More compelling personalities had taken over since, filling the air with their crude passion; and memories of harmony, laughter and exciting conversations or good-natured arguments, had been displaced by discord, mocking, superficial chatter or shattering scenes.

Nathalie looked at Felix as he gazed towards the downs, and even the actual man was no longer quite real to her. She was now so wrapped up in, and numbed by, the conflicts that raged round her, month after month, that Felix's gentleness came from another world, remote and inaccessible. There was so much that seemed incomprehensible now, so many things she could not talk about, that even Felix seemed a stranger. Though every part of him was familiar, and even beloved, she beheld him as though from behind a thick, glass wall.

As he walked slowly back to the house with his arm round her shoulders, he talked about his life in Washington, and gave her news of mutual friends. When they got to the kitchen, Nathalie said: "We've got someone coming to tea—one of the worthy ladies of the village. Can you face it?"

"I don't think so. When can I see you without worthy ladies?"

"I don't know, really." She could not explain that something so simple was insuperably difficult, and hedged: "Where are you staying, by the way?"

"With the Cunninghams, in West Compton. Do you know them?"

"I've met them." Vera disliked the Cunninghams, and Arthur did not trust them, so they had remained mere acquaintances. "How long are you down for?" she added.

"I must get back tomorrow night, as I'm going down to Chequers on Sunday."

"Could you come to lunch tomorrow? Arthur doesn't work on Saturdays, and he'd like to meet you, I'm sure."

She knew that there would be a fuss if somebody were asked to a meal without her husband being consulted and cajoled first, but she did not care. Felix made her feel brave, if a little apprehensive.

"Yes, I'll do that. Then perhaps I'd be allowed to take you for a walk afterwards?"

"I doubt it," Nathalie smiled. "I have a wildly jealous husband,

and if you suggest any such thing, he'll come after you with a knife between his teeth and a horse-whip in each hand." She wondered if Felix would ever have believed how nearly true that was.

"How much does he know about me?"

"That you're an old friend of the family's—apart from what he's read in the papers, that is."

"About us, I mean?"

"Nothing. Now, you can just sit down there while I get this tray ready," she added. Felix preferred to walk about and explore, however.

"It's all much the same as it used to be," he said, "but I don't remember *this* sort of thing." He lifted a lace mat and looked through it against the light, crooking the little finger of the hand that held it.

"They're not quite Olga, are they," Nathalie giggled. "They moved in with my sister-in-law."

"Oughtn't they to go on the backs of chairs, though?"

"You're thinking of antimacassars. Vera has some somewhere, I believe, but these are 'doilies'." Felix said nothing. "I'm quite an expert on middle-class frippery now, as you can see," she went on.

He was examining a large pile of mats on the kitchen table; she had brought the whole lot out, as the different sets had got mixed up.

"You're not going to use all those, are you?" he asked.

"Of course! Must do things proper, or else what would the neighbours say? One here, and one there. You'd be surprised how they get used up."

"Like this?" Felix asked, putting one between each cup and saucer.

"That's the idea. And one under each sandwich."

"Why not *in* the sandwiches?"

"Why not, indeed! And why not one on top of the jam sponge, as well as underneath it. Here's a nice, knobbly one that would look pretty."

"I think you'd look pretty with this one on your hair." As he solemnly placed a doily on her head, he remarked: "You've changed your parting."

"Fancy you noticing."

"Are you surprised?"

She did not look at him, but said: "I think you should wear one as well."

"All right." He laid a lace mat on top of his head with both hands, and then asked: "Are they wearing them straight this year, or a little to one side?"

"Slightly tipped over the forehead, I believe."

"Like this?"

He bent down to look at his reflection in a window pane, and as he swung round, his elbow knocked over a jug, spilling milk all over the tray.

"Blast! Darling, I'm *terribly* sorry."

He looked so childishly dismayed that Nathalie felt a small pang.

"You see, I'm just as clumsy as ever," he smiled.

She started laughing then, remembering Felix's clumsiness. His endearing, human capacity for making a fool of himself had provided many an incident in the old days, and a whole batch of small memories were suddenly illuminated for her.

"I'd completely forgotten about your clumsiness," she giggled. "Oh, Felix, how on earth do you manage, now you're so grand?"

"I'm always in trouble. One social black after another. I drop ice-cream into the laps of lovelies at banquets, trip over the toes of elder statesmen in the middle of delicate negotiations, and send glasses flying out of people's hands during diplomatic receptions."

They were both laughing quite helplessly now. "The worst incident," Felix went on, "was on one of the first occasions I had to address a U.N.O. meeting. Every network from coast to coast was geared up for me. I could see the floor writhing with endless black eels as I picked my way over to the right microphone, and I knew, I just *knew*, that I'd never make it without falling flat on my face!"

"You should have tried it on all fours."

"By the time I thought of that, it was already too late. Oh dear, it was so shaming—until I realised how much you'd have laughed, and then I felt better."

"Thank God you haven't changed!" Nathalie exclaimed, and suddenly she began to cry. Felix immediately put his arms around her.

"Olga told me things weren't right with you," he whispered. "I couldn't bear to think of it."

Nathalie gently released herself, for she found his tenderness so disarming that it frightened her. Having been shackled for so long, and so thoroughly, there was a risk of complete disintegration if she gave in to any feeling at all now.

"It's all right," she said, smiling at him, and holding both his hands.

"Really?"

"It's just the excitement of seeing you again, I expect." Yet, after that first glimpse of him through the kitchen window, there had been no excitement, or feeling of any kind. She noticed a certain look in his eyes, sorrowful and uncertain, that at one time had always made the whole of her go out to him. Now, however, although still clinging firmly to his hands, she merely looked away. It was at this moment that Vera appeared at the kitchen door with Elizabeth in her arms. She was looking at them with distrust and hostility, but Nathalie did not worry, and said with surprising assurance: "Hello, Vera. I hoped you'd be back soon. You haven't met Mr. Hamilton, have you?"

Felix removed the doily from his head as if it were a bowler hat, and shook hands with Vera, saying: "How do you do?"

"How do you do?" Vera said, smiling grudgingly.

"And this, I suppose, is Elizabeth," Felix said. "Hello there!" The child stared at him without a smile. "She's like you, Nathalie," he went on.

"People often say how like her father she is," Vera said, rather coldly.

"There's quite a look of Nathalie as a child about her. She was a solemn little thing, too—sometimes, anyway."

"Felix is an old friend of the family's," Nathalie explained. "He first knew me when I was five or six."

"Really?" said Vera, and it was difficult to imagine that she was interested. Then, abruptly, her manner changed. She had turned to leave the room, her expression hard and set, but suddenly, she wheeled round with an almost coquettish smile.

"How stupid of me," she fluttered. "When you said 'Mr. Hamilton', I didn't realise, at first. . . . Won't you come into the drawing-room? I'll see to the tea, Nathalie."

"It's all right. Felix has to go in a moment, anyhow."

"Well, all the more reason not to entertain him in the kitchen. I was so interested to read your speech at the Anglo-American dinner. I'll just see to Elizabeth, and then I'll join you." She tripped out of the kitchen and up the stairs, but by the time she came down again, Felix had already left.

Vera became extremely agitated when she heard that Felix Hamilton was lunching at Walton House the next day. Nathalie had not seen her like that since the Baroness's first visit, but this time there was a difference; she herself remained unperturbed by Vera's nervousness, and Arthur became irritated with his sister. He had lately begun to snap at her quite often when she was too fussy, or failed to respond to something that pleased him. On that particular Saturday morning, he told her to stop interfering, and to show a little more respect for his wife's capabilities. Nathalie had become quite a skilful and enterprising cook, and Arthur was often complimentary about her progress. She had learnt how to make the sort of fish-pie that tasted of rank flannel, instead of such concoctions as eels stewed in red wine; watery Irish stew that kept the fatty flavour of mutton and onions, and did not turn into something like cassoulet; and such straightforward sweets as treacle tart and castle pudding, rather than fruit salads laced with kirsch, or caramel cream extravagantly made with real eggs. This was the first occasion on which he positively took her side against Vera, however.

In spite of all this, the luncheon was a success, and Felix completely charmed his company. He had that rare gift of being human and unaffected, and yet at the same time completely civilised. Vera liked him because he was distinguished and did not make her feel a bore, and Arthur because he was important and yet made him feel clever. All this goodwill was to prove helpful a few days later, when the Baroness rang up to invite Arthur and Nathalie to a luncheon she was giving for Felix. Arthur accepted this invitation with a readiness that surprised Nathalie, for she did not realise how stimulated he was at the prospect of being among a gathering of celebrities. They arranged to make a day of it, and go to a theatre in the evening, and when they set off, even Vera's rather soulful farewell could not dampen his high spirits.

When the Baroness stayed in London, she usually borrowed a flat belonging to some American friends of hers who were hardly ever in England, and it was there that the luncheon was being given. The Bateman-Browns arrived before anybody else. The moment they were inside the front door, Nathalie was struck by the smell, which she thought of as the emanation of international good living, and it seemed to her an age since this had been so familiar to her as to be an almost unnoticed part of her existence. The Baroness could never quite confine the smell of cooking to any kitchen. In other hostesses, this would have constituted a social black mark, but in all her abodes, there was invariably something more personal than the mere whiffs that float out of first-class restaurants in the early afternoon. Besides a smell of food which was obviously not English, combined with certain kinds of cigar smoke, coffee and good scent, there was a freshness which could perhaps be traced to the quantities of flowers she was always surrounded with, or the clean wool of carpets, or even the lavender soap in the bathrooms.

On that particular day, with the sunshine pouring in through the large windows, Nathalie felt it to be almost intoxicating. Just as she and Arthur were shown into the drawing-room, the Baroness came in from her bedroom. That day, everything about her had been drawn firmly upwards, instead of sagging rather carelessly, and she looked magnificent. Her hair had been done in a coiffure above her head, and rinsed a vivid mauve. Both her slanting eyes and her full mouth turned upwards with her smile, and she was firmly corseted and swathed in an elegant dress, instead of merely being covered in several pieces of clothing. As she walked towards them, holding out both her strong arms, and exclaiming: "My dear children! How lovely to see you!" she was everything that is warmth, assurance and vitality, and made both of them feel that they were the favourite guests. When Nathalie had hugged her, Arthur kissed her hand with a flourish. As she went through the list of her guests, he became happier and more excited. He had heard most of the names before, and looked forward to describing the party to Vera afterwards.

The Baroness had had much practice as a hostess, and being aware of her nephew-in-law's sensitivity, she took care that he should not have a chance of feeling left out. After spending a few minutes with the guest of honour, Arthur found himself part of first one small group, and then another. He had had a dry martini on arrival, and took a second one while he was talking to Felix. They were strong, and he lost all the nervousness and shyness which had bothered him when the room had first started to fill up. Then, finding that his rather satiric description of a senior common-room dinner was holding several people's attention, and even making them laugh, he had yet another drink; when he was in this euphoric state, he could hear himself being supremely witty and intelligent. It was not until sitting down to eat that he realised how tight he was. His brain was functioning more than well, but his limbs seemed to be a long way away, and he also had difficulty with his focussing. "Drink's an odd thing," he reflected. "There are times when two or three double gins do the trick, and others when half a bottle of the stuff, even washed down with cider, makes no appreciable difference." He had once worked out a theory that a man got as drunk as he intended to, regardless of how much he drank. "But surely I never intended to get quite as plastered as this today?" he thought. He felt it essential to follow, and reply intelligently to, what the woman on his right was saying to him, and he looked at her intently. She was good-looking and beautifully turned-out, but she terrified him. He was intrigued to know what was really going on behind that immaculate make-up and that Mayfair voice, but doubted if he could ever know. "Would I find out if I made love to her?" he wondered. Then he decided that even if he made this woman—or any other of her kind—so helpless with desire that she was on her knees to him, still she would never really break down. "What bitches they all are," he reflected. "The whole pack of them, even Vera and Nathalie."

At that thought, however, something like a small pang struck him. Nathalie, he thought, was not quite like the rest, and he suddenly felt that he needed her reassurance. The effect of the cocktails had begun to wear off, and left him feeling acutely depressed, as gin always did. He became bothered, not only by the sophisticated women on either side of him, but by the whole gathering in general as well. Most of the men were better dressed than he was, except for one M.P., whose notoriety was partly based on his proverbially shabby attire. It irked Arthur to be the most insignificant man present, and he looked across at Nathalie to catch her eye, so that he should not feel so much on his own. She returned his wink with a smile, then seemed to forget about him again, and went on listening to the man on her right, apparently absorbed in what he was saying. Arthur had not seen her so animated since they had first met; yet, though she still looked absurdly young, she now had a woman's poise. He suddenly stiffened with a strong pang of jealousy. It was not the man next to Nathalie he resented, so much as her remoteness from himself, and the way she fitted so effortlessly into this company. He wondered what she could be saying to absorb someone as eminent as Sir Cuthbert, and decided that she must be relying on some sort of secret sex signalling to hold his attention. Maddened that he did not know what they were discussing, he reflected savagely that she was as much of a bitch as all the others after all.

By the end of lunch, Arthur felt better. It had been a good meal, and the effect of the gin had been counterbalanced by liberal quantities of two excellent wines. Coffee was taken in the drawing-room, in small groups that the Baroness had again carefully manœuvred, but she was unable to prevent Arthur from sitting down with Nathalie, who was talking to a French Embassy Attaché and his wife.

"I was just telling Nathalie," said Jules Marron, "that the first time we ever saw her was when she was a little girl one summer in the South of France. When would that have been, Clothilde?"

"Well, let me see . . . Nathalie was about ten. . . . It must have been . . . oh, la, la . . . how many years ago? . . . Fifteen?"

"Seventeen," smiled Nathalie. "I remember that summer very well, because it was the turning point of father's progress. We were having one of our poor periods, and had been lent a house near Grasse. Somebody turned up to stay with a Crown Prince or something in tow, and father did a portrait of him. He not only got £200 for it, but several other commissions as well. That was really how he started being famous."

She paused for a moment, looking back into that long since vanished world, when even Felix had not really existed for her, although he turned up from time to time. She remembered then that he had turned up shortly after the Crown Prince's visit, and went on: "Olga brought Felix Hamilton to stay soon afterwards, and father decided we must celebrate his good fortune. So we all piled into Walt's car and went to Talloires, on the lac d'Annecy —miles away but goodness, it was fun.

"Georges Bise?" asked Jules happily.

"No, Marius. We were very faithful to Papa Bise, even though the cooking at Georges' was supposed to be better in those days." She looked exhilarated as she laughed: "Do you remember the war of the poteaux, on the road that winds down to the lake from the main road? There was hardly a yard on either side," she explained to Arthur, "where father or son hadn't put a sign advertising their respective restaurants. Felix wanted to pinch a couple, but Walt got pompous about it."

"Oh, he was a gay one, that Felix," chuckled Jules Marron, remembering several escapades before the war. And Clothilde added, looking fondly at her husband: "You were naughty boys together, you two!"

Nathalie only half heard them, however, for she was still thinking about the lac d'Annecy. "Is it all still there?" she asked sadly, looking down at her hands. "Presumably the lake must still be, but are the Bises still fighting it out?"

"Well, Marius has got the upper hand now," said Jules. "I was down there not so long ago, and it was as superb as ever. He does an omble chevalier braisé du porto that is marvellous, and there is a Roussette de Segssel that is mm—uh!" He kissed the tips of his fingers and flung them out in a Gallic gesture of appreciation.

"I wonder if I shall ever go there again," Nathalie said, almost to herself.

"But of course! Why not?" Jules and Clothilde said almost simultaneously, and with such enthusiasm that she looked up and smiled. She noticed then that Arthur had drifted away. He was with a small group of men round Felix Hamilton, and she could see, by the way he held himself, that he was feeling disgruntled and aggressive. She rejoined him as soon as possible, and he returned her smile in the exaggerated manner that still succeeded in making her feel apprehensive.

Before she could say anything, however, Arthur turned to attend to the discussion at hand, and so she watched Felix instead. She saw then that he had changed during the previous few years; yet the only marks of age on him were his greying hair, and pigmentation marks on the backs of his hands. He appeared completely convincing in the role of a distinguished statesman, and yet looked less gaunt and worried than when she had last seen him. Even his shoulders, which had always had a tendency to roundness, appeared less bowed.

Nathalie was especially susceptible to shoulders. In a man, they seemed to her more expressive than speech, or hands, or even eyes could ever be. Once, when praying in church, she had looked down at the rosary dangling between her hands, and something had happened. The Crucifix, no longer a small ivory and silver ornament, had suddenly dominated everything, and the straining gap between Our Lord's shoulders and the horizontal bar of the Cross had become so real to her that she herself had felt the pain of it. Her own shoulders had begun to ache agonisingly, and even her arms to hurt, as though they, too, had been twisted and pinned at that cruel angle. This experience impressed her profoundly. After it, she felt able to know not only men's characters, but even their destinies, by the shape, and set, and carriage of their shoulders. There were countless varieties even among the arrogantly square, bovinely tough, commonly held, timidly braced, pensively bent, bureaucratically stooped, humbly rounded, heavily sagging and many others. All seemed to her unconscious and individual betrayals of the man within.

Watching Felix's shoulders now, she suddenly remembered, quite clearly, each curve and every detail of them: the colour and texture of the skin; the exact position of the freckles; the mole on his right shoulder blade; the small scar near his collar bone. It astonished her that she could think of all this with so little feeling, but at the same time, she was grateful; it helped to dispel the suspicion that perhaps her previous life with Felix was partly responsible for her failure as Arthur's wife.

Felix was describing the last conference he had attended, at which, yet again, a measure of agreement with the Russians had proved impossible to reach.

"I marvel at your patience with those blighters!" a former Cabinet Minister was saying, "but I sometimes wonder whether you're right. Can't go on letting 'em get away with it, like that."

"Complete deadlock is a state which must be avoided, almost at all costs," Felix replied. "We must preserve some lifeline of contact, some basis for negotiation—even if only to be able to withdraw it in a real emergency."

"Ah, there speaks the diplomatist! You've learnt the ropes

very thoroughly, I must say. I don't remember you ever taking that sort of a line when you were at Balliol!"

"That is a crack!" Felix laughed, and turning to the others he explained: "Tony remembers the time he was in office, not long before the war, when I publicly denounced his policy. I was a staunch Liberal, in those days, and it seemed to me that both the Conservatives and the Labour Party had got things all wrong."

"Are you still a Liberal?" Arthur asked, and something in his manner made Nathalie fearful.

"As a point of principle, rather than of politics," replied Felix good-naturedly. "Actually, I've never been much of a politician, but even I realise that liberalism as a political creed is obsolete, nowadays."

"Isn't it rather obsolete in every way?" Arthur asked. His awareness of Nathalie's anxiety excited him, and he added: "One thing the war taught us—those of us who fought in it, anyway—was that the Liberal way of life is nothing more than a nursery fairy-tale. It's no more real in terms of adult life than a discussion about sauces is to a starving man."

"As things are now, perhaps," Felix said. "But then movements of thought must be viewed in their proper contexts. Remember that the Liberal idea had a vigorous and significant start. It stood for the intellectual honesty and human compassion that had been forgotten in the solid society of the nineteenth century. There was a crying need, then, for more truth and greater freedom, and that's why scientific progress also came under the banner of Liberal enlightenment. But as soon as the scientific approach became identified with materialism, instead of being principally a method for thinking objectively, the whole point of Liberalism began to change. Up till then, it had merely been part of a conflict between two factions of the same family. When the materialists took it over, however, the fight came out of the drawing-room. The issues are more complicated, and far more dangerous now than they were then, but the needs that gave rise to Liberalism still exist. Now that the materialists boast of a morality as dogmatic and narrow-minded as that of a Victorian maiden aunt's, it's time for a further step in enlightenment, and a new kind of freedom."

"Does that mean that you reject morality?" Arthur asked aggressively.

"Not at all, but I do mistrust 'systems', and 'mass movements', and 'isms' of any kind. I'd rather pin my faith to a more individual brand of responsibility. The Liberal way of life was once a step in that direction, but it's your generation, Arthur, that will have to decide what is needed this time. It'll need great strength, and understanding, and imagination—probably rather more than was ever required in the world before—so perhaps we should find a new term for it, too."

"I doubt if, philosophically speaking, a term could be found for such a nebulous conception," Arthur replied. He felt rising in him a rage that was in danger of making him lose all his self-control, yet he almost welcomed the tremendous sense of power this gave him. He was furiously resentful of Felix's confidently easy manner, his humane outlook, his experience: in fact, of all the things that had caused him to admire the man only a few days beforehand. Arthur wondered savagely what he knew about reality and of the problems that dominated most lives: of the basic passions, and how they could affect people; of extreme situations like war, when a man was forced to act quickly and violently, and "the fundamental values" became just an irritating catch-phrase. "Nathalie's his sort, too," he realised. "They understand each other, those two, and share memories of a life that bears no relation to reality. I'll teach her, though. I'm already shaking some of the nonsense out of her, but she'll have to crawl and bite the dust before really learning anything worth while."

Arthur's anger reached a climax when he saw Nathalie smile at something Felix had said, for his black reflections had prevented him hearing the remark.

"You all deserve everything that's in store for you!" he shouted. "How much violence do you people need, before you begin to understand what life is really about?"

For a moment, he stood swelling and trembling, his face savagely distorted. Then he suddenly turned away, and walked out of the room. After a moment's hesitation, Nathalie followed and caught up with him in the hall.

"Where are you going?" she asked. Arthur said nothing, but opened the front door, his expression still angry.

"Where shall we meet, later on?" she continued, but he went out without saying anything. On the landing outside the flat, she put her hands on his forearms and tried to make him look at her.

"What *is* the matter?" she asked.

He shook himself free of her and said curtly: "Absolutely

nothing. I just can't stand that atmosphere any longer, that's all."

"Shall I come too?"

He did not reply, but she could tell that he wanted to take her away, and said: "Just wait a second while I get my things."

As she turned again, the Baroness came out on to the landing, saying: "I am so sorry you have to go already Arthur, but we'll look after Nathalie for you."

"Well, actually——" began Nathalie, but Arthur said abruptly: "That is most kind of you. Many thanks for the excellent lunch," and started walking quickly down the stairs.

"Shall we meet somewhere before the theatre?" Nathalie shouted after him, but he did not answer. He was already lost to her sight, and she heard his footsteps crunching on the stairs, and then abruptly cease as he went out.

As she went into the flat again, the Baroness put an arm round her and said: "Would you like some more coffee, my darling?"

"No thanks. Olga, I am so——"

"As neither of you come up to London very often, Arthur must have a lot to do. I'm afraid my lunches always go on far too long. I had no idea it was so late."

Nathalie gave her aunt a quick hug, and then let herself be led to a group of people talking by one of the windows.

When all the guests except Felix had gone, he, Nathalie and the Baroness sat down and pulled the party to pieces, though nothing was said about Arthur. Listening to the other two laughing and backchatting, Nathalie felt lulled by a warmth that was comfortable, and yet strange. She decided that it was rather like having a hot bath, when the body was cold, but the warmth of the water had not yet reached beyond the outer skin. The sensation was pleasant, and sufficiently relaxing to make her feel drowsy. After a while, the Baroness rose reluctantly and said: "I must go and see Mimi. She is leaving for Italy tomorrow, and I promised to call in before four."

"Is it as late as that?" Felix said, looking at his watch. "I ought to be off too," he added, but made no attempt to move.

"Nathalie, my darling, will you still be here when I get back?" the Baroness asked. "I'll be in by six, I should think."

"I expect I shall be curled up right here and fast asleep."

"Good. You talk to her, Felix, or she really will fall asleep. Look at her! She's like a sleek little pussy cat!"

By the time Felix had accompanied the Baroness to the front door and said good-bye to her, however, Nathalie was no longer at all sleepy. When he came back to the sofa again, she was sitting upright, and feeling rather self-conscious.

"How much longer are you staying in England?" she asked.

"Till Saturday. I have to be at Lake Success next week."

"Oh, of course. You'll fly, presumably?"

"Yes. I don't enjoy it much, but it saves a lot of time."

"Isn't it amazing how quickly one can get about the place, nowadays?"

"Quite amazing. Have you read any good books lately?"

"Idiot!" Nathalie giggled. She could just see that he was smiling, but would not look straight at him. "Felix, I'm terribly sorry about Arthur," she said, more seriously. "I don't know quite how to explain it. He just gets like that, sometimes. Something bites away inside him, and he suddenly goes off like a rocket. I'm sure he didn't mean to be rude to you personally. In fact, he was saying only this morning how much he admired you." She waited for Felix to speak, but he was silent. Then she looked up, and saw him gazing at her with an expression that she recognised with her heart, as well as her head. He was smiling, but his eyes were serious, and he stretched out an arm towards her. She put her hand in his, and the warmth of this contact drew her—abruptly and entirely—out of her desert of solitariness.

It was not quite a return to their old relationship, but something which included all they had ever been to each other. The last few years had given them both new and separate loyalties and experiences, but one thing had apparently not changed, and the truth of their essential unity was now fully revealed. The world still went on around them, with all its richness and pressure, variety and perplexity, but none of it stood between them any longer, and the wall of ice that had imprisoned Nathalie suddenly melted away.

They sat for some time, her hand resting in his, without the need to speak. She was overwhelmed by his tenderness. It came not only from his affection for her, but also from the very nature of the kind of person he was. Their harmony was a gentle one, for their wills were tuned into one another, instead of being pitched in a battle for domination. It was precisely this mutual submissiveness that was dangerous; it filtered so deeply into the innermost core of their hearts that Nathalie instinctively began to brace herself against her feeling. She turned her head away from Felix and he, who had once known her every mood, whispered: "Don't look so worried." He got up, and stood looking out of the window. After a while, he asked: "Is there anything at all that I can do?"

"I don't think so. It's just something I've got to get through."

Then Felix turned towards her again, and she forgot about everything, except he who now held out his hands to her. Although her knees felt so weak that they could hardly support her, she stood up and fell into his arms. He kissed her quickly and said: "I've got to go. I should have been at the Foreign Office at four."

"Aren't you naughty!" Nathalie smiled, snuggling her face in his neck. At that moment, she was completely happy.

"Not nearly as naughty as I'd like to be."

"Well, you'll have to find someone else, then. I'm horribly respectable, these days."

"You don't mean to say that you're faithful to him, as well as everything else?"

"It's never occurred to me not to be. . . . Does that surprise you so much?"

He did not answer at once, but drew her to him and hugged her again. Then he said: "No, it doesn't surprise me at all."

Hand in hand they walked to the front door and he added: "Am I going to see you again before I leave?"

"I don't know, really," she hedged, suddenly realising that she could never make any plans that were not directly concerned with Arthur or Vera.

"Have lunch with me on Friday?"

"Two trips to London in one week!" Nathalie smiled. "What can you be thinking of? The sales aren't on."

"What are you talking about?"

"Cuts of meat and advantageous lines in biscuits. Doilies and sales. You don't know how the other half lives. It's shocking self-indulgence to do anything for the sheer fun of it."

"I'll send my car for you, if you like." Nathalie laughed out loud at this.

"That really would fix things good and proper. I can't tell you why it seems so absurd, but it just does." She could picture Vera's reactions as Felix's Daimler drew up at Walton House, and then drove off with her inside it. "One of my sister-in-law's favourite theories is that propinquity is the devil's own weapon."

"Would she suspect you of getting off with the chauffeur, then?" Felix smiled.

"She suspects everyone of everything, the whole time. It doesn't seem to make her any happier, though, poor thing."

"Well, in that case, I'd better pick you up here. One o'clock on Friday. All right?"

Nathalie knew quite well that it would not be all right, but equally, that nothing would stop her being there at one o'clock on Friday if she could help it. When she told Felix this, however, he looked a little worried.

"If it's going to make more trouble than it's worth..." he began. But she was feeling light-headed now, and said bravely: "Why the blazes shouldn't I have lunch with you? Of *course* I'll come!"

"Good. That makes me feel much better," he said, then kissed her good-bye and left.

Nathalie walked slowly back through the drawing-room again. She sat on the arm of the sofa, one leg stretched out in front of her. She kicked her shoe off, and wriggled her toes inside her stocking, examining the shape of her foot and her slender leg, not critically, but as though she had never seen them before. She looked at her hands and her bare arms, slowly stretching them out in front of her. Then, leaving her other shoe, she went to the window where Felix had stood a few minutes before, and let the sun warm, first her neck and her arms, and then the back of her. It was hot, but the first impact made her shiver. Her blood was tingling, almost singing, to such an extent that her head felt as though it were full of balloons. She laughed out loud, exclaiming: "I must have been absolutely mad to imagine I'd got over it." Relishing her newly-awakened awareness, she stroked the fold of a velours curtain, slowly and lovingly, breathed deeply from a bowl of roses on a console table, and saw, for the first time, the intricacy and beauty of the design on the carpet. She caught sight of herself in a glass and, putting her face right up to it, examined the moulding of her forehead, the line of her eyes and brows, the shape of her nose, the softness of her mouth, and the contours of her chin and neck. It amazed her that everything could have changed so suddenly, for nothing else seemed to matter now, except Felix. She no longer lacked the courage to look at her memories, and one image after another reminded her of how it had felt to be carefree; to laugh with friends, or exult in swimming, or dancing, or driving at night in an open car. Her past memories of Felix himself were shadowy, however, and the person who had just left now seemed the most real to her. It was as though she had fallen in love for the first time, and yet could remember another life, in which she had learnt quite a lot about love.

Nathalie arrived at the theatre soon after seven, hoping for a reconciliatory drink with Arthur before the seven-thirty performance, but although she waited until after eight, there was no sign of him. This surprised her, because his love for the theatre was the most reliable thing about him. The only times he ever stopped being at war with himself and everybody else were after he had seen a play that satisfied him, and even if the performance disappointed him, the drama was usually strong enough to hold all his emotions for a while.

At Paddington, it occurred to her that she had not asked for a message at the box office. She considered going back, and then decided that it was too late. It seemed almost certain that Arthur would only fail to attend a theatrical performance if he were drunk and, in those circumstances, he would scarcely leave messages at box offices. "How impossible he is," she said to herself, and began to examine in detail what had happened at lunch-time. "The trouble started because he somehow felt left out," she thought. "He neither fitted in with the past, as I did, nor with the present, like everybody else there. He always lashes out like a thwarted child when he feels at a disadvantage, but it's ridiculous that he can't control himself any better and learn to take things more philosophically."

Yet, although there was no justification for his bouts of tiresome behaviour, his unhappiness moved her. It was never the whimsical appeal of the lost that touched her most deeply, but the sight of suffering without understanding. She had first set eyes on him during another small party of her aunt's, and her instinct had said: "What an unpleasant person!" Yet, when they came to know each other a little, the fact that he was also the most tortured being she had ever come across became the most important one. Something in him had cried out for help without the hope that it could ever be found, and the whole of her had responded with love.

It was after eleven when Nathalie reached Walton House, and she saw with relief that Vera had already gone to bed. Having put the car away in the garage, she crept into the house by the kitchen door, praying that her sister-in-law would not come downstairs. "I'm so afraid of being heard, I might be a burglar," Nathalie thought with irritation. It struck her, then, that the east wing had never really become self-contained. Vera had made herself so indispensable in the house that she lived with them almost altogether. Mrs. Dennison had been replaced by a succession of mothers' helps who never stayed long, and when each in turn had left, Vera always rose to the occasion, showing an energy and efficiency which at times almost passed for goodwill. At that moment, Nathalie longed to have the house to herself, so as to enjoy in peace the visions from the past that suddenly filled the whole place. Having ascertained that Arthur had not yet got back, she opened wide the drawing-room windows and then sat straddling a sill, her feet touching the ground on either side.

The warmth of the night had let loose all the scents of the garden, which reached her from time to time, and light from the house filtered unevenly among shrubs and grass, showing up isolated flowers and mysterious chasms of darkness. Everything Nathalie saw, or felt, or touched, or smelt made her think of Felix, and it seemed to her inconceivable that in this house, where the patterns of their respective lives had first begun to intertwine, his influence had not always dominated everything else. During the last few years, she had from time to time remembered incidents in which he figured, but they had been pictures without dimension. Now they, and many others besides, came so completely to life that Felix was almost there in person. He seemed so near, and so vital, that she fancied she had only to put out a hand to touch him.

Wanting to go back to the start, she tried to remember her first sight of him, but could recall no actual beginning. It seemed as though he had always been an insistent part of her life; always arguing during meals, playing tennis, dropping in with girl friends, riding on the downs, or listening to music and playing the piano. She remembered one particular incident, which had happened when she was about eleven. He had taken her to St. Giles's Fair in Oxford, and she had become almost hypnotised by a stand where a girl had been on show, completely encased in ice, with only a place round her face uncovered. Nathalie had dragged Felix back to this, again and again, feeling a vague unhappiness. She had then begun to feel cold herself, developing goose flesh and a peculiar numbness in her toes and fingers; it was almost as though she too were in the ice casing. She had suddenly known exactly what it felt like, and unable either to go away, or to bear the suffering that this girl was so futilely enduring with convulsions and a dumbly miserable look in her eyes, she had begged Felix to do something about it. At first he had smiled at Nathalie's pleading, trying to lead her away, but then he had changed his mind. Leaving her still gazing at the girl, he had gone to talk to the man in charge and returned to say that there would soon be a break in the act.

"How, a break?" Nathalie had asked. "Do they saw her in half as well?"

"No, no," Felix had laughed. "I mean, an interval."

"Does she have to go on doing it afterwards?"

"Well, it is her job, you know."

"But it will take her *ages* to get warm again. She'll still be cold through and through, for *hours*. I *know* she will."

"He's going to ask her if she'll come back and have tea with us."

Years later, Felix told Nathalie that both the man and the girl had thought him quite mad, but that he had prevailed upon them to humour her childish foible. They had brought the girl, Ada, back to Walton House for an enormous meal, and the Baroness had received her as though she were an old friend. By the time they sat in the garden, Ada had almost lost all her suspicion and reserve, and had been touchingly appreciative of their hospitability, and rather amused at the child's passionate solicitude.

"Why do you do that job?" Nathalie had asked her.

"Well ducks, you've got to eat, you know," she had replied good-naturedly, and then, turning to Felix, had added: "I'd learnt that long before I was her age."

Before Felix could say anything, Nathalie had asked: "Are you rich, then?"

"Get rich at that job? Not likely! But I get by."

"We're poor, too. That's why I come to live with my aunt, sometimes. My father is a painter, you see, but then he likes painting. I can't see the point of being poor, if you're not doing something you like."

Felix had tried not to smile, but Ada had burst out laughing and exclaimed: "Isn't she a card!"

"But you don't like that ice," Nathalie had insisted, quite certain that this must be so; for although she herself was warm again, there was still a curious feeling in her hands and feet.

"Whoever said anything about like?" Ada had replied rather sadly.

Some time after that, Felix had received a letter from her. It was almost illiterate, but contained an effusive message of gratitude to himself and Nathalie. They had set her thinking apparently, though what about was not made clear. Anyhow, she hoped the kid would be glad to hear that she'd now got a job she liked, with no ice and three square meals a day, and she hoped this would find them as it left her. Felix had been both touched and amused; but, more than anything, he had been puzzled by Nathalie's reaction. Although the outcome of this incident had pleased her, it had not seemed to her in the least surprising.

Nathalie went on drifting through her memories, but the one that stood out most vividly happened many years later, during the war. At that time, she had had a job as an ambulance driver, and Felix had been working at the Ministry of Economic Warfare. They had managed to arrange a whole day off together, and planned to lunch in Oxford, and go over to Compton Fawcett after that. No one was in sight on their arrival at Walton House, and they had walked around familiar places in the garden, pointing out shrubs and flowers to each other like happy children, and wandering towards the gate in the end wall, from where the downs looked familiar and beautiful. They had just become lovers, and could still hardly believe in their new-found happiness, which was too strange and delightful to let them think beyond the present.

Then, walking back across the lawn, a curious thing had happened. A pigeon, suddenly dropping dead from the sky, had fallen on to the ground just ahead of them. Coming up to it, Felix had paused for a moment, and then, putting his arm around her shoulders, had said: "The dove of peace passing out at our feet, do you think? What a sinister outlook for us, sweetheart!"

It was at that point in Nathalie's reminiscing that Arthur returned. She heard him the moment he came into the house, and thought irritably how violent and noisy everything about him invariably was. To stop him spoiling the spell on the terrace, Nathalie went indoors and met him in the drawing-room. She felt curiously brave and almost detached about him now, yet there was a heavy and oppressive apprehension in her again.

When he came into the room, she could see by the hard brightness of his eyes that although he was not drunk, he had been drinking. He gave her a long look and then said casually: "Ah, there you are. What time did you get back?"

"About eleven. I caught the nine-fifteen."

He was going around the room tidying here, straightening there, and his movements were just a little too deliberate. She recognised his mood as one in which he would be affable for a while before striking. After a few moments, he said, without looking at her: "Pity you missed the play. It was really rather good."

"Did you go, then?" She was most surprised.

"Of course I went. Isn't that what we arranged?" His tone was not reproachful, and it had the effect of making her feel in the wrong. She said: "Darling, I'm terribly sorry. I got there at seven, and waited until eight, and after that I lost heart and went home. I thought you must have changed your mind about going."

"You didn't think of asking at the box office, I suppose?" He had left her ticket there, and having taken his own seat at a quarter to seven, never came out to look for her. This had not been malice, so much as an almost superstitious notion that if she really wanted to find him, she would.

"Well, I remembered when I got to Paddington that I hadn't, but it seemed pointless to go back then," she explained. "Goodness, how stupid of me! But surely you didn't go in before seven, did you?"

"It's perfectly obvious you never went near the theatre!" he exclaimed angrily, annoyed with himself for what he knew to have been childishness on his part. Moreover, he had missed Nathalie's company.

"But I did," she protested. "Why else should I say I had?"

"It's as good an alibi as any. Women are such liars, anyway." She knew that not to answer would make him assume her to be hiding something, and that if she did, it would only lead to futile bickering; either way, he would have a row if he wanted one. It seemed that the only hope was humour, since he had not yet lost his temper, so she took up his last remark with a smile, saying: "This woman's besetting sin was that she told the truth too much, do you remember? You used to give me terrible rockets for 'undermining illusion', as you called it."

He looked at her then, standing by the open window, with the light only down one side of her. He found her mysterious, as though half of her belonged to the night outside, and even her gentleness, at that moment, was strange to him. Had she always been so lovely, without his noticing it, he wondered, or had she changed lately? Had something specific changed her, or was it merely the effect of maturing age? What was she really thinking? Was she trying to conceal something? What a fool he'd been to hide like that! Had she really been at the theatre? Would he ever know for sure? She smiled at him again, and said tenderly: "You can't have it both ways, you know, darling."

Then, Arthur lost his temper.

"You think you're going to get away with it, don't you? but nobody's going to make a fool of me! Where have you been?"

"I've already told you."

She came away from the window, and he saw that she looked tired, and no longer mysterious and lovely. Although this reassured him, he made no attempt to check the momentum of his mood; his rages were a form of debauchery, just as his alcoholism was, and were allowed to take their course in case they revealed something in their depths.

"I repeat: Where have you been?" he said menacingly, coming nearer to her.

"I didn't budge from Olga's flat until it was time to meet you, and after going to the theatre I came straight home."

"A likely story!"

"Oh, for Heaven's sake! What do you expect me to have been up to in a few hours after lunch, anyway?" A sudden memory then came back to her of the excellent use she and Felix had often made of those few hours after lunch, and she felt a strong desire to laugh at the irony of life. Arthur noticed the slight twitch of her mouth, and when she suddenly looked away from him, the last of his control broke down. He reached out and hit her head, then slapped her across the face.

It was not the first time he had struck her, and he considered himself justified because Nathalie had, as he put it, "opened the innings" when it came to hitting. The fact that he was larger and stronger than she was seemed to him irrelevant and he frequently stated that since women insisted on going in for equality, they must expect it all along the line. Usually, he hit her because she refused to give in when some long and futile quarrel had dragged on interminably. The only alternative to argument in these fights that she could understand was silence, and Arthur resented that even more; he would continue to nag in such a way that any silence would have been broken sooner or later. What he wanted her to do was to grovel and convince him, both that he was right, and that she was no good. Nathalie was incapable of this kind of masochism, however, and usually ended by bursting into tears of misery and frustration.

This time, however, things did not go quite the same way. Rather to his surprise, Nathalie hit him back, and they began to fight, both of them completely possessed with rage. He was too strong for her, though, and as she could not adequately defend herself with her fists, sought to do so with her tongue. Backing away, she began to curse him. He watched her, fascinated, for he had never before seen her completely lose control of herself. She looked so ugly, distorted by anger, that he wondered how he could ever have been troubled by her loveliness.

"Why can't you leave people alone?" she shouted. "Isn't it enough that you lie, and cheat, and even steal? Oh, yes! I know you pawned that diamond ring of mine! Don't you get enough satisfaction by doing people down and being dishonest in every way? Can you really not be happy unless you're the centre of some row or disturbance, the more violent the better?"

Arthur's own anger had now been switched off, and he said quite calmly: "Apparently you've got some spirit after all! It makes a change, anyhow."

"You're very pleased with yourself now because you've made me lose my temper, aren't you? You want to drag everybody down to your own filthy level, and then perhaps you'll be happy! Or will you? I can't see that appetite of yours for decadence and destruction ever being satisfied!"

Arthur just looked at her without saying anything. Then he saw that she was beginning to relax, so he said sarcastically: "Go on. If it makes you any happier, that is."

She was no longer angry, however, but miserable and frightened. "Why do you want to destroy me?" she asked. "Why have you always tried to strip me of everything?"

Now that she was calmer, she relapsed into her usual uncertainty, and that made her incoherent. Although knowing what she meant, it was impossible for her to express it, and Arthur was able to beat her in battle every time. She made one last effort, however, protesting: "You pretend to love me, but you make me feel that everything about me is always wrong—everything. The things I say, the things I do, my ideas, my friends, even my clothes. Everything."

"I have known you to be critical of others too, you know."

"Yes, of course. But criticism is not the same as completely deflating. After all, people differ. At least I let others live their own lives and do and think what they want. You, on the other hand, have to get at every nook and cranny of me and destroy each bit, one by one."

"How can one destroy a nook or a cranny? It doesn't make sense."

"You know perfectly well what I mean." She felt herself getting angry again. "You take unscrupulous advantage of the fact that I'm committed to you, and even in love with you, to defeat me at every turn. Why? That's just what I can't understand. What possible satisfaction can you get from destroying somebody you're supposed to love?"

"How little you know about life!"

"That doesn't answer my question. Why do you want to destroy me?"

"My dear child, you're exaggerating absurdly. Still, I must make allowances for the fact that you're not altogether English."

He knew that his patronising exasperated her, so he went on: "Besides, destruction is not so reprehensible in itself, and often has some phoenix-like qualities. It's a pity you were never educated, or I might have been able to explain several historical examples to you."

His references to her haphazard upbringing was one of his

stock ways of belittling her. Becoming discouraged then, and aware of the hopelessness of the whole situation, she said imploringly: "Must this go on, year in and year out? What do you want of me? You know I'll do anything for you, but you make it so difficult to understand what it is you want. You can't really want to kill me, can you?"

He saw that she was abject and unhappy, and as he had got her under his control again, felt that he could afford to be kind to her.

"It's for your own good, darling," he said. "You know, destruction can be a healthy, and even a creative process, like pruning a garden of weeds and dead wood, so that the good shoots can grow strong and beautiful. There's something missing about you, as you are now; I don't quite know what it is, but if we go on hacking away through the undergrowth, we may stumble on something worth while. You're a failure at the moment, but that's no reason for giving up hope."

This last attack was too much for Nathalie. She began to cry, not so much with despair, as with disgust and exhaustion. It had been a long day.

Arthur wallowed in such a display of remorse after this particular scene that Nathalie found it comparatively easy to tell him about her luncheon-date with Felix, and he put no serious obstacles in her way to keeping it.

When she reached Hyde Park Gardens the following Friday, there was a note from the Baroness saying that the latter was sorry to miss her niece, but might run down to Walton House on Saturday, if that would be convenient. Composing an answer to this was one way of passing the time, and Nathalie wrote out three notes before she finally left one on her aunt's desk. The last half-hour was almost impossibly difficult to get through. By the time the front door opened, she was feeling sick, and sat down on the arm of a chair. For a moment she feared that Olga had returned, and then realised that Felix must have borrowed a key. He came in from the hall and stood in the doorway without saying a word. His eyes looked as they had done during those few moments on the sofa, but now he was no longer smiling. He paused uncertainly where he was, and Nathalie knew then that he felt exactly as she did. With only the look between them to support her, she slowly rose to her feet and went towards him.

Some minutes later, he managed to say: "Don't you think we'd better have some lunch first? I've taken the afternoon off."

"Well, that's pretty plain, anyhow," Nathalie laughed, stroking his hair, his face, his ears and his neck. She wanted to recall every detail of him by touch, as well as by sight.

"Ouch, you're tickling!" he laughed.

"You used to like that."

"Oh, you are a terror! A little, Tartar terror!"

Every word, every gesture brought back some memory and drew them together, again and again. After a while, Nathalie asked: "*Are* we going out?"

"Hungry?"

"There's only one thing I want to eat right now," she whispered, and he answered this in his own particular way, then said: "Come on, Terror. Out we go."

"Where are we going?"

"Need you ask?"

For a moment she was puzzled, and then exclaimed: "Do you know, I don't believe I've been near Charlotte Street since." It seemed incredible that she never even thought of those innumerable evenings they had spent together at the White Tower, often with friends.

"Do you remember that autograph book, with messages in every outlandish tongue imaginable, and how we fooled old What's-his-name?"

"It was your idea, you monstrous girl." They had written a whole line in hieroglyphics invented on the spot, and had much enjoyed the consequences. "Well, do we go back?" Felix asked.

Nathalie was suddenly afraid. "One can never go back," she sighed, putting her arms around him. "And anyhow, this is something quite new."

She realised then that the gap between their ages had disappeared. Those twenty years had never really mattered, but they had been there. Now, they no longer had any significance at all. "Besides," she went on, "the food may be rotten, or the old boy may not recognise us, and it was never a place for lunch, was it?"

"Where would you like to go, then?"

"Let's go and kill a ghost at the Ivy!"

They had had their last restaurant meal together there, a luncheon someone had given on the eve of Felix's departure for America.

"All right. But I doubt if they'll let you fill your bag with rolls, just because you've forgotten to get any bread for breakfast!"

This brought back another memory which made them laugh helplessly.

"I must try to remember that you're now too grand to risk scandal," Nathalie giggled. "I can see the headlines in the *Express*, can't you? 'Minister's mistress maudlin.' And then something like: 'Sentimental Associations with Rolls.'"

" 'Mr. Felix Hamilton, British minister—without portfolio—now in charge of E.C.A.E., and visiting Britain at the moment for consultations with the Cabinet, had a curious experience today. . . .' "

" 'Mr. Hamilton explained to the proprietors of the Ivy Restaurant that he was demonstrating the principles of supermarket catering to his escort. Mr. Hamilton is at present a resident of Washington, U.S.A.' "

" 'Pretty Miss Corrand explained to our correspondent that during the war she had been Mr. Hamilton's . . . er . . . housekeeper, and had frequently had to dine out in order to obtain adequate supplies of bread. It was her memories of those hard, but happy times that had made her forget herself, and she wished to offer her sincerest apologies.' "

"Not Miss Corrand any longer, however."

"No." Felix turned away, with the rather evasive look he had when he was worried.

"Nor so pretty either, for that matter."

"You don't look very well, I must say."

She was slightly taken aback by his downrightness, living, as she did, in such a fog of dishonesty most of the time. Felix had never paid her futile compliments, however. He did not need to, for he so frequently betrayed what he felt by a look, or a gesture. As he held her in his arms now, for instance, his eyes troubled with concern, she knew, without a doubt, that he was completely on her side.

"The least I can do is to see that you get a decent lunch," he said tenderly.

"And the most?"

"I'll show you later."

He smiled, and taking her by the hand, led her towards the front door.

There is something about a tête-à-tête meal in a good restaurant that lulls, reserves and stimulates intimate conspiracy. Good food and wine relaxes and inspires, and the insulating hum of surrounding conversation adds to the dreamlike and detached quality which makes proximity seem a promise, or a fulfilment, but never static. The play of sex transcends the senses, then; it is anchored in worldliness, yet soars and explores in realms beyond the world.

The conversation of Felix and Nathalie throughout luncheon that day could have made sense to nobody but themselves. At one minute, they would be talking about politics or personalities, and then a look or a remark would suddenly plunge them into their own private universe again. Nathalie was greedy for details of anything that concerned Felix, and wanted to fill in as much as possible of the time that had passed since his departure from England. When he talked of his work, it became obvious to her that she now lived in a vacuum. Not being an intellectual, she had always absorbed her pictures of what was going on through other people. To read the newspapers, or books and periodicals, meant nothing to her, if she could not hear the issues involved being discussed. Having, before she married Arthur, always been surrounded by people who, however ill-informed they might be, at least thought and felt deeply about what went on in the world, she had developed an instinct for detecting the bogus, and had spotted early that both Vera and Arthur only had genuine feelings about what directly concerned them. Since it was at times expected of them, however, to offer opinions about what went on elsewhere, they did so, but always trimmed their statements to suit whoever they were with.

As Felix talked, Nathalie realised what true humility he possessed. He did not regard his achievements as a credit to himself so much as an increased challenge and responsibility. He did not see himself as a nucleus of power in negotiations which were attracting world-wide attention, but rather as someone in the fortunate position of being able to give abundantly of what skill and understanding he might have. It occurred to her, then, that true greatness came almost by accident; a man gave himself entirely in service of some kind, and whether or not the world recognised him was a secondary consideration. To be ambitious merely for the sake of eminence or greatness, and not even for achievement, as Vera was, betrayed a dangerous and self-centred sense of purpose, which might well destroy its sponsor in the end.

When Felix had been describing a party at the White House, she began to think of other parties, which they had attended together, and asked: "Do you still play the piano?"

"I try to as much as I can, but it's not so easy, these days."

"Even so, I daresay you'd still be able to get a job playing in a brothel."

It was an old joke between them, and they both laughed, spontaneously and simultaneously. Felix had, in fact, as an impecunious young man, managed to cover the cost of extensive travelling by relying on his talents as a musician.

"There's always that to fall back on, I suppose," he smiled, "but I've rather lost touch with the current versions of boogie-woogie. I seem to get more and more classical in my taste, as I get older."

"I'd like to hear you play the Chromatic Fantasia and Fugue again, I must say. Or would I? I'm not sure I could risk it, actually."

"What does that mean, exactly?"

"I can't bear music, these days." It was the one thing that still had the power to filter through her defences; to relax her, or pull her apart, and make her think of all she preferred to forget.

"Funny. I'd have said that you could never live without it."

"I'm not living," she answered quickly, and then, seeing Felix look upset, she added: "Pay no attention. That's just the kind of crack I can't resist."

Felix was not convinced, however, and, after a moment or two, he said: "Do you want to talk about it? You can, you know."

"It's far too boring. I'd much rather forget about it for a while, and talk about you."

"I do wish I could help."

"You do, simply by being. As long as I know that someone like you exists in the world, it helps me to keep a sense of proportion."

He accepted her decision, refilled their wine glasses, and began to tell her about a trip to Canada he had made some months before. She was immensely grateful for his respect. Arthur would have taken a similar remark as a challenge, and pounced on her vulnerable spot, using it as the basis for an attack.

As Felix had dismissed his car, they took a taxi from the Ivy. He tripped, just as he was getting into it, and that started them both laughing again. Nathalie became almost hysterical, until he said: "Stop it, you ridiculous creature," and began to kiss her. Then she did stop.

She had never before wanted anybody so desperately and made no attempt to conceal it, yet once they were inside the flat, and really alone, she became self-conscious and said: "If women are not supposed to reach the age of passion until they're thirty-five, I shudder to think what I shall be like by then."

Felix sat down and drew her to him, running his hands gently up and down her hips. He did not look at her, but she could see a little white patch on each of his cheek-bones. Then he said almost inaudibly: "Don't you think we've waited long enough, now?"

She wanted to take him in her arms, to feel his head on her breast, to lose herself in loving him, until they were both relaxed and confident again, but she heard herself say: "I don't know, really. . . ."

His eyes half closed, his head began to sway backwards and forwards, and the white patches on his cheek-bones became distinct triangles. She could not bear to see him so overcome, and every part of her longed and longed to push aside the remaining restraint between them; yet, she could not move. Finally, it was he who broke away, and standing up, took her to the window with an arm around her shoulders.

"It's so silly," she said. "I'm absolutely on fire for you, and yet . . ." He could have overcome her hesitation and made her forget everything except themselves and their moment, but she knew he would never force her into anything against herself. Eventually, they decided to go for a walk in the park, and having circled the Round Pond twice, they sat down on a bench by the Long Water.

It was full summer, now. Almost overnight, after a shower of rain, the blossom had dropped off the trees, the leaves were quite out, and the greens were darker, and no longer new. People walked about as though the delights of summer were their right, instead of being awed by the miracles of May. Felix was playing with Nathalie's hand when he exclaimed: "What on earth is the matter with me! Since when have I allowed a little modest reluctance to stand in my way? I must be getting old."

"You always did have integrity. I'm only just beginning to learn what a rare quality that is, but it's nothing new for you."

"Well, it's a damned nuisance, anyhow."

He went on playing with her hand, stroking one finger after another with a characteristic clumsiness that touched her.

"I do wish you weren't so unhappy," he said at last. "It makes me feel so guilty."

"Why guilty?" she asked, feigning surprise, although knowing quite well what he meant.

"Olga gave me a rocket for leaving you what she called 'dry and high'."

"Well, it would be difficult to say which one of us let the other down most." It was part of his dearness, she reflected, that it did not even occur to him to reproach her for what she had done.

He wanted to know then: "Would it have made a difference if I'd asked you to wait?"

"I don't really know. If you had, I suppose I would have been in a different state of mind and wouldn't have felt the impact of Arthur in quite the same way. As it was, even your letters made me feel . . . well, they didn't seem real, somehow."

Felix suddenly buried his face in the palm of her hand and groaned: "Oh, God, what a bloody fool I am!" Both this gesture and the expression on his face, when he looked up again, were so guileless and defenceless that Nathalie had a sensation of fainting. Again she wanted to take him in her arms, and yet could not move, but grasping both his hands in hers, she gabbled: "You mustn't think that. It was my fault. I should have had more faith, but I didn't want to be a nuisance, you see."

"A nuisance?"

"I didn't realise you'd want me in that way. Oh, I knew how you felt about me, but you never actually said so, you see."

"I'd said it to so many people, never really meaning it, but with you it was different. It always had been different with you, and I couldn't use any of the same old clichés or worn-out endearments. . . ."

"I know that now. I understood then, I think, but I was such a baby, in some ways."

Felix seized on this as being relevant and illuminating. Making a great effort to speak unemotionally, he said: "That was the point, you know. I felt I hadn't any right to hold you down—or rather, hold you back. Besides, I was afraid."

"Whatever of . . .?"

"All you still had to go through, I think. Even though I'd been through most of it and was ready to settle down, you were just at the beginning of everything, and *so* young. I was not only afraid of letting you down, but jealous of your future as well. I worried about all the others who'd love you, and how you'd handle them, and about your learning to tackle pain—even about what you'd feel for me when you were say, forty-five, and I was an old man of sixty-five. . . ."

"A darling old man. . . ."

"Perhaps . . . but old. I felt that you'd never get old, and that frightened me too. You're womanhood incarnate. There's compassion in your heart, wisdom in the depths of your eyes, healing in your arms, strength in your voice, courage in your vitality . . . the works, in fact. At forty-five, or sixty-five, or even a hundred and five, you'll merely have increased, and learnt to use the powers that you have now. You're child, woman, and goddess all in one, and the fact that in those days you weren't in the least aware of it made the responsibility seem quite terrifying."

"Why on earth didn't you tell me all that then?"

"There wasn't time. They only gave me twenty-four hours, if you remember." He made an effort to be gay again and added: "I was too busy seeing I had enough clean shirts to take with me."

"And handkerchiefs. . . . Do you remember how you had a cold, and I boiled about a dozen until they were dry and brown, and had to be thrown away?"

"Even a Tartar terror can't expect passionate declarations in those circumstances!"

"Tartar terrors are very demanding, as you should have realised."

"Oh, no, they're not. At times they lash out, but at heart they're sweet, and tender, and loving, and so unselfish that it puts one to shame."

"Nonsense! It's merely that they know how to 'reculer pour mieux sauter'."

"My little, Tartar terror!" He dropped her hand and looked away. "Nathalie, I do love you, you know. I always have done, in one way or another."

She said nothing, and looking down at her lap, plucked intently at a piece of grass, while he added: "I suppose that, with my usual ineptitude, I've left it too late to say that?"

Nathalie could not trust herself to speak for a while. Then she answered softly: "Perhaps people who have really found love can't always be together. Perhaps real love belongs to some greater pattern which we can't see, but which makes sense in the long run. It may be that what we created together is necessary for something else, to help us give to, or do, something which is important. I'm not really sure, but it must make *some* kind of sense, even if not by the standards we know." Felix took her hand again but said nothing; the tenderness and intimacy of such physical contact was as reassuring and important to him as it was to her. "Well, anyhow," she added, "I've caught up now."

For a moment he was puzzled, and then he smiled. They had often joked about the difference in their ages when she did not catch a reference, or recognise a tune, or know of some person who had been part of the background of his earlier youth. "Will I ever catch up?" she used to ask him, "or will you always be such a know-all?" And he would answer: "The older we get, the less difference it will make. You'll see."

He had always talked as though they would be together, one way or another, all their lives, and she had also taken this for granted, in the days when the outside world had not demanded to be adjusted to their own private one. Circumstances, however, had caught them unprepared in their contentment and forced them apart, and now they had separate directions to go in, if only physically speaking.

"Come on," Felix said, drawing her to her feet. "Time's up."

He had to be at Downing Street at six o'clock so they walked towards Marble Arch. Those last moments were becoming so tense that they both looked forward to being apart again; yet they sought to prolong the end, and crossed to an island in the middle of the street. There, they stood together for a while, looking out across the park without speaking, his arm around her shoulders, and the vehicles swooping noisily all round them. Then Felix signalled to a taxi and it drew up in front of them. He did not say anything, but she was so much a part of him, that the gentle hug he gave her before taking his arm away conveyed everything to her. She smiled at him quickly and then, without looking back, climbed into the cab, which was soon lost in the traffic.

Two days later, Nathalie and Arthur sat on the terrace after breakfast, reading the Sunday papers. He always turned first to the theatre criticisms, and often supplemented these with apt and illuminating comments of his own, but he also shared Vera's inordinate interest in crime and scandal. They both knew the details of every murder case that had been reported for the past thirty years, and would go over these minutely, comparing the various techniques and skills of killing and dissimulation, as well as the rhetorical intricacies of legal proceedings.

As Vera came out to join them, Arthur said: "There's more evidence about the Meadows' case. Apparently with the last one, he wrapped her guts round the bedpost before leaving her. Rather a neat touch, don't you think?"

"They never tell you the interesting bits in the week, do they?" Vera said.

"Only in *The Times*, but you have to use your imagination there. They don't display the facts in the same way." Later, he said to Nathalie: "I should be most interested to know at what point he raped her," but he did not dare say this in front of his sister. She now looked away at the garden, exclaiming: "What a lovely day! Oh, do look! The columbines have started to come out."

"Has our Doris finished with her rag, do you suppose? There's bound to be quite a lot about it in that." The mother's helps were encouraged to take in papers which Vera and Arthur also enjoyed, but would not order for themselves.

"I'll go and see," Vera answered, and meandering towards the herbaceous border, she disappeared slowly round the corner of the house.

Suddenly, Nathalie said: "I think I'll go to Mass this morning." Arthur looked up, surprised. "What's the matter with you?" he asked.

"Nothing. I just want to go to Mass, that's all."

"Why? You never have done as long I've known you."

"All the more reason why I should start again, then."

She did not quite know herself why she wanted to go. There seemed to be no reason why her present mood should take her like that, for although most of her intermittent schooling had been in convents, she had never felt particularly religious. Her first communion had not been an extraordinary or elevating experience, and she had never wanted to be a nun. Her mother had been pious and devout, but she had never known her, and her father had been strongly anti-clerical. His religion had been a combination of generosity and hard work. He gave away every penny he ever earned, and his career had left him little time for anything else; in fact, the Baroness once observed that he only noticed his knighthood because it had forced him to take a day off from his painting.

Arthur had put down his paper and was looking at his wife with mistrust. After quite a long time, he said slowly: "What kind of act are you cooking up now? You come back from London in such a filthy temper that you hardly say a word all evening. Yesterday, you pretend to have a headache——"

"It was no pretence——"

"Don't interrupt! As I was saying, you pretend to have a headache as an excuse for sulking, and now this. Does lunching with your boy friends usually give you religious mania?"

Nathalie felt so exasperated that she could not trust herself to say anything.

"Well?" Arthur insisted. "Can't you even speak, now? Or are you simply preparing to burst into tears, as usual?"

She did her best to appear unaffected by his sarcasm, and merely asked blandly: "Do you believe in God, Arthur?"

"What did that man give you to eat on Friday? Are you sure you're not suffering from food-poisoning?"

"You haven't answered my question."

"Because it's an impertinent one!" Arthur jumped up and started pacing the terrace. "I'd like to know what you imagine *you* know about God," he shouted. "You, and all those phoney 'liberals' of yours. 'God is love', I suppose!"

"I should think that's very probable."

"'Beauty is truth, and truth beauty.' 'Beauty, truth and goodness.' 'Faith, hope and charity,'" he said in mincing tones, and then added angrily: "All this wrapping yourselves up in catch phrases and getting intoxicated on irrelevancies has nothing whatsoever to do with God, or life, or anything else that makes sense. You people and your higher judge! You make me sick! You're just a lot of elephant-washers. Does your precious Felix wash elephants in his spare time to keep him so happy? Happy Ham! That suits him rather well, doesn't it?"

Nathalie began to feel acutely depressed. She had been so overwhelmed by her love for Felix that all the disappointment, frustration and sordidness of her life had no longer seemed real or important. Now, her surroundings were closing in on her once more. She wondered how the world could ever achieve any kind of tolerance or harmony if individuals made such a failure of getting on together. It seemed unlikely that nations, strangers with conflicting interests, would ever learn to co-operate in peace if civilised people who lived under the same roof and spoke the same language were unable to understand each other. With a sudden longing to get away from Arthur, she stood up too, and said: "Well, that seems to be the end of that conversation," before going indoors.

When the Baroness arrived at Walton House the following Saturday, it was at once obvious that she was not in a good mood. Nathalie was sufficiently familiar with the workings of her aunt's temperament to be aware of the effect on her of such a hot day, following several late nights, and including perhaps a touch of indigestion after a too rich lunch. She knew that the Baroness's stays would suddenly have felt too tight, her shoes too small, and her face too fat; and the reflection staring back at her from the looking-glass would not have seemed like a fine figure of a woman, held together by incredible vitality, but rather that of a flabby, futile old hag who had once been young, and much beloved.

Usually, a good sleep, followed by a bath and a gossip, could make the Baroness unable to understand ever feeling so low. On this occasion, however, instead of being able to give herself up to this relaxation, she had to endure a tedious journey, and look forward to the treacherous atmosphere of Walton House. Only the complications of altering her car-hiring arrangements, and a special desire to see Nathalie, prevented her putting off her visit. She wanted to assess, before this had worn off, what effect Felix's reappearance had had on her niece.

It was unfortunate that Vera should have chosen that day to invite the parson to tea, and this was probably one more cause for what happened later on. A collection of circumstances can often seem meaningless if taken one by one, but viewed in combination, they may give the impression of compelling inevitablity. There was nothing compelling about the Reverend Leonard Cox, yet his effect on the Baroness was inevitable. He was dark and willowy, and his Christian spirituality took a mystic rather than a muscular form; he had a passion for Wagner and Blake and an embarrassing admiration for the Lake Poets. In conversation, he would put his face too close to whoever he was talking with, as though drawing that person into an exclusive conspiracy. Moreover, the rituals of elaborate tea-parties had always made the Baroness impatient. She regarded tea as a drink, not a meal, and considered that to take food in the middle of the afternoon was too soon after lunch, and yet spoiled the appetite for dinner. Also she was invariably exasperated by the smugness and self-satisfaction with which hostesses enjoyed their power behind the apparatus of tea-making, and the tipping and pouring of pots, clinking and passing of plates and cups, seemed to her absurdly trivial yet so absorbing as to rule out conversation.

To the Reverend Leonard Cox, however, afternoon tea was the pivot of the civilised life, and he flattered himself that he could assess people's breeding by the way in which they served it. Not for him the hurly-burly of the café, with stale muffins, tasteless cakes, and the tired repertoire of a three-piece orchestra. With his visions of gracious living (the proverbial Edwardian tea-party on the lawn, with disciplined children in white muslin, appearing under the eyes of their nannies), and his memories of languid occasions as an undergraduate (when he was sometimes taken to visit the fascinating houses in the neighbourhood), the tea ceremony still provided him with the most effective form of romantic nostalgia. Tea in his own home was the last meal of the day, and therefore substantially different. Even he realised that the Ecclesiastical Commissioners and the donors of the local living were more to blame for this necessity than his wife (who bore the heavier, and least spiritual part of their burden), but the fact remained that it was impossible to be gracious sitting round a kitchen table over earthenware crockery, and in the company of children who were neither disciplined, nor had nannies. Besides, tea that aimed to nourish, rather than refresh, and therefore included sausages, fishcakes or thick paste sandwiches, was not afternoon tea at all, but high tea that was eaten, rather than taken. There were several houses in the village where tea was always taken, however, and the paraphernalia of silver accoutrements and numerous plates of colourful food both dazzled and soothed him, as well as enabling him to indulge his sweet tooth from time to time.

Len Cox approved of conversation as it reminded him of his Cambridge days, but he had never found it quite so disturbing as it became on that particular occasion. The Baroness was effusively charming, but made him feel uncomfortable, for although he was attracted by vitality, he disliked being swamped by it. When she started talking about the psychological effects of occupation during the war, for instance, he found it difficult to know what to say. He thought her rather "morbid" to suggest that neutrality stunted the development of a country, as well as its people, and that even the British could not understand what it was like to have had the enemy in the front garden. Vera passed him the Fuller's walnut cake and the Baroness, seeing him take another piece, suddenly turned to him and asked, with a smile that was a little too brilliant: "What do you think, Mr. Cox?"

"It's hard to say," he faltered, abandoning the morsel he was just about to put into his mouth. "I rather feel we should all be most thankful that we were spared."

"Do you suppose that being buffeted about by disaster corrupts a man? Or just diminishes him? Or can it, perhaps, have a strengthening effect?"

"I'd say it depends on how well able he is to resist it. We none of us can do more than our best, can we?"

"I have a friend of mine staying with me at the moment who was in Auschwitz not long ago—the concentration camp, you know."

Concentration camps had become legitimate grounds for expressing such a strong emotion as horror, and both Leonard Cox and Vera allowed themselves to exclaim: "How dreadful!" Vera added brightly: "Where exactly is it? I never know whether it's Southern Germany, or Poland?"

"Don't be idiotic, darling," Arthur exclaimed. "That's not the point."

Vera sulked for the rest of tea, but for once he hardly noticed, and turning to the Baroness, he asked: "How does someone start again, after an experience like that?"

"That is just what Maria is trying to find out. She was luckier than most, but even so, it will take her some time to recover. Her health is still very bad at the moment, and of course that is bound to affect her mind."

Len Cox, who had by now managed to eat half his piece of cake and was feeling that he must not let the party down, fastened on to an intellectual milestone that he was able to recognise.

"The Greeks felt that very strongly," he said eagerly. "I mean, the interrelation of the mind and the body."

The Baroness gave him one veiled, but not altogether friendly look, and then paid no more attention to him. Turning towards Arthur, she said: "We still know so very little about the mind. The priests have had their theories for a long time, and the doctors have developed theirs, but neither can really provide a full understanding of the problems we are up against today. I knew a Tibetan lama once who insisted that materialism in the West had killed our capacity for scientifically developing the most important aspects of the mind and soul. He made it all sound quite reasonable, I must say. Domination, corruption, destruction, persecution, perversion and all the rest of it, are as old as civilisation, but up to now they have existed only in isolated or detachable instances, and could be written off as what you English call 'bad form'. But now that they have all been used as instruments of government, there is a new problem, and we shall have to face that, sooner or later. Imprisonment, or even physical torture, have proved insufficient weapons for power-hungry dictators because people can retain freedom of mind in spite of them. But what safeguard is there against the far more sinister dangers of mental mutilation?"

Arthur was both interested and excited by all this. He said: "You know, I've always been fascinated by societies in which evil was the norm, and what we would call 'decency' was frowned upon. It crops up periodically, I suppose, but it's so extraordinary to think that a mark of respectability, of keeping in with the herd, is to behave in a way which we would consider caddish. . . . There is this to be said for those periods in history, though. They were at least vigorous and vital."

"Isn't it rather misleading to mistake violence for energy?" Nathalie asked, spotting another clue to the make-up of Arthur's character. His reaction against the devitalised and thwarting atmosphere of a milieu which regarded sanctimonious respectability as the key to a better life had developed in him a fascination for vitality of any kind, and she began to understand why violence seemed to him not only permissible, but even laudable. He felt a great admiration for the proud ruthlessness of the Italian Renaissance, for instance, as well as for the self-pitying introversion of nineteenth-century *maladie du siècle*, seeing in these movements not only relief from social limitations, but also a chance of fulfilment in revolt and action. The war had provided him with more reality than he had been able to bear, but his first meeting with the Baroness's set had rekindled his earlier romanticism with the promise of a freedom which it had once symbolised for him. Nathalie realised that she herself had been a disappointment because her kind of freedom, which was the same kind as Felix's, was of a different order, and one which Arthur could not in any way accept. He understood neither the meaning of, nor the desire for dedication of any kind, and confused tolerance with weakness; humility with indetermination; mercy with obtuseness; and ignorance with innocence.

The Baroness, however, especially in that kind of mood, had a vitality of a sort that appealed to him. He was delighted with the slightly cruel way in which she suddenly caught the Reverend Leonard Cox in the middle of a chocolate biscuit, and said: "Do you believe in evil, Mr. Cox?"

Len Cox could hardly have been more startled if she had said: "Do you believe in God?" but being determined to put up a good show, he answered jocularly: "Doesn't do to make fun of Old Nick, you know!"

The Baroness's expression conveyed that this remark had been a mistake, and he tried to redeem himself by adding: "There's certainly a great danger in losing sight of the spiritual values."

She looked at him for quite a long time, and asked: "Did you ever meet Rasputin, Mr. Cox?"

It seemed unlikely, but she appeared to wait for his answer as though trusting him to reveal some interesting points about this controversial figure. Len Cox, however, had to admit that he had not had the pleasure.

"There was evil incarnate for you!" the Baroness exclaimed. "I can't tell you how, or even why, but when that man was present, you just knew that he was the devil."

"The Empress didn't seem to know it," Arthur said.

"Ah, there are some people who make natural victims for destruction. They love it. It is possibly the only force that can make them feel alive. You often find that with Germans."

Len Cox had just started on a slice of coffee layer cake, but he realised that some sort of attack on integrity had been launched, and felt it his duty to come to the rescue.

"Come, come," he said. "Most people are agreed, these days, that there are good Germans, just as well as bad ones."

The Baroness smiled sweetly at him and cooed: "You are so gentle, Mr. Cox. It must be such an asset in these times of violence."

The Baroness had tasted blood, however. At dinner, that evening, she began to talk about Felix Hamilton, exclaiming: "What a pity he has to live in the United States!" Vera's smile suddenly became uncertain, and Arthur looked as though he were on the defensive. "What a delightful person, he is!" she went on happily. "You know, one of the most remarkable things about him is that he is so extraordinarily well balanced."

"Briefings on personality-balance are no doubt handed out with instructions on policy," said Arthur. "The Ten Commandments on how to be a good, all-round diplomatist, British pattern. I expect there's a standard issue of various things such as golfing or tennis cups, leather-bound volumes of Dickens and Jane Austen, and even recordings of classical music."

"You naughty boy!" the Baroness smiled, conscious that she

was at last making some headway. "But you know, Felix was like that long before the Government had anything to do with him. He is that rare specimen, a person of promise who has continued to fulfil himself."

"He's certainly rare," Arthur bristled. "How people like that continue to delude themselves into surviving as they are in the world today quite intrigues me. He may be an energetic diplomatist, but he's an Edwardian museum-piece as well."

"What rubbish!" Nathalie exclaimed. "One of the great things about Felix is that he still hasn't got stuck at any point. His philosophy may not be yours, but he never stops reassessing it in terms of what's going on at the moment. He'll always be far more in tune with reality than either you or Vera." She had spoken without meaning to, and now saw her husband looking at her with anger, her sister-in-law with hatred, and her aunt with an expression that was unmistakably triumphant. Arthur said coldly: "If it weren't so pathetic, it would be quite amusing to hear you setting yourself up as an authority on reality."

"I just meant that I've known Felix longer than you have, that's all," Nathalie faltered.

"And does that give you an exclusive understanding of him?"

Nathalie did not want to say any more, for apart from finding it unpleasant to discuss Felix in this atmosphere, she was afraid of giving herself away. "Well, does it?" Arthur insisted.

The corners of Vera's mouth were turned down, but her eyes betrayed the exultancy she always experienced when Arthur and his wife were at cross-purposes with one another. In a tone of voice that sounded determined to spread sweetness and light, she said: "I think it quite suitable that Nathalie should show respect for the older generation. I expect Mr. Hamilton was always very kind to her."

The Baroness suddenly seemed to swell, and towered over her end of the table. This combined example of Arthur's cruelty and Vera's condescension struck her as the last straw, and she said slowly:

"I don't think you quite realise how well Nathalie knows what she's talking about, in this case. After all, she was Felix's mistress."

Nathalie made a hushing gesture in her aunt's direction, then bowed her head and waited for the storm to break. Arthur was too amazed to be angry. Vera, however, seemed to be profoundly upset. She spluttered and gulped for a moment, and then suddenly stood up. Her face was completely distorted, and she began to cry out hysterically, in an absurdly high-pitched voice: "Disgusting . . . disgusting!" Then she fled from the room, still yelping.

The Baroness turned to Arthur, and asked: "Hadn't you better go after her? In that mood, she might do something silly, and that would be a pity, wouldn't it?" Without saying a word, or looking at anyone, Arthur slowly rose to his feet and left the room. Although he was worried about Vera, he also needed to get away by himself, to work out what his reactions were to be.

Left alone with Nathalie among the debris of the dinner table, the Baroness looked at her niece, who was still sitting head and shoulders bent over her lap.

"I've never known such a house for scenes!" she exclaimed. "I'm sorry if I've gone too far this time, my darling, but really, I do believe that even if I were to say 'The sun is shining', that would be given a *double entente*."

Nathalie suddenly began to sob, and pushing aside her plate, put her arms on the table and let her head fall on to them. Crying as though she could never stop, she was scarcely aware of her aunt's reassuring endearments.

When Nathalie took up the Baroness's breakfast the next morning, she found her aunt sitting up in bed. This tousled heap of cheerful vitality contrasted oddly with the beautiful and perfectly-manicured hands, covered with rings, that lay serenely on the bed-clothes.

"Here you are, you monstrous old mischief-maker," she smiled, putting the tray carefully down on the bed. "You ought to choke over every mouthful."

"But why? It looks delicious!"

The Baroness poured out her coffee, and exulted over the first sips of it with noisy gluttony.

"What would I do without coffee!" she exclaimed, and then added, somewhat more cautiously: "How is everybody, this morning?"

"Arthur's all right, funnily enough, but Vera the villainous virgin has one of her headaches."

"Oh dear! I'm so sorry."

"Hypocrite. You couldn't care less."

"Nonsense! I don't like to see suffering that is not necessary. That is why I plague your life so much, my darling."

"I thought Slavs considered suffering so good for the soul."

"Ah yes, when it must be a part of living. Life is so tremendous"—she flung out her arms in an all-embracing gesture—"and so complicated, that it is not surprising, when people try to live fully, that they get their fingers burnt. That is not a bad thing, even. It makes them stronger and wiser. But to suffer in running *away* from life all the time, like Vera does, is just stupid. And it affects others, too. That poor Arthur! He will not survive if he does not shake her off."

"She has her points, you know. If she hadn't, I'm sure Arthur would have seen through her long ago."

"My dear child, you don't realise how catching fear is. She makes him cling to her like a little baby by making him frightened too. If you can overcome that, you will win, but remember that she had a good start."

"It's odd, isn't it, considering how kind she is, in some ways."

"Kind! Kind! What is this word 'kind' that the English always use? People can be horrors—malicious, or just deadly bores—but you are expected to forgive them everything because they are so 'kind'. And all it means is that they can't mind their own business."

"Whereas you never interfere in anything, do you?"

"Well, at least I don't blackmail people into gratitude by insisting on doing them good turns they don't want! This being 'kind' is a most terrible form of self-indulgence in the frustrated, and they hide behind it when their consciences trouble them. How often have you seen wrecks of what were once good people, pathetically scrabbling around to find ways of being 'kind'. 'She is always so kind,' people say. 'She gave up everything' to nurse her father, or look after her mother, or feed the cat next door or something, but do you think that is real kindness? No! It is just cowardice and hypocritical self-righteousness. Len Cox is 'kind',

I am sure, but just look at him! He talks about the spiritual life as though it were a secret society. I'm sure he is really a Freemason. Pour me some more coffee, my darling. You know, the really pathetic thing about all these embryo Boy Scouts is that they begin by behaving as they do because they are afraid of pain, and they end up by suffering more than anyone. How did you find Felix, this time?"

"Very kind."

"You silly child! No, no sugar now—I am getting too fat. He seemed well, didn't he?"

"You know damn' well he seemed quite marvellous. That's half the trouble. Arthur finds it difficult to make him look a fool."

"What a pity that boy is so jealous. Felix could be a good friend to him."

"Even after what you let out last night?"

"I told nothing but the truth."

"The one thing Arthur finds almost impossible to face, and that Vera cannot bear in any circumstances."

"And how could I know that he was not already *au courant*? It's a fantastic way to live. I shared everything with my husbands, all of them. Is Arthur afraid that you are still in love with Felix, perhaps?"

"Probably."

"And are you?"

Nathalie walked over to the window so that her aunt could not see her face, and said cautiously: "Does one ever 'get over' things that have been really important?"

"My poor darling!" the Baroness exclaimed. "Have you told Arthur?"

"Told Arthur what?"

"That you're leaving him." Nathalie shook her head. "What are you waiting for?"

"You don't understand." She hardly understood herself. The most perplexing part of her state of mind was an immense renewal of tenderness in her feelings towards her husband. Overcome though she was by this strangely powerful love for Felix, it no longer turned her into herself. She felt a need to radiate outwards, to bring order to her immediate surroundings and give out something of the reassurance, faith and happiness that she was so suddenly and strongly experiencing herself. Even Arthur's own attitude since the previous evening mystified her.

He had been shocked and aggrieved by the Baroness's disclosure, indignantly demanding why this affair had been hidden from him, and Nathalie had reminded him of his constant refusal to discuss her past, which was almost as though he considered her life to have started from the moment of their first meeting. Yet, when she had told him all he wanted to know about her association with Felix, his sarcasm and abuse became superficial. She gradually understood that these revelations, far from poisoning her relationship with him still further, had in some way, and for the first time, impressed her husband with a kind of respect for her.

"What don't I understand?" the Baroness asked.

"It's jolly complicated this business of love, isn't it?"

"Is it?"

Nathalie turned round, picked up the breakfast-tray to put it on a nearby table, and then sat down on the bed.

"Isn't it rather odd," she said slowly, "that loving one person very much, and very . . . very *well*, if you see what I mean, should make one feel somehow more responsible for other people?"

"You're growing up, my darling."

"But Olga, I feel so extraordinary! The pain of being without Felix is in some ways worse than it's ever been, but somehow it doesn't matter any longer. I thought I loved him before, but that was almost trivial compared to what I feel now. It makes me feel grateful, and humble and strong, but also terribly ashamed, because I realise that I've given Arthur absolutely nothing. If I could only love him the right way, and enough, everything would straighten itself out. We know so little about love, though. It's like some huge mountain, most of which is hidden from us by cloud, but if we became capable of knowing the whole of it, I'm sure all the troubles of the world would be solved. Because of Felix, those clouds parted for me just a little, and I've caught a glimpse of that whole. . . . Does all this sound completely crackers?"

"It's how people feel when they get religion, I believe."

"I can understand that, because it's made God seem a reality to me for the first time. Are you religious, by the way? It's never occurred to me to wonder before."

The Baroness laughed, and patted Nathalie's hand.

"I'm just an earthy old sinner," she said, a little wistfully. "I also have loved a great deal, but I've never had any talent for asceticism. I enjoy the world and the flesh far too much, and it's never even occurred to me to resist any kind of temptation. To me, the only really unforgivable thing is causing deliberate or unnecessary pain."

Nathalie laughed too, buoyed up by an exhilaration that seemed a positive force in itself, flowing and fluctuating. Hugging her aunt, she exclaimed: "Oh Olga, I *do* love you so! You're so strong that you don't need to be afraid of anything—not even yourself."

Almost as soon as the Baroness had left Walton House, Nathalie felt depressed again. Her moods began to alternate so violently and unpredictably that she sometimes wondered if her sanity were in danger. For several weeks she was tossed between extremes of ecstasy and gloom, hope and despair, resolution and uncertainty, tenderness and disgust so often that it completely exhausted, and even frightened her. Arthur, meanwhile, continued to treat her more considerately than before. He still cursed and complained, but no longer seized every opportunity to belittle her. The volatility that possessed her, however, made her incapable of profiting by this change of attitude, and a fear of failure began to obsess her again. Once or twice, she longed to see her aunt, but the Baroness had gone to Paris, and it never occurred to Nathalie to visit her there. Finally, on an impulse, and driven by a desperate desire to talk to someone, she decided to call on the nearest Catholic priest, who lived in the next village.

The ugly church that the Roman Catholics built at West Compton in the middle of the nineteenth century stood not far from the splendid Gothic edifice which had once belonged to them, and which Father Francis prayed they would one day recover. The priest's house, which was joined to it by a long, covered passage-way, was in the same style, and looked bleak and uninspiring.

Almost as soon as Nathalie had rung the door-bell, Father Francis stood smiling in the doorway, saying: "Come along in."

He was not tall, rather bald, plump, and his robes looked uncared for. Although she was aware of the contrast between the homeliness of this figure and the dignity of the priest she had seen celebrating the Mass in all his glory, what impressed her most forcibly at that moment was the smell of soup that pervaded the entire building. It was not soup such as is usually found in England; neither the pasty concoctions that pass as thick, nor the more watery, but equally flavourless brews in the *consommé* category. It was more like a rich, succulent, peasant potage, lovingly tended for hours, or sometimes days, and mysteriously blended with herbs, game, garlic and even wine.

"What a wonderful smell!" she exclaimed. "It reminds me of a place in Normandy I used to stay in as a child. Have you got a French cook?"

"No, no. My Mrs. Morris has such bad varicose veins that I let her off as much work as I can, these days. I just make a soup like that, and by adding a few things to it from time to time, it lasts for days."

"Where did you learn to make soup like that?"

"My mother was Belgian, and I did my training in a seminary not far from her old home."

"That accounts for it."

She suddenly felt quite at ease with this little man. His simplicity and directness, as well as his obvious good-will, made her feel that, however puzzled he might be, he would nevertheless listen to, and accept what she had to say. Yet, when he asked, "What can I do for you, my child?" she suddenly had no idea where to start. It was not the prospect of revealing her innermost thoughts to a stranger that worried her, but a fear of distracting his attention to irrelevancies. It seemed to her vitally important not to lose sight of the core of her problem. Father Francis seemed to sense her hesitancy, and asked: "Are you a Catholic?"

"I suppose so. I've received some of the Sacraments of the Church, but it's only just recently that I've begun to think about it at all. This question of love has become so perplexing."

She took a deep breath, and plunged into her problem. Father Francis watched her with sympathy while she talked, but his expression remained completely enigmatic. She could not tell whether her words seemed to him gibberish, or were striking some response. Even so, the mere effort of voicing her thoughts made them seem clearer to her.

"I'm afraid all this sounds rather muddly," she said, "but I find it so hard to explain things. That's one of the troubles, too. You see, here I am, faced with these problems, and I haven't any equipment for dealing with them. What am I to do? I'm not particularly intelligent, I've never had any education to speak of, and apparently I haven't got a very strong character, either. I just don't seem to have the courage to love my husband enough, although I want to be on his side. I must be too frightened of what would happen if I put myself entirely at his mercy again. I feel this is a lack of faith, and yet I can't help it. It also worries me to realise that there must be many others in the same boat. After all, it's only the minority that has the mental equipment to work things out rationally. What happens to all the rest who are more like me, and yet have just as grave problems to tackle? In fact, it's the simple and guileless who are far more likely to make mistakes and drift into messes, and who are yet least able to understand what's happening to them. It doesn't make sense to me."

"What makes you think you are so inadequate?" Father Francis asked, looking at her so straight that she could not hold his gaze.

She shrugged her shoulders and said, "Well, I just am." It was not a question of thinking, but of knowing. She had always been just a sweet little thing among a galaxy of strong and brilliant personalities. Everybody had loved her, but she had always accepted, just as they had, that she had no talents except a capacity for being nice to people. Now, Vera and Arthur had made even that seem pointless. Yet, here were circumstances that required more than she could ever command, if they were not to defeat her in the end. She tried to explain all this.

"I think you're being not only unfair to yourself, but to God as well," Father Francis said. "Why should you suppose that He loves you so much less than any of His other creatures?"

"Do I suppose that?"

"It seems like it."

"I thought I was merely recognising my limitations."

"You're making an excuse of them. Why should you suppose that you have so little courage? You're quite as good as anybody else, including your husband. Why should you therefore have less courage at your disposal than others have? You have no right to think so little of yourself. God will give you as much as you ask for, if you put your trust in Him."

Nathalie felt that if this priest was going to talk in catch-phrases, it would be no good; yet, because he was so obviously sincere, she said: "That's getting to the crux of the problem. However much I may put my trust in God, I'm still afraid of what my husband could do to me. He's so much stronger than I am in every way, and cleverer, and more unscrupulous. Yet if one is to believe what one is told about love, it ought to be able to conquer not only my fear, but all those other obstacles to his own well-being as well. Why can't I love like that?"

Father Francis paused for so long that Nathalie began to blush and think she had spoken too foolishly. Then he said quietly: "There are very few people indeed who can give the full answer about love. For the rest of us, it's just a permanent struggle towards light and truth, and it's a lonely struggle. Is it the loneliness of that path that worries you, my child?"

"I don't think so. I've always been used to solitariness." Besides with Felix somewhere in the world, she was never completely alone.

"Adversity makes solitariness more difficult to bear," he said, "but remember that there is an excellent precedent for that situation. No suffering of ours can ever compare with His."

"Yes, that's true, of course. . . . It was different for Him, though. He was God and Man in one. But what's the use of a true allegiance to God, if it cuts one off from humanity in general? Is that so very much better than losing sight of Him because of a desire for complete identification with one's fellow creatures in all their misery and baseness? How can one remain in full contact with both?"

"There's no answer to that, except love," said Father Francis. "Love of God, and His Church."

"I thought the Church had the answer to everything, and that it was such a comfortable, thought-saving cushion to fall back on. That's what both her friends and her enemies so often maintain, anyhow."

"There are anaesthetising catch-phrases to be found in almost every dogma and philosophy, but the Church discourages muddled thinking and takes a long-term view. You see, there must be a background and framework to individual striving. The Church is the mother that we all of us need, to keep us from the despair of utter loneliness. She helps to remind us of the love of God, so that we may keep the trust and faith of children. Without these, life becomes a joyless thing, and no individual can hope for real fulfilment."

"Does so much depend on the efforts of individuals, then?"

"That, and the Grace of God."

Nathalie suddenly felt a wave of the wildest elation she had ever experienced. This attitude connected up with something else, something that she knew about; it became part of a pattern of which she could now see a fragment, but most of which was still hidden from her. She became eager to find out exactly how Father Francis felt about all kinds of things. In some odd way, he reminded her of Felix; for instance, in his belief that salvation would not come through the influence of a mass movement. It was true, he admitted, that a certain teaching had created a movement in which the foundations of our civilisation rested, but that was the example, the prototype. Every other mass movement had bred disciples who had misunderstood, and then perverted the message of the mastermind. Nathalie tried to make him admit that even the Church had suffered that fate at times, but he would not concede that the Church, being directly God-inspired, could be considered in the same category. He did imply, however, that such thoughts were not strange to him, and that all the adherents of the Church had not necessarily listened to guidance.

Yet it all seemed so complicated to her. If co-operation and example were recognised to be necessary influences on behaviour, how could these states of mass hysteria and dishonesty be guarded against? Father Francis maintained that there was a way, but that each individual had to understand and work out his own obligations, according to his circumstances and capabilities. Single examples of true behaviour, and especially sacrifice, could do more good than any amount of preaching and exhorting. In the end, this brought the priest round to his original point. He once again emphasised that Nathalie had no right to disparage her own worth or importance; the more she believed in God's love for her, he told her, the more surely He would strengthen her faith, and develop whatever He had given her in the first place.

Before she left, Father Francis persuaded her that she should take Communion the following Sunday. He sent her over to the Church ahead of him, saying he would join her in the confessional a few minutes later. She was too distracted to pray wholeheartedly, and nervous that she would forget the words of the Confiteor, for it was so long since she had used them. Yet once she had started on her Confession, everything suddenly seemed easy, and she felt strangely at peace. The priest was no longer the person she had been talking to, but a mysteriously impressive and impersonal authority. When he had given her absolution and had said: "God bless you, my child, and go in peace," he turned his head towards her, adding in an ordinary voice: "And pray for me too, will you?"

A contributory factor to Arthur's increasing well-being at this time was the success he was having at the Oxford Stage Club. This company employed a number of professional actors, but it was run by several University people who themselves frequently took part on the acting side. It was one of the best known out-of-town theatres in the country, and several successful London plays owed their good runs to first productions there.

Arthur had gradually become more and more absorbed by his interest in acting. At first, and with many misgivings, he had self-consciously undertaken to do one or two small parts. Then came the day when, playing the Fool in *King Lear*, he had suddenly found himself in what he was doing, and for the first time in his life, felt close to the heart of whatever he was trying to find. On a stage, artificially lit, heavily made-up, and playing the part of another person, he was nearer to an awareness of reality than he could ever remember being. The strange feeling of power he had over his audience intoxicated him far more than any amount of drinking had ever done, while at the same time leaving him unbelievably clear-headed. Finding that he could make people laugh, or grow tense with apprehension, gasp with terror or slacken with sadness, he was sure, during those fully satisfactory moments, that he could do anything with them. The relaxation of tension all this gave him influenced his domestic life accordingly, and for the better.

It was true that this part of his life was also being made easier just then by Nathalie herself. A remarkable change had been apparent in her for some time. Arthur traced it back to the time of her "confession" about her past, and would joke that a clean conscience was obviously something she had badly needed, but Nathalie knew that nothing had been the same since Felix's visit, and her subsequent call on Father Francis. At any rate, she had been getting prettier and gayer ever since. Arthur appreciated a dignity and a depth of personality in her that he had not perceived before he knew about this important episode in her past. Being for the moment satisfied with his own life, what he took to be signs of mystery and aloofness in Nathalie no longer irritated him, and even enabled him to enjoy playing the role of a man of parts, married to an interesting personality. He began to invent little explanatory tabs when speaking to people of his wife which were not untruthful, but gave an inaccurate impression. He started to drag in the names of now eminent people Nathalie had once known (including Felix), implying that they were all close family friends. "Lady Hooper was discussing that Charity Ball with my wife last week-end," he said to someone, for instance, after they had passed Lady Hooper in the street, and Nathalie had commented: "She once had her portrait painted by my father." And after telling him of a conversation she had once overheard at a luncheon party years beforehand, he was heard to say: "The Foreign Secretary told my wife all about that Treaty several days before the announcement was made." Nathalie found all this ludicrous. What bewildered her most, however, was that he made no attempt either to hide such remarks from her, or to explain away their bogus nature.

Arthur was so carried away by his histrionics that he not only believed in them himself, but also exhorted Vera to play up to them. It was an attempt on his part—his first—to reconcile his hankering for bourgeois security and respectability (of which Vera was a perpetual monument), with those of his needs, desires, aspirations and perspicacity which did not fit easily and permanently into such a state. However, since the change in Nathalie, it was no longer only Vera who could give him that security. His wife had developed a reassuring serenity, and seemed quite content to take part in the rhythm of an ordered life. Not even Arthur could now say of her that "she had no idea", or that she was unmethodical or untidy. In fact, in many ways, she had beaten Vera at her own game. Meals were always ready on time, but she did not worry, as Vera did, if they had to be kept hot because people were late. The ordinary routine of the house went on, but unlike Vera, she could drop everything at a moment's notice, and organise herself into sudden changes of plan without fuss. She still took far less interest in clothes than Vera did, but she now always looked neat. Vera, in fact, found it more and more difficult to make herself indispensable, for Nathalie was not only efficient, but considerate as well.

It was hardly surprising, therefore, that Vera should choose this time to reopen the question of her holiday with Arthur on the Italian lakes. None of them had yet been away from Walton House, and when she suggested that it might do Arthur good to take a few days off, he agreed, but without committing himself. Two days later, she brought the subject up again. This time, he said it was impossible for him to get away, and suggested that she should go by herself, or with a friend. Vera burst into tears and rushed upstairs, but Arthur remained adamant, even though he followed her up as usual to calm her down. A week after that, however, he announced that he had been given the lead in the Oxford Stage Club's performance of *Othello*, and that since rehearsals were to begin the following week, he could not go away.

As soon as he had said this, Nathalie jumped up and gaily flung her arms around him, as full of laughter and excitement as a child. Vera simply went on sitting, smiling rather falsely.

Arthur was infuriated by her general refusal to react to any stimulus unless it suited her, and found her inertia quite as compelling as active vitality. Even when she was in her bedroom behind closed doors, waves emanating from her somehow jammed the atmosphere of the whole house.

"Well?" he asked, at last. "Can't you find anything to say? You might at least congratulate me."

"I'm sure it will be very nice," Vera answered, without enthusiasm. The next morning, she woke up with a bad headache.

The first night of the Oxford Stage Club's performance of *Othello* was in September. There was a mixed and rather wild party after it, and when that was over too, the three Bateman-Browns returned home in tired, but contented silence. It was late by then, and Vera went straight to bed. When Arthur was saying "good night" to her, he was still too elated to notice that she was drooping rather wistfully, in spite of her apparent cheerfulness.

"Well?" he said eagerly, hoping that now they were alone, she would have something encouraging to say.

"Well?" Vera smiled, still a little withdrawn.

"Did you enjoy the party, darling?"

"They were an interesting lot of people, I suppose."

"I'm sorry I couldn't spend more time with you, but there was so much to attend to."

"It doesn't matter. I don't see so much of you these days in any case. You mustn't let this acting hobby overtax your strength."

Arthur now saw that her smile was forced, but he felt so confident that he hardly feared the potential danger hidden behind it.

"What did you think of the show?" he asked. "What I really mean, of course, is 'What did you think of my performance?'" She was the only person who had not praised and congratulated him that evening, and he could not be satisfied without a tribute from her.

"I thought you were good," she answered, but with a restraint that maddened him.

"Is that all? Since you obviously have no enthusiasm, haven't you at least got some constructive criticism?"

Vera paused for a moment, and then said: "There was just a line in the fourth Act, when you were talking to Iago, that you did not get right. You should have put the emphasis on '*again*', and said, 'I'll not expostulate with her, lest her body and beauty unprovide my mind *again*', and not 'my *mind* again'."

"Is that really all you have to say?"

"I think so. It seemed to go very well."

Later that night, Arthur complained to Nathalie about this incident, while he was cooking himself a large quantity of bacon and eggs in the kitchen. "And that's all she could find to say about it!" he exclaimed. "Like some schoolteacher looking at a French translation to see that the accents are in the right place, but not being able to understand what the piece is about. It would be funny if it weren't so tragic, to coin a phrase."

"Poor Vera," Nathalie smiled.

"Poor Vera, indeed! And what about me?"

"I should think you've had quite enough adulation for one day."

"You thought I was all right, didn't you?"

"You know quite well I was in floods of tears by the end. It's true that Desdemona's performance was so uninspired that it made yours seem all the more outstanding, but even so, you were quite remarkable. What was so impressive was the tremendous sense of restrained power that you gave. Othello is usually played by a large man, to give just that impression, but with you, it didn't matter at all that you're not twice the size of everybody else in that cast. The moment you were on the stage, you dominated it—always—and one could almost hear the conflict inside you. I felt as though I were being constantly pitched between doubt and trust, fear and love. . . . Oh, it was quite shattering!"

"That's my girl. That's the sort of thing I like to hear."

"You wait until you hear what the critics do to you!"

The critics were unusually encouraging, however. Most of them were kind, though not all. One of them referred to Arthur's amateurishness, and another accused him of being melodramatic. Arthur, however, in common with most artists, preferred to be slanged rather than ignored, and he was delighted with his notices as a whole. Putting down the paper in which he had just read the last of them, he said exultantly: "This is it, you know. You can't imagine what it feels like. I feel so strong, I could do anything at all, at the moment. Everything begins to make sense, past as well as present."

"Like getting religion."

"Is it? Is that how you felt?" But he did not wait for an answer, for there was so much going on inside him that he needed to sort out, and yet could not quite express, or even get hold of. It was a bursting into being of emotions he had been vaguely aware of for years, but which had now acquired order and authority.

"There are so many other parts I want to play, now, and yet I feel I know nothing," he went on. "Why on earth didn't I start with it all years ago. This cursed war! And yet, you know, it may be that I had to go through all that's happened to me in order to be able to become a real actor. You can't convey an emotion you've never even seen, so perhaps it had to be like this. . . . Why are you looking at me that way?"

Nathalie smiled, but she was on the point of tears. "You're exceeding my wildest dreams," she said softly. "I've prayed so much that you'd find the way to fulfil yourself, and resolve your conflicts."

"My dear . . . there are no words," he whispered.

"Do you mean to say that you're actually speechless? That's a thing I'd never dared hope for."

"I suppose when you really mean a thing, you can't say it. It hardly needs saying, in fact. We both of us always knew things would come right in the end, though, didn't we?"

"This isn't the end, it's the beginning." Arthur got down on the floor and put his head in Nathalie's lap. "What can I possibly do to show you how grateful I am?"

She gently stroked his wiry hair, and answered: "Just go on working hard at what obviously gives you so much satisfaction. That's all I ask."

"Can you forgive me for what I've made you go through?"

"And no more of that, either! No more dramatics in the home, now you've got a respectable outlet."

"But do you forgive me?"

"Even when I've resented you most, I've never held anything against you, so forgiveness doesn't come into it."

It was a few days after this that Arthur arrived home one afternoon earlier than usual, and roared for Nathalie even before he was out of the car. Vera was in the kitchen, arranging a tea-tray, and went straight to the back door as soon as she heard him.

"How nice to see you back so early," she smiled, but he paid no attention to her except to ask: "Where is she?"

"Upstairs with Elizabeth, I believe." A moment later, Arthur came clattering downstairs carrying the child and with Nathalie following them. He put Elizabeth down and said to Vera: "Keep an eye on her for a moment, would you? I've got to talk to my wife." Then, with a short: "Come on" to Nathalie, he strode into the garden. He did not say a word until they had reached the river, but as soon as they sat down, he burst out: "You'll never guess, so I'll tell you. I've been offered a contract by the Old Vic."

Nathalie had never seen him look so young. All the lines in his face now contrasted strangely with a new clarity and directness in his eyes. It is not unusual to see people with unblemished faces, out of which peer old, or tired eyes, but a face which is heavily lined by worry and nervous tension, and yet frames eyes that are young and eager, makes a curious effect. Nathalie stared at this new Arthur.

"It's about the best training there is, isn't it?" she said at last.

"Easily."

"Well, when do you start?"

"I haven't got as far as that. The moment I got the letter I had to tell you, so I rushed home."

Nathalie noticed the look of uncertainty that was beginning to dim his eyes again.

"It's so tremendous that they think I'm worth it," he added. This note of modesty seemed completely incongruous, and yet she remembered that in his rare moments of strong, but happy emotion, Arthur now invariably became touchingly young. Several times, lately, he had looked like that while making love to her, and it had been hard to believe that her trembling lover was the same man as the remote or grasping person she had previously known. At that moment, he was like a schoolboy who was wondering whether he really deserved to get his first-eleven colours.

"It will be what your biographers will call the turning point of your life," she smiled.

"My life seems to fair spin with turning points." Again he looked so unburdened that Nathalie dared to ask: "You want to do this, don't you?"

"If it were just a question of want, well, it's the only thing for me. In fact, I've never until now known what it was to want something with complete certainty, but . . ."

"If that's how it is, then there are no 'buts'."

"On the contrary, there are several: there's you, and Elizabeth, and this house, and . . ."

"And?"

"It would mean giving up my job in Oxford, and the Old Vic pay very little, you know."

"Actors do have families, after all."

"Even actors who don't start learning their business until they're over thirty?"

Determination suddenly hardened Nathalie until she was almost lightheaded with confidence. She was now engaged in a struggle of which her husband's plight was a symbol. It was not only compassion for him that moved her, but also a sense of solidarity with all the thinkers, dreamers and visionaries who were kept tethered to a sense of reality that was not their own. These speakers of truths and seers of light, these crusaders for harmony in life, for a greater perception of the universe, for an order not made barren by frigidity, for a heightened sensitivity, were continually being defeated because they were children in worldliness. It was only the rare man whose sense of purpose was so strong, or for whom the intangible world was so real that he could stand exile from the majority. For the rest, the best was an uneasy compromise, and the worst was a complete capitulation to fear, both their own and other people's. At that moment, Nathalie felt such a love for humanity that she was confident of having the power to overcome Arthur's doubts, even believing that, once he was set in the right direction, the world would eventually be the richer for it. For the first time in many years, she remembered that Felix had once said to her: "Somehow, in however small a way, you'll leave the world a better place than when you came into it. Of that I am convinced." At the time, the words had hardly impressed her, but at that moment it was as though he were actually there, speaking them, and giving her the courage to throw herself wholeheartedly into a fight which, at that stage, had to be a battle for domination. Pitching her will to triumph over Arthur's, she turned to face him fully, and said quietly: "It's not nearly so complicated as it may seem. To start with, we'll let this house. That'll give us the extra money we need. We can take enough stuff from here to set up in a small flat in London, and still leave it well furnished."

She paused for a moment to see how Arthur was taking this. He did not look at her, but said: "Go on."

"Then you can give up the college without any qualms and devote yourself entirely to the stage. You can spend a few years learning the ropes, and after that, there'll be no holding you. Oh, darling, it will be marvellous!"

Arthur looked at her with an expression of wonder and hope that reminded her of Elizabeth gazing at a Christmas tree.

"Do you think it really can be done?" he said at last.

"Why ever not?"

"What are we going to do about Vera?"

"I'm sure she'll be just as delighted as we are. After all, being so attached to you, she's bound to welcome something which makes you so happy. She must understand how important all this is for you."

Nathalie did not really believe this, and was fairly certain that Vera would be difficult. Yet, she instinctively felt it best to be optimistic, and reflected that there would be plenty of time for getting tough if necessary. Arthur said nothing, but he still looked hopeful, and she went on: "Vera can come and see us as often as any of us like, but we're going to set up on our own. You're a big boy now, and it's time you went into long pants. You can blame it all on me, if you like."

This assumption of responsibility on her part was exactly what Arthur wanted, for he was quite prepared to be shaken loose from Vera, but had not the strength to do it himself. Now Nathalie was, in fact, proposing to do the very thing for which he had married her in the first place. With eagerness they began to make plans. They would find a flat, the smaller the better, so that there were as few household chores as possible, and not too far from a park. Elizabeth would go to school, and they would have a wonderful life. They would soak themselves in lovely culture of every kind, for art was the thing. It amazed them that this was the kind of optimistic talk that undergraduates indulged in, and that yet, even with all their future in front of them, they should both have so much salutary experience behind them. Life seemed to them unbelievably wonderful, and the whole world belonged to them.

"And when I'm properly established, we can move back here," Arthur said. "We'll have a terrific flat in London, but this will be our real home, and we can have masses of fascinating people to stay. It will be carrying on the tradition of the house, won't it?" Part of his elation was that he now felt, for the first time, that he would himself be able to give Nathalie a taste of the life that she had once known. He would be a vital part of it, and no longer just an uneasy and insignificant onlooker.

"We'll tell Vera this evening," he added. "And I'll write to the Old Vic tomorrow."

"Why not write straight away? Then it will be done." Assured as she was, Nathalie felt it wiser not to take any chances; Vera's reaction might be softened by the knowledge that the decisive step had been taken, and that there was no question of discussing anything.

"You must allow me to keep some of my more harmless

bourgeois prejudices," Arthur replied. "One of them is that it's always best to sleep on a decision before acting on it. Never answer an important letter the day it arrives."

After dinner that evening, Nathalie made an excuse to leave Arthur and Vera alone. He was reluctant to see her go, but she insisted on it, being convinced that this was necessary to his self-respect; he had her support, but he must be able to follow up important decisions on his own. Even so, she was extremely nervous about the outcome of this conversation, knowing that for all his energy and aggressiveness, Arthur was weak. Vera's total lack of scruple did not make her a subtly calculating creature—indeed, she had little control over her emotions—but being totally self-centred, she stopped at nothing to get what she wanted.

Arthur was with Vera a long time, but when he rejoined his wife, he was convinced that all was well.

"You were quite right," he said. "She's almost as proud of the offer as I am."

"Did you tell her you'd definitely decided to accept it?"

"I made it quite obvious."

"Did you tell her in so many words?"

"In the interests of tact, I said the letter had not yet gone off, but that you and I had already worked out our plans. I outlined these to her, and she seemed to have no objection."

"Does she realise that she won't be living with us any more?"

"Oh yes. In fact, she's got ideas of her own. She thinks it would be nice to get a cottage by the sea somewhere, and not too far from London. In that way, we would have a pleasant place to spend week-ends in, or dump Elizabeth, if necessary, and Vera would have a London *pied-à-terre*."

"That sounds quite admirable."

"So you see, she's not such an ogre after all."

"I've never thought that. It's just that . . . well, you know what I mean."

"Don't I just! But all that's finished now."

"My, what a big boy you're getting to be!"

"We must all be especially nice to her, though. She doesn't have much of a life, really, apart from us."

It occurred to Nathalie that Vera had not made the best of what she had got. Then she immediately felt remorseful, for she and Arthur had so much to be thankful for, and Vera was, after all, being thoughtfully co-operative. Perhaps they had not really been fair to her, she reflected, and with more intelligent effort, it might even be possible to become real friends. One of Vera's greatest aids was the capacity she had for inspiring other people with a sense of guilt.

When Nathalie woke up the next morning, she found Arthur sitting on her side of the bed with a bunch of roses in one hand. "For you," he said, as soon as she opened her eyes.

"Thank you, darling."

"Where would you like them?"

"On my dressing table, please."

Arthur suddenly got bored with his gesture, crammed the flowers into a tooth-mug, and said: "I thought I'd let you choose the vase you preferred. They are lovely, though, aren't they?"

"Beautiful. Last roses of summer?"

"Pretty well. Would you like some tea? I'm afraid it's got rather cold, but I can make some more."

"Don't bother just for me, I've never really taken to it. Have you been up long, then?"

"I woke up at five, and I've been reading *Henry V* ever since." Now that Arthur's vitality had a direction in which to project itself, there was no limit to the amount of work he could get through. That morning, he had left his reading from time to time to absorb one passage after another, and weeded one of the rose-beds, mended the broken leg of a chair in his workshop, and polished the car. It was now after eight, but he still felt full of energy.

"I'll cook the breakfast," he said. "What are we having?"

"Bangers."

"Good. I'll do some bacon with them, shall I?"

"Don't be so extravagant! How do you think we're going to afford bangers *and* bacon at one sitting?"

"My, my, what a thrifty little housewife we've become!"

"You've made a proper monkey of me, haven't you? I can see you now, complaining to your arty friends that I'm such a dragon. 'I'm afraid she thinks that meals ought to be on time,' you'll apologise; or you'll scoff: 'Would you believe it, she insists that we have clean sheets every now and again.'"

"Well, nobody could say that you haven't responded to your training. I'm prepared to give you a reference any time you like, now."

Nathalie threw a pillow at his head, and said: "Get out, you conceited brute, but don't you dare make the coffee! That's one thing you've never had to teach me, anyhow!"

Arthur laughed and went out, singing an aria out of *Aïda* rather loudly, and not quite in tune. He stopped to look in on Elizabeth, thinking that he would take her down with him and save Nathalie the trouble of dressing her. When he picked the child up, however, he found that she was wet. Not quite knowing what to do, he held her out rather gingerly for a moment, and then dropped her back into the cot. As soon as he turned round to leave the room, she started howling, but he quickly closed the nursery door behind him, and went down to the kitchen.

After Arthur had left for Oxford, there was a certain tension in the atmosphere. Nathalie and Vera both knew that they would have to discuss the future, yet each was unwilling to broach the subject. It was not until nearly tea-time, when Vera had had her afternoon rest and Elizabeth was playing on the lawn, that Nathalie finally said: "Arthur seems thrilled about this new job."

"It was certainly flattering to have had such an offer. It will give him confidence in his acting."

Nathalie felt a slight apprehension, making her aware of the need for caution. She was not sure what to say next, but finally tried: "He'll feel at home with the whole business in no time. He'll be getting the best possible experience at the Old Vic, anyhow." Vera said nothing, and Nathalie could see that her mouth was pursed and turned down at the corners. Conscious of her heart hammering absurdly, she added: "I'm sure it won't be long before he's doing really well."

Vera began to fiddle nervously with a pair of secateurs she was holding and then, without looking at Nathalie, she said: "I'm afraid he's let this whole business rather go to his head."

"Well, it is exciting." Nathalie's heart was beating wildly, as she suspected what her sister-in-law was getting at; it was no surprise, but a bitter disappointment. "I hoped he'd have come to his senses by this morning," Vera added wistfully.

Nathalie felt a wild anger harden her, but judgment told her that control and caution were now more imperative than ever. In spite of her qualms, she still felt much of the confidence of the previous day; it was now vital not to spoil everything by stupid tactics.

"Poor boy," Vera was saying. "He does lay himself open to disappointment, with his enthusiasms."

Nathalie felt her anger grow. It was "poor boy" when Vera wanted to brow-beat him into doing what she wanted, but when it suited her better, she became the helpless sister and he was then expected to be big and strong. "This is something more than just an enthusiasm," she said firmly.

"I wonder how much help it is to him to let him indulge too much in this sort of daydreaming. I know men have to be humoured a little from time to time, but even so . . ."

"Were you humouring him last night, when you discussed future plans with him?"

"I'm afraid Arthur seems to have taken all this rather seriously."

"It is serious." Never had Nathalie found it more difficult, or more necessary to remain calm and matter of fact. "And he has quite made up his mind to go through with this. In fact, by now he'll probably have written to accept the offer."

"I doubt that. He promised to leave things open until after the week-end."

"You can't stop him. You have no right to stand in his way, like this."

"My dear child, I've never stopped Arthur doing anything, even if I have given him advice when he's asked for it. Surely, it's an excellent thing that he should be cautious, though?"

"Don't you try to pull the wool over my eyes. I'm not Arthur, and I'm just as unimpressed by your soft soap as I am by your tantrums. You know perfectly well that you have the power to wreck this scheme if you choose to, and you've made it obvious that you're not keen about the idea."

"There's no need to scream at me like a fishwife! If that's 'keenness', then I consider it more dignified to be without it." Vera looked indignant and sulky, and the fiddling with the secateurs became almost intolerably irritating. Nathalie tried a new line. "Do please back him up and encourage him to go through with this," she pleaded. "You must have seen how much it all means to him. He's been a different person since he got his teeth into this acting, and if you believe in him, you must be certain that he can make a success of it. Couldn't you just tell him to go ahead, and give him your blessing? It'll make *all* the difference to him. Couldn't you, Vera?"

But Vera never felt compelled to take part in any discussion; if it did not go the way she liked, her participation in it was merely removed. This happened at that moment, so Nathalie went on desperately: "He doesn't drink at all, now—not in the way he used to, I mean, and he hasn't . . ." But there were things that it was not possible to say to Vera. "I mean, he's so much more at peace altogether. Surely you want him to stay that way? If he doesn't go through with this, I shudder to think what will happen. He'll start drinking again, and this time it will be far worse than ever before."

"Are you implying that Arthur drinks?"

"You know quite well what I mean."

"Well! I call that a dreadful thing for a young woman to say about her husband."

Nathalie could have screamed with rage and frustration, but she said quietly: "Be that as it may, *will* you encourage Arthur to do something he's so obviously set his heart on?"

Vera said nothing and looked sulky again.

"I can see it's not what you would have chosen for him," Nathalie went on, "but surely you understand that people differ? What suits one person is not necessarily a good thing for another. Lots of people get through life without ever knowing what their purpose is, but Arthur is lucky enough to have found his. Can't you accept that, and respect his decision? It's so obviously right for him."

Vera got up, and looking at Nathalie with hatred, she said coldly: "How can you know what's right for him? What do you really know about Arthur? I've looked after him ever since he was a baby. I've seen him grow up, and I know everything about him. He's not always been easy, but that was just being young, and the war. He would have settled down quite nicely, if it hadn't been for you. It's you who are at the bottom of all this. If it hadn't been for you, he'd still be in that London job, and doing very well, by now. You're the one who unsettles him, trying to drag him down to the level of that set of yours. You'll just succeed in ruining a fine man with all that acting nonsense."

"It's *not* nonsense. It's the only thing Arthur's ever really wanted to do."

At that, all Vera's restraint broke down and she whined: "You just want to get rid of me. You don't like me, and you're encouraging Arthur in this so that I shan't count in his life any more."

"That really is nonsense, but you must admit that it's not unusual for a man to want to live just with his wife and children. You'll still see a great deal of each other."

"I wonder if you realise what it's like to know that you're not needed. It's a terrible feeling to be getting older and older, with so little to show for it, and nobody to care."

Nathalie was both embarrassed and revolted by this exhibition of self-pity on the part of the usually suave Vera. Even more overpowering, however, was her sudden glimpse of the utter bleakness and barrenness of her sister-in-law's whole personality; this woman might be selfish, shallow, unscrupulous and blind, but in whatever way these defects were of her own making, the result was a pitiable dissatisfaction and loneliness. Nathalie knew that she had been defeated by compassion and said: "Vera, please don't feel like that. Arthur thinks the world of you, you know that. He'd never do anything that made you really unhappy."

Vera smiled bravely. "I'm sure everything will work out for the best, so there's no need for us to get so agitated," she said. "Let's have a cup of tea, shall we?"

Vera was a great believer in brewing and sipping cups of tea as a means of dealing with problems. In this way, they could be shelved, rather than solved.

During the next few days, Arthur would say nothing definite about the progress of his plans. He seemed buoyant and optimistic, but no longer so relaxed. Vera was being gentle and obliging, yet there was a tenseness in the atmosphere that made Nathalie afraid of participating in the issue. Once or twice, she forced herself to ask Arthur whether he had written his letter of acceptance, but he would not be direct with her. Patting her on the head and forcing a smile, he would say something like: "There's no need for you to worry," or else: "You must let me handle things in my own way."

Days passed, and then weeks, until Nathalie felt she could bear the suspense no longer. One evening, she asked Arthur how long the offer would stand open.

"What offer?" he asked, and although for once he was looking at her, she could make no contact with his eyes at all.

"Don't be so silly. The offer from the Old Vic, of course."

"Oh, that!" Arthur said, looking away.

"Arthur!" She was trembling with anguish at his complete refusal to meet her. His attitude was not a new one, yet after all their excitement and discussions, it now seemed absurd. She could not think of anything coherent to say, and merely added: "Don't be like that."

Arthur smiled: "Take it easy, now. I think you must have been overdoing things today," and left the house.

She was really frightened. At one time, her first reaction would have been to try to get at the root of the matter; now, she found it wiser merely to hold on and make everything appear as normal as possible. To her great relief, he came back in time for dinner, apparently sober, and the rest of the evening passed in at least superficial calmness. Later, however, lying in bed and unable to sleep, she said: "Darling, I must know whether you've changed your mind about the decision you made."

"It was just an idea, never a definite decision."

"Come off it. Did you ever answer that letter?"

"What letter?"

"The letter from the Old Vic, of course."

"Was there one?"

It had not occurred to her that perhaps the offer never existed, but remembering now what an expert he was at bluffing, she said: "Are you a most outrageous liar and hypocrite, or just a coward?"

"All of that, I shouldn't be surprised," he answered mildly. Then, with a boyish defiance that touched her, he added: "How could you let me make such a fool of myself? You must have known how impossible the whole idea was. Why did you let me go on with it for so long?"

"Because it didn't seem in the least impossible to me, nor does it now."

"That's just the trouble with you; you're so hopelessly impractical."

"Vera's been at you, quite obviously."

"You leave her out of this, but at least she helped me to realise what a fool I was. You're no help. You just encourage irresponsibility."

"Can you really have forgotten all we talked about? All the plans we made? All the confidence we had? I've never seen you like you were then. It was wonderful!"

"Yes, it must have been gratifying to see me make such an ass of myself."

She realised that it was disappointment making him angry, but unfortunately anger is much the same, whatever its cause, and he began to curse her thoroughly. He blamed her for allowing him to know such hope, to get so near the supreme dream of his life, when he must necessarily lose it again. She should, he maintained, have protected him from such bitter disappointment, and she would be called to account for whatever result this disillusion might have. "Still, how can you possibly understand!" he shouted. "There's only one thing women ever want, and they're not at all fussy where they get it from. Bitches, all of them."

Not along after this scene, Nathalie realised that she was pregnant again. Afraid of telling Arthur in his present mood, she decided to wait another month before doing so. She now knew enough to be able to conceal her attacks of nausea and fainting fits, and in any case, Arthur was too preoccupied to notice much of what was going on outside himself. It seemed imperative that this issue about his future should be resolved before he knew anything about the baby. In the days that followed, he became more and more affected. Putting on extravagant displays of enthusiasm about trivialities, he would delight for minutes on end about the shape and colour of a plant, or the flavour of some dish that Nathalie had cooked, or the rapidity with which Vera was knitting him a jumper. He was submissive and considerate in a way that she found embarrassing, but Vera glowed with satisfaction. Her whole response seemed to say: "Arthur is himself again, at last. It's merely a question of knowing how to handle his difficult moments."

To Nathalie, however, this comedy of manners was utterly distressing, and she sensed in him not resignation, but despair. Once, she thought that if they went up to London, and Arthur could breathe the atmosphere of a theatre there, he would recover some of his old enthusiasm. She suggested this jaunt as casually as possible, and he acquiesced at once, saying with icy politeness: "Certainly. What would you like to see?"

"Whatever appeals to you, darling. I don't really mind!"

"It was your idea. Haven't you any suggestions?"

They looked through the list of theatres in the *Evening Standard*, but Arthur had some reservation about every play Nathalie picked out. Finally, she asked him to recommend something, but he replied: "You're the one who suggested going up to London, not me. You don't seem to know what you want." Then, knowing quite well what she really had in mind, he went on: "I suppose you think that seeing a London theatre would give me ideas again," and noticing her embarrassment, he added: "You're a real help, I must say."

"Arthur, you can't go on like this." After their interval of hope, an evil that she had previously learnt to accept as necessary now seemed intolerable.

"Like what?"

She knew how useless it was trying to make contact with him when he decided not to be co-operative, but she could not resist saying: "Either go through with the plans we made, or else resign yourself to the fact that you've given them up, but not this—this bogusness, all the time."

"I do think that lampshade is pretty. You really are developing excellent taste, my dear."

"It's been there nearly six months, and that's not what we're discussing. . . . Oh well, I suppose the majority never get what they want in this world."

"It's a pity that you should have had to learn that at my expense."

"But that's because most people don't really know what they want, and even those who do, don't always have the chance of getting it."

"That's right, turn the knife in the wound."

An instinctive compassion pushed her towards him with

outstretched arms, but seeing him turn away, she checked herself, sat down on the dressing-table stool, and said: "Darling, I do see that perhaps it was impossible for you, but never mind. There may be another, better chance later on, and in the meanwhile, you can get lots of practice in Oxford."

Arthur sat silently on the edge of the bed, leaning forward with his forearms on his knees, and looking at the floor. She warmed to her argument and continued: "It's quite possible that in a little while you'll perfect your technique enough to get offered a leading part straight away. That wouldn't be such a risk then, would it?"

"I shan't be doing any more acting."

"Why ever not?"

"Why! why! Why do you always talk like a third-rate journalist? Why don't you get pencil and pad out, while you're about it, and jot down my replies to be used as evidence against me later on?"

Nathalie was aware that by taking some definite action she could calm Arthur; that if she could only disregard his hostility and talk to him firmly, it would counteract his irritation, and perhaps even control his misery. Being too aware of what he was feeling and suffering to be able to dismiss it as nonsense, however, she remained still and silent and realised, with a sense of the bitter irony of life, that somebody more thick-skinned would have been far more successful with this self-pitying, self-centred, yet genuinely unhappy man. Arthur began to stride up and down the room, saying: "I'm just not that sort of person. Either I throw myself into it altogether, or I don't touch it. I can't just *play* at it. I owe it to my family to be a success, not just dabble at something after hours." He could see himself as a promising actor, or even a struggling one, but not as an unobtrusive and aspiring amateur, only half-hoping for eventual recognition.

"Never mind about your family. Think of your vocation."

"I know your set never mind about family, but I happen to have a sense of responsibility. I have my wife and children to think about."

"But supposing your wife and children are proud of your acting?"

"Both you and Elizabeth would soon stop being proud of me if the bills weren't paid."

"And if you had a son?"

For a moment he looked quite different. "A son . . ." he said blandly, and then scowled again: "But I haven't."

It was then that she told him about her pregnancy, afraid to do so now, yet equally apprehensive of what the consequences might be if the news were kept from him any longer. As he already had one child, and the principle of having children had been established, it seemed unlikely that the shock would be as severe now as it had been the last time. She had often wondered how he would take it, but the only reaction that she had never expected was utter amazement. He looked at her now as though the idea of having another baby was quite incredible to him.

"How can it be?" he said at last.

This was no moment to point out that their few weeks of hope that summer had been happy in every sense; indeed, it would have been more surprising if this had not been the result.

"We never planned this," he went on, and still she could not be quite sure what he felt.

"It just shows that 'safe periods' are not so safe after all," she smiled, betraying such a lack of confidence that he immediately pounced with: "You did it on purpose!"

"It takes two, you know." Again she tried to smile.

"If this is what that religious mania of yours——"

"This is the kind of accident that can happen to any young couple."

"You did it on purpose! Oh, don't think I'm such a fool as all that! You encourage me to give up my job, and then spring something like this on me! You want me to be a failure, so that you and my children can gang up against me."

"Arthur, stop that! It's quite preposterous." She was sufficiently angry for him to recede a little now, and he watched her while she went on: "It was just as much your doing as mine, and you know it. You can't put all the responsibility on me. Besides, there's no reason why we shouldn't have another child, especially as you've decided not to make any changes in your life. Why on earth are you getting so cross, anyhow?"

"I was not creatively conscious when that child was conceived."

"Perhaps God thought that a secondary consideration when He put it there."

"Oh, yes, of course! I'd forgotten that you're on such hobnobbing terms with the Almighty. We can't all have a direct line with God, can we?"

"Please, darling, do be a little less childish. Whether we planned it or not, we're going to have a baby. Isn't that rather exciting? Can't you just accept the fact, and make the best of it?"

Plead as she might, however, Arthur could not see it that way. To him, this was merely a dirty trick played on him by life, and the final stage of his defeat. He protested again and again about having been cheated of creative consciousness. He accused Nathalie of being either irresponsible or malicious, and even took credit for being the only wise and prudent person in the family.

As the weeks went by, his rancour merely increased. This new life seemed to him a reproach, a reminder of his failure to exercise control over his own existence. Every sign of it stimulated his resentment and increased his sense of hopelessness. His reaction was not violent as it had been over Elizabeth's conception, but the more wounding because of his sustained, cold hostility. He and Nathalie were really enemies now, and not merely two people battling their way towards some basis of mutual understanding. They were in totally different camps; she on the side of life, he against it.

All this went on for two months. Vera rose to the occasion again, and her bland self-assurance during this period was so unruffled that Arthur looked to her for reassurance. She became a go-between, a smoother-out of difficulties that were kept alive by being constantly made light of. Once she stopped feeling ill, Nathalie developed a self-protective technique of only concentrating on immediate problems. She experienced a sense of responsibility about this forthcoming infant that Elizabeth had never inspired in her, and was determined that it should never feel unwanted.

This new serenity provided the last straw of irritation to Arthur's discontent. Rigorously imposed self-discipline, and the scrupulous avoidance of any awareness, except for the visible details of existence, had begun to bore him for some time; being essentially an actor, it was necessary for him to change the whole key of his performance from time to time. His genuine despair had given way, first to self-pity, and then to bitterness. He no longer saw himself as a buffer or mediator between the two ways of living that Nathalie and Vera represented, but as the victim of life itself. He saw life as embodied in women; symbolically in Vera, by virtue of the control she managed to exercise over him; and actually in Nathalie, because she was pregnant. Any sign of agreement between the two women at this time made him feel all the more the victim of a conspiracy. He thought it would be a typical blow of fate if Nathalie were to be delivered of another daughter, so that there would then be four women against him. Yet, he wondered, supposing his second child were a son? He tried to imagine himself as the father of a boy, and the thought of this new role both excited and awed him. He considered a male offspring not so much as a companion, or even a fulfilment of his own, unrealised ambitions, but rather as an ally; there would then be at least one person on his side, against all this self-contained stronghold of womanhood. He began to recall his relationship with his own father, which had not been that of an ally; he himself had not taken his parent's side against Vera, who had despised and dominated them both. A wave of guilt and fear, so strong that he could not tolerate it, bore him straight out into the nearest pub. For the first time for many months he got extremely drunk, but on this occasion, did not follow it up in his customary way. Now, there could be no kind of oblivion for him in his usual form of debauchery, for his problem had become more specific. Drunk as he was, he was able to return home, not quite knowing what he wanted, yet obeying his deepest instinct.

By the time he finally got to Walton House, it was after eleven. He was annoyed to find his wife still up, yet would have been even more irritated if his defection had passed unnoticed. Nathalie had had her bath, and was heating up some milk in the kitchen. There was a visible swelling under her dressing-gown now, and she had all the beauty and remoteness of a pregnant woman who is proudly bearing the marks of a new life, but has not yet become ungainly. She seemed quite unabashed either by Arthur's lateness or his condition, and her very acceptance of timelessness and tragedy, added to the mystery in her. He felt that nothing he could say or do would perturb her, and this impression of inviolable strength, combined with the tenderness of her smile, unnerved him. For a moment, he was tempted to go down on his knees to her, to let her take his head on her breast, as she had sometimes tried to do, to sob and sob until his heart burst wide open, and he surrendered at long last. Then he pulled himself together, and his momentary temptation to weakness was replaced by a hate so powerful that he could have killed her, then and there. He turned away so as not to betray the battle of his emotions, and Nathalie asked him whether he wanted anything to eat. He remembered that he had not dined, and as he sobered up, his passions became less violent and his senses more compelling. He was now not only hungry, but tired as well, and accepted gratefully that she should cook some bacon and eggs for him. Then she sat down opposite him, sipping her milk while he ate, but her composure unnerved him. He could not endure silence at the best of times; it always seemed to him noisy with reproaches, rather than peaceful with an understanding that made words unnecessary. At that moment he needed to be assured that everything was all right and that his impulses had flared unnoticed, but Nathalie seemed far away, although so benign that even he could not accuse her of sulking.

After they had gone upstairs, she went first into the nursery, to see that Elizabeth was covered up, and then followed him into the bedroom. She did not get into bed, however, but picked up a book and went towards the door again, saying: "I'm just going downstairs for a bit, because I know it disturbs you if I read in bed."

"I think you should get some sleep."

"I know, but I'm not sleeping awfully easily just now, and I find that if I have some hot milk and then read for a bit, that usually does the trick."

Her detachment maddened him. He said: "And supposing I tell you to come to bed?"

She went out of the room without replying, and he caught up with her at the top of the stairs. She stopped, and looked at him with an expression which he could not fathom, blank and yet secretive, saying: "I shan't be long, and I promise to be quiet when I come in again."

"I want you to come to bed now."

"I shan't sleep if I do."

"I'll make you sleep."

He had not made love to her for months, but now he could not stand her independence and wanted to make her submissive. She turned to go downstairs, but he caught her and tried to embrace her. He noticed that she shuddered instinctively at his touch, but her tone was gentle as she said: "It's very late, darling, and I think we both need some sleep. You go to bed, and I promise you I won't be more than ten minutes."

Arthur started to shake with rage, and exclaimed:

"You'd never say that to Happy Ham!"

He noticed that this remark affected her as nothing had done for a long time. She actually blushed, and then looked away, saying: "Felix would never try to stop me reading downstairs if I wanted to, so the question wouldn't arise."

"Even so, he'd only have to lift a finger, and you'd be flat on your back, with your——"

"At least his breath wouldn't reek of stale gin!"

Everything in Arthur broke up then, and began to reel and spin, sway and swing, burn and prickle, and sting. For a fraction of time, he saw himself as though from a very long distance, and then even that control was gone. He began to hit Nathalie, first across the head, and then on her body, but even when she was down on the floor, he could not make her break down. Although braced rigid against his blows, with her arms up to defend herself, she seemed completely indifferent. He hit her again and again, determined to make her capitulate somehow; to force her to lose her temper, or cry, or at least fight back, but instead, he saw her actually smile. Then she said: "You really should have married a sensualist, you know. It's such a pity to waste all this," and even his subconscious control deserted him. She was near the wall, by that time, and he began to bang her head against it, again and again.

"You're in love with Felix Hamilton, aren't you?" he gasped violently. "You've always been in love with him, haven't you? You deny it, but it's true. Admit it, you bitch! Admit that you're in love with him! Admit it for once, you double-crossing little hypocrite!" When he finally stopped, she was too weary to prevaricate in any way, and in a distant voice said: "Of course I love Felix. I always have."

Arthur let her go and stood upright, saying: "Ah, at last! A grain of truth, at long last."

Nathalie slowly got to her feet, light-headed with exhaustion and relief.

"I could have loved you so much more, but you never let me," she said. "Until Felix came back, I never really realised how much he meant to me. Now, I shall love him all my life. I could have walked out on you last summer, knowing what I did about you, yet I didn't even make love with him. I came right back to you, with more affection than ever before, and full of remorse and determination. I must have been mad."

Arthur had a glimpse into extremes of passion and heroism that were strange to him, and which made him wildly jealous of his wife's experience. He came towards her again with one arm raised to strike, but without flinching, she said coldly: "You've done that once too often already. I've come to my senses, now."

"What do you mean?" He was suddenly frightened.

"This is the end for us. I'm leaving you."

"You don't for a moment imagine he'd take you, with one child and another one on the way, do you?"

"Odd as it may seem to you, I don't even want him to. I'm off men in general, now, thanks to you. My idea of heaven is to be alone with my children: to wake up in the morning without wondering what sordidness I have to face that day; to sit down to meals without my stomach going into cramps of apprehension; to come home, even if it's a third-floor back in Bayswater, without being braced against gloom, or disapproval, or drunkenness, or disaster; to be able to sleep. My idea of sheer bliss is never to have to set eyes on either you or Vera again. It's not much to ask, dammit."

Looking despondent and deflated, Arthur said miserably: "It was bound to come to this, I suppose."

Nathalie's sense of relief was big enough to suppress a pang of sympathy for him, and she asked: "You won't be bitter about it?"

"No, no, of course not." It almost looked as though he were going to be reasonable; then he added: "Besides, it should make an interesting case."

"I don't see why it shouldn't be quite tidy. It could be done on desertion, or something. Strange as it may seem, that happens every day."

Arthur looked at her with an expression of amusement. "I can just see the headlines now," he said slowly. "Minister's Moll—no, that will be in the American papers. Over here, it will just say 'Minister's Friend'. . . . There's such a wealth of meaning in that word 'friend' when it's handled by the Press, don't you think?"

"What exactly do you mean by that?" But she knew quite well; just as she knew that he would draw this moment out for as long as it would stretch, playing with her as a cat plays with a mouse, before finally destroying it.

"'Minister's Friend in Divorce Court'," Arthur went on. "That would be in large black type. Then the sub-heading would be something like: 'Old Romance Dies Hard', or perhaps simply: 'Adultery Denied.' Stark, but to the point."

"That's absurd! It can easily be proved that, ever since the war, Felix and I haven't even been in the same country for more than two or three days. You wouldn't have a leg to stand on." Her agitation was so obvious that it intoxicated him. He was dominating the core of her emotions through Felix, and aware of every aspect of his power. He smiled, saying: "It's just the kind of news item the papers lie in wait for. Think how Whitehall would lap it up, too! *And* the old ladies! 'How dreadful' they'll all say. 'Never thought this kind of thing happened among decent people—it's too horrible', and then they'll dig everywhere for all the details they can get hold of. I can just see Lady Bates now."

"Even you couldn't be such a swine," Nathalie said hoarsely.

"Language! Tut, tut. What would Happy Ham think of his little song-bird if he heard her using words like that? I'm sure you'd never talk to *him* that way."

She realised that it would be useless to point out that such mud-slinging would only make Arthur look the fool in the end; he knew quite well that Felix could not afford the publicity. Even so, she said: "I don't for a moment suppose you'll believe me, but I've never been unfaithful to you. I can't honestly think why not, but I haven't."

"What a little innocent you are, aren't you? I suppose you thought I'd behave like a perfect gent, and let you have it all your own way."

At one time, Nathalie would have been indignant, or even shocked at his cruelty, but now she merely resigned herself to defeat, and said coldly: "If you've quite finished, I shall now go downstairs and read."

Arthur's control slipped again. "Go then," he roared. "Go to hell, for all I care!"

He hit her once more across the head, with all his strength.

She was standing at the top of the stairway, and lost her

balance. He put out an arm to catch her, but was too late. On her back, and head downwards, she bumped all the way down the stairs, and when he reached her, she was unconscious.

Nathalie lost her baby that morning, but it was another twenty-four hours before she was sufficiently conscious to know it. Slowly opening her eyes, she returned reluctantly to awareness and an accompanying feeling of loss and pain. She put her hand on her stomach, and its flatness was all the confirmation she needed. When the doctor's serious face bent over her, she smiled at him, and said: "I know."

The doctor took her hand to measure her pulse, and asked: "How are we feeling now?"

"I always adore doctors when I'm ill. I trust them completely. Is that very rash?"

For answer, the doctor pushed a thermometer into her mouth. Everything stopped for that sacred half-minute, and the presence of other people became apparent to her. She was in her own bedroom, but a hospital nurse now stood looking at her from the foot of the bed, and holding a small board.

Nathalie felt too tired to meet that soulless, yet penetrating gaze, so she shut her eyes again. When the thermometer was removed, she said: "It was inevitable, really, when you come to think of it."

The nurse tiptoed out of the room, and the doctor sat down by the bed and asked: "Would you like to see your husband, now?"

Nathalie kept her eyes closed and said nothing. "If I stay like this, without speaking," she thought, "he will go away. They will all go away, and let me die in peace. It's never as easy as that though. There's always something, or someone, making demands, so that one can never be left alone. One is a single, solitary unit, and yet never without ties." Nathalie's head ached, but the pain there seemed at one remove from herself, and not really oppressive.

She moved it a little to be more comfortable, and then realised that it was insulated. Putting up her hands, she felt the bandages, and opened her eyes again to say: "What's all this?"

"You cut your head a bit, but nothing much. The most unsightly of your bruises are the least serious."

She began to remember all that had happened and with it, the mesh of cause and effect; intrigue and confusion; loyalty, and whatever it was that made husbands and wives protect each other. It was now necessary to check up on Arthur's account to be able to stand by it, so she asked: "What exactly happened?"

"How much do you remember?"

Nathalie felt herself being drawn out of lethargy and languor, back into the tenseness that was needed to be perpetually on guard. Wondering how much the doctor knew or had guessed, she said carefully: "Nothing much. I think I must have fainted and lost my balance, or something."

"Apparently, you went downstairs to get some milk. There was a broken cup and saucer at the bottom of the stairs. Your husband said he offered to fetch it for you, but you refused, saying the exercise would help you to sleep. Then he heard a crash, and found you unconscious, having apparently fallen all the way downstairs on your head."

Nathalie shut her eyes again, thankful to have got past the first hurdle. Then she heard the doctor ask again: "Would you like to see your husband now?"

"My head aches so much, at the moment." Indeed, the pain had got suddenly worse, and was now part of herself. "Could I wait a bit longer?" She hoped that by holding out, death might reach her before Arthur could.

"Yes, of course. Just as you like. He seems tremendously upset, though, and is anxious to see you as soon as he can."

Her mind reflected: "To hell with him! The least he can do is jolly well wait until I can face him, considering," but her instincts aroused her compassion. She suddenly knew what Arthur must be experiencing in fear and remorse, and that only she could reassure him. The doctor went on: "I'll give you a prick to relieve the old head a bit, and then we'll see how we feel when we've had a spot of shut-eye. How would that be?"

"That would be wonderful. I love you, doctor. I love anybody who makes decisions for me, so long as they're the kind I approve of. Who makes decisions for doctors, though? Remind me to ask you that some time, will you? Later on?" She sank back, relaxed again, and then lost consciousness, for the injection affected her almost immediately.

As soon as the doctor had given Arthur a sedative to calm his nerves, he left the house, promising to return after lunch. He said that the patient had now taken a turn for the better and was having a peaceful sleep, and since this would do her more good than any amount of doctoring, there was nothing to be gained by his staying. Meanwhile, Nurse Parker would hold the fort, and the best thing Arthur could do was to take a hold on himself. The danger had virtually passed, and peace and quiet all round was the order of the day. Could he leave things to Vera until he came back?

He could. Vera, who for once really was being needed, thought of everything. She arranged for the house to be cleaned so that there would be no noise near Nathalie, organised the meals, and asked the Hammonds to have Elizabeth for the day. For a while Arthur, who was both exhausted and dazed, felt grateful for the efficient normality with which life was organised around him. Vera did not question him about what had happened, but reassured him by insisting on the details of their usual routine.

As the effect of the sedative wore off, however, every minute seemed longer and more barren, and he got bored with the understanding that was growing between Vera and Nurse Parker over every fresh pot of tea. There seemed to be a conspiracy to keep him downstairs, and he resented this more and more. When he and Vera had had their lunch and Nurse Parker was about to come down for hers, he firmly announced his intention of staying with Nathalie while Vera rested, adding that the sickroom was, after all his bedroom, and the patient his wife. Both the women objected, but they were no match for Arthur; he became at once resolutely manly and flatteringly charming, and got his own way without much difficulty.

When Arthur saw Nathalie lying so unnaturally still, so small, so sallow and so grotesquely bruised, he fancied that she was dead. The idea of death stimulated him not only to grief, but also to a passionate desperation that seemed infinitely revealing to him. He had experienced a sufficient variety of emotions to be able to imagine any one of them extended and all-absorbing, but always at one remove, as though they were happening to someone else. Only through a sense of absolute power over other people could he experience passion, however; only then, could he feel so totally absorbed that he was on the threshold of losing his own identity, while at the same time possessing a clue to reality. This intoxicating sense of power had come to him, fully and fruitfully, while he was the central figure on a stage; then, he had known a promise of fulfilment, a sense of reality, that he could otherwise only get near through destruction or death.

As he stood by his wife's bed, Arthur suddenly realised how much he would miss her. Although the pain of his grief was almost welcome for the thoroughness with which it overwhelmed him, he could no longer imagine his life without her. Wilde had said: "Each man kills the thing he loves," but even Arthur could no longer concentrate on literary similes to his situation. He was now like a small boy who has gone too far in a game, and is miserable and frightened at the consequences. With an unguarded moan, he threw himself on to his wife, sobbing: "Forgive me. . . . Forgive me. . . . I wasn't worth dying for." When Nathalie opened her eyes and took her husband in her arms, he cried: "I thought you were dead. Oh thank God, thank God!"

Nathalie said nothing, but merely held him to her. It was the only response she could make, as she was still too drowsy to speak coherently. Even when he was not talking, however, Arthur made demands, and before long, the weight of his sobbing head on her shoulder became too much for her to bear. She whispered: "Could you move a bit? I'm afraid I'm still rather weak." This shifting of attention from his state to hers acted as a kind of detonator. He did move, getting on to his knees beside her, and clasping her limp hands to his face, but now a torrent of words poured out of him. He grovelled in remorse, demanding to be forgiven, passionately declaring that he could not live without her, and exhorting her to assure him that their love was so great as to be worth dying for. It was not a scene in their usual sense of the word, but equally exacting. She tried to meet him, to respond to him, to calm his fears, but the effort was too much. She was crying quietly, completely exhausted, when the doctor came back and turned Arthur out of the room.

"I really can't . . ." Nathalie tried to say, when her husband had gone.

"It's all right, little lady," the doctor said. "If you weren't so weak we'd move you to hospital, but we'll just have to do the best we can here, I'm afraid."

All the rest of that day, Nathalie lay relaxed, aware that neither Arthur nor Vera could get to her. She felt extraordinarily odd. The combination of pain-relieving drugs and extreme physical weakness seemed to cause her mind to freewheel, yet she had a sense of immense control. She knew that the outcome of all this depended on her; that it was for her to decide what to think, or even do, and whether the next piece in the jig-saw puzzle should complete the whole pattern of her life on earth, or only a decisive part of it. She knew that she would have to chose whether to sink into unconsciousness and out of this life, or stay in the indeterminate borderland of wandering fancy, or make the effort required to reorganise herself completely.

Towards evening, Nathalie asked for Father Francis, and this caused a fresh outburst of energy from Arthur. There was a smell of death in the house now, which stimulated in him a profound reverence for all the details of the situation. He had himself asked the priest to say a Mass for his wife that morning, and now took it for granted that Father Francis had come to administer the rites of the last Sacrament. Nathalie, in fact, merely wanted to talk to her confessor but the situation was now out of her hands. It neither surprised nor awed her to find others also aware of her closeness to death, for only the core of the crisis, and not its causes, or outward manifestations, seemed to her to have any reality. She submitted to the rites wholeheartedly and with humility, but when she and the priest were alone, she said: "I wanted to ask you something. Is death good, or bad?"

Father Francis thought that she was frightened, and tried to help her by replying: "It is something that happens to all of us, when we are ready to be called."

"Yes, I know, but that's not what I mean." She felt an exciting strength soaking into every part of her now, right up to the fingertips, and leaving her brain miraculously clear. "Natural death is all right," she went on. "One could almost say it is a sort of reward. But death is not always like that. When men murder each other, or slowly throttle the life-force out of each other, that is death too."

"It is not death as ordered by the Almighty. Those who take on themselves to abuse His power get their punishment in the long run."

"But if death by violence or destruction is bad, why is it the kind of end that so often comes to saints and martyrs?"

"You cannot attach a moral qualification to it. Death is a fact. It is destruction which is bad, and that can end in death, but not necessarily. It's true that saints and martyrs are often overcome by a form of destruction which ends in death, but that is the mercy of God interfering. He sends death as a release, when destruction has gone too far to be bearable."

"Who decides how much is bearable?" Again Father Francis sought to reassure Nathalie, and whispered: "God is infinitely merciful, my child. You must put your trust in Him."

"But at what point does someone decide that even God's help cannot make life bearable?"

Father Francis hesitated before saying: "A man is not always responsible for his own death." He thought Nathalie had not heard him, for she slipped down into the bed again, pitiably small and frail, and her face became like a mask. Then, in a clear, loud voice, she suddenly exclaimed: "I wonder . . ." before taking a step out of time.

There are many ways in which this phenomenon can come about. Love or disaster, supreme happiness or extreme sorrow, or some other key, may cause a complete unlocking of all the doors of time and space, so that in entering the intangible world altogether, everything becomes visible. This flash of vision may be a complete process of creation, development, enlightenment and fulfilment; sometimes, even the pivot of an entire existence on earth. It happened like this with Nathalie, while Father Francis went to find Arthur and the doctor to bring them upstairs again. The regular poundings of her pulse were transformed into a long strip of kaleidoscopic images, passing rhythmically rather fast, and extremely vividly. They represented scenes out of her life and the pattern of their progress was intricate, yet in geometrical proportion. Out of the first dozen or so, squared-off and self-contained, the most important would survive to appear in the next series, and the earlier ones disappeared. In this way she gradually got nearer to the present, although the most significant episodes of her past still reappeared, evenly spaced out with events of many years later. Her sense of timelessness was conscious and things that had happened twenty years beforehand took the same place in importance as quite recent events. Time, in fact, seemed an irrelevant concept, just as did the whole of her life from where she now stood, and what she now knew. This promise of a great and complete revelation was not yet quite fulfilled, but she knew that it soon would be. When the final picture of the long film of her life had flashed on to the screen of her consciousness for the last time, she would go through to whatever realms of light and enlightenment lay beyond. She could already see something of that radiance, and it filled her with a sense of peace and completeness that she had previously only suspected. The light was incredibly bright, but without the coldness or deep shadows of a strong glare on earth, and out of this aura came a woman, who stood in front of her holding out both hands. Nathalie did not recognise her but she knew by her eyes, her smile, and her gesture that here was the prototype of all tenderness, bringing the assurance of absolute understanding and security.

The girl sat up, holding out her hands to the woman, and was about to let her take them, when she hesitated. The thought of Elizabeth was a reminder of something unfulfilled. She wondered what the child would have instead of her, for even with the legend of a tragic love behind him, Arthur would always be too centred on his own problems to be a real father, and Vera was cold and barren. Where would Elizabeth learn about warmth, tenderness, compassion and laughter? She was not yet three years old, and in the many years ahead of her, only her own mother could help her, a mother who would now be beginning her genuine maternity.

As she hesitated, the woman disappeared and the light grew dim again. Nathalie lay down, and went back into time.

BOND OF PERFECTION

Part Three

Nathalie braced herself against the winter cold and alighted from the Oxford bus. It had begun to rain, so she ran the few steps to "The Traveller's Rest" and gratefully passed into the warmth and brightness of the saloon bar. She said "Good evening" to Bill Corker, greeted several more people, and then made her way to the corner where her husband was sitting. Having ascertained in Oxford that he had not been there that day, Nathalie now found him where she had expected to. His eyes were rather glazed, but it was not yet possible to tell whether he was more likely to sober up, or get still tighter.

"Hello, darling," she exclaimed brightly. "This certainly is the right place on a night like this."

Arthur kissed her hand, but said nothing. Her entry had struck him like a shaft of light, and he felt too moved to speak. Whenever she was away from him, he became afraid of never seeing her again, and her every reappearance impressed him profoundly. "I'll just get myself a drink," she added, and Arthur handed her his empty glass and said: "Same again, please."

Nathalie went to the bar, and asked for a sherry for herself and a beer for Arthur. He had been drinking gin and tonic, but did not question her choice. After a few minutes, he merely asked: "Well? And how was business, today?"

"I've been promoted. I'm to model the modes as well as sell them, now, though I doubt whether that's going to make either North Oxford or Cowley open their purses any wider."

Nathalie had been working for some months in an Oxford

dress shop, as the Bateman-Browns needed money. After her miscarriage, over two years before, she had been weak for a long time, and her slow recovery had run them into a good deal of expenditure not catered for by the National Health Service. Apart from this, with the cost of living steadily rising, they found it difficult not to spend beyond their income. Those were the explanations they talked about, and with which they made Nathalie's decision to take a job seem plausible; after all, plenty of people found themselves in the same predicament these days. Both Nathalie and Arthur knew, however, that their main problem was the disproportionate amount the latter spent on drink, but this fact was never mentioned outright.

When the possibility of Nathalie working had been discussed, Vera had been discouraging, as well as doubtful; and Arthur, for once coming out of his coma of complaisance with whoever had spoken last, supported his sister's point of view.

"People who've never earned a single penny in their lives don't just go out and get jobs," he had exclaimed, maintaining that there was a whole hierarchy of rank and influence in any career, and to get in by a side door, it was essential to be either on the spot, with the maximum amount of competence, qualifications and determination, or else to have contacts in high places. Nathalie, he had pointed out, was uneducated, not particularly intelligent, and a child when it came to practical matters. Moreover, none of her contacts in high places were likely to help her in getting the sort of job that she either needed, or could hope to hold down. He and Vera had both praised her sentiments, but had told her to forget the whole thing and concentrate on making joints of meat go further, and finding even more advantageous lines in biscuits; she could also save by doing without help in the house, and of course there would always be Vera to rely on.

Nathalie, who had learnt not to talk without thinking, and then hardly ever to say what she really meant, had thanked them for their advice, and then gone off to ponder over the problem on her own. Little as she felt the reality of money, two factors became obvious: firstly, that even with Vera's regular contribution to the household expenses, Arthur could not go on indefinitely spending over £12 a week on gin without getting into serious debt; and secondly that even if she did cut down on the food bills (and Elizabeth was a growing child) or managed without the few hours a week of domestic help, their income would be increased less than if she earned some money herself. Either Arthur must give up drinking so heavily, or she must find a job; that much was certain. It was almost as certain that the second alternative was the more practical one. What then, Nathalie wondered, could she do? Having examined herself critically, she came to the conclusion that her only marketable assets were a willingness to do things thoroughly, and her figure. Arthur had complained much about her skinniness, but now it struck her that she had the measurements suitable for a model. Without telling anyone, she walked into a newly-opened dress-shop in Oxford and asked for a job.

It may be true that providence keeps a special eye on fools; or that emergencies endow people with exceptional gifts of charm and verbosity; or perhaps it was simply that the manageress of Martine Modes Ltd. took a liking to Nathalie. At any rate, she was considered usable and taken on, then and there, to get experience in the shop first, while she learnt the rudiments of modelling on the side.

When Nathalie had come home with the news of this job, starting at £8 a week and with prospects, there had been consternation at Walton House. Instead of being glad that she had triumphed despite her handicaps, Vera had seemed quite dismayed. Was this enterprise really worth it, especially as Nathalie was not very strong? she had asked. Had she offset her expenses—fares, lunches, and more domestic help—against an already meagre salary? All kinds of difficulties about the organisation of the house had then arisen. They were genuine, yet could easily have been made insignificant, for Vera always analysed situations in a way that could not be called unreasonable, yet made no sense, and Arthur had developed this technique to such an extent that Nathalie sometimes thought that one of them must be going mad. Latterly, however, he had seldom bothered; he knew that his wife saw through him now, and in a curious way, found this a relief. On that occasion, however, irked at the idea of Nathalie being away from home so much, he had joined in. "What will happen to Elizabeth?" he had asked. "What about the shopping? And is Vera to do the cleaning when Mrs. Thomas has her shocking rheumatics and doesn't turn up?" He had firmly declared that he would not stand for his sister being used as a charwoman.

Nathalie had had an answer for everything. Although it had seemed to her absurd to generate so much thought and energy on what was, after all, merely the shell of their lives, she took special trouble to safeguard herself against every objection. With calm and unprecedented authority, she had made her arrangements known, and there had been immediate capitulation. It was then that Mrs. Dennison had moved into their orbit again, and Vera in some way knew that this time she could do nothing about it. Nathalie might be going out to work, but she had become mistress in her own house.

On that winter day, Nathalie had looked forward to sharing her good news with Arthur and Vera. She was pleased, partly because this was proof that she was not completely useless, but also because the increase in her salary would be a help; as there were now openings for free-lance work as well, this might be more than doubled.

The evening did not quite work out as Nathalie had hoped, however, for Arthur went on drinking. Getting more and more hazy, he sat on in the warmth of "The Traveller's Rest", unable to make the effort to move. Nathalie's news had dissipated the last shred of his self-discipline, and he responded by abandoning himself to her. This was not only a tease, but also the self-indulgence of leaving everything to some other person: he did not trust her absolutely, but put himself absolutely at her mercy. It had happened before in this particular way, and heavy though Arthur was, Nathalie had been able to help him home. That night, he was past even that, however. By closing time, he was incapable of talking coherently, or even standing up alone. Bill Corker understood the situation, and while rounding up dirty glasses from the table, whispered to Nathalie: "Hang on a mo', and I'll give you a hand. Not to worry."

She smiled gratefully at him and waited until after closing-time. Then she and Bill between them got Arthur back to Walton House. It was an inconvenient, rather than a difficult, process. Arthur was quite drunk, but not yet beyond that stage of being completely incapable with drink. If assisted, he could still make the effort to stand up, or take a step; he could still decide whether to abandon the slight effort that held him back from passing out, but did not choose to do this until he had arrived at the house. Then, an instinctive caution advised him that the best way of avoiding Vera was to put himself entirely in the hands of his escort. He was dimly aware that Vera would object to the idea of Bill Corker putting him to bed, but decided to laugh it off by saying that he had fallen, or been knocked down by a bicycle or something. Tomorrow, though; at that moment, all he wanted was oblivion, and he gratefully let himself be overcome by it.

When Bill had left, Nathalie went to find Vera, knowing that her sister-in-law would be glad of reassurance, however little she might believe what was told her. As long as appearances were maintained, and normal routine and trivialities observed, Vera could make herself think that everything was really all right. She was fond of saying that tomorrow was another day, and the morning was always wiser than the evening. Nathalie could see so clearly that everything was really all wrong that she found this ostrich-like optimism more pitiable than irritating, but it seemed to her too unimportant to grudge. Basically, there was no understanding between the two women, but they had learnt to live with one another. Since Nathalie had begun to stand up to her, Vera's resentment had been replaced by something nearer respect; and once she even told Arthur that she had to admit the girl was a sticker. Moreover, being unable to endure solitude, she needed the reassurance of her sister-in-law's company, now that her brother was so strangely lost to her.

"I don't think Arthur will want any supper," Nathalie said. "He's got a bad headache, and it will do him good to sleep it off."

"Would you like something to eat?" Vera asked. "There's some fish pie in the Aga, and a little soup I could heat up."

"Thank you so much. I'd love some soup, anyhow."

Nathalie was not at all hungry, but now that so much depended on her, she could not afford to take any risks with her health. They went to the kitchen and she told Vera her news, now too tired to take any pleasure in doing so.

"It will make all the difference financially," she stressed, knowing that this point was most likely to appeal to her sister-in-law. Vera immediately said, "Well done! I hope it won't be too much for you, though. You look so awfully tired."

"It's the end of the week. I'll be all right by Monday, though."

"You must have a good rest tomorrow and Sunday. I don't really know how you manage."

"It will all be more interesting now, even though it may be harder work. I don't mind that, though. I think boredom is far more exhausting than anything, don't you?"

This was not the kind of remark that Vera was prepared to

follow up, however. She merely smiled, and said: "I think you should get some sleep now. I'll see to the washing-up."

"Right. I'll just lay the breakfast things, then."

Nathalie awoke the following morning when Arthur brought her a cup of tea in her bedroom. She still did not like tea, but it seemed less trouble to drink it than argue, for this ritual was part of a pattern of living that he insisted on. Although Arthur had woken early, he had slept deeply, as he could only do when he went to bed drunk. He felt relaxed and rested now, and this was the only time in the day when he was what is usually regarded as normal.

He kissed his wife and asked her how she had slept.

"Fine," she lied. "And you?"

"Extremely well until six, but then I don't need much sleep at my age."

No mention was made of the night before. Arthur had given up either wallowing in remorse, or asking whether he had made a fool of himself; these occasions had become far too much a part of their lives. He did not often end the evening by passing out, but on the other hand he was seldom sober.

"I've been reading Chesterton," he said, opening the book in his hand. "Listen to this."

He read an extract from the autobiography, giving an account of a surprise visit Hilaire Belloc once paid to Henry James, and then exclaimed: "What a golden man he was!"

Nathalie smiled, and said: "I adore his sense of humour, and the way he quietly builds up to things."

"It's wonderful, isn't it? One can just see it. The more the shaggy and uncouth Belloc yells from the garden, the more disdainful and precious Henry James becomes." Arthur laughed happily. For a moment he was in the mood Nathalie loved best in him, and full of vigorous enjoyment and perception, but his confidence and vitality seemed to explore and expand, until suddenly it reached a crisis and exploded. Then he said petulantly, "Chesterton was a notorious drunk too, you know, so it would not seem to be quite such a handicap."

"I imagine he was the person he was in spite of, rather than because of, that. Anyhow, he went on the wagon after going to live in Beaconsfield, didn't he?"

"Only because he had a really appreciative wife who knew how to take care of him."

Nathalie remembered another occasion, on which Arthur had slanged Frances Chesterton for dragging her husband away from all that he cherished most in life, but she did not say so. It had been during a tirade in which he set out to prove how handicapped great men were by wives, maintaining that Tolstoy, Wagner, Irving and many others had all been blighted with intolerable humiliations by their women. Now, however, he went on almost seriously: "She understood the responsibilities of being married to a genius, and devoted the whole of herself to him."

"It's a responsibility, all right. I won't quarrel with you about that!" Nathalie smiled, and to her relief, Arthur smiled too, saying: "And I've got a wife who can't even make tea! I'm going down for another cup. Do you want some more?"

"No, thanks. I must get up. Is Elizabeth awake?"

"Yes. Shall I bring her in?"

"Oh, do. Saturday mornings are bliss, I must say."

Arthur went out and she lay down again, to enjoy for a few moments the delight of not being forced to get up, or scramble to catch the Oxford bus, or plan ahead before things caught up with her. She looked round her room, and the familiarity of line and colour, as well as of the view through the window, made her feel contented. Arthur had moved to a bedroom of his own during her illness and had never returned, and this new scrap of privacy made her surroundings seem all the more attractive.

There was a fumbling at the door-handle, and then the door slowly opened. It stood ajar for a moment, and suddenly, with a giggle, Elizabeth jumped into the room and leant up against the wall.

"I'm dressed," she smiled, waiting to be admired.

"So you are! What a lovely surprise."

"I dressed myself."

"What a big girl you're getting! Shut the door, and come and kiss me good morning."

As Elizabeth came towards the bed, it became apparent that she had put her shoes on the wrong feet, and she now walked as though the victim of some terrible deformity. Nathalie held her hands out to her daughter and said: "Jump."

Elizabeth jumped, but landed where she had started from, so she climbed up to sit by her mother. Nathalie hugged her, and said: "Good morning, sweetheart," and Elizabeth responded dutifully, rather than enthusiastically. She was still not a demonstrative child, although frequently revealed a deep affection for her mother indirectly. As she looked at her now, with her big eyes which were the same pale blue as Vera's, but the slanting shape of Nathalie's, and her thin little mouth smiling shyly, she asked: "What you doing?"

"Being lazy."

"Lazy Mummy!"

"What are we going to do today?"

Elizabeth stopped smiling and looked blank, as though the effort of making a decision had enclosed her in some trap. She said nothing, so Nathalie went on: "Are you coming shopping with me?"

This was a rhetorical question, because Saturday morning shopping expeditions were the highlight of Elizabeth's week, but it had the effect of making the child beam happily.

"And see the kittens at the farm?" she asked.

"If you like."

"Can dolly come too?"

"Of course."

Elizabeth slipped off the bed and went purposefully towards the door, walking without difficulty, now that her shoes had been changed round.

"Where are you off to?" her mother asked.

"To get dolly ready," the child replied, and left the room without looking round.

Nathalie lay back in bed, giving herself another ten minutes before getting up. Thinking about her daughter, she wondered whether all parents worried and puzzled so much over their offspring. She no longer felt detached from Elizabeth, as had been the case before her illness, and the child seemed to enjoy being with her. Her occasional bouts of unresponsiveness were trivial, yet her timidity was at times more than could be attributed to modesty, or even fears natural in a child. Nathalie remembered that she was afraid of venturing to the garden gate by herself, or using the back stairs, or strangers who came to the house, or of being left alone in one of the outbuildings, even for a moment. When something went wrong for her, she did not protest loudly and openly as most children did, but went pale and rigid, her mouth closed in a tight little line.

Although Nathalie was tired, and had, as so often, awakened with a slight headache, she began to plan her day. After breakfast and bedmaking, she would have to sort out a suitcase of old clothes in the attic, and find contributions for a village jumble sale. Then, before cooking the lunch, there were groceries to be ordered from the village shop for the following week. After lunch, she would have a short, but much-needed nap, and then go for a walk. These expeditions—along the river, or through the fields and copses of the countryside, or even as far as the downs—soothed and invigorated her as nothing else could. The rhythmic exercise, and the feeling of freedom, refreshed her whole system. At these times, her mind belonged to nobody, and there was no need to respond in whatever way was appropriate to Arthur, or Vera, or her employers. On leaving the village, there was a certain point at which she always said: "Now I can start." From then on, she would begin to think. Her object was to combine the maximum amount of awareness with a vigorous discipline. She wanted to be unafraid of facing anything; to be able to perceive all the facets of her experience and remember the light and shade of every person she had ever known, every place she had ever visited, every conversation or book she had ever followed, and every incident she had ever witnessed. It seemed to her vitally necessary to be able to face all things with imagination, but no sentimentality; honestly, but not bitterly; subjectively, and yet with detachment. Ever since her convalescence, she had been possessed by an insatiable desire to sort out reality from illusion, the core of any situation from its details, and the evidence of inevitable patterns in life from the decisions made by individual will power. Even if it was cold, or pouring with rain, she went out, if only for the comparative warmth of returning to shelter afterwards. When she got back to the house, they would have a late tea, and then play with Elizabeth for an hour or so.

Up till that time, the day would be comfortable, and often enjoyable, but what happened afterwards could not be predicted. When Nathalie took Elizabeth up for her bath, Arthur would also stand up and say something like: "Well, I think I'll just take a little stroll." It would be impossible to know at what time he might return, how much he would have to drink before he did, or even what effect it would have on him; the sight of Nathalie being falsely cheerful and Vera looking tragic with anxiety could set him off in a number of ways, none of them restful.

As Nathalie dozed and dreamt in her bed, there was a loud knock at the door, and Mrs. Dennison came in, barely waiting for an answer: "That's right!" she beamed. "Just you 'ave a nice lie-in while you can."

"Hallo, Mrs. D. You're early today, aren't you?"

"Well, I thought I'd give meself time, so as to give you an 'and with that attic."

Mrs. Dennison's determination not to miss that job if she could possibly help it amused Nathalie. Although she never actually asked for anything outright, she was a blatant scrounger. Whenever she said: "It's about time I changed the shelf paper in that cupboard", or "There's a shocking amount of moth about, I'd better put some fresh newspaper in them cases", Nathalie would know that this was just an introduction, a seeking of sanction to proceed. A short while later, she would come in with something in her hand and her eyes shining with greed, saying: "You don't want this tea-pot, do yer? It's all chipped. 'Course, it would be all right for those wot don't 'ave posh company, but *you* couldn't use it, and it's only cluttering up the china cupboard", or "Whoever does this moth-eaten pair of trousers belong to? Not Mr. Brown, surely. Funny thing, Sid was saying only this morning that 'e could do with an old pair of bags for touching up the cottage in. Gets 'imself in such a mess when 'e's doing odd jobs."

Now, Nathalie said: "I haven't had breakfast yet. You'd better just whip round downstairs until I'm ready."

"I done the drawing-room, but 'imself's in the library. Still, 'e'll be taking 'is little walk any time after ten, so I can do it then. Cor, you don't 'alf look pale."

"It's my natural colour. You can do the nursery while I get up."

The rest of the morning passed according to programme, and although Arthur returned for lunch rather late, he was in an equable mood, and enjoyed his food. Then he went up to his bedroom and slept until tea-time. Nathalie's after-luncheon rest was shorter, but extremely revitalising. Waking after an hour, she felt calm and energetic, and getting up immediately, she tidied herself, and went to the nursery. Elizabeth was asleep, her head on one side, framed by her arms, which were lying back, crooked on the pillow. At the sound of the curtains being drawn, she moved. When Nathalie let down the side of the cot and whispered her name, her eyes opened. For a moment or two, she blinked and swallowed, trying to focus on the world around her. She looked unseeing at Nathalie, and then, suddenly recognising her mother, smiled slowly, and began pushing back the bedclothes with her feet. Nathalie helped her to stand up, and then lifted her out of the cot. Holding her daughter closely, she experienced a strange satisfaction in the warmth of this firm and relaxed little body. Once, when looking after one of the Hammond children, she had thought that most babies were appealing when still half asleep, if only because of their completely unguarded trust. Now, she knew that there was something different about one's own; an animal response, due principally to smell, that enabled a blind woman to recognise her own child.

Elizabeth gave herself to her mother's embrace for a moment and then struggled, saying:

"I want to dress, now."

"All right, sweetheart."

The child only had her frock, cardigan and shoes to put on, so although she insisted on doing it herself, this did not take long. Nathalie was only allowed to help indirectly, but as she distracted her daughter's attention, she said: "You know, you're getting too big for that cot. We'll have to find you a bed to sleep in."

"A big one, like yours?" Elizabeth looked a little startled.

"Well, not quite as big as mine. Perhaps you could have the one I had when I used to stay here with Aunt Olga."

Elizabeth said nothing, and looked at her mother uncomprehendingly.

"This used to be Aunt Olga's house, you know, and when I was a little girl, I often stayed with her here."

Neither the past nor the future concerned Elizabeth as yet, so she merely said solemnly: "I like my cot."

"If you go on sleeping in it much longer, your feet will hang out of the end, like Mrs. Tiggiwinkle."

"Not Mrs. Tiggiwinkle, Mummy."

"Well, you wouldn't be very comfortable if people came and hung their washing on your feet, would you, now?"

"No—o," Elizabeth said, without a smile, and then again added solemnly: "I like my cot."

"Well, supposing you keep your cot in here to put all your dolls in and you have a new bed."

Elizabeth paused to take this in, and then beamed.

"Can I have my new bed tonight?" she asked.

"Well, we'll see," Nathalie began, but remembering this to be the most unsatisfactory of answers in childhood, she added: "I'll ask Daddy to help me move it after tea. Will that be all right?"

Elizabeth agreed, and mother and daughter went downstairs together, like a pair of happy conspirators.

Vera was in the drawing-room reading *The Times*, and went to the door the moment she heard them.

"Could Elizabeth stay with you a moment while I just get her outdoor things?" Nathalie asked her. She always made a point of insisting on the child's attachment to her aunt so that the older woman should not feel altogether neglected. Vera's attitude to her niece had changed perceptibly, however, ever since Elizabeth had become fonder of her mother, and it was with indifference that she now said to her: "Come along, then." Turning to Nathalie, she added: "Going for a walk?"

"I am, but Elizabeth is going to play with Sally Milton."

Vera's mouth pursed visibly. "I can't help feeling she's such a common child," she said.

"Do you think so? But Elizabeth must have some companions, and anyhow, they're very good friends." Nathalie smiled, but she felt annoyed, for Vera always found some derogatory criticism to make about any child with whom Elizabeth played.

When she was alone with her niece, Vera turned to her and said coaxingly: "Wouldn't you like to stay with Aunty Vera this afternoon, and we'll go down to the pond and see the baby swans?"

"Sally and me's going with Sally's granny," Elizabeth said happily.

"But will Sally's granny give you some sweets?"

Elizabeth looked blankly at her aunt. "Would you like a sweet?" Vera went on.

"Yes, please." Elizabeth smiled and put out her hand.

"Well, you stay with me, and you can have any sweets you like."

"I can't, 'cos I'm going to play with Sally."

"If you just tell Mummy you'd rather stay with me, I'm sure she'll let you."

Elizabeth looked blank again for a moment. Then she said stubbornly: "I want to play with Sally."

"I want! I want! . . . Nice little girls don't say 'I want', and Aunty Vera doesn't like little girls who aren't nice."

Elizabeth said nothing, but her eyes were quite vacant. "You want Aunty Vera to like you don't you?"

Elizabeth still did not speak, so she added more sharply: "Don't you?"

The child whispered "Yes" without looking up, trying hard not to cry. "Well, then! We're going to have a lovely time. We'll do all kinds of things that that silly Sally and her granny would never even think of. I tell you what. When we've bought the sweets and seen the baby swans, we'll go down to Miss Bradley's, and perhaps she'll let you look for the eggs. You'd like that, wouldn't you?"

At that moment, Nathalie came back into the room with Elizabeth's coat, gloves and bonnet. The child ran to her mother and burst into tears.

"Sweetheart! What on earth is the matter?" Nathalie said tenderly, drawing her daughter towards her.

"I want to play with Sally," Elizabeth sobbed.

"But you're going to play with Sally, you silly muggins. I'm just going to put these on for you, and then we'll be off. Were you getting tired of waiting for me?"

Elizabeth stopped crying, but went on clinging to her mother, while Vera hastily explained: "She must have misunderstood something I said. Now Elizabeth, you mustn't be a cry-baby, must you, or else what will Sally think? I keep forgetting what a tot she is! She's still only a baby, really, isn't she?"

Nathalie took one look at Vera's twisted, bitter mouth and hungry eyes, and then became totally absorbed in her daughter. She hugged her again, and murmured to her, until the child was reassured. Then she took her out.

When Vera was alone, she picked up *The Times* once more and tried to read. This time, however, the newsprint was swimming about all over the page and her hands were trembling badly, so she put the paper down and went out to do some gardening.

The garden had changed character so completely in the previous two years, that even the Baroness had noticed it. Shrubs had been drastically pruned back, and the herbaceous border was still half-empty, and no longer so bright. Several more flower beds had been dug, but none of them were ever fully planted, and what blooms there were had been arranged in rather monotonous municipal park symmetry. The most disturbing of Vera's changes, however, was her abolition of many trees, including a yew hedge that had taken sixty years to grow, a favourite old May tree, a weeping willow down by the river, an apple tree at the side of the house, and a young copper beech. Arthur agreed with Nathalie that all this was rather sinister.

After tea, Nathalie asked Arthur to help her move a bed into the night nursery, and he became almost as excited as Elizabeth. It was one of his delights to shift furniture around and create a new atmosphere in the surroundings. Sometimes his efforts were not a success, and he would eventually change everything yet once more, but more often he showed great imagination and ingenuity.

On this occasion, he entered into the spirit of the adventure to such an extent that it was not only a bed that was found for Elizabeth, but an entirely new arrangement of the room as well. While he moved tables, chairs, and pictures from all over the house, Nathalie swept up little piles of dust and litter that had lain undiscovered and undisturbed for some time, and Elizabeth ran happily backwards and forwards, getting in the way and clapping her hands.

Her joy and Nathalie's admiration were deeply satisfying to Arthur, but it was not enough. He told Elizabeth to call her aunt, so that she also could admire the results of his handiwork. Vera came upstairs to look at the new nursery and stood at the door, holding Elizabeth's hand, with everybody's eyes looking towards her; the child's eager and expectant; Arthur's challenging, and almost insolent; and Nathalie's, detached and observant. For a moment she hesitated, and then said quietly: "It looks very nice."

"Is that all you can say?" Arthur asked sharply.

"I really do think it's nice."

"Can't you sound as though you meant it?"

Vera left the room and went downstairs again without another word.

"You women and your flouncing, you make me sick!" Arthur exclaimed, flinging his hammer to the ground.

"Don't take on so, darling. I think it's wonderful, and so does Elizabeth. Don't you, Muggins?"

"Ooh, yes! Now can I put my dollies to bed in the cot?"

"Yes, but you'll have to be quick because it's past your bed-time. Darling Arthur, you are so clever. I never know how to arrange a room so it looks right."

"It is rather fine, isn't it? Rich, but not gaudy. Thirsty work, though."

"Yes, and you're nearly fifteen minutes late," Nathalie smiled. "The boys will be getting worried."

"That'll never do. I've got an important darts match to-night."

"Have you really? Who against?"

"Long Barrow. Most of them are a lot of damned Papists, so we should be able to beat them quite easily."

"We'll see about that!"

"Why don't you come too? I'll play so much better if you're there."

"I ought to put Elizabeth to bed."

"Vera'll do that. She'd be glad to—provided you ask her politely, that is."

"She does so much already that I feel I ought to do my share at week-ends. Besides, I see so little of Elizabeth."

Arthur began to look sulky, so she added: "I tell you what. I'll be quick and come on afterwards. I could be with you by seven."

"I know what that means. You'll never come."

"I will. I promise."

"I want you to come now."

"Darling, please be reasonable," Nathalie tried to cajole. "You know what an effort it is for me to be a good mother, so don't undermine my morale."

"What about being a good wife? Isn't that important too?"

"Of course it is."

"Well, what about making a little effort at that, for a change?"

"I can do both, if you'll just wait half an hour for me. Let's both put Elizabeth to bed, and then we can go out together."

Arthur was determined not to make a fool of himself by allowing anybody to get round him; besides, this was a challenge to his authority.

"Are you coming now or aren't you?" he demanded.

Nathalie met his glare coolly and steadily, and then said quietly: "Not now, Arthur, but I'll be at 'The Traveller's Rest' by seven."

"I shan't be there."

"Where will you be, then?"

He did not answer, but turned round and left the room, clattering downstairs and then slamming the front door behind him.

Nathalie hesitated, and a moment later, turned back to her tidying. It seemed to her that the only possible thing to do was to drown in the details of the next few hours, and hope that even though it was Saturday night, they would somehow pass without catastrophe. She turned to Elizabeth and found her sitting quite still, staring at nothing.

"Well, Muggins? Are your babies all in bed?"

"No. You put them in."

"I'll help you, but you must be there too, because I'm sure they want their Mummy."

When Nathalie had read to her daughter, tucked her up, and kissed her good night, she went out to look for her husband. He was not at "The Traveller's Rest", nor at the other two pubs within easy reaching distance. Nobody she talked to had seen him that evening, but Bill Corker suggested several places where she might try. Feeling suddenly discouraged and rather cross, however, she decided to go home again, knowing that if Arthur was determined to give her a wild goose chase, she was no match for him. With a faint, but vain hope that he might have returned meanwhile, she reached Walton House again by nine o'clock.

Arthur did not get back until after ten, however. He was drunk, but only enough to increase his appetite, and began to eat his dinner with enjoyment. To start with, nobody talked much. Silence in that atmosphere was as dangerous as it was uncomfortable, however, so in order to cover it up, both Nathalie and Vera made trite remarks. Finding things to say which could not be taken as controversial in any sense was not easy, but both women had had much practice at this in recent years. If Arthur was in the mood, however, he could twist almost anything to make it sound provocative or stupid. With his strong dramatic sense and his total lack of scruple, his ingenuity sometimes became quite fascinating, however cruel. Nathalie had learnt to regard these outbursts with detachment, partly because she was so used to them, and partly as a means of self-protection.

Vera, on the other hand, was not so philosophical. If she abandoned herself to a moment, she could see neither backwards nor forwards, and quite lost her head. If she was emotionally roused, she felt compelled to express herself, and did so, instinctively and passionately, whatever the consequences. She, who had once been able to control Arthur merely by having a tantrum, now found it impossible to bear the same type of outburst in him. She would slump into silence, her face sallow and flabby and her colourless eyes misty with misery.

On this particular evening, Arthur was laughing with Nathalie about the darts match and the people who had taken part in it, and there was something ominous about his amiability. Suddenly he turned to Vera and said: "You haven't got much to say for yourself."

Although half expecting some remark of this sort, she was unprepared for it. With a doleful and appealing look which whetted his huntsman appetite, instead of tempering it, she answered bravely:

"I was listening to your interesting conversation."

"Conversation implies joining in and taking part in. It's neither a lecture, nor a spectacle. Hence the name."

Vera looked down at her plate.

"Well?" Arthur insisted. There was no answer. "Darling?"

"What."

"Don't you agree?"

"I'm sure you're right."

"Why don't you join in, then, and say something worth hearing? It would be a nice change."

Nathalie said quickly: "Darling, how can you expect anybody

to get a word in edgeways, when the two of us are jabbering away sixteen to the dozen."

"You be quiet," Arthur said, still towering over Vera. "I want to know what my sister has to say for herself. Why is it that in any public house I happen to visit, I can get really excellent conversation, whereas in my own home I am surrounded by morons? And yet the people I meet there are neither particularly well educated, nor particularly clever. Many of them haven't even had half the advantages you two have had, but they make stimulating and intelligent companions. Why is that, do you suppose?"

Vera went on eating in silence, her head bowed over her plate, but Nathalie said brightly: "You've brought up a point I've often wondered about. Is there a difference between cleverness and intelligence, do you think?"

Arthur swivelled his torso round towards Nathalie with ominous deliberation and said ponderously: "That's more like it. Yes?"

"Well? Do you think there is?"

"Make your point somewhat clearer. Enlarge on it."

"It seems to me that people who are good at details—I mean, people who can pass exams, or write learned treatises on abstruse subjects, and so on—don't necessarily have common sense. I mean, somebody like Mrs. Dennison, who can write only just enough to fill up a pools coupon and couldn't remember a logical proposition if you paid her to, yet has something which probably enables her to cope with many of the grimmer problems of life far more effectively than Professor Snooks or Director Bloggs. Is it wisdom, do you think? Or resilience? Or just lack of imagination?"

"That's quite a good beginning. Now then, darling. Over to you. What do you think about all this?"

Vera made no comment, and Arthur went on: "Have you nothing to add at all?"

"What would you say?" Vera tried.

"I'm asking you. It's high time we heard what you think about things, and I'm tired of doing all the talking. Now then: would you say that there is any difference between cleverness and intelligence?"

This was the kind of remark that left Vera cold, for ideas neither stimulated nor challenged her, and her sullen cringing inflamed Arthur. If she had shown some traces of robust good humour, he would have left her alone. What he found intolerable was her automatic condemnation of anything she did not understand, and the self-pitying way in which she exclaimed: "I'm afraid I don't know what you're talking about, half the time," irritated him to excess. His eyes began to glitter dangerously as he said: "What an extraordinary remark for a clever—or is it intelligent? —woman of the world to make. It's a simple enough proposition, after all, and if you haven't any views yourself, can't you at least take an intelligent—or is it clever?—interest in what other people think?"

"I did ask you what you thought," Vera protested, with petulant resentment.

"Oh, what does it matter, anyhow!" Nathalie said. "We're none of us being particularly intelligent *or* clever at the moment. Shall we play Lexicon after dinner, even though Vera can beat the pants off both of us when it comes to spelling?"

"Don't change the subject," Arthur said coldly. "I want to get to the bottom of this. Now then, darling. I should really be interested to know what you consider to be conversation. What do you talk to people about? I know you better than to believe that you discuss the kind of things that most women do when they get together—you'd hardly be in a position to, anyhow. In that case, what do you talk about?"

"I should have thought you'd know that, after all these years."

"That's just it! It always seems to be me that does the talking. All I can ever recall you contributing are moans about the shortages, or extremely boring anecdotes which I have heard umpteen times before."

"Don't you dare talk to me like that," Vera exclaimed, with vehemence rather than fervour. Her hands began to tremble and her face puckered at the forehead, and round the eyes and mouth. "You're dreadful! Horrible!"

Nathalie tried to catch Vera's eye, but the latter was too upset to notice.

"Insults are hardly an acceptable form of conversation," Arthur said with deliberation. "No wonder you have no friends."

"How dare you!" Vera wailed, and at the same time, Nathalie said firmly: "Arthur, that's enough. There really are limits, and you've gone beyond them."

"Do I detect an echo of Happy Ham? Or is this merely a case of 'Up the Guides!' 'See your knots are properly tied, girls, or whatever will the Chief say. And no dirty words, please. We don't like that sort of thing here.' Ha!" Arthur sneered. "All that was needed was that you two women should start ganging up against me."

It went on and on. Nathalie tried to distract Arthur's malice to herself, but he was not to be side-tracked so easily. Her apparent imperviousness, and her growing tendency to laugh, rather than cry, during his outbursts, made her an increasingly unsatisfactory target. She tried to encourage her sister-in-law by such interjections as: "Pay no attention and he'll stop," or "It's you now, but it'll be my turn tomorrow." Once or twice, Vera tried to make light of some wounding jibe, or ridicule her brother's conduct, but she could not sustain any resilience. She showed injured nonchalance at an affront to decency, rather than passionate revolt against injustice, and her obvious suffering seemed to stimulate Arthur to greater and greater excesses. He became so absurd that it was almost impossible to take him seriously, yet his nagging was as wearing as water dripping on a stone; trivial, but impossible to ignore. He had goaded Vera before, but never beyond the point where she began to lose all reason. This time, it seemed as though he were impelled to go to the utmost limits. From time to time, partly as a result of Nathalie's efforts, he would seem to withdraw a little, and the women breathed more freely, but this was all part of the game; he only allowed escape in order to pounce again. After Nathalie had chattered for a while, and Vera, trying hard to be brave, turned back to her food, he would suddenly spring to the attack once more.

Vera's resistance, which usually dissolved more quickly, cracked this time with a force intensified by accumulated effort. Putting down her knife and fork, she began to bang her fists slowly up and down on the table, chanting hysterically: "Leave me alone! Leave me alone! Leave me alone!"

The look in Arthur's eye, at once hard and elated, was almost mad, but he spoke quietly, saying: "I only wish I could. Still, I notice all this doesn't seem to put you off your food. How lucky you are to have such a constitution!"

The limit had been reached. Vera jumped up, snatched the bread knife, and plunged wildly at Arthur. He made no effort to get out of the way and faced her without even flinching, but Nathalie caught her sister-in-law's hand before it struck. Without saying anything, she took the knife away. Vera sat down, and with her head in her hands, went on sobbing.

"We'll all have some coffee, and then I think it's high time we went to bed," Nathalie said firmly. Arthur, taking a moment or two to recover, exclaimed: "Really, darling, what a bungler you are! A bread knife is no use, it's far too blunt. The carving knives are in the drawer behind me, as you should know."

Vera's sobbing rose to hysteria. With her hands clutching at her hair, she rocked backwards and forwards, wailing loudly. Her flabby puckered face was a devil's mask of distortion, so sickening to watch in its anguish that Nathalie could not bear to look at it, and went over to this wracked creature, trying to calm her with a firm hold on her heaving shoulders. Vera could not be reached, however: she shivered slightly at being touched, and then went on yelling, even louder than before.

"I should keep away, if I were you," Arthur said, "or you'll get your throat slit. She likes you even less than she does me."

"Shut up, you filthy swine! Vera . . . Vera, dear. Don't. . . . Please."

"That I should live to hear you cooing at Vera!"

Somehow Nathalie persuaded her sister-in-law to quieten down, and then to let herself be taken to her bedroom, paying no attention to the wild remarks that kept on coming all the way upstairs, such as: "I can't bear it any longer," and "I shall kill myself."

She boiled some water in the nursery kettle to fill a hot water bottle, and by the time this was done, Vera had undressed and got into bed. She seemed remarkably composed again, and grateful for Nathalie's solicitude.

"You are kind," she said, easing the hot water bottle down to the bottom of the bed with her feet. "I think you're wonderful, the way you handle everything. I really do. I don't know how, or why, you stand it."

"I'm his wife," Nathalie exclaimed rather bitterly. Then seeing Vera flinch, she added quietly: "It's all right if you stand up to him and look as though you meant it."

"I can't help being upset. It's all so horrible."

"Yes, I know, but don't show it. It's fatal to let him see how much he's hurting. He only stops if he thinks it's having no effect."

"But how can he be so cruel! Can't he see how unhappy he makes me?"

"I think he's more unhappy than either of us."

"He couldn't be more unhappy than I am. Nobody could."

"Oh, I don't know. I always feel that whatever one may be going through oneself, there must surely be people who have far more to put up with."

"I haven't even that consolation. Nobody has ever had to bear as much as I have."

This combination of self-pity and egoistic obtuseness struck Nathalie as being so grotesque that she could not reply, and the compassion that she had felt for this desperate and defeated creature now began to thin out a bit. Yet she was touched by the pathos of this woman who might have been an attractive and generous person, but whose passion had been thwarted and turned into some cold, devouring fury.

"Would you like a hot drink?" Nathalie asked.

"No, thank you."

"I'll put some Ovaltine in a thermos for you, and leave it in here, just in case you wake in the night."

"I shan't sleep anyhow."

"Well, I'll give you one of my sleeping pills. I find them a great help. Insomnia can be a habit, and very often if you think you can't sleep, you don't. These break the cycle, as it were, and they leave no after-effects."

She fetched the Nembutal, and Vera swallowed a capsule without hesitation.

"There now," Nathalie fussed. "You won't know a thing until I bring you some tea in the morning."

"You ought to get some sleep as well. You must be exhausted. I don't know how you keep going the way you do."

"There's not much alternative, is there?" Nathalie replied ruefully. "Shall I open the window?"

"Please."

"Anything else I can get you?"

"No, thank you."

"Sure?"

"Quite."

Arthur was still in the kitchen when Nathalie went downstairs again. He looked up as she came in, and it was at once obvious that he was both apprehensive and ashamed. He watched her clear the supper things away in silence, and after a while asked anxiously: "Well? Is she all right?"

"I expect so. She seems quite calm, now, and I've given her a sleeping-pill."

Her voice was toneless, and both her manner and her expression quite non-committal. Arthur went on trying to make her abandon this disinterested neutrality, but she was feeling disgusted with emotion, and continued to do her chores without saying much. Following her into the dining-room, where she was putting the silver away, he said irritably: "She must be mad to go at me like that. Do you think we ought to consult a doctor?"

He had calculated well. Nathalie, now too tired to temper her reaction to Arthur's outrageousness, dropped everything and turned towards him.

"I thought I'd seen everything as far as you're concerned," she said furiously, "but you're beyond belief. Not only do you give an exhibition of the most revolting sadism, but you then try to make out that other people are to blame for the consequences. It's absolutely—— Oh, what's the use! The only surprising thing is that I can still be surprised and appalled at anything you do. But I really think you surpassed even yourself, tonight."

Arthur was curiously soothed by this outburst. It was part of his sickness to crave punishment for his excesses, and he had been unwilling to let this one be passed over so easily. Indignant as she was, Nathalie noticed that he looked relieved, though he answered: "This really is the last straw. For years you've been bellyaching because I've taken Vera's side against you—so you've maintained, that is. But now that there are signs of it being the other way round, you're still not satisfied. What *do* you want?"

With a part of her, Nathalie could not help marvelling at Arthur's ability never to be at a loss. Yet, although his ingenuity was so often devilish, there were times when it seemed difficult to be certain that he was being totally dishonest. "Does he really suppose," she wondered wearily, "that by treating Vera so harshly he can somehow make things better between himself and me?" All the anger had gone out of her voice when she replied: "This is utter nonsense. Leaving your brutality out of it for the moment, why do you have to take sides at all? Why is it that you never seem able to be on good terms with both Vera and myself at the same time?"

"I should have thought you knew all about that by now."

"Yes, I suppose I do. But if you understand it all too, isn't that half the battle won?"

"No, I understand only too well that she's a bitch, and deserves all she gets." Then he exclaimed with exasperation: "Dammit, I thought you'd welcome such signs of emancipation!"

"Not like this. For all her sweetness, I wouldn't trust her further than I can spit, but there's something terribly pathetic about her. Whatever it is she got for selling her soul to the devil doesn't seem to be any good to her. It's bad enough when you bully me, but with her it's inexcusable, somehow. Have you absolutely no pity at all—for other people, that is? Why can't you be strong in a gentle sort of way? Firm, but kind."

"Like Happy Ham, I suppose." Nathalie looked away quickly. "Oh, Christ! You're just as bad as she is, trying to make me into something I'm not, all the time. What chance have I got, when you neither of you will leave me alone. I'm just not allowed to have a personality of my own."

"Would it be thwarting your personality too much if I asked you not to incite people to murder?" she asked gently. "As you yourself pointed out, Vera would make an extremely messy job of it, anyhow."

Arthur smiled too, as he answered: "Am I to be deprived of my only remaining means of self-expression?"

"I'm to be blamed for this, in fact?"

"Of course."

"As with everything else, *d'ailleurs*."

"Naturally! That's what wives are for."

When Nathalie was in her bedroom, and alone at last, she forced herself to go on thinking about the evening. Arthur was a brute, though a wretched one, and Vera was imbecile, though pathetically so, but what about herself? For the first time, she felt thoroughly ashamed of her detachment. It had once seemed creditable to learn to control the emotion of her reactions, and to project an awareness of her own suffering into attempting to understand other people's. She even found a satisfaction in her increasing ability to withstand the myriad assaults of someone cleverer and more determined than herself without cracking. Now, however, this complacency seemed to her so indecent that she feared corruption. It appalled her that she should have got through that evening without being shocked, and could manœuvre a scene of that kind with so little effort. It was one thing to learn to absorb pain and accept evil, but quite another to become basically hardened to them; there could be no virtue in perspicacity and tolerance, if these simply added up to a proud boast about an impotent feat of endurance. "And yet," she wondered, "what else can I do?"

The knifing incident took its place in a long list of disturbances and calamities, and cleared the air for one of the more peaceful phases of life at Walton House.

At the same time, however, it gradually became obvious that Nathalie's hours of work were becoming far more erratic than previously. Her schedules could not always be known beforehand, and it happened more than once that she had to break a luncheon appointment with Arthur, or return from Oxford without him. Occasionally, she was able to take the afternoon off, but equally often, she was kept late at a photographer's session, or modelling in a show.

At first, this did not seem to matter. It was something new, and therefore rather exciting for all of them. Besides, there was more money coming into the family. Then, as Nathalie became more successful there was more work, and her absences from home prolonged. Her own appearance went on improving so that she was now not only attractive, but strikingly so. Her hair had been cut short, which showed up her long neck, and the shape and set of her head. She now used more make-up than before, but it was applied effectively, and with skill; and for the first time in her life, she had begun to dress elegantly.

"How splendid that she should be doing so well," Vera exclaimed one evening, looking at a photograph in *Vogue* of Nathalie in a ball-dress. She had a genuine admiration for success of any kind, but since in this case there were complicating factors, she added: "Who would have thought it was the same girl?"

"The same girl as what?" Arthur asked, rather sharply.

"As the one we first knew." She could not bring herself to say "As the one you married."

"Is there a sinister implication in that remark?"

"Of course not," Vera replied in her most soothing voice. "I merely said she had changed. A lot of people do, after all."

"You don't—ever." Having said this, Arthur smiled. He was still on his good behaviour to make up for his quarrel with her, and Vera chose to take the remark as a compliment.

"Perhaps that's because my feelings for you never change," she said, smiling affectionately.

"In spite of everything?"

"In spite of everything."

They were sitting in the drawing-room, drinking sherry before dinner; even Arthur, who had not touched gin for nearly a month. Nathalie was working late, and was not expected home before the last bus got in at eleven o'clock. In spite of the blazing log fire, the lights of the room were soft.

"What is she doing this evening?" Vera asked after a while.

"Who is she?" Her assumption of this unspoken, but most real, contact in their trains of thought annoyed Arthur.

"You know I mean Nathalie."

"Well say so, then. She's modelling summer playsuits for overseas buyers."

"At this time of the year?"

"Apparently they have to get their orders in months before the appropriate season."

"Where is the show?"

"It's not a show, only a private viewing in the Oxford Town Hall."

They watched the glow of the fire for a while, and then Vera said: "It's a great compliment to Martine Modes that overseas buyers should come all the way down to Oxford for their models. I should have thought they had wholesale houses enough to choose from in London."

"It's connected with a London firm, I understand. Nathalie did tell me the name, but I can't remember it at the moment."

"Oh, I see."

Again Vera paused for a while, before saying: "It must be tiring for them to have to work as late as this, but I suppose they can all go on to a late supper somewhere."

"Talking about late suppers, what about ours? I'm hungry."

Vera jumped up immediately. "Come, give me a hand with the trolley, then. I thought we'd have it here, by the fire."

"What a good idea. That will be nice." Arthur stood up too, and they went out together.

They had cleared the dinner things away and were just beginning a game of cribbage when Nathalie came in, almost an hour before they had expected her. She was a little tired, but her accentuated pallor suited her, and her eyes looked huge and bright. Arthur was delighted to see her, and welcomed her cordially.

"Come and sit by the fire. You look cold," he said, pushing his chair round for her.

"I'm all right now," she answered, sitting down, "but it was fiendish trying to look happy in beach wear in this weather. You cannot imagine how cold and draughty that Town Hall can be."

"Lots of orders?" Arthur asked.

"We'll know in the morning, after Martine has been in cahoots with Head Office."

"Have you had anything to eat this evening?"

"Yes, food was on the house tonight." She stretched her legs out and sat back, saying: "Oh goodness, this is nice."

Vera noticed how compact and smooth she looked in the firelight, and said: "You're back earlier than we expected. Have they put on another bus?"

"No, I got a lift. One of the buyers is staying with friends in Henley, and offered to drop me on the way."

"This is hardly on the way to Henley from Oxford."

"I suppose it isn't, really. Still, you know what these Americans are. They think nothing of driving a hundred miles for a cocktail, and England seems to them pocket-size in any case."

"Well, if you'll excuse me, I think I'll go to bed," Vera said abruptly. She wished Nathalie good night and turned to leave the room. As Arthur held the door open for her, he said: "I'll say good night now, as you may be asleep by the time we come up."

"I shall be reading for a while."

"Even so, I'll say good night now."

"All right."

"Good night, old thing. Sleep well."

"I'll try to." She paused to smile, and went upstairs.

Sitting near the now evenly glowing fire, Arthur and Nathalie talked quietly about the respective ways they had spent their day. Arthur told her about the party given for an eminent visitor who had just been given an honorary degree, and made her laugh with his quick sizing up of every idiosyncrasy in the contrast between the worldly men of public affairs and the dedicated pedants of learning. "The visitor somehow didn't go down with a swing," he smiled. "Perhaps that was because he referred to the hors d'œuvres as 'horse ovaries', and maintained that Jesus Christ would never have got past the MacMahon Act. It's hard to realise how prim dons can be, at times."

When Nathalie talked, he watched her intently. It seemed incredible to him that such a lovely creature was his wife, and should continue to be so. It also amazed him how clear-headed and competent she had become. Vera had been quite right in saying she had changed. He began to feel a vague uneasiness, and wondered how much she had changed in less obvious ways, and what might be going on that he did not even suspect?

"Where did you say you had dinner?" he asked suddenly.

"Dinner?" She had to make an effort to remember, as it was a long time since she had eaten anything, but her hesitation increased Arthur's misgivings. "Oh, we had something before the show at the office. It was a glorified snack, really, but all rather grand, and quite adequate."

"Who is 'we' exactly?"

"The girls, and one or two of the buyers who are old friends of Martine's."

"Including the American?"

"The American? Oh, the one who gave me a lift, d'you mean? No, I don't think he was there. . . . No, he wasn't."

"You don't seem very sure."

She saw that Arthur was working himself up into "one of his moods" as Vera would have put it, and answered quietly: "There was a good deal of coming and going. I had to think for a moment."

"Think what you had said already, so you could stick to your story?"

Nathalie became exasperated. "For Heaven's sake don't start nagging now," she said. "This is so cosy."

"I won't nag, but you may as well realise that I'm not quite such a fool as you think." Then he added with a superior smile: "I appreciate the lengths you go to to make your stories convincing, but you'll have to do better than that."

"Better than what? Are you maintaining I've made it all up about this evening? . . . Are you?"

Arthur had not meant to let things go as far as this. He had merely wanted to throw in a warning dart of disquietude without committing himself, but Nathalie had a habit of never letting anything pass. However, there was no turning back now, so he decided he might as well make a job of it.

"I don't believe there was any show tonight," he said. "In fact, I have reason to believe that you had a *tête-à-tête* dinner with somebody—probably that American." He did not really believe this, but felt that if he confronted her with a definite accusation, he might trap her into giving something away.

Nathalie answered coldly, "Why don't you ring up Martine and ask her, then?"

"And make a fool of you? I know the meaning of loyalty, even if some people don't. Besides, she's obviously in the plot too. You hard-bitten career women have to stick together." His indignation grew, and fanned his suspicions and jealousy until he began to think that she really must be hiding something. "Anyhow," he said at last, "do you expect me to believe that buyers would come all the way to a potty little firm in Oxford, when there are first-class wholesalers galore in London? It doesn't make sense."

Nathalie jumped up and put her hands on Arthur's shoulders. "Darling, stop this," she said firmly. "Stop it at once. I'll make a deal with you. This evening is to be reported minutely in the *Oxford Mail*, with photographs, full names, and all the details. If you still don't believe me after next Friday, we can open up this discussion again. How's that, now?"

Without looking at her, Arthur answered coldly: "I never bargain."

"Oh, don't be so pompous!" Nathalie, now tense with apprehension again, sat upright, and Arthur jumped up, exclaiming angrily:

"Don't you dare talk to me like that!"

"Not only pompous, but absurdly childish as well."

The defiance he had once longed to find in her, together with her contempt, which he found unbearable, now unbalanced him completely. His eyes growing even smaller and harder with hatred, he lifted an arm, and moved as though to strike her. Without even twitching, she glared at him and said: "If you so much as lay one finger on me, I'll leave you tomorrow. This time, I mean it."

She did, and he knew it. He backed away again without touching her, and said: "So that's it. That 'American' as you call him, is in fact Happy Ham, isn't he? Is he prepared to risk the scandal now, do you think?"

"And don't start that again, either. You know quite well that Felix was married over a year ago. Since his wife is expecting a baby and he hasn't set foot in this country for over two years, I think you'd now have some difficulty in finding any solicitor who'd take on your case."

Arthur looked surprised, and said: "You have begun to learn about life, haven't you? But please do leave just the same, if that's how you feel. Elizabeth will be quite happy. In fact, at her age, she'll soon forget you, and just as well, too. It can't be much of an example for her to have a mother with so many suspicious—er—'outside interests'."

Nathalie suddenly felt inordinately tired, and her defiance vanished. All she could say was: "You make me sick! I'm going to bed. Good night." Without looking at him, she went towards the door, and then heard him say: "You must admit I have every reason to be suspicious. It's most unlikely that anybody as passionate as you could live without sex, and as you don't get it from me, you must get it from someone."

Knowing, even then, that she should have paid no attention, yet she stopped and turned towards him again. The demands of the flesh had not been quietened without a struggle, and this reminder of a recurring sense of futility now goaded her into saying slowly and angrily: "I've never been unfaithful to you, and I haven't got a lover. If you can't, or won't, take my word for it, there's nothing I can do to prove it."

"There is one way," he said, and suddenly he was by her side. She would have left the room then, if he had not put out his hands to stop her. "Sleep with me tonight," he said. "Then I'll know there's no one else."

"Surely, according to your idea of women, that would prove nothing."

"Oh, yes it would, even with you. I'd know straight away."

"Has it occurred to you that too little enthusiasm might simply show that I don't want you?"

"Will you sleep with me, or won't you?"

"No, I will not!" Ever since the loss of her baby, the idea of physical contact with him had revolted her.

"That proves your guilt, then."

Nathalie's voice rose in exasperation.

"It merely proves that I don't want to sleep with you. The only point would be either as an expression of mutual love, or in order to have children, and we've stopped pretending about either of those."

"And what about my rights as a husband?"

"Your rights as a husband, indeed!" she fumed. "How dare you treat me like one of your tarts!"

"You're my wife and I want you. I have a right to."

He put his arms around her and tried to kiss her, but she recoiled with such obvious and violent revulsion that he was taken aback. At first, he looked surprised, and then quite disarmed. His moments of genuine emotion were so rare, so incongruous and so strangely defenceless, that they were startling. He was completely pathetic as he said: "Am I really so repulsive?"

He was indeed. With detachment, she observed his hair, now lank and straggly; his bloodshot eyes, seeming too close together; his sagging skin, that looked florid and pock-marked. Nothing about him touched her any more, but realising that she had wounded him at the source of his manhood, she opened her arms to him.

Later, when Arthur was asleep, Nathalie realised that the person who lay beside her was now a complete stranger. To him, physical conquest was not an expression of love, nor even a search for it, but a means of revenge. With his grudge against the world in general and his dissatisfaction with himself in particular, love had become synonymous to him with hostility; he saw it as a battle-ground for domination, and pleasure as an ultimate means of degradation. During their brief summer of expectation, it had seemed, for a short while, as though this eternal combat between man and woman might be replaced by a tolerant understanding that could have strengthened both of them, not only in their unity, but also individually. They had, in the past, shared physical ecstasy without ever becoming really intimate, yet many moments had given them hope of something deeper. Now, she knew that nothing could ever help them to break through the defences and hypocrisies that the previous years had intensified, instead of diminishing.

Nathalie longed for Arthur to return to his room, so that she could be free of pretence for a few hours, but he was sleeping heavily. Suddenly, the bed, which no longer seemed her own, became intolerably frowsty; getting up, she put on her dressing-gown and slippers and went downstairs. She drew back the drawing-room curtains, and in spite of the cold, leant far out into the clean air of the winter's night.

The loneliness which had almost stifled Nathalie upstairs now became a sharp and penetrating pain. It seemed to her fantastic that copulation should be referred to as "intimacy"; it could, as she knew, be the sweetest and most profound expression of closeness, but she felt that nothing in the world brought on a more terrible sense of solitude than this kind of physical contact with someone who was otherwise remote. Then, to her acute unhappiness was added self-disgust, for reluctant as she had been in her first moments of proximity with Arthur, the animal in her was still powerful enough to have made the experience eventually not only tolerable, but even physically satisfying. This seemed to her a betrayal of some sort. It was the ultimate example of her ability to exist on a dual level of consciousness, for one part of her had remained sadly detached, watching another self writhing with pleasure. Even her awareness now seemed to her reprehensible, a symptom of yet another intensification of her isolation and her loss of innocence. Innocence reaches out and embraces without question or self-consciousness, giving without thought, and receiving, rather than taking. In the aware, ignorance may take the place of innocence, and it has a hunger of its own, a hunger that seems insatiable.

Breathing deeply of the purifying air, Nathalie no longer felt surrounded by enemies, but it was from a deep and nauseating despair that she prayed: "Dear God, what weak and complex creatures we are. Help us. Help us out of our hells of loneliness. Help me. Help me to become all of one piece, and at peace with You. Help me to know what I should do, and from Your grace, grant me the courage to do it."

That evening marked the beginning of a new phase of jealousy in Arthur. He had known jealousy all his life in a multitude of ways, direct and indirect. As far as Nathalie was concerned, ever since the beginning of their marriage he had resented her background, her innocence, the people who were fond of her, and even her womanhood. Now, as well as this, he became jealous of what she herself might be doing or feeling. Previously, he had always known he controlled her at heart, whatever he pretended to the contrary. Now, however, he just did not know what was going on, and could not even check or control Nathalie's movements. She always had plausible reasons for being late, or going away, but he often wondered whether they were true, or if she was making a fool of him by telling lies. His resentment grew all the more vigorous because he made no attempt to counteract it. Instead of letting reason come to his aid, he was convinced he had every right to feel as he did. The more sorry he felt for himself and his position, the more worried he became; and the more he worried, the more injured he felt. He questioned all her appointments, every business or social contact she made, even her means of transport. Previously, he had often rifled her desk to look at her private papers. Now he opened her letters before she did, and sometimes tore them up before she herself had read them. Occasionally, he told fantastic lies to keep her at home and stop her going to work. It was a tribute to his histrionic skill that, in spite of everything Nathalie knew about him, he got away with it the first time. The police had rung up, he said, about a crime that had been committed during the night. He could not tell her now what had happened; it was too appalling, and he had given his word to the inspector. She would find out soon enough, however, and he hoped her stomach would be strong enough to take it. The detective wanted to question everybody in the neighbourhood, and she was not to leave the house until he said so. It took her until lunchtime to find out that this was a hoax. The second time, he hid Elizabeth, saying she had had an accident, and had been rushed off to hospital. Even after Nathalie knew this to be untrue, she continued to worry. There was a curious compulsion about Arthur's acting, and it was almost impossible not to be dragged into his world, even when the voice of reason could be heard condemning all along.

Arthur's jealousy was not precise enough to be attributed to any one factor. He did not really fear, as he maintained, that Nathalie had lovers, or that she was salting away money in secret in order to leave him; that she made fun of him to people he did not know, or even that others were developing aspects of her personality that he had never discovered. Nor did he resent, to any great extent, having lost a love that he had never really wanted. It was the loss of his power over this particular human being that he could not accept. People had often been thrown out of his life, and some had even walked out of it of their own accord. In all these cases, however, physical absence had not affected his importance; had he chosen to, he could still have swooped down on his victims, confident of being, if not adored, at least obeyed. This situation was in reverse, however, for here was somebody continuing to live within his orbit, yet no longer subject to his influence. Worse than that, this once diffident nonentity had not only survived all that he could do, but had then blossomed into a fascinating and self-sufficient person.

Arthur began to drink heavily again, and his dislike of everybody was now scarcely veiled. The only person he found tolerable, in fact, was Vera, for she remained calm and wise during those difficult weeks. Vera's vitality and confidence always increased immeasurably when things were difficult between Arthur and Nathalie, and feeling that her brother needed reassuring, she set about doing this in her own way. She had an animal link with him which enabled her to tell, in spite of her obtuseness, what worried him specifically. When Nathalie was late, or otherwise unaccountable for, she would say: "She's so attractive now that people are bound to want to take her out, but I'm sure she only plays up to admiration because it's good for business," or "I'm certain we can trust her, you know, even though she was brought up with no moral sense, and made some bad mistakes when she was young." Arthur pretended to ignore these remarks, but they left their mark, and meanwhile, his appearances at his job became more and more obviously intermittent. At first, he would simply take a day off now and then, saying that he had a touch of 'flu, or work that could more easily be done at home. Then he would spend the day without unwelcome interruptions, reading a little, sleeping a certain amount, and drinking a lot.

When Vera began to worry and nag about his being away from the office so often, he developed a different means of escape, and idled away the day in Oxford, instead of at home. He would stay in one pub or another until it closed, and then go to sleep in a cinema, or an armchair in the Randolph Hotel lounge. In the afternoon, he might stroll in a college garden, or the Parks, or spend an hour or so in Blackwell's. Occasionally, he would drop in for a gossip with a colleague, but his contact with people was now more difficult than ever, and all these occupations were merely ways of filling in time until the pubs opened again.

Nathalie met Arthur whenever she could, and as often as possible they returned home together, but one evening, towards the end of February, she could not find him anywhere. Although he had come into Oxford with her that morning, he was not at the Mitre at five-thirty, where they had arranged to meet. She waited until after six, and then did the rounds of his favourite haunts, but he had left no messages anywhere. Assuming that he must have gone home earlier, she decided to catch the seven o'clock bus. It neither surprised nor hurt her that he should be so casual with her; she was far too used to his ways even to wonder why he had not left a message with Martine. She did not worry either, supposing that he would either be at "The Traveller's Rest" or already back home.

Arthur was not at "The Traveller's Rest", but Nathalie was so tired that she decided to wait there a few minutes before going on. Strangely enough, the saloon bar was empty except for her, and she welcomed the chance of a short rest in such quiet surroundings.

"What'll it be?" Bill asked her. "Spot of Jerry's Frontier, as per?"

"I don't really feel like sherry tonight. It's rather liverish, and I've got a slight headache. What do you recommend? I'm whacked, but I don't like spirits. Difficult customer, in fact."

Bill looked at her with mock solemnity, and said: "Leave it to me. Shot of bubbly for you. Just the job. It'll set you up so's nobody can get you down."

He disappeared into the cellar, and Nathalie had to wait until he came back before protesting: "That sounds all very fine, but I don't know what it will do to the family finances if you get me into the habit of drinking champagne."

"This is on the house."

She understood the combined friendship and chivalry of Bill's gesture, and accepted it gratefully.

"There," he said, as he poured himself a glass as well. "It's quite cold enough from being in that perishing cellar, but I'll put what's left on the ice. Now drink up. There's a good girl."

They silently toasted each other, and by the time she had

drunk even half the contents of her glass, she began to revive.

"I've never thanked you properly for being so sweet, the time you helped me with Arthur," she said.

"That was on the house, too. Corker's the name, you know."

"You're a jolly corking Corker, if you ask me."

"Look, if ever you're in a jam with him—at the house, or anywhere else I can reach you—just whistle, will you?"

"That's terribly nice of you, but I really don't see why you should bother."

"Don't like to see people being pushed around, that's all. Never have done." He refilled her glass, and she protested: "Hey! No family can afford more than one serious drinker, you know."

"Do you good. Just what you need."

"I can't take much liquor at the best of times, and when I'm tired, it's risky for me to touch it at all. It won't do if *I* start coming in glassy-eyed and hiccoughing."

Bill looked at her for a moment, and then asked: "Why do you put up with it?"

The wine was beginning to make Nathalie take a light-headed view of things, but suddenly she became clam-like with caution. It was useless to deny anything in front of Bill, who had now been involved on the inside of her private life, but she said non-committally: "One man's meat, and all that."

"You're a jolly attractive girl—as pigeons go, that is—and there's nothing that I can see to stop you having a whale of a time, if only you'd cut loose."

Nathalie diverted Bill's meaning by explaining to him how fully occupied her time was, these days. He had his own theories, however.

"Truth is, women just revel in filth," he said. "The more refined they seem, the lower they like to sink."

"It's not really what you'd call fun, Corky."

"I've seen it again and again. Oh, I could tell you a thing or two."

"Maybe that's true for women who can't enjoy their fun in any other way, but I'm rather straightforward in that sense."

"I've seen you come in here with bruises and black-eyes, and yet smiling up at him so sweetly. No woman would put up with that unless she liked it. Or perhaps you think you can reform him? But that man's a shocker in any language. You're wasting yourself for nothing. No good can come of it. You mark my words."

Nathalie had finished her second glass of champagne by then and felt benign and inspired. Keepers of public houses seemed to her to have the same combination of sympathy and impersonality as priests and doctors, and wine always made her feel expansive.

"I'm in love with someone else," she said suddenly, and a little too loudly. "What helps me most to keep going is feeling that I'm earning his respect, and even his admiration by not giving in. At least, that's how it was at first. Now, it's something more than that. I've got a touch of religious mania as well, trying to serve God, to cancel out a fraction of the debt of sin in the world by a small contribution in sacrifice and suffering. I'd never have believed it possible, but it has a curious way of increasing all kinds of useful things, such as understanding and patience—even love. I can't help feeling that if I can break just one vicious circle, stop the sins of the fathers being visited on to the sons, just once, it's worth while. It's a big 'if', but I suppose there's still enough hope to weigh the scales on to the side of 'I hang on'. Or perhaps it's just that I'm too much of a coward to quit. You know, even if I left him, I feel I'd never really be rid of him. Or is it just the problem of evil that I'll never again be able to forget, or ignore?"

She was hardly aware of Bill now, and followed her own thoughts. He, however, ignored what he called her 'fancy talk', and tried to get back to essentials by asking: "Who's this other bloke? Any good?"

"He's an absolute corker. I've been in love with him ever since I was fifteen—on and off, anyhow. Isn't that an extraordinary thought?"

"Why did you marry Arthur, then?"

"That was during one of the off periods."

"I suppose he's married?"

"He is now."

"The old story, in fact."

"What on earth do you mean by 'the old story'?"

"Number of chaps I've seen who want to have their cake and eat it! A bloke may have a good home, a decent wife and nice kids, but no, that's not enough. He has to go and muck things up for himself, his family and some perfectly decent girl, as likely as not, with this eternal triangle nonsense. I know men. We're beasts."

"Well, it's not quite like that with Felix."

"It never is. It's always different when it happens to you.

Number of times I've had a girl weeping on my shoulder—always the corker, as you know—because some cad won't do the decent thing by her, and yet won't let her go."

"I meant that he doesn't interfere with my life in that sense for the simple reason that I never see him, or even write to him. We parted, as they say, several years ago, and since then we've only met once, when he was over here for a few days, two years ago."

"Where is he now?"

"He lives in America."

"Well, there's not much he can do to you from across the Atlantic! What on earth do you get out of it?"

What did she get out of it? Nathalie wondered, yet knowing that the pattern of her existence was meaningless without Felix. In the past, it was through him that she had first awakened to beauty and ecstasy, to a knowledge of the depths and dimensions of life, to the joys of discovery and sharing. In the present, his tenderness and respect had lifted her out of hopeless despair, and propelled her once more towards a faith in love. Even when the future must now be without him, yet his very existence, somewhere in the world, was an assurance that love was the core of reality and stronger than fear, more important than caution, truer than worldliness. Even the pain and misery she had known because of him were trivial, compared to everything else he had given her; all the worlds of light and delight, warmth and wonder, colour and contrast, melody and movement. In her love for Felix, universe transcended universe until the sight of God Himself seemed nearer.

Nathalie wondered how to convey all this to someone like Bill Corker, and finally said: "You wouldn't understand." Then, in order to cover up what might be taken as a snub, she added: "It sort of gets sublimated into other things."

"Well, what about sublimating some more of the old widow?"

Bill refilled their glasses for the third time, while Nathalie exclaimed: "I'm stinking already."

"It'll sober you up, then . . . 'sublimated', indeed! The trouble with you, of course, is that you're a Slav. Why didn't I think of that before? A barmy Slav! There was a White Russian girl I used to sleep with in Hong Kong, the most explosive armful I've ever had to do with. Christ, what a woman! Used to yell the house down every time I laid her. She had something, that girl, I must admit, but it gave me the willies. She cried when she was happy, and laughed when she was on the verge of suicide—which she was several times, while she knew me. After I was through with her, I said to myself: 'No more Slavs for you, Billy-boy.'" Nathalie was laughing wildly, and he added: "It wasn't a bit funny, I can tell you."

"It's you who make me laugh," she managed to say.

"What did I tell you? Here you are, with your life as mucked up as can be, and all you can do is laugh!"

Nathalie controlled herself enough to ask: "Would you rather I was in floods of tears, then?"

"You Slavs!" Bill exclaimed, and then added with great kindness: "I'd like to see you have a bit of fun, though. You deserve it. You're a nice girl."

"Is that what's the matter with me, do you suppose? But I always thought nice girls were a sort of combination of heartiness and primness—Betjeman tennis girls with a partiality for potted culture. Not me at all, I sincerely hope."

"Those are good girls. A nice girl is something quite different."

"Well, you're a corker anyhow, Bill. Now I must go home. Home! Home! I wonder if I shall ever know what that word means? Talking of 'bill', how much does he owe you?"

"That's no concern of yours."

"It is, you know."

"No woman should have to worry about her husband's debts."

"I dare say, but then things are what they are, and not what we like to pretend. Parents don't automatically love their children better than themselves, brothers and sisters don't necessarily love each other at all, and husbands don't always take care of their wives, or wives respect their husbands. Couldn't you dilute the gin a bit? Or even refuse to give him any?"

"And lose my best customer? He'd only go somewhere else to get it, and that would make it more difficult to get him home again afterwards."

"I suppose so. Good night, Corky. You're a dear, and thanks for the medicine."

She went out into the night, and groped her way through the dark and the cold. When she finally reached the wooden door in the garden wall, the squeak it made while opening was so familiar that, for a moment, the present chilliness of misery and apprehension seemed like a nightmare. "Surely," she thought, "when I'm through the wall, the house will again be glowing with light, warm with cosiness, and alive with voices and laughter. When the front door is opened, old Anna (Olga's German parlour-maid, who had died at the beginning of the war) will take my coat, and fuss because I'm cold. There'll be a faint, but distinct smell of delicious cooking, low and furry voices droning behind doors, and the bustle of people upstairs, getting ready for dinner. When I open the door of the main sitting-room, an enormous fire will be burning in the grate, and the room will be full of friends. . . ."

Even before reaching the house, however, Nathalie knew that she was dreaming of ghosts, and that the nightmare was the reality. Except for a light in the kitchen, the house was black and silent. The curtains of the drawing-room windows had not been drawn, and even though it was extremely dark, she could just see the dead outlines of furniture inside. Letting herself into the cold house, she went straight to the kitchen, the only heated room. Vera was having her supper, and said sombrely: "I waited until after nine."

"I am sorry I'm so late, I got kept today and missed Arthur. Is he back?"

"He's upstairs," Vera said, looking rather sulky.

"Is he very tired?" Nathalie felt annoyed with both Vera and herself because with anybody else she would not have hesitated to say: "Is he stinking again?"

"I have no means of telling. He went straight upstairs without speaking to me."

They had dinner, and half an hour later, Nathalie said: "I'll take Arthur some soup. He ought to eat something."

"If he wants food, he should come down for it. This is just encouraging him."

Nathalie said nothing, and merely heated up the soup before taking it upstairs.

Arthur's bedroom was dark, but she could just see him lying on the bed. Putting the bowl of soup down on the tallboy, she lit the bedside lamp, drew the curtains, and then went and sat beside him. He was not really asleep, and opened his eyes when she said: "I thought you might like some soup."

"Mm . . . lovely." He propped himself up on one elbow and managed to take a few mouthfuls, though his hands were trembling badly. "I was just having a little snooze," he added.

"Better now?"

"Much. I've got a lot of thinking to do, so I thought I'd better fortify myself a little." He took some more soup, and then propped himself into a sitting position, now fully awake. "There comes a time in every man's life when fate intervenes, and helps him to take a step which he might not otherwise be able to decide on for himself."

This pompous lucidity was sinister, and Nathalie became fearful of what he would say next. He was silent, so she prompted him with: "Tell me more."

"It seems that my job has now been found to be redundant, so my services are no longer required at the college."

"Well, that certainly is a challenge, I must say."

Arthur's manner suddenly became unguarded, and he took a letter from his pocket, handing it to Nathalie and saying: "They did warn me this might happen, but I never thought they were serious. Oxford's no longer what it was, if it can't tolerate drunks." He smiled, but was obviously frightened, and seeking Nathalie's reassurance. The most pathetic aspect of his drinking was that Arthur himself could not take it seriously, and in spite of the social problem named "the evils of drink", he saw himself as belonging to a distinguished minority. Now, however, the outside world refused to play up to his act, and he lost the last shred of his self-respect in passing through the transition from heavy drinker to drunkard. This fact impressed him with unusual sharpness.

As he sobered up, the fear that Arthur had managed to dismiss all day began to take hold of him, and fear, like love, feeds on itself, and spreads far beyond its own origin. He was afraid of the future, of financial difficulties, of himself, of public opinion and of what Vera would say. The only thing he was not afraid of was Nathalie, for regardless of all the insults, accusations, suspicions and jealousies that he had proclaimed, even those of the previous weeks, Arthur knew that she was on his side. At that moment, he wanted her to take complete charge of his life, to control everything he said or did, and take all responsibility off his shoulders. He relied on her to know what was best, and swore that he would abide by whatever she decided.

"Darling, it would be no good," she protested. "You may feel like that now, but it's not what you really want. You have far too much character to let anyone direct your life."

"No, I haven't. Please tell me what to do, and do it for me."

"If I so much as tried, you'd start kicking me for it." Then, at the same time as he said it, she added: "That's-what-wives-are-for," and they both laughed.

"No, to be serious, now——" she began again, but he interrupted her.

"I don't want to be serious, I want to lead an aimless, fruitless, hopeless and thoroughly enjoyable life, but nobody will let me."

"You're a big boy now, you know."

"No, I am not. I'm a frightened little boy who doesn't know what's good for him, and prefers it that way."

"All right then, have the courage of your convictions. I'm growing up fast, even if you're not, and I shan't let Vera stop you doing anything you want this time. Really."

"Can I drink myself to death, then?" he smiled.

"As long as you're not sick on the carpet too often."

"Will you drink with me?"

"No."

"There you are, you see! That's all the encouragement *I* get!"

They talked for a long time, sometimes chaffing, at times more seriously. Arthur at last began to feel better.

"Something you must remember," Nathalie pointed out, "is how young you are, even in years. After all, you're not yet thirty-five. Lots of people change their careers much older than that. You've got years and years ahead of you, still."

"Don't rub it in," he groaned. "The trouble is that I don't want a career. I've absolutely no ambition left, now."

"Damn it, you must do something! And not just because we need the money."

"But that seems to me the only possible inducement to work, for someone who much prefers being idle."

"Oh, Lord! Have I taught you nothing?"

"Quite a lot actually, though probably not what you meant me to learn."

His defeatism became less real and more and more an affectation, however. She would not allow him to seek solace in despair, or in despising those who did not appreciate him sufficiently, but sought rather to make firm his faith in himself. She wanted him to believe that his intelligence, his experience and especially his tremendous vitality still existed, and were only waiting to be put into use. Even his looks would not desert him, she maintained, if only he would take himself in hand. Eventually, he was confident that after a good night's rest, a new and promising phase in his life would begin. Then he heard Vera coming upstairs.

"What am I to do?" he panicked. "What shall I tell her?"

"Tell her that you've lost your job. Why not?"

"Don't be silly! I can't face up to one of her scenes now."

"There won't be one if you stop looking so apprehensive."

"I think I'll leave it till the morning. It would be more considerate not to worry her at this time of night."

"Won't she be waiting to say good night?"

"Why should she expect me to say good night, as though I were still a small boy. I won't be pushed around like that!"

"All right, then, don't go."

"But you don't know what reprisals she takes if I don't."

"I have a pretty shrewd idea."

It was obvious that Arthur would be unable to relax or rest until he had faced Vera. He finally agreed to do this, provided Nathalie waited in his room until he returned. He was not away for long, and came back smiling and jaunty.

"There," he said, getting under the eiderdown again. "Now I feel quite a man."

"It was all right, then?"

"Money for jam. She couldn't have been sweeter. I think she regarded my Oxford period as an unfortunate interlude, and seems to think I'm doing a public service by putting myself up for employment again."

"Did she say she was sure it was all for the best?"

"How did you know?"

"I've noticed that Vera trusts fate no more than she would a capricious woman, but that whenever it strikes powerfully, she becomes a sentimental philosopher. It's all part of her respect for success."

Arthur's morale did not remain consistently at this optimistic level. During the weeks that followed, he would vacillate from one attitude to another, unable to make any definite decision. Sometimes he was overawed at what had happened, conscious of himself as a man who had ruined everything with drink. At other times, he posed as an outcast with an understanding of life too deep to allow of a proper adjustment to daily existence. Either of those extremes involved a number of variations, and in all these roles he surrounded himself with a slight air of mystery. Only with Nathalie did he at first occasionally relax, but gradually, his fantasy worlds became so real to him that he was more and more difficult to communicate with in any way. He went through the motions of trying to get another job, but with neither enthusiasm nor conviction. Being on the books of the University Appointments' Board, he was given an interview from time to time. When he failed in these, he suffered momentary pangs of panic and self-pity, but he was never really surprised. Prospective employers were either discouraged by his reluctance to meet them halfway, or disgruntled by his arrogant attempts to make terms with them, and he always fell back on to feeling that if fate struck with sufficient power, and indicated an opening to him unmistakably, he would take it. Short of that, however, he saw no reason for putting himself out. Nathalie found him relatively easy to handle now, as he was usually docile, and no longer made scenes, but Vera became more and more disagreeable. She would complain that although Arthur was amiable and acquiescent, he hardly needed her (by which she meant that he did not cosset her when she sulked); that she suspected he was often "not himself" (by which she meant that he was drinking again); and that he no longer seemed to be "interested in anything" (by which she meant that he did not nag much at his wife). It generally happened that when Arthur and Nathalie were not in an obvious state of open warfare, Vera became acutely resentful, and this period was no exception. This time, however, her instinctively activating discontent became a catalyst in a series of chain reactions that she could not have foreseen.

Nathalie was to be sent to Paris on a job, and the Baroness had written to invite both her and Arthur to stay with her during this four-day period. He declined to go, however, saying he had an important interview at just that time and could not take the risk of missing, or even changing it. In fact, he simply could not be bothered to go away, and made the most plausible excuse that occurred to him. It made him tired just to think of the effort of packing, wearing tidy clothes, responding to new environments and people, and above all, organising his supply of gin so that it would not fail him. It was all too much trouble for nothing.

Nathalie went through the motions of trying to persuade him to come, too, even insisting that the change would do him good, but when he continually refused, she took care not to show her relief. Alone in her bedroom afterwards, however, she suddenly felt dizzy with excitement, and wondered if she might even be able to prolong her absence to a whole week. She thought with delight about seeing Paris again, and Olga's house there, and the friends she would get in touch with for the first time for years. Yet, in spite of her joy, she was harried by a small sense of guilt which seemed to her absurd. "Why on earth shouldn't I go away for a few days?" she said to herself. "It's part of my job, Arthur doesn't seem to mind, and Elizabeth will be all right, so what's the matter with me? Or has Vera got something to do with this? She didn't seem at all pleased at the idea of my going."

Vera was certainly displaying a concern that was far from pleasure. As soon as Nathalie left her alone with Arthur, she turned to him and said bitterly: "Is this wise, do you think?"

"What on earth are you talking about?" Arthur was irritable, but not aggressive.

"Well, won't she be exposing herself unnecessarily? I mean, in that sort of work, and in Paris. . . . Her judgment isn't always very reliable, and it would be a pity if she ran into any trouble."

"I don't suppose she'll come to much harm. She knows Paris like the back of her hand. She used to live there, after all."

His sister's opposition to this scheme made him ready not only to tolerate it, but to champion it as well. Vera had her trump card, however, and she played it then, quietly and gently, by saying: "Is Mr. Hamilton still there?"

"According to the papers, the conference he's been attending broke down over a fortnight ago."

"Of course it did. How stupid of me. He must be back in America by this time."

"What are you getting at?" Arthur roared, with a vigour that had become rare to him during the previous weeks.

"I merely wondered if he would still be there. After all, he is an old friend, and it would have been inevitable for them to meet if he were."

"Are you trying to make out that my wife has an assignment in Paris with Felix Hamilton?"

"No, no, of course not. Besides, the Baroness will be there, too."

This was hardly reassuring, but then it was not meant to be. In any case, Vera had said enough. She could now afford to relax and watch matters take their inevitable course.

At first, Arthur sulked. Then he worried, became excessively irritable, and drank more than he had done for some time. Finally, he blew up with a noise and heat, unprecedented even in that house. He was making up for lost time as far as abusiveness was concerned, but Nathalie wanted so much to go to Paris that this time she became utterly obstinate and simply went on packing while Arthur commanded her not to leave the house, and threatened that if she defied his authority, she would regret it for the rest of her life. It would have been easy for her to point out that if he did anything too violent or drastic, he might endanger the livelihood of them all, but even at that moment, she was unable to take such a mean advantage. Nathalie's anger merely increased in fact, as she realised how much she was faltering; she cursed herself for lacking the kind of hardness that would have enabled her to put Vera in her place, and disregard the anguish beneath all Arthur's bombast. Finally, she decided not to go, and breaking down, quite agonised with frustration, she sobbed and sobbed.

Arthur was a little taken aback, for this was no ordinary weeping, and he had never seen her cry like that before. She was not actually hysterical, so that he did not feel he should resort to slapping her, or pouring cold water on to her head, but she went on sobbing so pitifully and wholeheartedly that it almost touched him. Finally, he left her alone, and it was then that Vera rose to the occasion.

Nathalie heard her say something, and then looked up, trying to focus through her swollen eyes. Vera was standing by her, holding a cup and saucer.

"I've made you some tea," she said, smiling sympathetically. "I'm sure you'll feel better if you drink this."

Nathalie stared at her, and gradually her sobbing subsided. "This is the last straw," she said. At that moment, she hated Vera so much that she could have struck her; yet she was aware that nothing anybody could do, or say, would ever straighten out the evil in this woman. Determined to defeat her, even on such a small issue, she got up and went straight upstairs to finish packing. Ten minutes later, she had left the house.

Perhaps even then she might have had a chance, had she not decided to ring up Arthur from the airport. Having left without saying good-bye to him, she wanted to reassure him that she was no longer angry. He was so glad to hear her voice that it disarmed her, and she had to make quite an effort to tell him that she would be away for a week, instead of four days. He was reasonable and accommodating, however, and that made her feel even more wretched.

"You're not running away with Happy Ham, then?" he asked, without a trace of aggression.

"You know perfectly well I'm not. You must stop Vera putting these absurd ideas into your head."

"She's very worried."

"What rubbish! It's none of her business, in any case."

"Is he there, in fact?"

"Darling, I have no idea, but I don't see how he can be. He's far too busy to hang around for weeks on end doing nothing." Arthur was silent. "Are you there?"

"Yes."

"Besides, that's not the point. You must know that I'd never leave you in such an underhand way—or without Elizabeth, for that matter."

"You could always come back for her, I suppose. I never know what you're really thinking."

"I'll have to rush now—they're calling out the flights. Darling, please, *please* don't make such a fuss about nothing. Well, good bye. See you next Wednesday."

"Good-bye," Arthur said miserably. "Enjoy yourself."

She could never quite shake him off, however. Even when she discovered that Felix had left Paris a fortnight beforehand and wrote immediately to tell Arthur so, her husband's unhappiness still haunted her. She tried to distract herself out of it; to work and play, and talk herself into a forgetful stupor, but with no success. All that she did seemed unreal compared to what she had left behind at Walton House. On the third evening, she took stock of her mood and tried to reason herself out of it. "The plain facts are that I, a model, have been sent over to Paris by my firm on a job," she told herself. "I'm staying with my aunt at my old home, and for the first time since my marriage. What is so extraordinary, or sinister, about that? How on earth can a perverted bitch and a neurotic drunkard possibly draw me into their own filthy fantasies? I know why Vera did what she did, just as I know why Arthur so easily becomes half-crazy with jealousy and fear, but it doesn't make sense. And if I give in to their tantrums, it will merely be taken as evidence of guilt in their eyes. I see it all clearly enough, so I must just pull myself together, be sensible, and call their bluff. And I have every right to a few days' break!"

The moment the last show was over, however, she took the next aeroplane home.

The Baroness expressed both annoyance and concern at the sudden curtailment of Nathalie's visit to Paris, and went over to England herself, a week later, to see what was going on at Walton House. There had been a distinct change in the atmosphere there since her last visit. Previously, a rhythm of sorts had existed there, so that each of its inhabitants was always in direct response to one of the others, if only connected through strife. Now, even during meals the three Bateman-Browns almost disregarded one another. There were occasional half-hearted outbursts, but like a ritual that has lost both meaning and energy, they were without real consequence. Not even the Baroness's arrival made an appreciable difference; she was simply left to take her place as a fourth unit. Arthur, now always half-drunk, sat smiling and nodding, his eyes hardly focussing; from time to time, he made remarks which sometimes fitted in, and sometimes did not. Vera's eyes were misty with bewilderment, rather than alcohol, but her comments were so trite and shallow that the effect was as inappropriate. Nathalie was amiable, but her calmness seemed almost ominous.

The Baroness had arrived on a Friday night, and by Sunday, she was ready to burst. Even when she and her niece were alone together, they did not talk at all naturally. Nathalie looked tired and strained, whenever it was not necessary for her to assume an air of professional brightness, and responded to her aunt's remarks quite non-committally. The Baroness, who had never favoured the iron hand in the velvet glove technique, decided that the time had come for plain speaking. She further calculated that this could best be done away from the house, and on their way back from Mass at West Compton, suddenly said: "I am very worried about you, my darling."

"Oh, why?"

"You know very well what I mean. You can't go on like this."

"I'm in excellent health—a little tired, perhaps, but nothing serious."

"I was not thinking of your physical health."

"As long as that holds out, there's no sense in worrying about anything else."

The Baroness stopped, and put both her hands on Nathalie's shoulders.

"Being here this time," she said, trying to make her niece look at her, "is worse than living among the dead."

Nathalie's eyes, the colour of trout in a deep stream, became as flickering and elusive as this fish itself. She did not speak but looked away, so the Baroness let her hands fall to her sides again. Olga was uncharacteristically silent for so long that eventually her niece turned to look at her, and what she saw upset her inordinately. The Baroness was crying. Nathalie had seen her aunt howl with rage, or sob with the sickness of exhaustion, or even weep with luxuriant self-indulgence at the opera, but never had she seen her cry so quietly or so hopelessly, and looking like a ravaged and defeated old woman.

"Olga, darling! Don't. . . . *Please.*"

"It's so awful that you won't even *talk* to me now," sniffed the Baroness.

"I haven't really talked to anybody for a long, long time. It's not a reflection on you, it's just one of those things."

"Your poor mother! She trusted me. I was always the strong one, but I am not strong enough for you."

"What else can I do, but just go on hoping for the best?" Nathalie asked her, and now her voice sounded uncertain.

The Baroness's weeping suddenly stopped, and she said: "I must sit down. Walking is bad enough, but standing is terrible."

They found a tree trunk on the edge of a copse and made a seat of it, looking out over fertile, newly-planted fields. Nathalie saw that it was almost spring again, and that even the broken-down tree they sat on was sprouting with new life. She was surprised that there should be enough feeling left in her to experience a deep depression at this reminder of her own barrenness and futility.

"You've got to get out of it, my darling," the Baroness said with decision. "You must leave them before they kill you altogether."

"I can't just give up. Besides, how could I leave them?"

"Turn them out. It's your house."

"But where would *they* go?"

"You have no need to worry about that. It's you who are the helpless one in practical matters, not they. I expect Vera has made many economies—enough to keep them going, anyhow."

"I'm not so sure. She's paid quite a few of Arthur's bills. Sometimes, I think one of the main reasons he goes on drinking is because it's the only way he can stand up to her. It makes a mockery of all her little schemes. . . . Besides, you'd never get them out."

"They'd go soon enough if they had to pay the rent that house is worth."

"How sordid that all sounds!"

"Sordid? Is it more sordid than murder?"

"He doesn't hit me now."

"There are more ways of destroying people than by hitting them. I don't know what he's doing to you, but ever since your miscarriage you've been a different person."

"I've grown up a bit, that's all."

"No, that is not all. . . . You've become hard, and somehow bitter. If you hit back, fair and square, I would say 'Hurrah!' But you don't. You just nag and fret, or else stay completely detached. You're getting more and more like them, and that shows they are murdering you."

Nathalie was about to say, "Why must you always exaggerate so much?" when she realised that Arthur or Vera might well have made that kind of remark. And although she was so used to criticism now that it hardly affected her, this cry was from the Baroness's heart, and touched her own with unexpected vigour.

"One has to compromise with one's environment," she

exclaimed. "How can one possibly survive otherwise? It's one's experience that moulds one, not one's principles."

"One! One! Good God, you even talk like they do, now. Anyhow, what sort of future is this for Elizabeth? Have you thought of that?"

"I've thought of everything. Perhaps that's just the trouble. He'd never let her go, not because he loves her, but because once he's definitely fallen on Vera's side, he'll clutch at a sense of property. Anyhow, he knows the law is with him about her, whatever he does."

"Nonsense! He's only browbeating you if he maintains that. Elizabeth is a small girl, not a son, and this is England, you know, with the fairest justice in the world."

"It's not a risk I can take, though. I may not be much of a mother, but think what that child's life would be like if she were brought up by those two, or at best, shuffled between her parents. . . . No, it's better like this."

"Is it for her sake, then, that you're sticking all this?"

"I suppose so." A few moments later, Nathalie added: "No, I'm not being honest. Even without Elizabeth to consider, I still wouldn't be free to just walk out."

"But why?" The Baroness was now thoroughly exasperated. "I do not understand. What do you get out of it? Not money, not position, not protection, not even fun. Nothing! Is it sex, perhaps? But surely—— And anyhow, at your age you have no need to worry about that."

"No, Olga, it's not sex," Nathalie smiled. The Baroness's aggressiveness evaporated, and she said: "Please tell me, or I shall go mad," so pitifully, that Nathalie made an effort to be explicit.

"I suppose it's this continual will-o'-the-wisp of hope for him," she said slowly. "I can't help feeling that if I abandon him, he'll be altogether abandoned. I know he's difficult and often unpleasant, but he gets moments when everything is quite clear and terribly exciting. He doesn't ever quite put it into words, but I somehow get the impact of it, just the same. Then Vera steps in—or he thinks she does, which comes to the same thing—and everything clouds over and goes wrong. And when things go wrong with Arthur, they do so altogether. There'll never be any half-measures about anything he does. That's why, if ever the good moments were to outnumber the bad, he might get on to something which most of us can never hope to attain. I don't quite know what, but something well worth while, at any rate. Somehow, I remember those illuminating flashes, even when he's forgotten them. He's weak, you see, and at the moment there are two of us, in spite of everything."

The Baroness was silent for quite a long time, and then said: "Your father had a penchant for lame ducks, but at least they only took his money. They left him his soul."

"I am aware of what's going on, you know. That's something, isn't it?"

"Is Arthur really worth the sacrifice?"

"I'm tougher than you think."

"You're half dead already."

For a moment, Nathalie knew a great sadness, and her head began to thicken with sobs, but the habit of discipline was strong enough to dismiss all this. She said: "Can you understand what it's like to know someone else's misery so well that it almost becomes part of you as well? That their pain becomes yours, and your responsibility? When I was young, I used to feel that occasionally, but now it happens more and more. And it's not only a responsibility, it's a challenge. A challenge to fight death or evil, or whatever you like to call it. Life is simple enough for those who live by something. You, for instance, are in love with life, and Felix with a cosy humanist God of love, and even Vera has something, because she loves herself. These passions become basic and motivating powers. But Arthur has nothing. He doesn't care a fig about anything, or anybody—not even himself, now. It needn't be like that, though. That's not what God made him for."

"And will it bring him any nearer God to destroy you?"

"Perhaps he won't. Perhaps in time, with prayer and patience, he may learn to believe in himself again, but in the right way, this time."

"Can it be that you love the horror?"

Nathalie paused for so long that Olga repeated her question, and then she answered: "I'm not sure that I know what love really means. The Bible talks about perfect love, but how on earth are we to achieve it, or even recognise it? If ever I've loved any person, it's Felix. With him, I've known a wholeness of mutuality, and awareness, and ecstasy that somehow set the pattern of love for me for ever. He's still the one I most trust, and respect, and want to be with; yet, when he was last here, something kept me from him, although basically I belong to him as much as any human being ever belongs to any other. It still hardly makes sense, but I've begun to wonder whether perhaps love and responsibility aren't far closer terms than we ever suppose. Arthur is my responsibility in a way that Felix has never been. Probably it's because he's my husband, but it's also that Felix is strong, in spite of having his full share of human weaknesses. He has faith, and a sense of purpose."

"I wish he'd had enough ordinary sense to just take you away from all this," the Baroness exclaimed, with a bitterness that was rare in her.

"It wouldn't have solved anything; either for any of us, or as far as the general problem of love is concerned. St. Paul, who usually knew what he was talking about, said that 'Charity is the bond of perfection'. Well, that's all very fine for the balanced or the unimaginative, but what happens if that principle is taken seriously in an extreme situation? Or by a perfectionist who is either too obstinate, or too simple to think in terms of compromise? Does it mean, then, that if necessary, one must die for love, just as Our Lord did for us? But if people go around dying for each other, how will it all end? Logically, it doesn't stop at personal problems, but goes on to include wars, and revolutions, and sacrifices on a mass scale that become more and more ghastly, and make the purpose of life more and more difficult to see. Is that what He really wants of us? But with so much death and destruction, how can we survive with healthy souls? And who will be left to do the work? It's no answer to say that these cases are exceptional, because they do happen, and if they happen to the chap next door, it may be you next, however little you may want it. There, but for the grace of God, and all that. . . . Oh dear, it's all so difficult. What do you think, Olga?"

"I don't know, my darling. You've gone beyond me, now."

"Well, I suppose these things always have to be worked out in solitude, and perhaps people who have learnt something about love are meant to use whatever strength and wisdom they've acquired through it to help others. But how, dear God, how?"

"By fighting. Fight with everything you've got, and the more primitive you are, the better. You know, those two will respect you more if you stand up to them, than if you keep turning your other cheek."

"There was a time when I'd have denied that, but now I know it's true. They really feel that it's a sign of virtue to know exactly what one wants, and to get it by fair means or foul. The trouble is that it doesn't *solve* anything. I suppose I could—in theory, anyhow—get Vera out of here, but that wouldn't really liberate Arthur. That's not going to give him the strength to stand up to her."

"Why in Heaven's name did you ever let her move in in the first place?"

"Possibly for that reason. In fact, I had no option."

"And now you've twice the problem on your hands! Well, you must just fight her on her own ground, or else she'll get the better of you. The Veras of this world win because they concentrate like children on what they want, and kick and scratch if they don't get it, whatever the damage. Even if Arthur wanted to get away from her, she'd never let him, because it's not him she cares about, but herself. You must do something about it, or she will win."

"I still can't fight," Nathalie answered miserably. "I can't fight, and I can't hate. According to the books, that's supposed to be better than violence and venom, but it's not much use in the short run. . . . I get so terribly frightened, sometimes, never knowing in what particular way I ought to be on the look-out."

"But don't you understand, my darling? Charity is all very fine, but it's a tough world, and there's no sense in being sentimental about life. This is war, not a case for sweet reasonableness. One of you has to win, and why should you let it be her?"

"Why should Arthur be a battle-ground between two women, even if they do represent two ways of life? I can't make his victories *for* him. I can only stand by him while *he* fights and makes his choice. Anyhow, what right have I to say: 'I love you in the *best* way, and I'm the only one who really knows what suits you, so you must do as I say, or else.' Adults must be treated as adults, after all. If I really thought he'd be better off without me I'd leave him tomorrow, but much as I'd like to, I can't really believe that! Perhaps that's just cowardice on my part, because I can't face the fight to get out."

"It's all such a waste," the Baroness exclaimed. "And what will become of you? What will become of you, my little darling?"

"I know what will become of me if we stay here any longer, and I don't get luncheon ready on time, anyhow. There'll be endless grumbling and nagging, too, because the shoulder of lamb is too fat. If ever I do leave Arthur, it will be in order to live off tins of Spam and never have to cook another 'joint of meat' for the rest of my life."

The Baroness's visit to Walton House was effective, though not precisely in the sense that she had hoped. Her talk with Nathalie had revitalised the latter with a fresh amount of determination, since to actually state a case or a situation is often to see it more clearly, and she was persuaded to offer her nephew-in-law any help which would make it possible for him to get on his feet again.

Arthur then began to dream of another part that he might play, that of a man behind the scenes in high circles of London life. As he saw it, his occupation would not be specified, but he would be a man of mystery, a person with such vision and sagacity that all the great and eminent would consult him and treasure his advice before taking important decisions. After he died, his influence on his time would be unquestioned, however difficult to assess in detail, and his eminence would be comparable to that of such men as Machiavelli or Richelieu.

The Baroness had promised to talk to a few people who might be useful, and Arthur began to feel more sanguine than he had done for a long time. This lightened mood, combined with a new spurt of vitality on Nathalie's part, brought husband and wife a little closer together. They began to make plans which were vague and wild with optimism, but nevertheless provided something to look forward to, and since Arthur now became aware of his surroundings once more, he wanted everybody to join in with his new mood. Vera, however, remained unresponsive. When spoken to, she answered as though preferring to be left alone and never smiled, especially when the other two were laughing. Yet, in spite of her self-effacement, her presence was as oppressive as a lump of undigested porridge, and she exhausted the atmosphere by sapping up its vitality like a dry sponge.

"Can't you show some interest?" Arthur would say. "One would think you'd be pleased at the thought of my getting going again." Now that he was on good terms with one of his women, he was turning against the other.

"It's just that I'm worried about you," she would answer. "I'm only thinking of your own good." Her sulking was, in fact, a form of insurance.

The Baroness, true to her word, telephoned several days later asking Arthur to lunch with her the following Thursday. Nathalie came home early on Wednesday to see that his best suit was properly pressed. She had bought him a new shirt, a couple of linen handkerchiefs, and some prawns. Dinner was relatively gay. Being determined to take no chances, she saw to it that Arthur and Vera were not alone for long at any time that evening, and by insisting on playing chess and being rather coy, she contrived that he should say good night to his sister downstairs, and thus avoid the usual nightly session in her bedroom. When he eventually went to bed, he seemed in a good mood. Nathalie promised to make the tea the following morning, and although Arthur said that this would be running a risk, rather than enjoying a treat, he was obviously pleased.

When Nathalie took up his early morning tea, she found Arthur dead drunk, with an empty bottle of gin beside him. He tried to lift his head off the pillow, but the effort was too much, and it flopped down again. He smiled vaguely, trying to focus his swollen, bloodshot eyes, and then gave up, and turned his face to the wall. Feeling really sick with panic and despair, Nathalie left the room again, now quite certain that he would never get to London that day. At first, she thought of making an excuse for his defection, but could think of no convincing reason for a sudden change in such an important plan. Besides, although she had become skilful at concealment, she was no good at straightforward lying, and knew that the Baroness would never believe her. Indeed, the prospect of trying to explain anything to her aunt at that moment was more than she could face, so she sent a telegram instead, merely stating that Arthur would not be able to get to London as he was unwell. "Olga will know what *that* means," she reflected bitterly, "but what else can I say or do?" Then, having kissed Elizabeth good-bye, she left the house and went to work, forgetting to have any breakfast.

Arthur's drinking now became really serious. Even though Nathalie had been used to his excesses for years, she was amazed that there were so many more aspects of alcoholism than she had previously realised. The depths of degradation that her husband sank into would have appalled her far more if there had not been such a lot to keep her occupied: so much, in fact, that she had to take more time off from her job and this added to her problems, for less work meant, quite simply, less money.

Vera was so shocked and upset that she was numbed into helplessness. Not only was she of little practical use now, but she had to be soothed and reassured as well. For the first time in her life, she did not fiercely resent someone else doing things for her brother, thinking herself too sensitive to deal with such sordid horrors. She frequently praised Nathalie to her face for dealing with everything so magnificently, sometimes adding that she herself was too sensitive to be able to witness such brutality without cracking.

Arthur now spent most of the time in his bedroom, and drank round the clock. Whenever he began to recover from a stupor, he drank again until he passed out once more. At first, Nathalie thought that if she could check the supply of gin that came into the house and cut his consumption from two bottles a day down to half a bottle, she would be able to curb at least the excessiveness of his drinking. This notion betrayed her lack of understanding of the violence of Arthur's craving, however. He did not enjoy drinking any more. His physical condition was now so painful that it gave him an additional reason for seeking oblivion, and his sodden brain, when it worked at all, no longer revealed a panorama of fascinating and extravagant visions, but terrified him with its distortions. Therefore, he strove all the more to put himself beyond any limits, and Nathalie's hindrances were merely a challenge to his ingenuity. She was no match for the single-minded determination and inspired cunning of the drunkard, and although she discovered most of his hidden supplies in the house, he still defeated her. Once, he came upon her pouring gin down the wash-hand basin and sprang to snatch the remains of the bottle from her. At that moment she turned towards him, however, and something in her expression reached him, and made him pause. She looked neither angry nor reproachful, but almost glazed with exhaustion, as well as a kind of despair that matched his own. At this glimpse of what he had done to her his stomach almost retched in its craving, but he just said rather sheepishly: "Well, at least I haven't taken to boot-polish or hair-tonic yet. You must give me credit for that much, at any rate." It was odd little moments like this that Nathalie found even harder to bear than the really exacting trials.

This acute state of affairs went on for over a fortnight. Vera finally faced up to the situation, and even made suggestions for dealing with it. Arthur, she said, must not be allowed to have any money, and he should be forbidden to leave the house; in this way, he would be forced to stop drinking.

"Having no money would make no difference. He's an expert at living on tick," Nathalie answered. "Even now, he's not capable of going out much, or for long, yet he gets the stuff somehow. I suspect he organises a troop of small boys to smuggle it through to him from time to time. However many times he's caught, he'll always work out something else."

"You're too indulgent with him," Vera exclaimed. "He must be made to realise how horrible he is . . . how horrible it all is for us."

"Can't you see the hell *he's* in? He's got to be helped to overcome this with dignity, and not hounded or humiliated like some animal which doesn't keep in with the pack. All this locking doors and emptying his purses and general moral castigation is no good. It just adds to his degradation, and the more he feels the world is against him, the more ways he'll think up of fighting it, and wallow in his shame."

Vera shrugged her shoulders, saying unhappily: "It can't go on like this. . . . It *can't*. . . ."

Yet, when Nathalie answered, "That I do agree with. I think I'll go and have a chat with the doctor," she objected strongly, fearing a public scandal. "Besides," she added, "it's a question of moral delinquency, not physical ill-health. What can a doctor do?" She resented the idea of any outsider being admitted to their private shame.

"That's what I want to ask him. Doctors are professionally discreet, after all, and dealing with drunks is all in the day's work for them, in any case. He'll think of something."

Vera suddenly capitulated with almost confusing readiness, and when the doctor arrived, she received him with the mixture of coy deference and adulation that a small girl lavishes on a favourite uncle.

When the doctor found him, Arthur was lying on his bed in a semi-coma. He looked pathetically ugly. His hair, now dark with greasiness, was long and untidy; his glazed and lolling eyes seemed too close together; his nose was dark, and the rest of his colouring putty; his cheeks were cavernous, his twitching chin unshaven, and saliva trickled out of one corner of his mouth. The medical examination did not take long.

"Heart's dicky, of course," the doctor said to Nathalie, when he had called her back. "It's a wonder he's alive at all, though. He must have the constitution of an ox. I've injected him with a powerful sedative, so that when he comes to, the tension ought to have broken down and he should feel reasonably relaxed. He'll have interrupted the drinking cycle, anyhow. By this evening, I'll have made the necessary arrangements for him to go to a place where they cope with these things wisely and humanely."

"An alcoholics' remand home?" Nathalie asked.

"Not quite." The doctor mentioned a name, and Nathalie, having heard of it, exclaimed: "But that's a nut-house, isn't it?"

"We prefer to call it a psychological readjustment centre. Besides," the doctor added, "it seems to me that you could do with a rest too."

"What will they do with him there?"

"Get him over the first hurdle of physical ill-health, and then try to help him by psychiatric treatment."

"Rather you than me. My husband doesn't hold with psychiatry."

"Well, we'll have to see about that." The doctor put all his bits and pieces away again, and then said: "Now you can breathe until this evening. I want you to let me know the moment he wakes up, and whatever you do, don't let him touch any booze. He probably won't want it, but if he *should* ask for it, nothing doing, see?"

"It will be a pleasure, Doctor." She had hours and hours in which to explore all the hiding places, and to conceal Arthur's trousers. Callers would be screened and filtered as though Walton House were a Carmelite nunnery, and tomorrow, with Arthur safely in good hands, she would be able to go back to work again.

By the evening, however, it was obvious that things were not going to be so simple. Arthur woke up as planned, relaxed and quiet, and she telephoned the doctor, who came round immediately. It seemed, however, that he could not be taken away until he consented to it, or two others declared that he needed treatment. The more the doctor reasoned with him, the more stubborn he became. He refused to be "whipped away like this", as he put it; thanks to the injection, the worst was probably now over. He insisted that he felt well and calm, and would first regain his strength right there, at home; later, they could discuss what steps should be taken to ensure that all this did not happen again. The doctor tried what persuasion he could, and then went to find Nathalie. She was not surprised at the *impasse* which had been reached, but being so convinced that this was Arthur's big chance, she offered to try to make him see it too. He was clearly frightened at the state he had now reached, and that might help.

Not until she was alone with him, however, did Nathalie realise just how frightened he was, and as soon as she was in the bedroom, he betrayed himself, completely and shamelessly.

"Don't let them take me away," he whimpered. "They'll never let me out again. They do ghastly things in those places, you just don't know. You don't know how wicked people can be, you're too good to see it. I know I deserve all the punishment there is, but please don't let them take me."

She sat on his bed, and tried to soothe him with all the tenderness in her power. Never had he clung to her so frantically, and with a fear and a despair which she found difficult to counteract.

"Nobody can make you go unless you agree to it," she said quietly.

"Yes they can, if you and Vera say so. Vera would, just to serve me right, just to get her own back, but don't *you* let them. *Please* don't. I'll never touch it again, I promise with all my heart. You must know that this is a lesson that I'll never forget. You must believe that."

Nathalie almost did believe it, such was her desire to, and she was quite amused at her capacity for being taken in by Arthur, even after such a record of broken resolutions.

"Darling, I promise you won't go unless you want to," she said.

"Cross your heart?"

"Cross my heart."

"Do it, then." He was in earnest, so she solemnly complied, adding: "Even so, I'm going to try to talk some sense into you, and make you see that it would be for your own good."

It was no use, however. Arthur remained obstinately deaf and blind to all she had to say, and merely clung to her promise. In the end, she had to admit defeat and send the doctor away without him.

It was nearly midnight by then. Vera had gone to bed with a new kind of sedative, and Arthur, still not fully recovered from his injection, dozed off for a while. Nathalie undressed, and was about to go to bed with the doors of both their bedrooms open, when he called her. She put dressing-gown and slippers on, and went into him, asking: "How do you feel?"

"Not too bad. Thirsty, though."

"Now, then . . ."

"I don't mean that, silly. In fact, the mere thought of alcohol is quite nauseating. You couldn't bear to make some tea, could you?"

"Darling, this is the crowning moment of my life! I've waited years to hear you say that."

When she came back again, they sat, each with a cup in hand, and Arthur said: "You know, this tea is not only drinkable, it's actually quite good."

"What a pity it should take strong drugs to make you appreciate my tea-making!"

Later, she turned his pillow and tucked him up, and then opened a window.

"With your upbringing," he teased, "I can't think where you get all these hardy English outdoor-girl notions."

"Be that as it may, it's high time we let a little fresh air into here. Shall I turn this light out?"

"No, leave it on. I can't bear the dark."

"You will get some sleep now, won't you?"

"I'll try." She kissed him good night, but again he called her before she had got into bed.

"I'm frightened of being alone," he said dismally.

"Well, I'll just get a pillow and a rug, and sit by you in this armchair until you drop off. All right?"

"Lovely."

When she was settled, both of them finally dozed off, hand in hand.

At two o'clock the next morning, Arthur suddenly woke up, feeling terrified. The effect of the drug had quite worn off, and he was completely conscious. His panic was like an actual pain, icy and searing even into his brain. In spite of the light, it seemed to him that the room was full of ominous shadows. He kept catching glimpses of moving creatures, some large, but some even more frightening by being extremely small; yet, whenever he dared to face them, they would have moved elsewhere, and again be only just in the corner of his vision. As his terror increased, he felt a host of nightmare images and monsters waiting to take possession of his whole mind and soul. He found these too horrible to face, and could only brace himself against them with all the control he had left. He was sweating profusely, and his hands were trembling so hard that he could scarcely use them. At first, he tried to endure his torture alone, and without waking Nathalie, who was now asleep in the armchair. Then, two of the figures who seemed to be slithering and lurking around the room became more insistent than the rest. They came and stood just by his pillow, and petrifyingly near. For a moment, he pretended to ignore them; then, realising that they were between himself and Nathalie, and seemed to want something of him, his resistance suddenly broke, and he screamed. Almost immediately, she was by his side, and the figures receded.

"I'm sorry I woke you," Arthur gasped. "I couldn't help it."

"Have you been having bad dreams?"

"Much worse. Put all the lights on, will you?"

She did so. He slowly looked round the room, and then added: "That showed them. They've gone now."

"What?"

"All kinds of things. It's all right now, though."

"Would you like some food?" To Nathalie's certain knowledge, he had not eaten anything for twenty-four hours, and his diet for a fortnight before that had not been exactly balanced.

"I couldn't swallow a thing."

"Not even some more tea?"

"Later. You mustn't leave me alone now, even for a moment."

Nathalie fetched a book and began to read aloud to him. For a while he seemed interested, but soon his reactions became more and more forced.

"Would you like to go to sleep again?" she asked at last.

"All right. You can turn off the other lights now, if you want to."

They settled down as before, with Nathalie in the armchair, holding one of Arthur's still trembling hands. Propped up on several pillows this time, he lay back and closed his eyes, but within a few minutes he knew that the two figures were beside him again. He did not dare to look straight at them, but when he opened his eyes, he could see them, just out of full view, on his right. Again they were insisting on something, and again he called out to Nathalie. This time, he was not so easily comforted, however. The demons receded when she was actually with him, but would return the moment she was more than a few inches away again. Finally, the only way she could quieten him, even for short intervals, was by getting into bed with him, and holding him in her arms. Even then, every now and again, he would start moaning, and struggling, and begging her to make "them" go away.

"But who, darling? There's no one there."

"Yes, there is. Can't you see them too, or is it only because there's so much evil in me that I can?"

"What are they like?"

"Archetypes. Two of them. They want to get at me in some way, but I won't let them. As long as you stay with me, they don't really dare."

For hours and hours they fought and fought. Arthur was resisting complete possession by something that made him hysterical with terror, and Nathalie was instinctively aware that only her animal warmth could keep him from capitulation. Although she did not understand what was going on, it was the most complete and selfless dedication that had ever been asked of her. For a while, she ceased to exist as a thinking individual, and become an instrument of the will-power and vitality of life. Through this primitive and innocent contact with her, Arthur managed to remain alive and sane.

When daylight finally came, banishing the horrors of the night, they were both limp and grey from battle, but they had won. "Now I know there is such a thing as absolute evil," Arthur said. "That was it."

Nathalie reflected ruefully that it was only to be expected that Arthur should have D.T.s more colourfully and dramatically than anyone else. Yet it occurred to her that perhaps he was not exaggerating. "How can one person ever really tell," she reflected, "what chasms of panic, or black hells of distortion, another had to endure in terrible solitude?"

Nathalie only fully realised how frightened Arthur had been by his illness when he agreed to have psychiatric treatment. As he had always been impatient of doctors in general, and contemptuous of psychiatrists in particular, there could have been no surer proof of the hell he had seen.

It was arranged that he should visit a particular hospital in Oxford twice a week, and he set out for the first session in high spirits.

"What's the betting on my analyst having a nervous breakdown within a month," he said to Nathalie, and at Vera he cracked: "You'd better come as well. It would do you a lot of good." Vera actually smiled at this, for her confidence in doctors was now quite unrestrained. Their G.P. had not only given Arthur some medicine to keep him relaxed and stop him craving alcohol, but had also prescribed a sedative for her which enabled her to sleep at night without interruption, and got her through the day without caring much about anything. She had begun to take larger and larger quantities of this elixir, but the surgery did not, as yet, question her white lies about broken or mislaid bottles.

Arthur's optimistic mood lasted for some time. Always fond of talking about himself, he was now intensely gratified to be the centre of so much attention. Even the sight of a well-stuffed dossier with his name on it in jet black letters stimulated him, and he found the whole ritual and process of analysis so interesting that he gave Nathalie a blow by blow account of every consultation. Once so morbidly secretive, he now felt no need whatever for reticence, and spared her no detail. These tributes to truth and honesty would have been more gratifying to her if they had not been quite so tiring, for Arthur required the most exacting co-operation. She was not only expected to listen closely, but also to give her own views on the analyst's interpretation.

All went well for nearly three weeks, however; then, Nathalie came home one day to find Arthur extremely irritable. Some trouble had apparently arisen over the problem of guilt, for the doctor had maintained that if only Arthur stopped feeling guilty about his casual affairs and his sister's unhappiness, half the battle would be won.

"Well, why not?" Nathalie asked. "Doesn't that fit in with your conviction that the world has given you a raw deal?"

"If you're just going to be beastly, you'll be no help at all."

"Tactless perhaps, darling, but not beastly. You know you always have insisted that women who choose to behave as tarts deserve what they get."

"All women are tarts anyhow, but there are a few who have some kind of heart as well. It's the ones who are genuinely upset by their contact with me that I should be worrying about."

Nathalie remembered a girl working in a shoe-shop, who had come to see her one day, simply because a link with Arthur's wife was better than no contact with him at all. He had overwhelmed her with attentions until, having possessed every part of her, body and soul, this complete enslavement had bored him, and he had abruptly abandoned her. There had also been a dancer from a small, theatrical troupe. She had been a tougher proposition, but had eventually capitulated just as completely. Her reaction to Arthur's callousness, however, had been less meek. Bearing out the dictum that "Hell hath no fury like a woman spurned", she had sought out Nathalie to advise her to leave the villain she depicted in picturesque, and not altogether irrelevant terms.

Nathalie now said: "I thought you believed that violent emotional upheavals are salutary; that they enable people to take stock of themselves, face up to the reality of life, and enjoy a little excitement that might otherwise never have come their way—all that sort of thing."

"You're just as much of a bitch as all the rest of them, throwing things up at me like that. You know perfectly well that I've always thought it wrong to use people. The fact that I continually do so doesn't excuse me."

"Always" was a big word, and meant little in this context; yet, knowing instinctively that she must flatter him towards benignity and further acquiescence, Nathalie smiled brightly, and said: "That must have floored his nibs. I wonder how often he has patients who are so intelligently aware, in spite of having such serious problems. I rather wish I'd taken you on about that nervous breakdown prediction."

Arthur was immediately appeased. "We left that one for the time being," he said more calmly, "but it was over the question of Vera that the real trouble started. He spent a long time trying to make me admit that I wanted to sleep with her. Well, I don't, and never have done, and that seemed to disappoint him. When I asked him innocently if sleeping with my sister would stop me feeling guilty and cure me of jealousy, he began to look rather tired."

Nathalie smiled: "I wonder what Lady Bates would say if she could hear this conversation."

"She wouldn't believe it. According to her, this sort of thing could never happen to people she was ever likely to meet."

These difficulties over the question of guilt continued for two more consultations. Then Arthur announced that he was sick and tired of the whole business of psycho-analysis, and refused to go on with it any longer.

"There's nothing any psychiatrist can teach me about myself that I don't know already, or that you can't tell me, for that matter," he exclaimed impatiently. "I know I'm dominated by my sister. I know I killed her fiancé—partly because she egged me on, and partly because I was jealous of both of them. I know I can't stand her, and yet can't get away from her. I know she's so morbid about sex that it's affected me, and probably accounts for my attitude to women, and love and life, but what does all that prove? Nothing, except that I make my wife unhappy and drink too much. Yet, if I try and say any of this to that idiot in Oxford, he keeps repeating that everything would be different if only I shed my sense of guilt. Even I can't do that, though. I'm rotten in almost every sense, but I can't resign from all responsibility for what I've done, or what I am. We're all guilty, not only in our motives and our actions, but in our instincts as well. You can't laugh—or talk—that one off. Even the fact that we kill each other in wartime, and under orders, doesn't make murder any more excusable, so where do we go from here?"

"Perhaps you have learnt something after all—acceptance, maybe. Perhaps if you really do keep off the booze, you'll be all right, now."

"I'll let you into a little secret. It is not a sense of guilt, or frustration, or unhappiness that drives me to the bottle. I drink because I'm bored—bored to death with life, with the people round me, and even with myself. That's far too simple for any psychiatrist to accept, though, so they have to dig up all these complications which are not really relevant and, in fact, just add to my boredom. You see, unlike you or Happy Ham, I haven't haven't got any of these obsessions about wanting to be useful. To me, they seem pointless and excessively boring."

That evening, when Nathalie was at last by herself, she went on considering the problem of guilt, and wondered if Arthur had really been so implicated in the death of Vera's fiancé as he always made out. His craving for self-dramatisation was too complicated for her to understand, but she knew it well. The accident could equally well have been just that; an accident. To regard it as a symbol of man's guilt might be picturesque, but was it not perhaps being used as a covering for the less interesting shortcomings of cowardice and vanity? She knew that ordinary, human frailty was too dull for Arthur, and that he could never admit to a mere error of judgment. "And yet," she reflected, "we *are* all of us responsible, even indirectly, for what happens to other people. How much am I to blame for Arthur's present condition, for instance? At the time, I seemed to have no choice about marrying him, but shouldn't I have considered that it was perhaps my acute suffering at the loss of Felix that made the kind of challenge Arthur represented seem so compelling? It's hardly fair to turn round afterwards and say: 'That wasn't the real me, but just the fragments that managed to survive without Felix. Only your suffering was great, or real, or deep enough, to enable me to forget mine, but although I needed your violence then, it wasn't really my cup of tea. I can't live up to it, so I'm afraid you've got rather a raw deal. So sorry!' Presumably it's what's known as marrying on the rebound, and that's always supposed to be a mistake. Yet, aren't most people's lives based on a series of rebounds, of picking up the remains of one ended phase and starting again on a new one? Isn't that how evolution in general works, and can either blame or guilt be attached to such a process? Surely Arthur's had as good a chance with me as with anyone, but why has almost nothing but destruction come out of our life together?"

A few days later, Nathalie had a message from Arthur's psychiatrist, asking her to call on him. He had not quite given up all hope yet, and thought Nathalie might be able to assist him.

When this doctor at last joined her, in an antiseptic private waiting-room, she was surprised at the negative impact of his personality. This was due not so much to his ordinary appearance, as to the complete lack of warmth in his manner or attitude. At first, Nathalie thought that her failure to establish any contact with him was simply because she was not his type, but gradually she became more and more distressed. He talked about Arthur frankly and shrewdly, and yet did not seem to know him in any personal way. All that he said was true, but it could equally well have been applied to someone else.

Answering his questions as lucidly as possible, she tried to tell him what he wanted to know. It all took quite a long time, and after a while he stopped taking notes and merely listened, though with attention, rather than interest. Finally, he said: "That confirms several things I had already suspected. I'm afraid there's nothing we can do for him unless he's prepared to co-operate."

"But surely he's been doing that? I've never known him to concentrate on anything for so long, or so wholeheartedly."

"He's not really serious about it. If he spent less effort in trying to catch me out, and more in being straightforward, we might have got somewhere."

"You must have had 'mixed-up kids' before. I should have thought it was your job to straighten them out again, whatever way it takes them."

"He's no more mixed-up than you or me. All that's wrong with him comes from being vain, weak, cowardly and completely selfish. There's nothing I, or any other doctor can do about that as long as he's so arrogantly sure of being in the right."

Nathalie's illusions about sympathetic and wise psychiatrists were being knocked out one by one, but she was not yet ready to give up entirely.

"Isn't all that what you call compensation mechanism?" she suggested, aware that many of the reactions Arthur so convincingly wallowed in were part of a conscious pose. Trying to sound as humble and cajoling as possible, she added: "There's something there that's worth while. It seems such a pity that it should all turn towards drink and destruction. I'd be so grateful if you could help him." She smiled in a way that had made other men go weak in the knees, but the doctor betrayed no flicker of sensitivity.

"I think I'd better explain something about the system," he

began. "You see, what we do is to help people face up to themselves, and to understand what they find when they do so. After that, it's up to them. We can then advise on what we consider the most suitable forms of occupation, either as careers, if that's possible, or simply as hobbies if it isn't. We have a very satisfactory percentage of successful cases, but only among those who genuinely want to benefit from treatment."

Nathalie took a little time thinking out her next move. Then, she said: "Arthur said there was some trouble over the question of guilt. I believe he finds it difficult to abandon all sense of responsibility."

For the first time that afternoon, the doctor showed faint signs of animation.

"To indulge in a sense of guilt as he does is just a form of masochism," he exclaimed. "It has nothing to do with conscience. I tried to make him see that, and to get him to realise that his first responsibility is to himself. Only when he straightens himself out can he hope to be of some use in more general terms. I don't understand how anybody as self-centred as he is could resist an argument like that. It can only be because he just doesn't want to take all this seriously, or make any progress with it."

"Is there nothing you can do, then?"

"We're up against a question of character here, and that can only be changed if he wants it to."

"Can't you persuade him to *want* to change?"

"I'm afraid not. A man's will-power is the only freedom that can't be taken from him."

Nathalie suddenly stood up, and almost shouted: "Do you care what happens to him? Does it really make any difference to you what becomes of your 'unsuccessful percentages'? Do you know at all what sort of hell they go through, day and night? Have you any idea what they feel? Are *you* indeed at all capable of feeling?"

The doctor looked at her in amazement, and said quietly: "My job is to think, not to feel."

Nathalie had not meant to voice her disappointment, and she apologised for her bad manners.

"I'm afraid I had rather high hopes that something would come of all this," she explained. "Now, I'm wondering what's next."

"He may be all right if he gives up drink altogether."

"Perhaps. But then you know just as well as I do that he won't."

When she reached home again, Arthur eagerly pressed her for details of what the doctor had said, and what the two of them had decided. Nathalie felt tired, and said wearily: "It looks to me as though you gave him the full treatment. I've never known anyone less happy in their work—as far as you're concerned, anyhow."

Arthur was delighted. "Well, at least I've done a public service in teaching one of those chaps that not all the answers come out of books," he chuckled.

"I don't think he quite took it that way."

"Did he show any signs of a nervous breakdown."

"Not yet, but he seems to think there's nothing more he can do for you."

"It's about time he admitted that."

Nathalie paused, and then said carefully: "There's only the Church left, now."

"You keep your tame monks away from me!" Arthur was firm, but not annoyed, so Nathalie said: "I'll make a deal with you. As long as you keep off the bottle I won't insist, but the moment there's any sign of nonsense again, I shall unleash Father Francis on to you, and tell him to stop at nothing."

For a moment, Arthur looked disconcerted, and then he laughed.

"Done! But you'll have to see that my supply of medicine never gets dangerously low."

"In other words, I'll have to take all the blame if you start drinking again."

"Of course," they both started in unison. "That's . . . what . . . wives . . . are . . . for."

It was a little time before Arthur thought about alcohol again, for at first he was entertained by the ritual of taking a new medicine to relax his inner tensions. His health had improved so much that he now found it difficult to understand ever having given way so completely, and became convinced that, his equilibrium having been restored to such an extent, he no longer needed to worry about having the odd drink now and then. He went so far as to persuade himself that it would complete his cure to know that he could do so without danger.

Having decided that moderate drinking was the right course for him, in spite of what the psychiatrist might have said, he began to drink pink gins before luncheon and dinner again, and for about a week, never had more than two each time. When he got back to the house one morning and found that luncheon was not yet quite ready, however, he went into the library to have a third "short snort". He finished that, and then another one, and suddenly something broke within him. When Nathalie came to call him to table, she found him quite drunk. His book had fallen on to the floor, the bottle of gin, which had been nearly half-full thirty minutes beforehand, was now empty; and Arthur was lying stretched out on the sofa. When he heard his wife exclaiming: "Oh, *Arthur*!", he opened one watery and unfocussing eye, and said unsteadily: "Just having a little snooze." By force of habit Nathalie calculated how Arthur should be sobered up, how Vera could be shielded, and how Elizabeth must be kept away.

"Arthur," she said urgently, but he merely smiled, and mumbled sleepily. He was evidently docile, so she took courage to be a little firmer.

"Arthur, now listen to me," she tried again. "Pull yourself together, and listen to me."

He opened his eyes, but closed them again almost immediately.

"You've got to get upstairs. Make the effort just that long. That's all you've got to do."

"I'm tired," Arthur said. "Leave me alone."

"I'll fetch Vera, then."

She made as if to leave the room, and saw then that he was struggling to get up. Finally, he stood, swaying gently backwards and forwards, running his hands through his hair, and trying to pat down his clothes.

The pattern of such incidents repeated itself with only small variations. With a little help from Nathalie, Arthur managed to go up to his bedroom. Vera sat through lunch in almost complete silence, and then went to lie down with "a bit of a head", having taken an extra strong swig of her own sedative. Elizabeth went to spend the afternoon with Sally Milton, and Nathalie did her best to lose herself in a nervous orgy of household chores. At five o'clock, she went into Arthur's room and found him wide awake, rested and cheerful.

"It's all quite simple," he said, the moment she came in. "That was just the final fling before the real turning over of the new leaf. It often happens, in all manner of contexts; before being married, before taking religious vows; before any major step, in fact. What happened the other day was to make me decide, and this was a sort of sealing gesture. It's very hard to be the sort of person who reacts so wholeheartedly, but that's the price of sensitivity, I suppose."

Nathalie laughed, and exclaimed: "Anyone who can drink nearly half a bottle of gin in twenty minutes without a sign of a hangover afterwards can't really expect to be considered sensitive."

"Now you're just making fun of my peasant ancestry, which is what endows me with such a strong constitution. How typical of you to confuse that with my soul."

"Darling, please. It doesn't suit you to talk about the soul. Not your mystique at all."

"I thought it might please you, by reminding you of Happy Ham."

Nathalie no longer even needed to turn away to conceal the pang that references of this sort always gave her. Yet, her carefully acquired self-discipline could not prevent a softening, a relaxation of tension within her, that any thought of Felix always brought on.

"Will you go and see Father Francis by yourself?" she asked. "Or would you like me to talk to him first?"

"I thought you'd come out with that one, sooner or later."

"It would make a lovely new role for you to play. Just think of it: the brilliant young man, frustrated by this, that, and the other who tries everything, and then turns to the Church as the last resort."

Arthur pretended to ponder over this image, but as always, he had got there before her. Playing for time and effect, he said: "I foxed you on that one."

"Have you seen him already, then?"

"Ages ago. I've been taking instruction ever since you began to recover from your miscarriage."

She did not believe him, mostly because with his avidity for an audience, it seemed unlikely that he would have kept something like this to himself for any length of time. He sensed her incredulity, and added: "You can ask Father Francis if you don't believe me. I told him not to tell you, but it doesn't matter now."

Nathalie could no longer be so easily convinced, however.

"I don't get it," she said suspiciously. "That was more than two years ago. Are you still having instruction?"

She had guessed correctly, almost by instinct. After her illness, Arthur had sought out the priest a number of times, but these talks had petered out after a few weeks. "It requires a fair amount, one way and another, to get elected to any good club," he hedged. Then he added more aggressively: "But even so, I bet I know more about the rules than you do."

"What on earth do you mean by 'any good club'?"

"Just that. And the Catholic Church is apparently the best club, since it's older, stronger, richer, more powerful and more highly organised than any other."

"Is that all you understand by religion?"

She knew that he was not altogether speaking in jest, and was shocked by his attitude.

"You belong to the best club, which enables you to hob-nob with the right people, and get any extra shot of grace that's going, and from then on, you're in. That just about sums it up, doesn't it?"

Even now, she wanted to believe that he was joking to cover up his real feelings, but she feared that this was not so.

"Don't God, or even love, come into it at all?" she asked, wanting to say more, but being afraid to. As it was, this sufficed to make Arthur jump up from the bed and exclaim irritably: "Love! Love! Does anybody ever think of anything else? I'm bored stiff with all you people and your love! It stifles me, and if you think I'm going to go on wasting my time with that bore Father Francis, you're much mistaken. He's just as childish as the rest of you. Why can I never find any adults to talk to? You'd think a priest would be some help, wouldn't you? but all that one can do, when it comes to the point, is quibble about 'faith', and 'acts of contrition', and 'the infallibility of the Church', and even 'giving oneself'. I'm prepared to sign on the dotted line, stick to the rules as much as the next man, and give him one good mark in the book that records this traffic in souls, but apparently that's not enough. Give myself, indeed! Why should I give myself? I belong to myself. I'm me, do you hear, and there's precious little of that left, after all you vampires have had your whack! To hell with the lot of you, priests, women and children! You're all effeminate sycophants, anyhow, and if I want to drink myself silly, I will."

He was about to charge out of the room when he heard Vera coming along the corridor. Quickly jumping back, he quietly shut the door and then stood listening, a forefinger on his lips, imploring Nathalie to be silent. The sound of Vera's footsteps came nearer, and then receded as she went down the stairs, and into the kitchen. Arthur sat on the bed with a sigh of relief, and clutched his head.

"What *you* need is a nice cup of tea," Nathalie smiled. "Shall I ask Vera to bring you one?"

"Your capacity for hitting a man when he's down betrays your unstable racial origins!"

"Well, I'm going down to have some, anyhow."

"Don't leave me. Please."

"Come too, then. You've got to face her sometime."

Once more they went through the familiar process of Nathalie acting as a buffer between Arthur and his sister, Arthur and his conscience, Arthur and life. In spite of all they had been through together, she could still not understand why he was unable to carry off comparatively simple situations. This matter of standing up to Vera was beginning to assume a primary, almost obsessive importance in her mind, and she did not fully appreciate that he was even more hampered by his sister's despondency than by her tantrums. It was a vicious circle for him with guilt, alcoholism and Vera chasing each other round and round within his dark and tortured world. Nathalie could still make him laugh, however, and when she finally exclaimed: "Why on earth can't you stick to drugs, instead of taking to drink, like this?", he smiled, and consented to go downstairs with her.

It was no use, however. Vera's genuine unhappiness, as well as her sulkiness and complete lack of response, screwed him once more into a rack of tension that he could not endure. He left the house shortly afterwards to get extremely drunk, and started on another cycle of alcoholism which culminated four days later in an acute attack of gastritis. This was not as dramatic as his D.T.s had been, but far more sordid, though it did provide a short period of comparative quiet.

It was at this time, when Arthur was in bed, groaning with fear and physical discomfort, that the Baroness suddenly reappeared. The quality of her awareness was almost uncanny, and even from a distance she seemed able to sense what was going on. Walking into the house one morning, she simply exclaimed: "Vera must leave. At once."

"I've been thinking the same myself, lately," Nathalie replied. "But how? And where will she go?"

"She must arrange the details for herself. Are you nervous? I'll tell her, if you like?"

"No, it's not that. I'm just wondering how to make her understand. She never sees anything unless she wants to."

The Baroness became annoyed at this, and exclaimed: "Now don't start that, my darling. Just tell her to go."

"But I can't. I must explain somehow. She has a right to be told the truth, after all."

"The truth! There are people who cannot stand the truth. It gives them no satisfaction, only much uneasiness. She is not our sort in that way, and you have told me so yourself often enough."

"She can be reasonable, if only she's tackled the right way. It would be better for Arthur like that, too."

This time, the Baroness exploded altogether.

" 'Reasonable!' " she shouted. "How can she be 'reasonable' about Arthur when she never sees him as a man, but only has her private, romantic ideal. She pushes Arthur up on an impossible pinnacle, and then complains when he falls backwards on top of her. She doesn't love him, she just wants him—but without any 'nasty' complications—and yet you think she can be 'reasonable' about him. How could such a sour, self-centred bitch be reasonable about any man, anyhow. Can you see her admitting that men need tenderness, or encouragement, or interest, or respect? Can you see her giving herself with complete abandon while lying bathed in a man's tears? Or sheltering him in her arms with the love of a mother, and yet making him feel proud of his manhood? Or having such an understanding for his purpose that he thinks her judgment and admiration worth having? Of course not! Reasonable, indeed. She is a maniac."

Nathalie could not help smiling at this outburst, but at the same time she suddenly felt inordinately tired, and flopped into an armchair.

"It's too late now," she sighed. "I should have done it ages ago. What a miserable moral coward I am! How was I to know, though? How can one learn about this sort of thing, unless one sweats it out to the bitter end?"

"You'll never learn. You're too soft. Even now you can't take yourself to throw that terrible woman out, and yet she deserves much worse than that."

"She's so pathetic, all dried up with frustration and disappointment like that. You said yourself that she understood very little about anything, and you were right. It would kill her."

"She has turned you completely round her finger, just like Arthur. I'm going to tell her myself."

"Olga! Wait a moment." The Baroness turned round from the door. "If anybody is to do it, I must."

"I don't trust you. You're not even angry."

"No, but I'm desperate."

"Go and do it now then, and if she makes you feel sorry for her, I shall tell her completely what I think of her."

"You're an old monster," Nathalie laughed, and slowly left the room.

She found Vera in the garden, giving Jacob instructions to tear down an eglantine that had for many years struggled profusely all over a yew hedge. At first, Nathalie wanted to protest against this vandalism; the promiscuous flowering of the wild rose, set against the formal severity of the dark hedge, had always given her a deep satisfaction. The garden had been made Vera's province, however, and it seemed unjust, as well as inadvisable, to impose restrictions or reservations on this, whatever the consequences, but this incident served the purpose of hardening Nathalie's resolve. Without any qualms, she now said: "Will you spare me a moment? There's something I'd like to discuss with you."

Jacob, who disliked his task almost as much as Nathalie did, disappeared with what passed as rare tact, and she went on: "We've all been living on top of each other far too much, and for too long. I feel it would do you the world of good to take a really thorough holiday somewhere. Then, when you return, perhaps Arthur will have been able to sort out what he's going to do."

Vera gazed at Nathalie with eyes that were haunting, as well as haunted with fear, and asked in a trembling voice: "I don't understand. What are you trying to say?"

"Just what I have said. This whole situation is a strain on everybody. Arthur doesn't want to go away, and there'd be no point in that, anyhow—he'd meet himself wherever he is. I can't go, as I have to work, and that leaves you. It might be a great help to all of us if you were to get a new and fresh outlook on things, and come back with some bright ideas to guide us."

Vera started accusing her sister-in-law of turning her out, taking Arthur away from her, and making her feel unwanted and unloved. It was sufficiently overdone to arouse indignation, rather than pity, and Nathalie exclaimed irritably: "You're wasting your time with that sort of act. Both Arthur and I have had far too much of it already. I know you're unhappy, and hurt, and disappointed, but other people's feelings have to be considered as well. Is it so very unreasonable for a husband and wife to want to have a few weeks together on their own?"

Vera understood that being pitiful would not help her this time, so she resorted to haughtiness instead.

"All I've ever wanted is Arthur's happiness," she said emphatically, "and I think I have as much right as you have to decide what that is."

"Doesn't Arthur have any right to decide for himself?"

"Of course, if I'm not wanted I'll go, but I can't believe that would really be best for him." She was becoming tearful once again, and Nathalie found herself weakening.

"Vera, don't let's quarrel about this," she said. "Please try to see things a little from my point of view. I've compromised with your world, so why can't you come even a short way into mine?"

"You know I have no patience with that kind of talk."

"Only because you don't *want* to understand, but you could if you tried. I'll make an effort to be plain. You and I stand for completely different things. We want, like and believe in different things. When I first got to know you, I thought your whole way of looking at life was wrong, and somehow beside the point, but as time went on, I realised that I'd been just as prejudiced as you, in my own way. I then began to learn, not only the reasons for my instinctive mistrust of your set of values, but also that in certain ways I was wrong and you were right. My way, if carried to its logical extremes, becomes a sort of messy anarchy, which is also extremely wasteful. It's all very fine for my sort to reject materialism, but we're just as dependent on you 'practical' ones as anybody. My sort could never run a large business, or understand about the building of bridges, or plan a sewage system, or organise the construction of cars, or aeroplanes or washing machines; yet we're almost completely dependent on all those things which make life easier, and pleasanter, and help to remove the drudgery out of work. Through you, I also learnt the value of order, and all that that implies. There must be balance in everything, though, and my lot have their uses too, you know—perhaps not me in particular, but all the kind that helped to shape me. They contribute something in the way of ideas, and art, and all that provides, not only entertainment, but a deeper understanding of what makes people tick, and what we're all here for anyhow. Couldn't you admit that? Couldn't you, in your turn, try to accept some of the things that I think important?"

"Such as not knowing the value of money? Or the most disgusting moral conduct?"

"Such as respecting people you love enough to leave them alone. Don't force Arthur to choose between us. He's himself, first and foremost, and is not bound to go all the way with either of us. He must be allowed to develop in his own way of looking at things, wherever that may lead him, or he'll never become a real person. If he's pushed to an absolute choice, he might even walk out on both of us."

"He'd never leave me. You're trying to take him away, but he'd never leave me."

"Can't you see that what I'm trying to do is to make it possible for him to live with both of us, and not always be at war with one or other of us? That's not only unpleasant for us, but terrible for him. This kind of situation can't go on, with Arthur drinking himself silly, you resorting to drugs more and more, and me going off my head. There'll be some *really* terrible catastrophe, sooner or later."

"You go away, then," Vera sobbed hysterically. "We were happy enough, until you came along. You go away, and leave us alone again. Even now, he's perfectly all right when you're not there."

Nathalie was about to reply: "All right, then, I will," when she noticed her aunt hovering in the shadow of a cedar tree, only a few feet away from them. At that moment, the Baroness hobbled forward and went straight over to Vera. Quivering with suppressed fury but speaking quietly, she said: "Vera, I am now an old woman, and I have seen many things. I have also watched your little comedy for quite long enough to know what your game is. That is why you dislike me so much—because you know you cannot make me a fool as you do these two young people."

Vera immediately lost all her limpness and became alert and disdainful. "I will not stay here and be insulted," she exclaimed, yet remained while the Baroness said: "You will listen to me. It would be best if you go away, as you are not only ruining Arthur's life, but also—and quite deliberately—breaking his marriage."

"What an extraordinary thing to say, when I've given up everything for him."

"That is only a part of your possessiveness, but you are one of those women who must feel superior to men. You like to keep Arthur wanton and no good, just so that you can humiliate and despise him. Oh, I quite understand that it is a dilemma for you. If he does well, you are put in the shade; yet, on the other hand, it is only through his success that you can hope for any kind of distinction yourself. But you would rather do without even that if it meant Arthur having a soul of his own. You would rather rot with him, than have him standing on his own feet in life, and not one hundred per cent dependent on you. If you had any real love for him, instead of being so blind with passion for yourself, you would at least try to compromise with what Nathalie asks."

Vera, looking ugly with malice, exclaimed indignantly: "I've never heard such rubbish in my life!"

"You cannot bear the truth," the Baroness said loudly, "but one day it will catch you!"

"You foreigners always exaggerate so. You'll thank me later if I go now, and stop you making a further fool of yourself."

Vera walked away in the direction of the house, taking rather high, tripping steps, like a thoroughbred shying in noisy traffic. Seen from the back, her whole demeanour was one of outraged dignity. She could never be forced, even by the Baroness, to come out and fight in the open, and was the sort that gave women a bad name, sending out deadly shafts, but never answering for the consequences, and retreating behind a bogus façade of gentleness, helpless feminity, refinement and lies. As with all totally immoral people, there was no device, no weapon, no treachery too mean, or too low, for her to use in feeding the core of her own vanity and jealous possessiveness.

"When everything is done and said," the Baroness said wearily, "she is just a bourgeoise. You know, the English genius for compromise is a funny thing. Those who use it to make the best of both worlds become the most humorous, sane and discriminating people that ever were, and stronger than anybody. But when it works inside out, it makes them cling to everything bad. They get snobbish, obstinate and weak, and their brains go round and round. Nathalie, my darling, I don't know what will happen now, but I'm afraid I have to see Jimmy Featherstone before I go back to London."

"I haven't seen him for ages," Nathalie said. "I never seem to see anybody, these days." Then she remembered meeting him in the village shop a few days beforehand, when he had said: "Your aunt seems very anxious to see me about something. Any idea what I've done this time?" Now, she turned slowly to look at the Baroness and asked: "What are you up to?"

"Do you remember that Carruthers boy? Sophie Trafford's boy by her first marriage?"

"The one who couldn't dance and had extremely hot hands, do you mean?"

"He is so clever, poor boy. He has become a brilliant scientist."

"I'm not surprised. I remember him at lunch, one day, making a mark on the tablecloth every time a rather tiresome American woman said 'Yes', which she did about six times in every sentence. When everybody was getting up to go, he said clearly and loudly across the table at her: 'It may interest you to know that you have said "yes" one hundred and forty-six times in the last ninety-five minutes', or whatever it was. He should go far."

"He has just got a marvellous position at that atom place, not far from here, but he has a wife and three children, and they can't find anywhere suitable to live."

"So you're going to foist them on to Jimmy, are you? I'm not sure Lady Bates will like that."

"I don't suppose she will. Not at all." The Baroness said this without much regret, but it was to be some time before Nathalie realised exactly what she meant by it, so now she merely asked: "How will Jimmy feel about it?"

"Well, his house is too big for him, he is lonely, and he has not enough money. The answer is obvious, isn't it?"

"All the answers are always obvious to you!" Nathalie exclaimed irritably, but she did not remain exasperated for long, for the Baroness looked tired and defeated, and was beginning to show the frailty of old age. Nathalie kissed her good-bye with almost protective tenderness, suddenly aware that even this beloved rock of her own life was a mortal being. Then she went back into the house.

Arthur went to see Father Francis after recovering from his attack of gastritis, but although he now began to take instruction seriously, he experienced no deep sensation of conversion. It seemed to him that an institution as strongly established as the Catholic Church, counting as it did among its sons so many of the clever, rich and eminent, must offer some worthy challenge to his own despair. He hoped that by subscribing to the rules of the organisation and by paying deference to the details of this faith, the faith itself would eventually become a reality for him.

Nathalie began, little by little, to relax, and come off her razor's edge of armed vigilance, so that when the next crisis came, it almost caught her unawares. Coming into the library one evening, she found Arthur sitting with his head resting on his forearms, which were crossed on the desk in front of him. She could not see his face, and thought at first that he must be asleep, for he often tired himself by reading for hours during the night. Putting an arm round his shoulders, she kissed his forehead, and found that it was exceptionally hot. Arthur moved and opened one eye, and it was then obvious to her what had happened. Looking in a drawer of the desk, Nathalie found an empty bottle of gin.

"Darling," she said quietly, "come upstairs. You'll be more comfortable there."

Arthur began to sob and this surprised her, for in spite of all the scenes and affectations he resorted to, he rarely indulged in weeping. Putting both arms around him, she asked softly: "What's the matter? Tell me."

Arthur made an effort to pull himself together, and sensing

that for once his mood was genuine, she was deeply touched and disturbed.

"Arthur darling," she murmured. "What is it?"

He did not answer, and this very lack of response was so uncharacteristic as to be almost unbearably pitiable.

"Tell me what the matter is," she pleaded. "I'll do anything, give you anything I can, only please stop suffering. . . . What is it?"

"I want love," Arthur sobbed, without looking up. It was a cry that came from the very heart of him.

"If there's anyone special, go to her, only don't go on destroying yourself. Anything, rather than that. Is there someone you want?"

"Yes."

"Well, then, go to her, my darling, and with my blessing. You simply *cannot* go on like this. . . . Who is it?"

"You."

"But you've got me, you big silly. I'm your wife—remember?"

"I haven't got you. Perhaps I had you once, but not any longer."

He was sitting up now, once again in control of himself, and looking straight ahead. A little, bitter voice in Nathalie said: "When you had me altogether, you didn't want me, and now that I'm no longer completely at your mercy, you want me after all," but aloud, she said:

"I should have thought I'd given you ample proof of my loyalty."

"I don't want your loyalty, I want your love. Besides, it was to protect Happy Ham that you stayed, rather than because of me."

"That's not altogether true. Anyhow, all that was a long time ago."

"This is our moment of truth, and yet you're the one who is running away now. If you loved me as you should, you'd have died for me after your miscarriage. Instead, you decided to live, but without me, just to be a constant reproach to me."

"That's melodramatic nonsense!"

"If I asked you to jump under a train for my sake, you wouldn't do it, would you?"

"I doubt if I'd do it for anybody. Nor would you, for that matter."

"But then I'm not the one who sets himself up as an exponent of love. Besides, you'd do it for Happy Ham."

"He'd never dream of asking me to do such a thing, so the question wouldn't arise."

"But if you saw it was the only way to save him, you'd do it."

"In such a case, I'd do it for you, too."

"So you say. Yet two years ago you refused to die, when that might have been the only way to save me."

"And do you think that proves that I don't care a fig about you?"

Arthur did not take this up, which was yet another sign of the genuineness of his despair. Without any emotion in his voice, he asked: "Would you please tell me what it is that makes Happy Ham so irresistible? He's no cleverer, no better educated, no handsomer, no more amusing, even, than I am. Why, then, is he such a success—with you, and in everything else? It's the old boy net again, I suppose."

"No, of course it's not that! But these things can't be explained by logic," Nathalie hedged.

"Please tell me. I must know. There must be something." He smiled wearily at her, and added: "It's so seldom you get me in a reasonable mood, you'd better make the best of it while it lasts. What, to coin a phrase, has Happy Ham got that I haven't?"

Nathalie made a great effort, and said at last: "He gives."

"Of course! He who pays the piper calls the tune, in fact. Is it my fault that I wasn't born a rich man? And who was it, I'd like to know, who discouraged me from staying in a job where I had the chance of becoming one? That was the most inspired of vampire actions that I've ever come across, which is saying something. I congratulate you. I'd underestimated your strength."

Arthur's sarcasm showed that he was regaining a frame of mind more normal to him, but there was no turning back now, and Nathalie said: "I don't mean that sort of thing at all. I mean he gives himself, the very core of himself, over and over again, without counting the cost, or even expecting anything in return."

"Like you, in fact—a sort of perpetual, emotional diarrhoea, lavished indiscriminately on anything that can stand it. And if people get stifled, or just won't succumb, then you direct it all at some God or other."

The gin had relaxed Arthur sufficiently for his thoughts to be freely projected, but physically he was having difficulties in co-ordinating. His eyelids kept dropping, and his hands were trembling so badly that he tried to occupy them by making dogs out of pipe-cleaners.

"Some people are just made that way," Nathalie said unhappily. "They want to give. . . . They have to love."

"The most revolting self-indulgence, in fact," Arthur blazed. Then his defiance broke, and he added, again with a sob: "Why can't I love like that? Why can't I, instead of distrusting or despising people, or just getting bored with them? I've tried often enough, but it never comes to anything. I never know how you feel. I can't understand the sort of love that makes you prefer to suffer, rather than do someone else harm. I just don't understand the sort of love of God that Father Francis seems to feel. It's neither mystical escapism nor social convenience with him, as it is with that absurd Len Cox, but something simple and solid, for which he'd go to the stake quite cheerfully, if necessary. It just doesn't make sense to me. Why can't I love like that?"

"I wish I knew, Arthur. Oh, God, how I wish I knew!"

He went on sobbing, and Nathalie did and said all she could think of to comfort him, but she could not reach him.

"Give it all a chance," she pleaded finally. "Go on with this instruction, and unless you feel you really can't stomach the whole business, be received into the Church and see if it helps you. After all, you're not bound to accept either my view or Father Francis's. There must be as many ways of reaching God, or enabling Him to reach you, as there are people. Go on with it for a bit, anyhow."

Arthur gave in almost meekly. He was getting rather bored with this particular scene, and apart from that, he had developed a certain respect for Father Francis, and that struck him as a challenge. The instruction accordingly went on, and seemed to progress. Vera did not approve, but on the other hand, she did not actively disapprove. Now living in a remote and hazy little world of her own, out of contact and unresponsive to everything around her, the main object of her existence was seeing that her bottles of sedative drugs were constantly refilled. She used all her wiles and ingenuities to this end, even playing off against each other two doctors, the partners on whose panel she was a patient. The rest of the time, she wandered round the garden in a euphoric state, amiable and unhurried, digging up the more prolific plants, drastically pruning shrubs and trees, and even giving instructions to Jacob to clean up the wilderness on the far bank of the river (instructions which he characteristically interpreted as he thought fit).

It was arranged that Arthur should make his general confession in time to take his first communion at Corpus Christi. Nathalie went to early Mass that morning, and prayed for her husband's welfare with a whole-hearted intensity of dedication. The effort was exhausting, but left her feeling relaxed and peaceful.

Walking back afterwards, the beauty of the countryside reached and touched her with unusual intensity. She was vividly aware of the early morning mist on the distant downs; the peculiar grey-green shimmer of fields of barley; the bales, in never quite straight rows, of the first-cut hay, and the sounds of birds and cooing doves. When she reached the gate in the end wall and went through into the garden of Walton House, the magic changed and intensified. Myriads of small and intricate dewed cobwebs glistened on the lawns and roses bloomed everywhere, as though in defiance of Vera's ministrations. She walked by the river, looking into the cool, dark water, and loving the whole familiar pattern of the garden, and the way the house was set in it.

In this timeless quiet, Nathalie felt her deep attachment to the whole place, knowing how it had moulded her. Many houses stay just houses. They are built, looked after and lived in, but never become more than homely places of shelter, with no personality of their own. With a few, however, it is quite different. They retain something of the lives and tastes that have developed within them, some impact that eventually creates in them an essence of their own. They in turn then exist independently, solid and incorruptible, eventually influencing, rather than being influenced by, those who come into it. Walton House was more than a house, or even a home to Nathalie; more than the container or background for so many of her strongest memories; more, even, than a symbol of a way of life, or a distilled impression of a certain civilisation. It was all these, and yet something besides; almost an entity in itself, embodying an eternal tribute to womanhood and yet rejecting matriarchy, just as a piece of music or a poem could do.

As she walked towards the house, Nathalie's glimpse of the broader pattern melted with the morning mist, and she returned to her particular wedge of time present, but feeling stronger and calmer than before. Vera and Elizabeth were having breakfast, but Arthur had only had two cups of tea that morning, since it was required of him to fast before taking communion. He welcomed her as she came in, saying: "I'm warning you, here and now, that I shall want the most enormous breakfast the moment we get back from this pantomime."

"That's all in the best tradition," Nathalie smiled. "I ought to have baked you a cake."

"Ugh! Have a heart, darling! Not at this hour of the morning—really!"

"Would you rather have lobster and hot chocolate sauce, then?"

"You're taking a perilous risk, you know. I shall either spank you or have a very stiff drink, if you go on like that."

"In that case, I'd rather you spanked me, but it's a beastly choice to give a girl, in the circumstances."

"All's fair in love and war."

"Which is this, then?" she asked, suddenly apprehensive, for no reason that seemed apparent.

"Both, I imagine," Arthur answered blandly, and then went upstairs to have a bath.

By a quarter past nine, Nathalie had washed up the breakfast things, made the beds and seen to what preparations were needed for luncheon. Vera was to put the meat in the oven later on, and meanwhile was upstairs in her bedroom, tidying and resting in alternate bouts. Nathalie got Elizabeth ready, and then went to find Arthur. He was still in the bathroom, so she shouted through the door: "You are being a time! We'll be late."

"I got engrossed in Sartre's *Huis Clos*, but I shan't be long now."

"I think we'd better go. Elizabeth walks so slowly."

"Right you are. I'll catch you up."

This time, Nathalie's walk between Walton House and West Compton did not leave her slightly suspended. Most of her attention was being drawn more specifically by Elizabeth who from her child's eye level, could take in so many of the details of the countryside. For a while, the little girl was content to walk straight ahead, holding her mother's hand tightly. Then their path went through a patch of woodland, and she started exploring, though timidly, never leaving Nathalie for long. She picked some wild anemones, carefully inspected a mossed-over piece of tree trunk lying on the ground, and discovered some wild strawberries, which she ate with relish and excitement. Then she found a rather large hole under the roots of a tree, and nervously ran back to her mother.

"It must be some animal's hole," Nathalie tried to reassure her. "Who do you suppose lives there? The Flopsy bunnies? Or some of Rabbit's friends and relations?"

Elizabeth would not take part in the whimsy, however. "And, after all, why should she?" Nathalie thought. "That hole might just as well be inhabited by a fox, or a fierce animal, or even a Frankenstein monster, for all we know." They walked on, but even when they were already kneeling in the church, there was still no sign of Arthur. He came in at the end of the Kyrie, and without looking round, she recognised his slow, rather heavy footsteps as he came down the aisle. He genuflected and knelt beside her. She looked sideways to smile at him, but could not see his face, as he was holding his head in his hands. Only when they rose to go to the communion rail together did she realise that he was drunk. He was not incapable: in fact, on the contrary, all his movements were precise and measured, but his smile was a mask-like grimace, and his eyes had the look she knew only too well.

Nathalie became physically rigid, but her brain started racing, trying to get ahead of the moment; to control, or even determine its course. Yet, even as she received the Host, and cried from her weeping heart: 'My Lord and My God,' she knew it was too late and that there was nothing more for her to do. Arthur also received the Host, and as they returned to their pew and knelt down again, he gave her another grin, now triumphant and malicious.

Trying to survive the impact of her feelings, to stave off an actual physical agony that grew more intense at every moment, Nathalie read the Epistle for the day in her Missal, and saw:

"Whosoever shall eat this bread, or drink of the chalice of the Lord unworthily, shall be guilty of the Body and of the Blood of the Lord. But let a man prove himself; and so let him eat of that Bread, and drink of the chalice. For he that eateth and drinketh unworthily, eateth and drinketh judgment to himself, not discerning the body of the Lord."

Her hands and feet grew numb with cold, her shoulders ached, and a sharp pain in her side became almost unbearable. She was too overcome with suffering even to pray and simply knelt, with her face hidden in her hands, hoping for strength merely to move again. After a while, she became aware of Elizabeth tugging at her sleeve. Looking slowly around her as though returning from a great distance, she heard the child whisper: "Wake up, Mummy. It's finished."

Arthur had disappeared.

That evening, after having put Elizabeth to bed, Nathalie went to see Father Francis. He knew what had happened, but they did not discuss Arthur himself. To Nathalie, the latter was no longer just her husband and responsibility, or even a person with a particular problem. He had also become a catalyst, an example, even a symbol of a universal sickness. Her grief and disappointment were not merely personal ones, but extended to the sorrow of all the suffering. She was profoundly perplexed and quite unable to see what to do next.

"I can only think in paradoxes now, and even they're not interesting any longer," she told Father Francis wearily.

"Perhaps it would be better for you not to think too much, just at the moment," he said kindly.

Nathalie was already demented, however, and exclaimed: "Either a situation takes you with it, or you take it with you. There's nothing in between. There's no rest. I must decide. That's one more paradox, you see, like so many others; like 'It is within every man's power to resist evil, yet evil is absolute', or 'Wholehearted dedication is essential, yet enslavement is death', or 'Everybody is responsible for everybody else, yet solitude must be accepted as the natural lot of man', or 'Every man has an obligation to be self-sufficient, yet the pursuit of wealth is wrong', or 'It's essential to love without reserve, yet the more you open your heart, the more pain flows into it'. Both sides can be true, but which is it to be? Do I control, or does it kill me? Who decides? And when? And why? What were my big mistakes and how far back did I step out of the pattern? Or did I have no choice but blind obedience to a destiny I cannot see, led by a character

I cannot alter, and moulded by circumstances I cannot change?"

"Relax, child, relax. We'll drink some of this Beaujolais—it will do you good—and then we can talk, but sensibly." Father Francis took the bottle and filled two rather thick and cloudy glasses almost to the brim. Holding his up to the light, he exclaimed: "Look at that colour, will you! As warm and vital as the place it comes from. I spent some years as a priest in a village in Auvergne before being sent here, you know. The battle between good and evil goes on there too, just as it does everywhere else, but they have this to help them. It enables them to be benign, but without rotting their guts. I once worked out a theory about the wine-line. It's not nationality, or economic prosperity, or even religion that differentiates people, but the wine-line. Above it, you find a foggy, mystic, pagan romanticism; a coldness and hardness of the spirit; an aggressive masculinity in politics, and morals usually taking the place of religion. Below the wine-line, on the other hand, everything becomes at once simpler and more clear cut; softer, warmer and somehow more feminine, just as wine is more feminine than spirits. Yet, the same sort of problems exist in both regions, but merely come out differently. . . . That's the way. Finish what's in that glass, and then we'll have a little more. . . . There, now I can see that you feel better already."

"You're so good, Father."

"What makes you say that?"

"You put me in my place without making me feel a fool."

Father Francis refilled Nathalie's glass and said: "You know, one of the things I miss most, north of the wine-line, is talk. I don't mean intellectual discussions, but intelligent conversation about the ordinary things of life, and about human problems and situations. It's not that people here don't feel things, but that they're almost ashamed to do so, and it's difficult for a man to talk openly of what he is ashamed. That is one reason why I enjoy talking to you so much."

"I'm not making much sense at the moment," Nathalie sighed, but she was, indeed, feeling a little better; as Father Francis had predicted, the wine calmed and warmed her. She was still worrying at the core of her despair, however, and went on: "I'm beginning to suspect that love itself is destructive. What use has it been to Arthur, for instance? It's awoken in him echoes to which he can't respond, and that have plunged him into hell. If I'd tried less to be considerate and understanding, and had joined his sister in being narrow-minded and demanding, there would have been no dilemma for him. He'd have had no choice but to fulfil the ambitions we both pushed him into. He'd have developed some nasty habits on the quiet, of course, but we'd have been too obtuse to notice what went on behind our hypocritical façade of jolly trivialities. We shouldn't have cared, in fact, so long as the money was coming in thick and fast and the neighbours respected us. Our friends might only have liked us for what they could get out of us, but then we have no friends at all, now. After all, many people seem to get on all right, with no *raison d'être* except to keep themselves alive on a rather grander scale than the next person. They may not do much good, but then they don't do much harm, either—probably less than those of us who try to apply to life the standards of a game of cricket at an English public school."

Father Francis seemed to be thinking this over, but he finally said: "Another of my theories is that individual lives are rather like pendulums. When they are not very highly geared—that is to say, loaded without much more than the normal amount of talents—they can only swing a short way on either side of centre. They'll never have anything outstanding to show, whether for good or for bad. But the ones who have been endowed with an exceptional amount of vitality swing far more vigorously, and that means that they're capable of going high and far on either side. I think your husband is one of those. He could never have stayed swinging near to centre, and it was perhaps necessary for him to have you in his life, in order to help him determine his direction. It's important to realise that a person capable of great evil also has it in him to pursue great good. Many of the saints are an example of that very process, after all."

"And I failed him."

"His despair is great, and certainly rather terrible, but it's not hopeless. Most of the saints had periods of intense blackness too, which often proved salutary in the long run."

"But you've seen how it is, Father. He'll end up by either destroying himself or else killing me—and possibly both. What am I to do next? What can anybody do for him, since he really seems to prefer destruction and damnation? I'm not equipped for this sort of excitement. All I have to offer are the normal stock-in-trade of any ordinary woman: understanding and tenderness, and a warm body that once knew how to give pleasure, as well as to comfort. But that's not what he wants. He seems to think that if I'd died for him, that time he caused me to lose the child, I might have saved him. I failed him even there, though."

"Don't be such a romantic," said Father Francis. "Death may be a symbol of sacrifice, but it's not necessarily the ultimate end. There's been a lot of muddled thinking on that subject."

"Does that mean there's worse to come, then?" Nathalie smiled and felt considerably better, warmed not only by the wine, but also by human contact.

"Possibly," Father Francis answered. "It also means that there's always a future, and therefore always hope. Would you like some soup? It's onion today, and should be ready by now."

"I'd love some," Nathalie answered, even though she felt as though there were an air-lock just above her stomach, and any food she swallowed would bounce straight back again. They took their glasses and the bottle of wine into the kitchen, a far more agreeable room than the one in which Father Francis normally received. He set some thick white plates and large spoons on the wooden table, then drew up two Windsor chairs, saying: "Here, you take the armchair."

"I'd rather you sat in it," she said, drawing up the other one.

"Just as you like." He started cutting some pieces of bread, holding the loaf to his chest, and drawing a knife across the top of it. Then he put one slice on each plate and the rest in a basket, setting that on the table, as well as a hunk of cheese on a board. When he had carefully served the soup, they sat down.

For some minutes they did not talk and ate slowly, in peaceful silence. Then, Nathalie sat back and asked: "Who first said '*L'appetit vien en mangeant*'?"

"I don't really know, but it's certainly true in all kinds of respects. Some cheese with your bread?"

"Thank you." She ate a little more, before saying: "You know, the very intensity of evil must be proof of the existence of God. Only something as powerful as God could inspire the lengths to which the Devil goes in order to try and do Him down. Look at the way Satan strikes at the innocent, for instance—at people who are so far removed from him that often they aren't even able to recognise him. I suppose that concentrating on those who already half belong to him isn't nearly so much fun. It's too easy. He may use them as his own secret police to further his ends, but it's the ones who look as though they belong to the other side that he really wants, since as soon as he's sure of anybody, he loses interest. He's not a decentraliser, like God, and thrives not only on power, but on conflict as well. He thoroughly enjoys inciting the complete degradation of some human beings by others—in such a cunning variety of ways, too. Nobody could be as ingeniously sadistic unless he were up against very big stuff indeed." She saw Father Francis smiling, and added: "Don't laugh at me! Or am I being very stupid?"

"On the contrary, I was smiling because I'm so glad you feel better. You see, even your own despair was not so unshakeable after all."

"You know, there's one thing about the Devil for which I'm grateful. He's the only creature in the whole of Creation that I can't feel compassion for. I could spit in his eye quite happily, without wondering whether perhaps the love of a good woman might put things right." This time, Father Francis laughed out loud.

"But where is one to go from there, Father?" she went on. "And even more perplexing, how?"

"You know what my answer to that must be."

"Yes, but what about those who don't belong to the Church? Or those who don't even know about God? What about people like Arthur, who just *can't* love, apparently?"

"Even without the love of God, a knowledge of His commandments and the doctrines of His Church can provide a man's guide and strength. What he makes of those is up to him. It's his responsibility."

"I'm beginning to hate that word," Nathalie smiled.

They talked for a long time, until finally she felt courageous enough to go home and see whether Arthur had returned. Even now she put off coming to a decision until seeing him, and appreciating any new developments there might be. In this there seemed to be still another paradox: "Time waits for no man, yet it is only within time that situations can ripen, mature and come to fruition." She felt surrounded by brands of romanticism that all seemed inadequate, without herself having anything to offer in addition to them. What could she add, she wondered, to counterbalance Arthur's fashionable pessimism, Vera's dour moral rectitude, the Baroness's brutal defence of the life-force, or Len Cox's woolly reverence for goodness and beauty? Even Father Francis's mediaeval adoration for Mother Church now seemed inadequate. She was curious to know what would Felix have said to all this. He was not there to ask, yet she knew that his whole attitude would express, as indeed hers had to Arthur: "You're the only one who can decide. I'll stand by you with friendship and affection, but ultimately it's up to you, and don't rush your fences."

Her moment for decision had not yet come, however, for when she reached Walton House, there was still no sign of her husband.

Arthur was away nearly a week. When Nathalie returned from Oxford the following Friday evening, she saw a London taxi by the front door, and found the driver drinking beer in the kitchen.

"I've brought yer 'ubby back, lidy," he said.

"Thank you. Is he all right?"

"Better 'an 'e was, any'ow. One of my mates and me made 'im drink some coffee and sort of looked after 'im. Proper mess 'e was, too. Then we 'ad the devil's own job getting 'is address orf him, but I reckoned 'e'd be better orf 'ome than in jug. You don't want to 'ave nothing more to do with the police than you need to, I always say."

"How sweet of you to bother. Have you had anything to eat?"

"Well, I ought to be toddling back, but yer 'ubby said I was to see you about the fare."

"Yes, of course." She paid him, and then added: "Wouldn't you like a sandwich, or something, to take with you? It's quite a long drive back."

"Well, just a bite of bread and cheese, per'aps, but I'll cop it from my old woman if I stay out too long. She gets worried, you know, and that makes 'er proper carping."

Nathalie made the driver some cheese sandwiches, wrapped them in greaseproof paper, and then saw him off, thanking him again for his kindness. After that, she went to find her husband.

Arthur was in the library, simply sitting, and gazing straight ahead at nothing. This ravaged wreck of a man was so much a stranger to her now that she could even afford to remain unhardened against him. Without looking at her, he said despondently: "As you see, I'm still around. Even hell-fire didn't strike me."

"Where have you been?"

"Here and there. I don't remember, really."

"And you haven't found an answer yet? Even now?"

"No. And I'm too exhausted to think, or even talk, at the moment."

"Do you want some food?"

"No. Just sleep."

"Shall I make you some tea?"

"I'm going to bed," he said, and went upstairs, still without looking at her.

The next morning, Arthur seemed cheerful, though obviously rather tired. He made no reference to anything that had happened, and merely suggested accompanying his family on their Saturday morning shopping expedition. This happened sometimes, and now that they no longer had a car, he was most helpful, especially in carrying things to and from the bus. While Nathalie went into a grocer's shop, Arthur took Elizabeth with him. Nathalie was vaguely uneasy about this, but then immediately reproached herself; in the cosy normality of an English market town on a Saturday morning, it seemed absurd to worry because a man wanted to take his own daughter shopping with him. Nathalie did her errands, and then walked further down the street, towards the store where she expected to find Arthur and Elizabeth. Before reaching it, however, she spotted them on the other side of the road and paused, waiting for a chance to pick her way through the traffic, and across the street. They had not seen her, but suddenly Arthur looked as though he, too, was about to cross over, so she stayed where she was. She saw, then, that he was not sober, and a quick glance at the bulge of his game-pocket—the half-bottle of gin bulge—confirmed this. Paralysed by a pang of apprehension so strong that it might have been a premonition of disaster, she could not move, or even call out. There was, in fact, nothing to be done but wait. Elizabeth put her hand out to take her father's, and for a moment, he held it. Then, as he stepped off the kerb, he somehow lost his hold of the child. She came after him, trying to grab his sleeve, and then his coat, but he seemed to have forgotten about her, and went on walking across the street. Elizabeth was off the pavement as well now, and finding herself alone as a large car came towards her, she suddenly screamed.

To Nathalie, this cry was more terrible than anything she had ever heard, and it finally broke her. By the time she reached her daughter, it was obvious to her that the determining crisis had come. After lunch, when Vera and Elizabeth had both gone up to rest, she told Arthur that they had arrived at the end of their life together. Her anger of three hours beforehand was largely undisplayed, but so immense, and so deep, that it was to go on reverberating with chain reactions for many days, settling every issue with clarity, and helping her to carry out the details of her resolve. Arthur was not surprised, but even so, he said bitterly: "So much for all your clap-trap about love and religion. Does Father Francis give his blessing to this?"

"I don't know. He always tells me I have to make up my own mind about things, though in accordance with the teachings of the Church."

"And does the Church teach women to leave their husbands in the lurch when they've fallen on hard times? I thought she considered the family sacrosanct."

"She does, and it is. I think that's really why our marriage survived for as long as it did. While some kind of family life could go on, there was still hope, and it could have been a link between us, to make us both slightly less egocentric. I know I hadn't much of a clue about it to begin with, but I had a late start in learning. It means nothing to you, though. I used to think you weren't to blame, and that I must be more patient, but now I know it's no good. There isn't room in your life for children, or anything else that isn't principally a foil to you, and today you very nearly destroyed Elizabeth, as well as—well, as well as so much else."

"It's real Christian charity to fling the past at people, I'm sure."

"Charity or no charity, I can't go on where love always involves choosing. It's impossible having to choose between you and everything else all the time. Between your authority and what I feel might be right. Between you and life. Between you and God, even. It's not only all wrong, it just doesn't make sense. To me, love is all-embracing and branching outwards, growing and flourishing with all it touches. I'm just not made for your brand of all-consuming, destructive passion. I may not be a good Catholic, but the only thing I can do now is to try to see that Elizabeth has a better chance than we ever had. She'll probably have to learn most things for herself, and through her own mistakes, but at least she's still young, and there's hope for her."

"Does that mean that you've given up hope for me, then?"

"No, but it means that since you forced me to choose between you and her, I've chosen her."

"You'll fry in hell for such arrogance."

"I've no alternative." She was no longer afraid of him and sensing this, he knew he had lost his power over her. As she left the room, he said: "Well, well! The game really is up. Pity."

Nathalie went straight to Fawcett House then, to tell Susan Hammond that she was going to leave Arthur.

"And about time, too!" her friend exclaimed. "But what an odd girl you are. You've been dripping and wilting in that set-up for years, and now you announce this as casually as though you were suggesting a jaunt to the cinema."

"Will you have Elizabeth for a while? I've got to sell the house and find somewhere to live in Oxford, and I don't want her to feel more unsettled than she has to, poor lamb."

"Of course," Susan said warmly. "Annabelle will be delighted." Then, after a pause, she asked: "Must you sell the house, though? Why don't you let it—to start with, anyhow?"

"I've got to get right away, or I shall crack up. I want to go on seeing all of you, of course, but not here. When I leave here, I never want to come back again."

"You'll get over that in time, surely. Anthony and I could see to this end of the business side for you until you feel better."

"You're a darling, but it would be no use. I can't ever live in that house again, so there's no sense in hanging on to it."

"One never knows. . . ."

"I've got to make a complete break, and a clean one."

Susan looked so worried that Nathalie suddenly said desperately: "I do wish you could understand. I wish *somebody* could. The house will survive, but it must have people who can be a real part of it and look after it properly. That sounds ridiculously whimsical, I know, but I feel it strongly, and there are several reasons why I can't live there now, quite apart from lack of money. The first is because it's impossible to go on living in a home you've tried to make with someone, when that goes wrong. The second, because I've got to prove that the reason I failed with Arthur was not——"

"How can you talk of failing," Susan interrupted impatiently.

"The man is a useless drunkard, and that sister of his is a horror. That's all there is to it. The only real mistake you made was to stick it so long."

"It's not as simple as that," Nathalie protested, "but I'll try and put it in another way. There are plenty of people like Arthur and Vera, though their behaviour is not always so extreme. They're symbols of something that crops up again and again, in various guises. You can call it evil, if you like, but that's over-simplifying it, as very few of us are all of one piece. Anyhow, I've got to prove that the reason they haven't altogether defeated me is not because I have any kind of worldly security or materialist advantage, but because there's something stronger than evil. There are plenty of reasons why people become mixed-up kids, embittered cowards, neurotically self-centred, or even destructive under the guise of a high moral purpose, but I can only deal with the particular situation I find myself in. There's no real excuse for what's happened to us on grounds of intelligence or training—Arthur's far cleverer and better educated than I am, and so is Vera, for that matter. There might be as far as background, or even money is concerned, though, and I don't want them—or the likes of them—to have any excuse for what they're doing."

"But you can't help the background you're born with! You can't just pretend it doesn't exist."

"No, of course not. In fact, it's stupid not to take heredity into account. If that, as well as the circumstances of one's upbringing meant nothing, people would presumably never worry about what they did to their children. But I want to take it from there. I must prove that it's not material circumstances, but something *inside* people that counts in the last resort, so that these angry rebels can't just get away with blaming everybody else for their failure, and then lashing out so destructively. Perhaps it's a form of penance on my part—I mean, to deliberately give up something that means so much to me, not only personally, but also as a woman wanting to make a nest for her young. I have to fight on equal terms, though, and cut out all the Lady Bates in my surroundings—not so much to avoid reproaches from those I'm fighting against, as in order to encourage those who may also be suffering hopelessly and defencelessly. Does that make it at all clearer?"

"I wish I could say it did, but I'm afraid I'm rather simple. Or perhaps it's just that I've always been too happy. . . .

Talking of Lady Bates, by the way, have you heard the latest?"

"No, I don't think so."

"She's hopping mad because Jimmy's divided his house into two, and let half of it to an atomic scientist with a Chinese wife. She seems to have nightmares about the yellow peril spreading all over England from Dacron Court."

"What did she say?" Nathalie laughed, now remembering her last conversation with the Baroness. "Don't tell me, let me guess. I bet it was something like 'It does let the place down so'."

"You couldn't be more right!" Susan giggled. "What she also finds hard to stomach is that Mrs. Stinks-specialist is not only an Oxford scholar, but extremely decorative as well. Jimmy is delighted, of course, but I think Lady B. would almost rather have her tilling the soil with bare feet."

"Poor Lady Bates," Nathalie sighed, "she just has no idea at all where she is, these days, has she? It's terrible how some people have to suffer."

Nathalie betrayed an utter loneliness behind her jocular manner, and Susan said sympathetically: "Poor you!"

"I don't know. I'm dangerously exhausted and on the verge of hysteria at the moment, but in a curious way, I've never felt so strong, or so clear-headed, in all my life. Not that that's saying much, admittedly. And they do say it's always darkest before the dawn, don't they?"

Nathalie took one more action that day. The reminder of the Baroness softened her determination a little, and she wondered if her decision about selling the house had perhaps been a little high-handed. Her aunt was in Italy, so she sent her a telegram, saying: "Leaving Arthur. May I Sell House?"

The answer arrived early the next morning, and ran: "Delighted My Darling. It's Your House. Do Anything You Like But Not Change Your Mind."

During the next few weeks, the pattern almost developed itself. Nathalie received a number of offers for Walton House and finally sold it, not to the highest bidder, but to a family with which she felt in sympathy. They had appealed to her from the first moment of their arrival, and had paused to take in the atmosphere of the whole place before then making suggestions about the rooms and the gardens which she knew would be right. She also found a flat in Oxford and decided which of her belongings to keep, or send to auction, or put by for the Baroness.

Arthur stopped drinking and just drifted around, sometimes sorting out his own things, but mostly doing nothing. Vera, on the other hand, rose to the occasion with an energy and determination that had not been apparent in her for many months, and she now only used her sedatives in order to get a good night's sleep. She terminated the letting of her own little house in the Midlands, and arranged to move herself, her belongings and Arthur back into it. When her own side of the packing up had been completed, she ranged round Nathalie's province, trying to appropriate this carpet, or that electric fire, and living up to her reputation of one who could be trusted to keep an eye on practical matters. Arthur had already pawned a number of oddments such as little-used silver dishes, a Sèvres vase, and a Corot which had been in one of the spare bedrooms, and Nathalie had never commented on this, having considered them as much his as hers to dispose of. Vera's scrounging, however, especially in these circumstances, seemed to her a different matter, and did not improve her temper. This whole process of dismantling, in fact, was a severe strain on both the women, and their dislike for each other now flourished unchecked. Vera often exclaimed that the girl must be hard and heartless to break up her own home so deliberately, and Nathalie, determined not to betray how much the effort was costing her, affected an attitude of callous thoroughness, for as soon as her anger abated, she had to drive herself from one task to the next. Even though dazed by exhaustion, and restrained by a control that kept her sense of loss just out of sight, she still slithered in and out of reality, however, and it was hardly surprising that a quite trivial incident nearly caused her to break down altogether.

Vera and Arthur were to leave a week before her, and the day before their projected departure, Nathalie was sorting out books and trinkets in the library. She came across a carved, ivory cigarette-box that had been a wedding-present from one of Arthur's brother officers in Paris. Looking at it then, she had to push away memories that were too painful to face, and put the box on Arthur's pile of belongings. He came into the room shortly afterwards, and picking it up, said: "You have this."

"No," Nathalie answered. "After all, Nigel was your chum."

"He adored you, and gave it to both of us."

"But I'd like you to keep it." She suddenly wanted to weep; to give up, not only all she had undertaken, but altogether; even to die, for everything seemed impossibly, insolubly difficult.

Turning away from Arthur, Nathalie started looking through the books again, but her eyes were too full of tears, and her brain had started free-wheeling.

"Will you be all right, do you think?" he asked.

"It's a little late in the day for you to start worrying about *that*!" she exclaimed bitterly. "But at least there's one person who's coming out of this chaos thoroughly satisfied, anyhow."

Suddenly, Arthur said: "Darling, I'm not going."

"I'm afraid you'll have to. The Richardsons move in on the fifteenth."

"I mean, I'm not going with Vera."

"Well, you're not coming with me," Nathalie said apprehensively. "Get that *quite* straight."

She had no strength left for another battle, no strength for anything, except to somehow get through the next fortnight of packing, moving and heartbreak.

"You don't understand, silly. This is important." Arthur sounded amused, and turning to look at him then, she saw that he appeared tired, but unburdened and cheerful. "You've done it!" he exclaimed.

"Done what?" She was too exhausted to be anything but alternately bewildered and suspicious.

"It's suddenly all quite simple. I'm cutting and running, and she can either like it, or lump it. You needn't look so apprehensive. This isn't an act. It's revelation, at long last." Being Arthur, he could not leave it at that, however. This new part of his had to be padded, and set against a background, but it seemed wholehearted enough.

"Don't you see?" he went on eagerly. "The insistence of life is a far greater punishment for some people than the paralysis of death. Your leaving me, like this, is punishing me far more than your dying could ever have done, because it's costing you so much more. All because of me, you're not only prepared to face life alone, when even you now know how cruel and cold it can be, but you've also deliberately sacrificed a home that means so much to you. I suddenly understand the quality of your love because I'm touched by your suffering, and you're suffering because of me."

"My dear Arthur, I've been suffering because of you for years, and the only reason I'm going through with all this now is because it's preferable to putting up with you any longer." She spoke almost petulantly, yet could not help feeling a little tender at the sight of an Arthur now looking curiously transformed with joy.

"You still don't understand!" he exclaimed happily. "I always said you were very stupid, but perhaps you'll see it too, one day. You've liberated me!"

Even then Nathalie could not be sure whether this were one of his tricks, but she smiled as she said: "As long as I've liberated you out of my life for good and all, that's all right by me."

"You've got to do one more thing for me," he said. "Then your wish will be granted."

"I might have known there'd be a catch in it."

"You've got to be the one to tell Vera."

"Coward!"

"I don't believe in trying providence too high—not yet, anyhow. I'll pack up all I need in a couple of cases and slip out of the house tonight. Then, you can break it to her in the morning. Will you do this last thing for me?"

"Only if you take Nigel's cigarette-box with you."

He took the box, kissed her with unusual gentleness, and then went upstairs to pack.

After he had left the room, she could not help sobbing for a few minutes. Even that was a dangerous luxury, however, so she went on sorting out the books.

Shortly before midnight, when they sat in the kitchen over their last snack together, Arthur asked his wife: "Will you ever forgive me?"

"Don't start that again. Please."

"But will you?"

She thought for a while, and then answered: "I suppose in the long run that will depend on what you do with the future. You may have been liberated from Vera, but have you also abandoned your obsession with destruction and death?"

"There are so few people who can understand their fascination,"

Arthur said slowly. "The limitations of life are tame, compared to the exciting possibilities of death. Orpheus understood this sort of thing, but of course, it's no use telling you that—you've probably never even heard of him. Like him, though, I've always felt that response to the various mysterious forces of death must lead to revelations of all kinds, artistic as well as other wise."

"I wonder if becoming an actor would have helped you to get over that. I mean, if that means of expressing yourself would have canalised your thirst for power and revelation into a creative direction."

Arthur looked at her sharply, and said: "You and your living, and loving, and creativeness! That's been the real battle between us all along, I suppose, just as it is in the whole universe. Life struggling against death, creation against destruction, good against evil, even—or whatever else you like to call it. But both exist, and side by side, so it's futile arguing which is the best, or most important. And remember that death always has the last word, after all."

"I'm not so sure about that. . . . No, darling, I don't believe that's true. Perhaps the final test *is* whether people decide to live or to die, but there are *no* limitations for those who choose life. In order to know it and be part of it, they may have to suffer; to face every danger, accept every challenge, and absorb every pain. They may have to steer a rather uneasy course between two different ideas of man: the one, that of a humble creature with all his weaknesses, instincts, appetites, and energies not properly sorted out, and pushing him here, there and everywhere; and the other, that of a marvel of partly undeveloped resources such as reasoning ability, sensitivity, understanding, appreciation, nobility and wonderful creativeness. Perhaps all they can hope for is to progress a small step nearer to their likeness in the image of God, and perhaps all they can pray for is courage: courage to retain their faith, and accept pain, and laugh, and reconcile passion and reason, and not only recognise evil, but stand up to it as well; above all, courage to love. . . . But if that last prayer is ever fully answered, my dear Arthur, all your stinking destruction and death will count for nothing more than *that*!" She flicked her fingers, but the sound was muffled and feeble, so she added: "I never have been able to do that properly!"

Arthur smiled. "We are a couple of Dostoyevsky characters,

aren't we?" he said. "Well . . . I suppose I'd better go." He stood up and began slowly gathering his belongings.

"Wouldn't you like to take something to eat?" Nathalie asked, feeling rather stupid. "Some sandwiches, or something?" She could not look at him, and he did not answer, but kissed her lightly and then left.

Nathalie thought there would be some pleasure in breaking the news of Arthur's departure to Vera; a Vera who was now so obviously in control of herself and her own domain that she could no longer excite pity. The whole situation had become so extraordinary, however, that by the next morning she felt no emotion at all. It seemed to her as though they were all puppets now, watching themselves take part in a drama for which the words of the last act had already been written. She was not even surprised when her sister-in-law refused to believe that Arthur had left them both for good.

"I expect he's gone ahead to get things ready," Vera said blandly. "He always used to be so considerate, and he's now evidently being his old self again."

"You can shut your eyes to what's happened if you like, but you'll have to open them sooner or later," Nathalie answered, and then wondered if this were so; there seemed to be plenty of people who somehow managed to get through life without being aware of what went on, even under their own noses. Vera could easily be like the woman in the Mary Petty drawing who pointed at the portrait of a turn-of-the-century motorist, and said: "I keep telling myself he may be having engine trouble somewhere." Even when her belongings had left, and she herself was about to depart, she still confidently maintained: "I know he'll come back. He always has."

"But this time, I think it may be different," Nathalie replied.

Both these views expressed the attitude of the women who voiced them, rather than an accurate forecast. It was a fact, however, that whatever the outcome might be, Arthur was now on his own.

[illegible]

[illegible] would be much [illegible] to be thankful [illegible] ... her own [illegible] ... The [illegible] ... by the next morning [illegible] ... she was not [illegible] ... had ... refused to believe [illegible] ... for the good.

[illegible]

You [illegible] ... to what [illegible] ... through [illegible] ... their own [illegible] ... [illegible]

[illegible] ... whatever the outcome might be [illegible]